VALERIE BELGRAVE was born in
went on to study at Sir George W
Canada, obtaining a BA in Painti
Trinidad where she is a working artist                                         ...ing in
batik.

*Ti Marie* is Valerie Belgrave's first novel and, as with her batik and
fabric designs, the author seeks to promote a positive image of West
Indian culture through the popular medium of the historical romance.
The cover of *Ti Marie* features a batik picture by the author.

# VALERIE BELGRAVE

# TI MARIE

**HEINEMANN**

Heinemann International
A Division of Heinemann Educational Books Ltd
Halley Court, Jordan Hill, Oxford OX2 8EJ

Heinemann Educational Books (Nigeria) Ltd
PMB 5205, Ibadan
Heinemann Educational Books (Kenya) Ltd
Kijabe Street, PO Box 45314, Nairobi
Heinemann Educational Boleswa
PO Box 10103, Village Post Office, Gaborone, Botswana
Heinemann Educational Books Inc.
70 Court Street, Portsmouth, New Hampshire, 03801, USA
Heinemann Educational Books (Caribbean) Ltd
175 Mountain View Avenue, Kingston 6, Jamaica

LONDON   EDINBURGH   MELBOURNE   SYDNEY
AUCKLAND   SINGAPORE   MADRID   HARARE

First published by Heinemann International
in the Caribbean Writers Series in 1988

British Library Cataloguing in Publication Data
Belgrave, Valerie
Ti Marie. — (Caribbean writers series).
I. Title       II. Series
813 [F]            PR9272.9.B4

ISBN 0–435–98830–1
ISBN 0–435–98831–X export

Chapter Openings illustrated by Caroline Craig

Photoset by Wilmaset, Birkenhead, Wirral
Printed in Great Britain by
Richard Clay Ltd, Bungay, Suffolk

*To my mother, Josefita Celestine Charles.*

# FOREWORD

Trinidad is a small Caribbean island, less than two thousand square miles in size, although it is large in comparison to neighbouring islands.

It is a well-endowed island, with abundant oil and asphalt, fertile soils and a rich culture. It is the proud birthplace of what are universally accepted as West Indian art forms – the calypso, the steel band, the limbo, West Indian-style carnival.

Its peoples are drawn from many races, and indeed today the twin-island republic of Trinidad and Tobago prides itself on being an exceptionally cosmopolitan and racially harmonious nation. The early history of Trinidad has contributed greatly to its cosmopolitanism and also to its rich outpourings of art, for even in the dawn of its modern-day period (the late Eighteenth Century), it was a haven of liberalism and racial and cultural tolerance. I have set my fairy-tale of the beautiful coloured girl and her Georgian beau, a young Corinthian, at this early period in the island's history, a period when its liberalism was being sadly shaken.

VALERIE CHARLES-BELGRAVE

# A NOTE ON THE LANGUAGES

What would rightly have been the French patois (creole) of the slaves has been liberally translated into 'Trinidadian English', so that the colour and flavour of the language could be transmitted to the English-language reader.

Almost every conversation in the novel would have been in French or Spanish, except for conversations among the English themselves and for those conversations that take place in England.

# PROLOGUE

Sweat poured off Yei's face, distorted now in pain, and Bella renewed her efforts to keep her friend cool. Overhead the yellow, wizened branches of the carat palm that formed the roof rustled and whispered in protest as the sun pounded down mercilessly. For perhaps the first time in her life, Yei was losing her stoical composure; she moaned softly, mumbling what Bella assumed were her primitive prayers.

Labour had started early that morning. Yei had been at the Spaniard's hut, seeing to the children, when a sharp and unexpected burst of thunder had pierced the morning stillness. The great rumble, as if reverberating within her, had become a wave of pain.

It's too soon, too soon, she had thought, sudden panic sending her heart pounding wildly like a mocking echo of the great rolling noises in the heavens. She had hurried to settle the children, calling to the old African, Tía Roma, to help her, and then left hastily. She made her way towards some huts which were not far off.

'Bella, Bella! *Es la hora!*' she called.

A middle-aged, brown-skinned woman appeared. She instantly realised the situation and they went hastily inside the hut. Bella quickly made everything ready for the delivery. They said very little, intuitively hiding their mutual apprehension. Only their silence, the seriousness in their eyes and the intensity of their movements betrayed their ill-ease.

For hours Yei bore the pain silently until, unable to control her fears any longer, she said, 'Why now? Why now, Bella?'

'Is your first time, Yei, maybe that's why.'

'But I know I should go on for almost two more months.'

'Did you slip or fall? Did you get a fright?'

'No, no, you know I did not!' protested Yei, her voice hoarse and rasping.

'*Amiga*, I too do not understand it. So many deliveries you have helped with. You know everything even better than I. You are the one everyone looks to for help in sickness and childbirth. Do not be afraid now. All will surely be well.'

Bella's worried expression gave the lie to her consoling words.

Yei grimaced as another wave of pain attacked her. 'Oh, Bella, I don't understand it. Everything was as it should be, but I was always afraid . . . I was afraid all the time.'

'That's because the other women kept saying how you were growing too large so quickly, but you should not have made so much of their foolish comments. Maybe you miscounted your time. That would explain it . . . calm yourself, *amiga*. All will be well.'

Yei had been in labour for six hours now. Earlier, heavy rain had mercifully afforded her some respite from the oppressive heat, but it had stopped hours ago and the sun's power had mounted in steady, unrelenting waves, turning the little mud hut into a veritable oven. Now, at the hottest time of the tropical day, the cramps were urgent and excruciating.

Yei felt the urge to push. 'It's time now, Bella, this time,' she gasped.

Marshalling her limited strength, she forced her daughter out into the world. Bella's deft hands did what was necessary, and soon the air was filled with the lusty sounds of a baby's cry.

In exhaustion and relief, Yei sank back on the rough bed and closed her eyes.

'No, no, you must not sleep as yet – the afterbirth, Yei, one last effort, *amiga mía*.'

Yei roused herself at Bella's request but, as she did so, strong cramps and waves of intense pain, defying both their knowledge of this stage of delivery, engulfed her. The severity and unexpectedness of this attack, the lingering apprehension in her mind, and the exhaustion of the last six hours left her now in a state of real terror.

Gripping Bella's hand, she screamed, 'The pain! The pain comes again! What can it be? Something is wrong, Bella!'

The older woman tore her hands away from Yei's desperate hold and, thinking to assist with the afterbirth, discovered instead to her great astonishment the round, hairy crown of another tiny head.

'*Es otro, Yei, es otro! San José! Madre de Dios! Son gemelos! Gemelas!*'


It was the year 1777, on the tiny neglected island of Trinidad, lost on the southern tip of the Caribbean.

Yei laughed and cried and laughed again, when Bella presented her with her twin daughters; and Bella, instantly understanding, reciprocated her mirth, using laughter to throw off the tensions and anxieties of the unusual delivery.

But the birth of the twins was after Yei had already come to be part of the La Flores family.

In a sense, Yei's story, and that of the twins, started one day almost two years before, during the reading lesson . . .

# BOOK ONE

~

# *The Wild Flower*

## CHAPTER ONE

### I

Don Diego de Las Flores, trapped and bone-weary owner of the estate of Santa Clara, irritably slapped a mosquito from his sun-baked arm as he set his mouth in a firm line and insisted that José begin again at the top of the page.

Diego was a picture of long-suffering, beleaguered frustration. He was so tired, not just from the daily battle against the persistent weeding, the watering and coaxing of his recalcitrant cocoa crop, but from years of ceaseless, pointless toil on the land, work that essentially went against his naturally indolent disposition. He frowned and pointed to the letters in the primer in his seven-year-old son's grubby hand.

As the boy's voice stumbled over the unfamiliar letters, Diego looked around at his lands. Named after the patron saint of his wife, Santa Clara was nestled in the foothills of a range of low mountains which ran from east to west, spanning the northern section of this, the most southerly island of the Caribbean. It was a struggling and impoverished undertaking, as was the island itself. Oh, a natural paradise it could be, he knew. The natural bounty of the country was the only reason they had survived at all, for despite its decidedly strategic location, standing as it did at the gateway to all of South America, it was a neglected and godforsaken place. Perhaps it was just too far away from Sante Fé where the seat of administration was located.

What was he to do? No ships came, the few Indians who were left after the massacres, transportations and epidemics were almost all relocated to the missions.

'What we need is slaves, strong black slaves to work the cocoa,' he sighed, inadvertently speaking his thoughts out loud.

'But, Papa, there were some strong black men in Port of Spain,' came the unexpected response of the child.

'José, I was speaking to myself, but anyway, most of them are free men,' responded Diego. 'Trinidad is a refuge for anybody on the run. Slaves or no, they live just like us anyway. None of us have anything. How many of us are here? A handful of whites? And so many of us are already intermarried with Africans or Indians. My son, in a companionship of misery, there's little room for discrimination. Now, the lesson!'

The child read on and Diego returned to his ruminations. At a time like this, when the thirteen colonies of North America were at war with Britain, making a bid for independence, and every other island in the Caribbean was prosperous with slaves working the land, who could believe that after three hundred years of Spanish rule there wasn't even a proper town here? St Joseph could boast only a few mud huts, a church without a roof. Then there was Port of Spain. A town that was never founded, that had no council and no real name. *Port of Spain*, a description, not a name, even if the Governor chose to live there now.

Half-listening to the child, he idly took up a twig and drew a rough map on the earth – a map of North and South America with the islands like a necklace flung in the Caribbean Sea, and square-shaped Trinidad at the very end, a broken-off part of the mainland, very close to Venezuela.

'What are you doing, Papa?' asked the child.

'José, pay attention to your lesson, I've little enough time to spare for you. Come on, read, soon your mother will be calling you in and we have reached nowhere as yet.'

Reluctantly José resumed his efforts but, as before, Diego's mind drifted. He thought now of the desperation that had driven him here eight years ago, and the madness that had made him allow Clara to come. Clara, who was always ill and now going through her fifth insecure pregnancy. He thought of José whose education was so deficient. 'These lessons get nowhere. What I need is a miracle, a real miracle.'

'Papa, tell me what . . .'

'No José, we've wasted enough time today. Remember, I have no time tomorrow because I have to go again to the port. Come, now, pay attention!' Diego's voice was insistent and unyielding.

## II

The next day, unbelievably, Diego got his miracle. In fact, for a while he had many reasons to count his blessings. Not only had he found a tutor for his son, but his crops were looking promising and his Clara at long last was safely delivered of a daughter. After several previous miscarriages, Juanita's birth was a truly joyous event.

Diego's joy was boundless . . . but shortlived. Already weakened by the delivery, Clara succumbed to an attack of yellow fever.

Her death took the heart out of her husband. Diego was ready to give up, to let the jungle win the battle, take over his mind and his work. But no, there was José and the poor new baby, weak and sickly. It was quite apparent that she too was dying.

Today the baby lay in a twilight between life and death, watched over by the devoted old African. Diego could not stray far from his daughter. He walked agitatedly up and down the clearing in front of his home, his inner agony and helplessness marring his weatherbeaten face. His ragged clothing and deeply sun-burnt skin made him look as wretched as the humble thatched-roof dwelling from which he had just come.

In his early thirties, with dark hair, finely chiselled features, and a noble, determined chin, he was not an unhandsome man, but the struggle for his and his small family's survival had made any concession to appearance impossible and irrelevant. After a while, he stopped pacing. He stared with desperate eyes at the dominating mountains and then at the relentless jungle around, at the unending thick growth of trees, towering upwards, struggling to catch the sun, their trunks barely discernible through the tangle of shrubs and broadleafed creepers that wound their way upwards on every available trunk or branch. The snake-like lianas that entwined everything were as determined as the trees themselves to strangle each other in their bid for survival. Here and there the brilliant colour of a wild flower peeked out as if to lend some beauty, some fragrance or hope to the meaningless, menacing tangle of foliage. His life seemed to him as tangled, as incomprehensible, his path forward as impassable as the jungle that trapped his home on three sides.

Diego hung his head in abject despair.

'Pardon me, Señor Diego,' the tutor's weak, almost tremulous voice said. 'I know it is not a good time to disturb you, but if you will permit me a suggestion?'

Diego lifted his head slowly and looked at the young Frenchman. He was so thin that even his face seemed all bone. His nervous grey eyes were sunk in his skull, while his great height exaggerated his leanness.

His story must be almost as sad as mine, mused Diego. He certainly seemed a lost, desperate soul when he had met him at the port. He was shaking, sweat-drenched, stuttering with nervousness though in faultless Castilian as he struggled with his two crates of books. Diego smiled as he remembered how the captain of the little boat from Grenada had introduced him.

'You need books for your son's education? Well, ask that trembling palm tree over there, Louis Sauvage he's called. His blasted books almost sunk the boat in the Boca. Damned Dragon was rough today', he had said, referring, as Diego well understood, to the 'Dragon's Mouths', those infamous and treacherous narrow passages that separate Trinidad and a string of rocky islets from the Venezuelan mainland. Here the waters are notoriously choppy and the current very strong. They formed a natural defence, which partly explained why Spain had not lost the island long ago.

Diego had approached him, offering to barter for some books. He ended up taking pity on the lost young man and hiring him as tutor to his son, in exchange for food and shelter.

'About the baby, Señor,' continued the Frenchman, interrupting Diego's thoughts. 'There is a young woman whom you may not have noticed, for the overseer has only recently taken her on. I have heard that she is versed in the use of local herbs and medicines. She has quietly been helping many of your workers to overcome illness. Could you not let her see the child?'

'What do you know of this woman, Louis?'

'The woman is an Amerindian, Señor, very inscrutable. Miguel is the one who took her on to work in the cocoa. I heard too that she is part African. She looks like a mature woman but is probably no more than a girl. The natives hold her in great awe for her unusual silence and stature, as well as for her rare knowledge.'

Without hesitation Diego went in search of Miguel, the overseer, who like Bella was a half-breed Spaniard, one of several lost souls finding sanctuary at Santa Clara. He then followed Miguel to a nearby hut and waited as the overseer roused its inhabitants. In a short while Yei appeared at the entrance.

The golden orb of the sun had moved far down in the distant western horizon, and the inflamed sky sent colours dancing gaily between the shadowy clouds in a whimsical and flamboyant farewell to the tropical day. Don Diego, hands clasped together behind his back, legs apart in his familiar stance of authority, had turned his back to the hut and was looking at the sky, wondering at the insensitivity of nature to display such mocking gaiety in the face of all his grief.

As he heard the rustle of movement behind him he turned, taking his gaze too suddenly from the brilliance of the dying sun to the darkened doorway, and his ill-adjusted eyes alighted on what appeared to be a magnificent bronze goddess.

Tall and statuesque, of a heavy build, with smooth gold-tinged dark skin, crowned with a wealth of long, wavy black hair and draped in a loose, almost Grecian garment, the vision of Yei left him momentarily stunned.

His eyes soon adjusted to the fading light, and he half-smiled to himself as he realised the illusion they had just played on him. He proceeded to explain to her, with words and gestures, that his baby daughter needed the help of her medicines.

She came that very night to Diego's hut and, taking the two-month-old baby firmly in hand, banished all but Tía Roma, the old African house slave, from her presence. She then set about the mysterious processes that led finally to the recovery of the child.

## III

In the weeks that followed, Diego, still recovering from the loss of his wife and the near loss of his baby, turned imperceptibly towards Louis, whose frail, timid appearance concealed a powerful mind and a spirit as untamed as his name – Sauvage, the wild one. The Frenchman's perceptions and facility for acquiring knowledge and information filled Diego with growing respect, in spite of the republican sympathies he now revealed.

It was to Louis that Diego confided his joy at Yei's beneficial influence on the children, commenting on her strange magnetic presence and on her uncanny skill with the baby, and it was Louis who supplied him with more details of the Amerindian.

'It seems that her father was a strapping Mandingo, probably a runaway adopted by her mother's tribe. He must have died in some disaster or epidemic. That disaster probably forced her mother to flee and live on the fringes of white settlements until she too must have died from grief or whatever. Anyway, Yei just wandered in here one day.'

'And where do you think she learnt about medicines?' asked Diego.

'Apparently, healing was the profession of her mother's family.'

'Interesting . . . she has a second sense, or is it simply natural intelligence? She hardly talks and moves so noiselessly.'

'It's a characteristic of her people, I understand. In her it's even more like a . . . a natural elegance or other worldliness.'

'Well, we may never understand her, but the main thing is that she is good for the children,' concluded Diego.

# CHAPTER TWO

## I

At the time that Yei was entering Diego's humble household, the Spanish Court, which for so long had concerned itself only with the lazy task of gathering raw wealth from its vast and undeveloped colonial empire, began to sit up and take weary notice of the steady encroachment of the British navy into its colonial waters. The British, with an audacity seasoned by the threatened loss of their thirteen colonies of North America, were making steady inroads into Spain's South American possessions, first under the pretext of trade but increasingly in an openly aggressive manner.

Nudged by France, her virile and alert neighbour, Spain tried to rouse herself from her years of lethargy and incompetence and decided to take an interest in even the neglected island of Trinidad.

Towards the end of the year 1776, a royal decree was issued, permitting immigration to the island. A new governor was appointed and, soon after, Trinidad was placed in the legislative and military sphere of the Captaincy General of nearby Venezuela. A new day had dawned on the island.

A trickle of change and hope came like the life-saving breezes that defy the unrelenting sun and serve to make the islands more tolerable than the mainlands. For the first time in several years a ship called, and Diego had the chance to export some of his crop, to purchase supplies and to pick up a handful of slaves.

Casting off all signs of indolence, Diego began remorselessly clearing large tracts of land for cultivation. His obsession and his liberal treatment of the slaves inadvertently gained him their respect and allegiance. He was already predisposed to a form of tolerance unknown to more seasoned slave masters. Indeed, the horrendously oppressive and decidedly bigoted slave societies of the north had not as yet spread their tentacles to the lush shores of Kirie (as Trinidad was called by Yei's people).

With Spain's new interest in the island, Diego was able to export his second harvest and, for the first time, to realise some profits. He began thinking of building himself the proper house he had dreamed of with Clara: a modest two-storeyed house with a wide veranda, located on a gentle hill overlooking from one aspect the treetops of Santa Clara and, from another aspect, the magnificent Northern Range. There would be lavish lawns and flower gardens, in the middle of which he would plant a golden poui.

The house on the hill swiftly became a reality, and eventually the day came when Diego and his family moved in.

Whether Diego had had it in mind for Yei to become a full member of his family or just the official nanny, she became in effect indispensable to the running of the new establishment.

With José's influence she learned to speak French and Spanish. For, fascinated but frustrated by the limitations of her storytelling, he insisted that she stay with him through his lessons with M. Louis.

The once timorous Louis, now revealed as an incisive, volatile young radical, considered Yei's education a special challenge. Eventually overcoming her initial resistance, she proved an apt pupil.

At the same time Tía Roma, a retainer from nobler days who had accompanied Clara from Spain, deeply grateful to Yei for the survival of baby Juanita and touched by the Amerindian's willing deference to her, cheerfully taught Yei the running of a nobleman's establishment, about manners, customs and etiquette and generally about survival in the white man's world.

## II

About a year after she had first come to the rescue of the sick baby and had embarked on the role of foster mother to both of Diego's children, Yei – who although known to occasionally absent herself had never been known to so much as give a second glance to a man – became most obviously pregnant. No one could persuade her to identify the father.

Once the babies were born and it became clear that their father was either wholly or part white, suspicion naturally fell on Don Diego. It was certainly remarkable that he never dismissed Yei. However, these two little matched dolls, who looked like black and white versions of each other, were the instant delight of Diego's children and indeed of everyone on the plantation.

Yei, in her natural wisdom, included both José and Juanita in care of the babies. She captured for ever José's interest and affection by granting him the privilege of naming them. He called the lighter one Carmen, and the darker, Maria Eléna.

In no time it became clear that the twins were not identical, and indeed, although undoubtedly similar, they matured differently.

Yei and her daughters demanded very little, and in any case Diego knew that in the secluded estate of Santa Clara, nestled in the extensive and relatively remote Maracas Valley some ten miles east of Port of Spain, he could have found nobody else to befriend his otherwise solitary little daughter. Mixed households were not unusual, anyway. In that depressed land, coloured mistresses and coloured offspring were part of pragmatic compromise and made for survival.

M. Louis simply included them in his classes. In fact he became very fond of the twins, particularly of the little brown-skinned girl. In her early displays of intelligence and sensitivity, he saw a kindred spirit. Unlike the rest of the household who had chosen to call her Eléna, he took to calling her *ma petite Marie Hélène*, which was shortened to *petite Marie* and eventually to *'ti Marie*.

One day, when the twins were only two years old, he was out of doors with his charges. He noticed Eléna reaching down. Looking shyly at M. Louis, the little toddler pointed her chubby finger at the weeds at her feet.

She was indicating the sensitive mimosa plant, which, like the folding of butterfly wings, closes its miniature fern-like leaves, magically, at the slightest touch. Louis remembered part of a verse which he had once heard somewhere, and he bent down to her, singing as he touched the plant, 'Look, *ma petite*, 'ti Marie, 'ti Marie, close your door, policemen're coming to find you.'

The little girl was delighted with the game and her face lit up with a glow that warmed Louis's heart. Completely overcome by her innocent charms, he hugged her to him and said, '*You* are my 'ti Marie, my little sensitive plant. See, you are as delightful as the tiny 'ti Marie flower. How the name suits you! Little wild flower, 'ti Marie.'

# III

During these years, when the twins were growing out of babyhood, the French, mostly from Grenada, were migrating to Trinidad in modest numbers with their slaves. The island was beginning slowly to come to life, but this in no way affected the children.

Within the household, Carmen grew to look quite as Caucasian as Juanita. She was even held to bear her a certain resemblance, both having auburn hair and sparkling hazel eyes, Carmen's intense, sensitive personality proving perfectly harmonious with Juanita's sweet, lively character. Eléna, on the other hand, was not considered a beauty, but her reserved yet caring personality and her quick intelligence were endearing qualities. Without ingratiating herself, she would foster harmony around her. She showed a precocious maturity, being the least playful and the most academically inclined of the children. Were it not for her almost wayward sense of humour, her tutor would have worried at her serious-mindedness.

When the twins were five years old the ailing Tía Roma died, and Yei completely took over the reins of the household.

In the sixth year of the twins, when Eléna's intelligence and ingenuous personality were already evident, and Carmen's undoubtedly gifted singing voice was the joy of those who cared to listen, Spain again made an effort to attract settlers to the island. Charles III passed a royal *Cedula* on colonisation, a decree of wider scope than the previous one of 1776. This *Cedula* was aimed mostly at French colonisers of the other islands of the Caribbean.

That year Trinidad's meagre population rose to over six thousand souls. The French came, fleeing from their failed crops, from British persecution, from poor, depleted soils, or from their debts and mortgages.

Some of the immigrants were white families, but by far the greater number consisted of free blacks and mulattos, attracted by the promise of the *Cedula* to grant them land. Non-whites would get only half the white grant, but that was a generous offer to those generally oppressed peoples. Here, at least, their entitlement was assured and could even be considerable, depending of course on the quantity of their labourers; for with all these immigrants came thousands of African slaves, the number determining the size of land grants allowed their masters.

Apart from Louis's incomprehensible, forbidding declaration that development sometimes extracted a heavy price, these happenings had little, if any, effect on the lives of the happy family de Las Flores at Santa Clara.

Then one day Diego returned home, exclaiming to Louis, '*Gracias a Dios*, Louis, I met the new Governor today. Don José Maria de Chacon, a knight of Calatrava! No longer one of the scum of Spanish politics, but a real man, a man of vision!'

This Spanish nobleman, José Maria de Chacon, a linguist and a liberal, became well known and well liked by all but his fellow Spaniards. For naturally, in an island where they were fast being outnumbered, they did not like his equitable land distribution policy.

Many of these Spaniards left the island in pique, and those few who stayed were for the most part out of sympathy with the Governor. Finding himself isolated from his own countrymen, he welcomed friendship with Diego, occasionally making token protest over the indolent Diego's refusal to join the ruling *cabildo*.

Some evenings, escaping from the pressures of office, Chacon would visit Santa Clara. Since the house was not large, Eléna heard many of the gentlemen's conversations, learning of the wonderful improvements Don Chacon had instituted. They talked of the reorganisation of the country into districts administered by overseers or commandants of quarters, possessing civil and judicial authority. They talked of the establishment of a medical board and a port health doctor. They talked of marvellous improvements to the town of Port of Spain, of the relocation, at Chacon's expense, of the Río Santa Anna into the Dry River (a man-made bed at the foot of the low Laventille Hills that skirted the town.

They talked too of the construction of new government buildings, of a fort and mole on the Port of Spain waterfront, the improvements to public works and roadways and the construction of a proper carriage road linking St Joseph to Port of Spain.

The discussions that attracted Eléna's most serious interest, though, were those that dealt with Chacon's humanitarian projects: the establishment of new missions for the welfare of the Indians and the drafting of a new, liberal slave code. This code would protect slaves from harsh masters and neglect in their old age, allowing them to be instructed in the Roman Catholic religion and guaranteeing their right to live in families. There were to be regulations governing the quality of their food, hours of work, living quarters and punishment. Eléna began to understand a great deal, by inference, about all these matters. This 'Code Noir' was of particular interest to her, for already she had begun to pay special attention to Diego's slave population.

One day, however, she found herself the subject under discussion, as Don Chacon exclaimed to Diego, 'What a beautiful black child!'

'Who? Eléna? Why, she is no match for her sister Carmen!'

'Oh no, no! The other is fair, and has the obvious beauty of a mulatto, but this one is like a dark Spanish Moor, like a girl I once knew in Madrid. Her charm is still a sleeping bud, yet to open, but she will be a great beauty one day.'

Eléna could not believe her ears. She did not then know that Chacon himself had a mulatto family, nor that she possessed exceptional good looks. For her, it was the first time that anyone but Yei had called her beautiful, so she remembered Don Chacon and his kind, complimentary words long after he had left the island of Trinidad.

## IV

Reserved and industrious, Eléna spent her spare time reading from Louis's stock of books or sewing dolls and dolls' dresses for Carmen and Juanita. Happy with her own company, she loved to sit under a special tree which stood in an isolated spot by a little stream on the estate.

She was also very close to her mother, and would walk with her through the fields and forests, learning of her life in the tribe or of herbs and their uses and discovering the art of healing. It was to Eléna that Yei passed on a special pride in her mixed race.

By this time most of the Amerindians had drifted away from Santa Clara to the missions, but many more African slaves had been acquired. Under Diego's comfortable paternalism, they were relatively well cared for and allowed limited but indisputable freedoms. They were encouraged to marry, they lived in families, tended their own plots of land and sold their produce for their own profit. Without doubt they were a subjugated people, but they were never considered anything less than full human beings. Most of the time, however, the children of the 'big house' remained aloof from them with one exception: at the weekend, when they were allowed to tend their own plots, Eléna opted to accompany her mother who had formed the habit of joining them in the fields.

This unusual intercourse became a tradition. Yei was well regarded by the slaves for her healing skills, and Eléna especially revered as one-half of a twin – twins being of special, almost magical, significance to the Africans.

Yei felt no degradation in this activity. As she said to her old friend Bella, 'I live in the white man's way, but the Africans are more like me – more natural.'


## V

In the loving, nurturing atmosphere of Santa Clara, fragile, sweet-tempered Juanita thrived and grew strong; laughing, teasing José grew to manhood; and the twins blossomed into beautiful, sensitive versions of Yei. It was a gossamer world, an idyll of rare beauty, and no reflection of what was occurring on the outside. With the ugly convulsions of revolt and war that were taking place, Santa Clara might have been merely a poet's dream, or a fairy-tale spun to amuse a child's fantasy . . .

When the twins were just eleven years old and Juanita on the brink of adolescence, in the very year that José was proudly entering Chacon's tiny militia and the great man had been officially issuing the Code Noir, the bare-footed masses of Paris stormed the Bastille and set France aflame. When the twins were thirteen, that struggle reached the West Indies. The black masses of Saint-Domingue (later called Haiti), France's greatest colony, rose up in anger against their white masters. Four years later, revolution was fermenting in the islands of Guadeloupe, Martinique and St Lucia, and threatening to start in Grenada, Jamaica and St Vincent. Even more so now than during the American Revolution, the age of republican ideas predicted by M. Louis had dawned. The world began to tremble or rejoice at the cry of 'Liberty! Fraternity! Equality!'

By the time Eléna first heard of it, however, the struggle had long ceased to be merely republican against royalist. It had metamorphosed into full-scale war between France and her allies, and Britain and hers, with the Caribbean Sea as a chequered board on which the game of war was played.

In the Caribbean, the revolution undoubtedly brought new freedom and hope to the once hopeless, but part of its effect was rotting corpses, maimed bodies, abandoned plantations, terror, fear, suspicion, and a massive movement of people that was to have a great influence on Eléna's little island. Isolated to the south, still in its groping infancy, content in its unusual tolerances, Trinidad suddenly, about the year 1794, began to notice the seas growing blood-red around it.

The first inkling of these realities reached Eléna one evening as Don Chacon said: 'It was one thing, Diego, when they were honourable men coming here to escape some hardship. Now we get all manner of riff-raff, all manner of . . . of republicans!' Chacon spat out the word in distaste. 'Men with scandalous ideas, who will ruin us! Like they have ruined France!'

Diego heard Louis's sharp intake of breath and cast a restraining look at him, but Louis, now in his mid-forties, with grey streaking his wild, unruly hair and fine lines adding character to his sunken eyes, was not intimidated by Diego's speaking glance. His own brand of republicanism had conceded much to changing realities since his youth, but yet he clung tenaciously to unshakable principles.

'They call it a revolution,' he said in a challenging voice.

'Revolution? I don't care what they call it. They should keep it in France, not be instigating revolution here like in Saint-Domingue. To make it worse many of the slaves who are being brought in by white owners have seen how it was done there.'

Louis's sunken eyes took on a fiery glint as he responded, 'The slaves in Saint-Domingue needed no prompting from the Jacobins in Paris to realise their own suffering! And yes, what happened in Saint-Domingue can happen here. Trinidad is fast becoming just like that cursed land, a big graveyard for slaves! The Code Noir isn't stopping the atrocities of the royalists. We too are importing in large numbers, and slaves are being worked to death.'

'No, no, Louis, you have it all wrong. Diego, talk some sense into this fellow! My commandants of quarters are there to protect the slaves by enforcing the Code Noir. But I tell you, the planters are also afraid that the new coloured immigrants are going to infect their slaves with dangerous ideas.'

'Ah ha! Now we come to the real point. Coloured freemen, eh? Men who . . .'

'Louis, Louis, I have no fight with you,' interrupted Chacon. 'You're a philosopher. You read Voltaire and Rousseau, but you left France too long ago, you don't understand what men with poisonous ideas are capable of.'

'Put your fears to rest, then. Aren't the British transporting all republican suspects to Europe? They may have lost Guadeloupe, but St Lucia and Martinique are still British. You can rejoice – they are purging these islands of the taint of republicanism, soon there will be no men of "dangerous ideas" left to come here.'

'I do rejoice that the British are ridding the Caribbean of the French menace. Trinidad used to be a haven, a refuge, especially for the peaceful coloured man, but now it's the refuge of all the snakes and vipers of the pit of demons stirred up by the Jacobins in Paris!'

'Excellency, these are strong words, said without thought!' cautioned Louis, turning away in disgust.

'Well, we have had a frighteningly large influx of immigrants recently,' Diego quickly added.

'Yes, that is precisely our trouble. I have had to start questioning arrivals,' continued Chacon, 'because they are coming now from those very islands where the British are in power, and worse, from republican Guadeloupe, running . . .'

'Running from the British and the loyalist dogs who invited them to take the island!' interjected Louis with a near snarl in his voice. 'Obviously they are running to get some peace, and those running from the French, obviously they are not republican!'

'I don't agree. Look, coloureds already make up the majority of the population here. I mean, I have the greatest respect for coloured men, but I strongly suspect that this new lot is in league with that Victor Hugues.'

'But it may also be that the coloureds are coming here to escape the mere horror of recapture by French forces. When Guadeloupe was recaptured by Hugues, over three hundred people were killed, you know,' supplied Diego cautiously.

'Exactly!' exclaimed Louis. 'They may be running from war, running *from* republicanism, not running to spread it!'

'Louis, you don't understand. Some of these men may simply be agents of the very Hugues they pretend to fear. Don't you hear how they are addressed as soon as they land? It's "Hail *Commarade*!" That's what you hear.'

'You speak so scathingly of Hugues, he is the official commissioner of the government in Paris . . .'

'Don't talk to me about that band of brigands! The man is a murderer, a criminal!'

'So that justifies your inquisition?'

'I have no inquisition. Is an investigation an inquisition? That's a reprehensible thing to say, Louis.'

'I rather think that what is reprehensible is that the governor of a Spanish colony cannot see that Spain is a natural ally of France, and will be so again, and soon. Spain cannot sustain many more defeats like that of the first campaign of last year. King Charles is not that foolish, he . . .'

Diego sighed wearily as he listened to the Frenchman's comments, but he knew that Don Chacon, though troubled and confused, was not personally offended by Louis's ideas. And Louis, the crazy savage, had been right all along. This unrest, worry and suspicion were the price of development. *'Ay de mí!'* he sighed again. 'What drives men to such lengths? I've become too complacent and unambitious, too afraid of real poverty and too content with my small fortunes, to understand.'

Diego chuckled to himself as he got up to replenish Chacon's drink. As he turned, his eyes met Eléna's. He was startled, and more than a little shocked, by the intense look of concern written on her small brown features.

# CHAPTER THREE

## I

A week later, taking a message to Diego, Eléna knocked on the door to his study and entered. With some surprise, she noticed that her patron had been closeted with a personable young coloured gentleman who now looked arrestingly at her. She glanced away quickly and conveyed her message to Don Diego. He excused himself instantly and hurried out of the room.

As Eléna turned to leave, the coloured gentleman, dark eyes sparkling with interest, said politely, 'Won't you stay a moment longer, Mademoiselle?' He had risen to his feet on her arrival.

Eléna paused, stiffening as she regarded his dark, intense brows and well-groomed black hair waving away from his handsome forehead.

'Do you . . . er . . . live here?' he asked hesitantly, unsure of the status of a coloured girl in a white household.

'Yes, Monsieur, this is my home.' From years as M. Louis's pupil, her French was faultless.

The young man introduced himself as André Fontainebleau and proceeded to invite her to attend his parents' ball on Shrove Tuesday.

'You will be the guest of my mother and my sister, Yvette, who is about your age.'

His attitude and his address were decorum itself. Obviously this gentleman had been highly educated, probably in Paris itself, or in London, thought Eléna fleetingly.

'I . . . I don't know what to say, Monsieur,' she stammered, bewildered by this sudden, non-fraternal attention to which she was unused. She was saved from replying further, however, by the reappearance of Diego, breathing heavily and wiping the sweat from his brow. The invitation was repeated. Impulsively, Diego accepted on Eléna's behalf, explaining to the gentleman that Eléna was his daughter's companion. He concurred with him as to the exact arrangements.

Eléna hastened to excuse herself. She was dismayed, blushing furiously under her dark skin. Upon retiring that evening she felt calmer, and spoke of it to her mother. Yei raised no objections. She suggested that Bella would be a suitable chaperone for she knew full well that Carmen would be reluctant to accompany her sister.

Eléna spent the week working feverishly on her ball gown, her heart filled with barely suppressed excitement. She modelled it for a delighted M. Louis, who was full of avuncular praise for his pupil's handiwork.

''ti Marie, you will outshine everyone at the ball,' he said confidently as he waved her goodbye and rode off towards his own revelry in the town.

Carnival celebrations among the French had started long before, since Christmas some two months previously, and were now building up towards their climax on the Tuesday before Lent.

At nine o'clock in the morning on Shrove Tuesday, M. Fontainebleau arrived to collect Eléna. She was dressed simply in her customary white muslin and a dainty straw bonnet tied with a protective scarf on her dark hair. Accompanied by Bella, she stepped into the buggy and unwittingly into an adventure that would shake her from her secure little cocoon, foreshadowing the maelstrom that would one day engulf her.

## II

It was a glorious tropical day, breathing a spirit of *joie de vivre* with its intoxicating, sunny brilliance – a day to inspire a feeling of gaiety. It was carnival weather.

The sun blazed down. The few clouds in the sky only accentuated the intensity of the blue. The small company drove unhurriedly through the countryside where stretches of cocoa trees, with their many-coloured pods oddly placed on branches and trunks, were interspersed with yet untamed rain forests.

Sometimes sheaves of cane waved at them from the intermittent sugar plantations, or tall bamboos swayed and rustled in accompaniment to the sweet chirping of the birds. It was a heavenly day and Eléna was happy and excited.

The young gentleman asked Eléna to address him as André, and in a spirit of informality they conversed. In a while, on hearing that his family had come from the island of Guadeloupe, Eléna asked what life had been like there for them.

'The conditions of life there were very severe. We were humiliated at every turn. The whites got the best of everything and we, almost nothing. We could not even walk on the same side of the street that they used. There was harsh punishment for the slightest offence.' André paused, frowning thoughtfully as if the memory was still painfully alive in his mind.

Eléna was shaken, and she hastened to brighten the conversation. 'But here it is better, no? I know that because I often hear Don Chacon speak of people's rights.'

'Chacon is a good man,' responded André. 'Under the Spanish, the best conditions exist in Les Antilles. We at least have some civil rights, and we're treated with respect. I have even been offered a commission in the militia. The terms of the *Cedula* are fairly generous, and because of our large numbers, and I daresay our fair amount of wealth, we can live with some security. That is not to say that most of us are wealthy. Many are only skilled workers or smallholders, but enough of us are well off.'

'Somehow you don't sound as cheerful as your words,' commented Eléna astutely.

'I see that I have to be careful when speaking to you.' The young man chuckled softly. 'I'm sorry, it's just that I often wonder how long all of it will last. Things are not quite as easy-going as they once were.'

'Do you feel insecure here, then?'

'Well, with Spain still aligned with Britain, and so keeping the wolves at bay, and with the French dominating this island and making it therefore rather less than a prime target for the republicans, we are safe enough here . . . for now . . . But how long do you think it will be before Spain allies herself with France?'

Eléna's errant scarf danced in the breeze, stretching playfully to include André in its wayward jig. The young man smiled, capturing it and handing it back to an apologetic Eléna.

He continued, 'As good as he is, Chacon is already showing his rising panic over the war, the internal French rivalry – for there is that too – and the growing number of coloured immigrants.'

'I believe he has appointed a committee to examine all new arrivals,' commented Eléna.

Surprised at her continuing interest in the conversation, and her pertinent comment, the Frenchman continued: 'That is correct. What's more, he has already deported some that he didn't like. I'm afraid sometimes that one day he may entirely lose sight of the fact that coloured people have nothing to gain by creating a revolution in the one place that is a haven to us.'

'But his fears arise from the greater fear that coloured people will join with the slaves in revolt.'

André laughed, but not derisively. 'That won't happen, but by their strictness the Grands Blancs may just provoke what they fear. Many of us, you see, are sympathetic to the promises of the revolution, but mostly what we want is control over our own lives. It was the same in Saint-Domingue. Free coloureds had won the legal right to vote, but the Grands Blancs refused to allow them to use it. They took up arms, and after that the slaves revolted.

'The fears of the white royalists may influence the Governor and

19

everything may change. But Chacon's fears should centre on the British, on the lack of defences in the island. Oh, but who knows the future? Today is too lovely a day for such thoughts. We should be talking of happy things. *Mon Dieu!* We should be speaking Castilian for your chaperone's benefit.'

Eléna smiled stiffly at him, some of her happiness dissipated by the discussion. But the bacchanalian carnival sun was still dancing joyously in the radiant sky, and even the trees swayed in merry abandon. Here and there along the way, faint sounds of merriment blown on the wind reached them, kindling Eléna's curiosity, and stimulating her sense of anticipation. By the time they reached the lively town she was gay once more, and looking forward to the entertainments of the day.

What a day it turned out to be! On arriving at André's home, they were greeted by the antics of his jovial friends as they promenaded down the Fontainebleaus' steps into the streets to the accompaniment of their noisy music.

Bella, just stepping out of the carriage, pursed her lips and frowned in disapproval and apprenhension. Plump arms folded across her ample chest, eyes alert and challenging, she looked to all the world like a haughty, formidable duenna.

Eléna laughed, as amused at the revellers' antics as by the set of Bella's face. They were ushered indoors.

André's father, plump, prosperous, greying and very much the gentleman, greeted the arrivals with the exaggerated chivalry of one already in a festive mood. His mother, buxom and exceedingly good-natured, was effusive in her graciousness and smiling hospitality. Yvette proved to be a thin, perky young girl of sixteen, lively but evidently prone to illness, constantly cautioned by her watchful attendants. More and more joyous bands of revellers converged on the house, bringing their music and infectious gaiety with them before disappearing with rousing salvoes, dancing off to carouse at other houses with other friends.

Entertainment was the order of the day. André's father in his generosity had granted his slaves permission to celebrate by performing that morning. The Maître de Cariso – the calypso singer – sang his ingenious songs, the '*bel tamboyes*' enchanted with their drums, and the slave women danced the *bèlè*, their version of the stately minuet.

Never was there a dull moment. When the activity was not inside, it was out in the streets and Eléna watched with the guests as bands of masqueraders paraded. Observing the antics of such a group of white revellers, she encountered the first sobering note since their arrival.

Kings and courtiers, priests, monks, devils and warriors made up the band. Then Yvette called their attention to a white man disguised as a field slave.

'Yes, he's pretending to be a *neg jardin*', agreed André, hugging his sister comfortingly. Then it was his turn to become unnerved, for they had spotted a masked reveller gyrating in a most vulgar fashion so that Yvette hid her face and ran inside. It was a white woman dressed in the douillette, mouchoir and foulard (the colourful overskirt, gay neckerchief and turban of the French creole mulatress).

'Why must she make such rude gestures? It's so vulgar! André, is that how they really see us?' asked Eléna soberly.

'There's that interpretation, I suppose,' André replied, stroking his chin thoughtfully. But privately he wondered if it was not a sly, twisted comment from an aggrieved party on the white man's notorious penchant for coloured mistresses.

That evening there was the ball. Eléna had never seen such a gathering of beautifully dressed ladies and handsome gentlemen or heard such music. Never had she received such compliments – for her ballgown was quite outstanding – or been the object of so much male attention. The night was perfect. There was an odd moment, though, when André was introducing her. He referred to her as 'Eléna de Las Flores'.

'De Las Flores?' she repeated, in confusion. 'No, *De las Flores del Campo*,' she added, smiling.

' "Eléna of the wild flowers",' repeated André, gazing at her with undisguised admiration.

It was late into the night when the ball finally ended and Eléna climbed wearily up the stairs, surrendering herself to Bella's kind assistance. She sank gratefully into a sleep of contented exhaustion.

## III

With morning came sobriety. Eléna accompanied the Fontainebleaus to church to receive the symbolic crosses of ash. A hearty breakfast followed. At the table Eléna enjoyed their solicitous hospitality. They were a proud, formal, yet easy-going family. Mme Fontainebleau freely admitted her love for cooking, speaking conversationally of the uselessness of her many servants in that regard. M. Fontainebleau, Eléna learnt, was the owner of not only a small sugar plantation near the town but of a thriving import business as well. He bristled with pride as he told Eléna of the successes of his undertakings and of the high regard in which he was held by the Governor and other people of note in the country. His obvious pomposity amused but did not revolt Eléna. She realised what such regard meant to a family who had come from the degrading conditions that André had so sketchily described to her. She listened politely, even though in her inexperience she could find no words with which to praise their achievements.

It was nearly afternoon by the time she and Bella took their leave, amid many entreaties to return soon for a proper visit. They set out once more in the open carriage, with André, for Santa Clara.

The afternoon was calm, and looked as surfeited as Eléna felt. Even the constant twitter of the birds was slower, mellower, less frenetic. Different from the day before, but beautiful. Or was it just her imagination? Eléna was content and settled down comfortably in her seat in the carriage to enjoy the leisurely ride eastwards and the friendly conversation with André.

'André, I must tell you that it was a wonderful experience, I wouldn't have missed it for the world,' she began.

'The day was greatly enhanced by your presence, Mademoiselle', replied André gallantly, in good humour.

'You are very gracious. Your family too. I enjoyed meeting them very much.' She smiled across at him. After a quiet interlude she spoke again. 'I've been thinking about this carnival all morning. To go through so much hard work and effort just to enjoy yourself, to have everything just right. But that is what makes a celebration like your carnival so wonderful. In a strange way it makes complete sense. I mean, to be able to say, for once, we'll put our efforts into just being happy and frivolous.' Eléna laughed, a little embarrassed by her own audacious speech. She glanced shyly again at the young Frenchman.

'Don't stop now, your philosophy is fascinating!' he said encouragingly.

'Do you know, I've never been frivolous before yesterday.'

'Oh no, you make yourself sound so solemn. However, I do detect a strong spirit of fun even in . . .'

André never got to finish his sentence. Suddenly the peaceful afternoon was shattered by a horrendous, blood-chilling cry.

'What is that, André? What can it be? Someone is in pain! Someone is hurt! It must be! Oh, go faster, please go faster! Someone needs help!'

André increased speed. The carriage rounded a bend in the road and they came upon a scene of such horror that Eléna involuntarily stood up in the moving vehicle and started screaming wildly and uncontrollably.

In a clearing at the side of the road was a black slave, cringing helplessly in the dirt. Tearing into him, ripping at his flesh, were two large, ferocious dogs.

Torn skin, blood everywhere. Desperate, hopeless screams assaulted the newcomers. Two armed white men stood at ease. They looked on, unmoved by the spectacle, like waiting vultures. The slave's voice rent the air with his pleas. The white men made no response.

Lips set in a firm, angry line, hands tensed, André was intent on driving past. He knew only too well the viciousness of some white slave-owners. Eléna would not allow him to do so.

'Stop, André! Oh stop! We can't just ride away. We must plead for him, we must get the men to let him free! Oh let him alone! Call off the dogs! Let him alone!' she cried hysterically.

'Eléna, sit down! For God's sake, sit down! We cannot interfere! I cannot stop! You don't know these men as I do!' shouted André, as he urged his team forward.

But Eléna was beyond reason.

'You can't just drive away!' she screamed, grabbing the reins and struggling with André.

Rather than fight her, he allowed the team to slow down. She threw herself out of the vehicle, recklessly intent now on stopping the cruelty herself.

André scrambled after her, trying to restrain her, yelling to a bewildered Bella to calm her charge. 'I'll see to it! I'll see to it!' he conceded.

He did not know exactly what he could do. This was none of his business. He knew it was foolish to interfere, but the girl in her naïvety would surely think him a coward, for ever, if he just rushed past as he had intended. He could at least pretend to enquire, make a small gesture. After all, he was just starting a promising courtship. He had to appease her in some way.

He thought quickly, deciding the best course was to be very polite and respectful. He would merely ask if there was anything he could do to secure the release of the victim, or to assist in some way. He conjectured that there must have been an attempted uprising and the men were making an example of this unfortunate slave. Perhaps he had been the leader.

He approached the white men cautiously. His face was ashen with fear. He got no opportunity to say a single word.

Seeing him advance, one of the white men rushed up. He took a massive swing with his gun and levelled a stunning blow to André's head, sending him face down in the ditch.

Eléna saw, and her hysteria knew no bounds.

Nothing in her experience had prepared her to deal with such a situation. Where were reason, good sense, humanity?

Involuntarily, she began screaming again.

Her screams, the tortured yells of the slave, Bella's frantic pleas, the wild noises of the dogs, the protests of the horses in that long moment became a deafening roar of anguish which reverberated through the air, stabbing the once beautiful day with frenzied intensity. Eléna began to stagger.

The white men lurched forward, and grabbed at both women. One held Eléna roughly. He slapped her about the face, snarling profanities. She struggled, limbs flailing wildly. Her clumsy resistance incensed him more. He imprisoned her hands, grinning lecherously. He grabbed her collar, swiftly dragging her down on to an embankment. With one brutal movement, he tore away her garments.

It was then that Eléna lost consciousness.

For an eternity she seemed to be fighting off grotesque, human-like forms. Kings with tarred skins, wild abandoned women with swinging hips, and well-dressed young men with faces like vicious dogs. Struggling frantically, she was sinking further and further into a dark, gloomy world of hideous colours, forms, insubstantial grinning faces. Purples, yellows, murky pale creatures engulfed her as her clothing fell apart.

With a desperate effort, she mustered all her strength. She lurched forward, awake! And into the arms of her mother.

There, magically, was Yei, right at her bedside, holding her close.

'Yei, Yei, what happened? Did they . . . Yei, did they . . . ?' Eléna was unable to complete the question, not knowing how to voice her fear.

'No, no my child. Apart from your bruises, you are unharmed.'

Eléna's troubled eyes searched her mother's frantically.

Yei shook her daughter, saying emphatically, 'Eléna, listen to me, they did not violate you, they did not succeed.'

Eléna succumbed to a flood of uncontrollable sobbing. Yei hugged and comforted her.

Finally, able to speak again, Eléna asked, 'What happened, Yei? How did I get here?'

'M. Louis saved you, my child. He arrived in time.'

'And Bella?'

Her mother looked away.

'Yei, tell me!' she demanded.

'I may as well tell you then . . . He was not in time to save my dear old friend. Bella is dead, Eléna. She fell in all the confusion and broke her neck.'

Yei's voice held a sad resignation and Eléna looked with horror at her mother's controlled but anguished face.

'Oh no, no, no, it can't be!' she moaned, rocking her body in desperation. 'How did M. Louis know, Yei? Where did he come from?'

'He had just come in from town. When he saw you weren't at home as yet, he went to look for you. Thank God, he did not wait! He has gone now to report the incident.'

'What . . . what of André, Yei? Is . . . is he . . . dead too?'

'No, no, my love, no. He was saved. He recovered and has been taken home. All will be well, love. We'll take care of you. You are a strong girl. A very strong girl. You will be all right and you will soon forget.'


# IV

Eléna, though soon recovered, did not soon forget. She did, however, renew her acquaintance with André and they continued to be friends, with him calling on her frequently at Santa Clara. Despite his efforts, though, their conversation was never that of lovers. Eléna would always steer their thoughts to an impersonal course.

She would ask about the cruelty of the royalists and protest that the Code Noir ought to protect the slaves.

'But who is to carry out the law, Eléna? Not the very same masters of torture who came from places like Guadeloupe that I told you about? Aren't seven out of the ten men of the *cabildo* French royalists?' replied André.

Eléna would grow determined – never, never would horror and injustice touch the slaves of Santa Clara, not while she was alive! André made many attempts to interest her in himself and in his growing feelings for her, but she turned every attempt back to her compelling new interests. When it was not the realities of slavery, it was the French government's recent abolition of slavery in French territories or the tensions growing in the island, or Spain's recent neutrality in the war (the partnership with Britain broken, as Louis had foreseen), or the threat of British invasion in spite of the island's neutrality, or the state of the local militia (in which, like José, André was now an officer), or the revolt in Grenada and the attempted revolts in the other islands.

André realised that she has been badly scarred. He understood finally that it was not yet a good time to press his suit. The spark that he had hoped to kindle had gone out of her. He decided to bide his time, never suspecting that when the spark burned again it would be a different fire, stronger, steadier, to be kindled by someone else, a stranger, unexpected, unsuitable, appearing briefly on the stage like a bit player in a travelling show.

# CHAPTER FOUR

## I

Far from the sunny island of Trinidad, where already forbidding clouds were gathering and threatening to rain terror on the backs of slaves and free men alike, in a world so completely different as to be incomprehensible to those slaves already dying on plantations, in a luxurious London drawing-room Lord Vantage was sitting impatiently.

This distinguished member of the British aristocracy, the ninth Earl of Vantage, was awaiting the arrival of his delinquent son, the Honourable Barry Wingate. His Lordship, a sober, portly man in his early fifties, sat pensively, thinking of the misdemeanours of his youngest son. His face was set in a heavy scowl which every member of his vast household had reason to dread; for Lord Vantage was an easy-going man, slow to anger, but once roused his wrath was just as slow to cool.

Incumbent of the prosperous seat of Vantage in the county of Kent, Lord Vantage had, on his precipitate ascendency to the title, been firmly sat down and lectured by his mother.

The Dowager Lady Vantage had proceeded to press home to her son the urgent necessity for a union between himself and an acceptable daughter of the British aristocracy. The Dowager did not hesitate to explain that the purpose of her admonition was not simply to assure his future happiness (although she certainly wished as much for him), but, much more importantly, to assure the succession of the title, lands and properties of the noble house of Vantage. In a word, the necessity for an heir. His mother was most importunate about it, not just because he was her only son but particularly since she had taken the sole other heir, her late husband's younger brother, in great dislike.

There was no disputing the fact that his mother was perfectly right, and in a short time the ninth Earl took to wife the Lady Marjorie, heiress to the considerable fortune of the Davenports. Their marital union was blessed with not one but three healthy sons in rapid succession. This number more than adequately satisfying their need of heirs to title and property, Lord and Lady Vantage thought to pack up their nursery and settle down to the enjoyment of watching their sons grow to manhood.

It was therefore a most unexpected and, as Lord Vantage himself cried, 'a vulgar' shock, to learn five years after their third son was out of leading strings that Lady Vantage was expecting yet another addition to the family.

Not being an unkind or unreasonable man, His Lordship sought to console his equally distraught wife with the assurance that this time it would surely be the daughter she had longed for.

With the maddening perversity of nature, however, the baby turned out to be yet another lusty boy.

Fair, where the other three had been dark, and with the most beguiling blue eyes, like deep pools of icy water, he was born in the very same year that Yei gave birth to her twins. Already solid, he steadily increased in weight, growing into an athletic and healthy infant. Unlike his elder brothers, who all had peculiar quirks of their own, he was a well-adjusted and playful child with a gratifyingly quick intelligence. Consequently his parents soon overcame their disappointment at his sex and proceeded to spoil, and indulge young Barry, as he had been named.

The Honourable Barry Wingate, spoilt as he was by a household staff of twenty-one servants, his three elder brothers and his parents, was a surprisingly kind and sensitive child. Though full of energy, boisterousness and mischief, he had a kind heart for animals, children and underdogs as well as a remarkable tolerance and respect for adults.

He was a joy to his doting grandmother, the Dowager, with whom he loved to spend school breaks and summer vacations at Grenmill, her ample estate in Somerset. The estate, left to her by her father, was her sole unentailed property. She was therefore free to dispense with it as she willed. It was everyone's belief that this inheritance would fall to Barry, for the bond between the two was unmistakable, and it increased rather than diminished as the child matured.

To the Dowager, Barry was an unexpected spark sent to brighten her old age. Her Ladyship had neither in her youth – nor her advanced years – been accounted a popular person among the members of her class or among her sex. She had the reputation for being a rebel, a bluestocking, and she was considered 'fast'. She was known to say exactly what she thought on most subjects, holding unpopular views on many. She was indeed far too well educated for a mere woman, and even in her later years when it was not necessary, she was an avid reader. She had in her day held her own ground against many great thinkers of the age on such controversial topics as exploitation of the poor, child labour, the excesses of the Court, the abomination of the slave trade and the oppression of women, to name but a few.

There were limits to Her Ladyship's revolutionary zeal, however. She would argue fiercely for the liberation of the slaves, but would not consent to dismiss her own servants. She would rail against a society dominated by men but would not have agreed to pass the reins of power to women.

It is noteworthy however, that for her era she was a genuine liberal with enough sincerity to allow logic and good sense to overcome prejudice in many cases. The fact that she had not been ostracised from society was due, of course, to her vast wealth (which came not only from her marriage), to her exceptional beauty as a young woman, and finally to her powerful husband and, subsequently, her powerful son.

On many a summer evening the young Barry would sit at her feet in front of the fireplace of her informal sitting-room at Grenmill, discussing and debating the issues of the day.

'Grandmama, why do you say that we must not always think like aristocrats?'

'Because, my dear boy, that sort of thinking is what got Louis and Marie Antoinette into the Tuileries where they are now. They're virtually prisoners, and I daresay in grave danger of their lives. Monarchs cannot simply care about their own kind and do nothing to alleviate the poverty of the common people, just as I cannot overlook the people of my village. We must be able to place ourselves in the other person's shoes, and feel for the other.'

'Most of the poor have no shoes, Grandmama,' chuckled young Barry.

'*Touché!*' she smiled, fine lines radiating from her bright grey eyes. 'But you know full well what I mean. I was speaking metaphorically.'

The young boy sprawled full out on the Persian carpet, propping his chin with the palm of his hand, and asked, 'Is that why you are against the slave trade?'

'That wretched business! I hate to even think of it. When I read some of the reports of how the slaves are transported from Africa, the horrible conditions.' She shuddered, the silk Indian shawl on her elegant shoulders shimmering in the firelight. 'Those blacks may be ignorant, but they are not animals to be so treated, Barry.'

'But they are silly and primitive and, ugh! So ugly. They have no notion of religion, or even civilisation, Grandmama.'

'Well, I'm glad to see you're so interested in them. I'll have to get you some literature on the subject. Just the same, your bull terrier is hideous, yet you treat him well, and he is not a man who can speak and think. I think that white men have forgotten that they were once primitive too and lived in caves. Slavery is a dirty business, Barry, a dirty business.'

Their small discussions in time grew to be interesting debates in which the sharp-witted, knowledgeable Dowager held forth on many topical issues. Yet such discussions at his grandmother's fireside were not really taken seriously. They were no more than pleasant pastimes, as much of a game as pitting one's wits against an opponent in a wrestling match or a game of cards. Barry loved these quiet evenings as much as he loved frolicking through the woods, playing games of cricket, taking care of his pet animals, or romping with his elder brothers. The issues were never thought about after the holiday.

When Barry left to return to school, his grandmother would gaze after him lovingly and say, 'What a beautiful, sensitive child! What a wonderful husband and father he will make, and a perfect master for Grenmill.'

As Barry grew to manhood, however, this sensitive side of his character was soon overshadowed by a youthful exuberance which manifested itself in a spate of mischievous and delinquent escapades.

## II

While the children of Africa on the other side of the world were writhing under the boot of the most brutal form of slavery ever known to mankind, and some were already struggling under fierce tropical skies to free themselves from that unholy bondage, certain young aristocrats in Britain, untouched by those eventualities and quite heedless of the war in which their country was then engaged, were wallowing in the excesses initiated by the Prince of Wales.

Barry, following the highest example, therefore, and seeking as well to emulate the youthful exploits of his notorious eldest brother, Graham, fell in with a bunch of hell-raising companions calling themselves the Rovers: a gang of over-indulged young aristocrats, fun-loving but callous, who happened to be his classmates at Oxford.

The Rovers, with their ever more daring practical jokes, were the bane of anxious mamas, and the terror of the eating places, taverns and clubs of the towns surrounding Oxford. Barry gained a bad reputation which resulted in several warnings and pointed suggestions made to him, or worse, to his father. But the genuine mutual love between Barry and his parents, and his basic good nature whenever he was at home, seemed incompatible with vague tales of his misdemeanours in an age already tolerant of excesses.

Nevertheless, he seemed to be propelling himself towards disaster, and disaster met him in the form of one Annabella Claymore.

Barry's contribution to the disrepute of the Rovers was not particularly in the line of womanising, but was mostly as a result of his unquenchable sporting enthusiasms. He fancied himself a budding Corinthian, and would do anything to prove his skill with the whip, his excellence as a sharpshooter or his dexterity in the ring.

Annabella Claymore, cousin of one of Barry's cronies who went by the soubriquet of Ruggie, and sister of one Viscount Clifford Claymore, stepped into Barry's life during the Christmas season of 1795. The association continued on Barry's occasional visits to London in the weeks that ushered in the New Year. Lord Claymore, taking advantage of the eligible Barry's obvious infatuation and, mindful of the imminent collapse of his Jamaican plantations, colluded with his sister to entrap Barry into matrimony. The scene had been carefully set. It took place on a weekend when Barry and Ruggie had come down from Oxford at a party at Lord Claymore's deceptively lavish home. Barry was caught in a clearly compromising position with the temptress, and Clifford, in the presence of witnesses, demanded that he marry his sister.

Although Barry was young and limited in experience, he was not so easily duped. He was quite aware that Annabella had been seducing him, and not the other way around. He therefore laughed in Clifford's face and declared flatly that he would do no such thing.

Clifford had not expected such a reaction. Barry was not quite the lovesick fool he had expected. This was not at all the way they had planned it, but in the presence of witnesses he was forced to defend his sister's honour. He stepped forward and flicked his fingers in Barry's face. 'You'll meet me for this, young man,' he snarled. 'Name your choice of weapons, tomorrow if it suits you and have your second contact mine. Sir Edward Morley would undoubtedly stand with me.'

'And I'll stand your second, Barry,' added Ruggie loyally, looking defiantly at his cousin.

'Very well. Ruggie, pistols, tomorrow. I'll expect you at dawn. Good evening, gentlemen.'

Arriving home some twenty minutes later, determined to retire to bed immediately and put an end to a disastrous day, he was met at the front door by Williams, the old family butler, who informed him that his father requested his presence in the library. Such a summons was not to be ignored.

Handing Williams his hat and cane, he was ushered into his father's presence.

Lord Vantage was not alone.

'Ah, there you are, Barry. I'm glad you're home in time to meet your Great-Uncle Wilfred.' The two gentlemen shook hands as Barry wryly reflected to himself that this was the notorious Wilfred, the bane of his grandmama's life.

Wilfred Wingate was the younger brother of the eighth Lord Vantage, the very brother whom the Dowager had held in violent dislike. Her aversion to Wilfred stemmed, however, not so much from those many character blemishes she was wont to enumerate, nor from the fact that as a young man he had squandered his inheritance. In fact, it was her bitter disappointment that someone who was associated so closely with her could have become an active participant in the notorious and reprehensible slave system. For that was not only how Wilfred had chosen to regain his wealth but how he chose to live.

'What brings you home, Sir?' asked Barry conversationally.

'Time to take my eyes off those lazy niggers in that blazing sun, what! Not that it's easy to leave, m'boy! Always so much there to do. I'm not one of those "absentee owners", you know, and what's more I have two plantations to see to.'

'What's the size of your holdings there, Uncle? I believe you produce sugar. Grenada, is it?'

'No, no, left that cursed island years ago, when m'wife Marta inherited her father's estate in Barbados. I have two plantations in Barbados. I live on one, in an adequate residence, very adequate with about two hundred slaves.

'Why don't you come down with me, m'boy? There's a lot of good living to be had there too', he chuckled and leaned mischievously towards Barry. 'Not all those slave women are repulsive, you know, and they certainly can't trap you into an early marriage,' he added unwittingly and guffawed, continuing, 'What say you, m'boy? Nothing like a trip to the Indies to prove your manhood!'

Smiling politely, Barry replied, 'Tempting offer, Uncle. I'll give it some thought.' Barry of course, had not the slightest intention of so doing, for he was totally unaware that the fates had already decreed his future in which the Caribbean and the reprehensible system of slavery was to play a vital part.

As the events which followed unfolded, his grandmother, deeply saddened by them, consoled herself by thinking that at least disruption at an early age meant one would be flexible and adaptable, and therefore better able to deal with unaccustomed difficulties, deprivations or danger. And she prided herself that she, at least, had imparted to him some sense of objectivity that ought to stand him in good stead, no matter what.

# III

The following day Barry rose at four-thirty in the morning, since the duel was to take place at dawn. He dressed and left the house. Ruggie was awaiting him in a carriage. Saying little, they set off through the city. Soon they were passing through Piccadilly and arrived at Hyde Park.

The dawn had by then fully broken and the sky was rapidly lightening. They heard the sound of an approaching carriage, which rolled to a halt a short distance from them. Clifford and his second, Sir Edward Morley, descended, with the doctor. Ruggie and Sir Edward conversed for a few minutes.

The seconds did their duty. Both gentlemen refused to apologise or back down in any way.

'If you are ready, gentlemen,' Sir Edward called out. Barry selected his pistol. Ruggie said, 'Good luck, old chap.'

The duellists stood back to back and moved forward as the paces were counted. They turned on the command and fired. At the end of it all, through the smoked-filled air, Barry could see Clifford sprawled on the ground, while he himself felt a stinging pain in his upper arm. 'My God, Ruggie, I aimed too well, Clifford's badly hurt,' he shouted.

Ruggie and the two older men bundled Clifford's prostrate bulk into the carriage which immediately set off at a spanking pace. Ruggie rushed over to Barry, dragging him away into his waiting vehicle.

'The shots may have been heard, we've got to get out of here fast, before anyone comes!' he cried.

But they had already been spotted, and by none other than a member of the Bow Street Police. Everything happened very quickly after that. The man raced after them, demanding that they stop. Ruggie would have none of it. 'We've only to ditch this carriage, he may not have spotted us,' he offered.

Barry's reply was not at all optimistic. 'Good God, Ruggie!' he exclaimed, looking behind him. 'Did you see who the Runner was? It's Carlton – who tried to arrest me in that rumpus we kicked up last time we were in London.'

'You can't mean the same Runner who swore to get even with you?'

'The very one!'

'Now we're done for! Do you think he recognised either of us?'

'I can't be sure. One way or another, I'll have to get out of town fast.'

# IV

Although duelling was a not infrequent pastime of the rich in Britain, and persisted long after Barry's encounter, it was in fact outlawed, and had been so for some fifty years. Since it helped many an aristocrat to save face, however, it retained its clandestine popularity with the upper classes. Although undoubtedly dangerous, it did not often end in death, fatalities resulting in only one out of every thirteen meetings. As chance would have it, Clifford was one victim that proved the statistic.

Barry had been nicked in the arm and needed immediate, if minor, attention. By prior arrangement, because of the scratch, they drove to Ruggie's rooms. That was just as well, for after having tended the wound, changed clothes and hired a new carriage, they arrived at Mayfair to discover a strange man pacing up and down in front of Lord Vantage's home.

Drawing away quickly, they were able to escape detection. It was clear, however, that the police were on Barry's trail. His disreputable past had caught up with him. He had in fact been recognised by Carlton. The man was not about to forget the humiliation he had suffered on a fateful day when the law had succumbed to the influence of a certain aristocrat, running to the defence of his notorious son and his friends. Nor would Carlton forget his other encounters with those rascally youths who were constant thorns in his side.

Barry and Ruggie stayed hidden all that day. Towards nightfall, judging it safer, Barry approached the house once more. Although there were no signs of untoward surveillance, he took the precaution of entering at a more secluded side entrance. Once inside, he came upon the butler, Williams, who confirmed his worst fears. The man Carlton had been to see his father.

'Do you have any idea what I can expect now?' asked Barry of the kindly old retainer.

'Sorry, Mr Barry, the picture looks gloomy. His Lordship's been in a towering rage these last six hours.'

'I'm going up to my room to change. Kindly tell him that I'm home and will be down to see him in a short while.'

'Very well, sir. Please permit me to wish you good luck.'

'Thank you. I'll be needing it this time.'

## V

The Earl of Vantage glanced once more at his watch, then put it away. It was fifteen minutes since Williams had informed him of his son's arrival in the house. His anger, which had mounted steadily all day, had by this time been transformed to a numbing fear over the future of his much-loved son.

When Barry finally entered the room, Lord Vantage rose and started pacing.

'This is a fine mess, Barry,' he began by way of greeting, 'Do you know that Claymore is dead?'

Barry started visibly. 'No, no, I didn't, Sir.'

'What are we to do now?' asked his father helplessly.

'I apologise, Sir, for causing the family such distress. Would it help matters at all if I told you that it was not of my deliberate making?'

'I'm aware of the circumstances. I had a chat with Sir Edward a short while ago. Why didn't you come straight to me, boy? Together we might have avoided this. What's to be done now?'

'Short of going on trial and facing a prison term, the only other thing I can do is go away for a while.'

'Standing trial with your reputation may well mean a prison sentence. You'll have to leave town, and Oxford – there's no gainsaying it – but is there any place you can go where you won't be readily detected?' asked His Lordship more to himself than to the tense, pale young man standing solemnly behind him. 'You can't go to any of our houses nor to your grandmother's at Grenmill, that's for sure.'

'Perhaps I should leave the country, Sir.'

'Drat it boy! You can't go to France now. There's a war on there and there's no time to arrange for you to go anywhere else.' Lord Vantage paused, and then a new thought occurred to him. He sprang around and declared, 'But you *can* go to the West Indies! Wilfred sails at dawn tomorrow from the port of London.'

'But isn't there a war on there too, Sir?'

'Oh in Saint-Domingue and those other islands, but not in Barbados. No, it's safe there. Give me a little time to look into this matter. I may be able to sort things out so you can safely return before long.'

There was a mad rush to escape. There were some tense moments before he boarded the ship, heavily cloaked and uncomfortably defeated, but the fates had had their day. On a bleak morning just before the spring of 1796, Barry Wingate sailed out of England on the *Norfolk*, bound ultimately for the island of Barbados.

# CHAPTER FIVE

## I

Barry looked dubiously around the tiny space which he was to share with Wilfred for the next few weeks aboard the *Norfolk*. He wondered whether a prison cell would have been much worse. Excusing himself, he left Wilfred and went up on deck. Once there, he stood leaning on the rail, a lost and forlorn figure. The bitingly cold wind tore through his hair, sending it streaming backwards. Though he felt the chill through to his bones he did not move: torturing his body as his mind was tortured. He gazed with unseeing eyes at the expanse of nothingness ahead. He thought that the future was as bleak and chill as the wind and as formless as the horizon.

'What a damned rotten mess, to be cast adrift in a hopeless place like the West Indies,' he mumbled into the wind. He regretted many things, but most of all his inability to bid his grandmother farewell. 'I know how hard she will take it, that the fates threw Wilfred in my path. Fate! I wish I had faith!'

'You look as melancholy as I feel, standing there. Is there nothing we two can do to cheer each other up?' a friendly voice asked.

Barry turned and saw a man of medium height, slim and well dressed, who was probably in his late twenties. His long, slim nose and high brows gave him an air of distinction.

'Fred Whiteways is the name. Care if we join each other in our misery? I always feel the same utter dejection and hopelessness every time I set sail, it doesn't matter for where.

'It's the human condition, you know,' persisted the gentleman. 'Going away makes one feel the passing of time, the passing of one's life more acutely, but it has its positive side too. It gives one an idea, a glimpse into the all-seeing eye, or what you will. I mean, you move from one place which you know, and go to another, which you get to know. You almost become omniscient, you see.'

A philosopher, by George! thought Barry. He introduced himself and accompanied the interpolater to the ship's dining-room, where they sat at a small table, sipping glasses of rum.

Their conversation faltered at first, for Barry was unnaturally uncommunicative. After a few drinks his companion's real or philosophical melancholy inclined him to open-hearted loquaciousness and he volunteered. 'I'm off to Grenada, you know. Was there before, some years ago. Nice place if the damned Europeans would leave it alone. All the islands, I'd say! Bloody hell-holes! Man preying upon man. War, revolt, rebellion, floggings, killings, rapes. Can't imagine why m'sister ever wanted to stay there.'

'Where? In Grenada?' asked Barry, curiosity getting the better of his moroseness as he sensed a story about to unfold.

So it was that Barry learnt the history of Fred's sister Kathy, who in rebellion against a domineering and oppressive father had eloped with a man she did not love because he was going far away to the West Indies. Fred was now on his way to rescue her, for her husband had been killed in the uprising. Their father, quite reformed by his daughter's rejection of him, had sent him on this mission of mercy.

'She's quite a bit older than me, you know, but from what I gather m'father was very strict with her. Virtually kept her prisoner in our castle in Northumberland, never allowed any suitors. Once when on holiday she did start a liaison but he violently broke it up and she never got over that. Strange, he was never that strict with me. Ha! He's so desperate now for me to marry, he'd probably not mind whoever I chose!'

'Is your sister all alone on her plantation then?' asked Barry, opening up with genuine concern.

'Not exactly, slaves and overseers and so on. She does have a son too, although he's been away in Europe. Like us, he's probably on his way back, I'd imagine, but then, he's not much use in a crisis; arty type, you know. Point is, huh! I doubt that she still has a plantation!'

'Is it that bad there?' asked Barry.

'Oh yes, my melancholy friend. Don't you know the Caribbean is the battleground of the European powers? And, too, French republicans have their lackeys at work. The place is crawling with troublemakers – officially freed French slaves, ex-slaves from the revolt in Saint-Domingue, free coloureds demanding rights! British islands are not immune, my friend, there were uprisings in both Jamaica and St Vincent last year. Now Grenada's been changing hands every few years, you see. Of course, the last time the French captured it in '79, they did so with the aid of the resident Frenchmen. It's been in British hands since the recapture of '83, so the French have been viewed with great suspicion and treated as such. With Victor Hugues in the Caribbean now, the malcontents everywhere are getting assistance and encouragement.'

'Who is this Hugues?' asked Barry.

'Official representative of the government in Paris. A West Indian mulatto, no less. He has a fleet, men with arms, and the mandate to take the revolution to the West Indies.'

Whether it was the rum or not, Fred seemed an open, easy-going fellow, and despite the serious implications of their discussion Barry began to feel his depression lessening.

'So, my friend, you see I am expecting anything, but you should have nothing to fear. Barbados is as peaceful as heaven on earth. The climate is warm and that's a delight after the fogs of London. There's certainly rum aplenty! So drink up. No point in our being blue-devilled over things we can't change.'

The two gentlemen soon became fast friends. Barry had found in Fred the type of friend which Ruggie may have become, but which he had never really had: a man experienced enough to have overcome youthful recklessness and young enough to retain a zest for life.

It was not long before Fred knew Barry's story. Ironically, the mere act of telling it coloured the circumstances of the duel if not its outcome with a humour that Barry had not previously detected. Just that cheered Barry enormously. Therefore in laughter, good companionship, mutually interesting conversation and plenty of strong drink, Barry's depression vanished. The narrow confines of his cabin seemed less imprisoning. He was even able to tolerate Wilfred's presence, and he actually began to look forward to the 'adventures' ahead.

The day finally came when their ship docked in Bridgetown's beautiful harbour. Like a large emerald, the island of Barbados sparkled before them, lush and peaceful, almost perfectly flat, its gentle rolling undulations like well-crafted facets in a gem. Black men were everywhere, their bodies glistening in the sun, as they saw to the business of receiving the ship. Here and there, white supervisors stood, legs apart, whips poised, suspicious eyes keenly surveying every effort and everywhere the noticeable presence of the military.

'Isn't it beautiful, what! barked Wilfred. 'Barring the bloody, lazy niggers and the bloodthirsty French, these islands would be heaven on earth. Ah, there's Marta waving. Wave to her, Barry. There, she's seen you!'

37

Barry dutifully waved and then, excusing himself, went in search of Fred.

'This is goodbye, then?' he said to his friend.

'Not just yet. It will take me a day or two to arrange passage to Grenada. Then, by God, I'll be back with Kathy, she must want to leave by now! Her fingers or her rosary beads ought to be worn out from overuse!'

'Rosary beads? You're of the Roman church?' asked Barry in surprise.

'Yes, although I'm a sort of fallen member. We're Irish really, didn't I tell you? Well, we've lived most our lives in England. Moved there when my father inherited his title. Mother was of the Catholic Irish. When she died, Kathy clung to the religion, even in the climes of Northumerland. It was the one indulgence my father allowed her. I've friends here so we'll come back to resuscitate ourselves before heading home. I think our paths will cross again – in fact, I'll look you up tomorrow.' They shook hands and parted.

## II

Wilfred's house, a fine Jacobean mansion with an imposing façade and all the trappings of an English stately home, including chimney and formal gardens, was situated on a slight elevation overlooking the plantation.

Palms swayed and rustled in the wind. Birds sang sweetly. Afar off, the gentle sea sparkled and shimmered as it kissed the land. Barry was completely enchanted by the beauty of the island.

'You are right, Uncle,' he said at dinner that first evening. 'This must indeed be the most perfect spot on earth.'

The next day, however, Barry was to encounter the other side of the coin.

After a good night's rest he rose, breakfasted and was fussed over by the plump, red-faced and ebullient Marta. She was as profuse in her offers of hospitality as in her hunger for gossip about England. Many were her questions about the latest fashions and fads, about the Prince of Wales and his many exploits, his recent wedding and his attachment to the remarkable Beau Brummell.

Hours later, Marta's curiosity sated for the moment, Barry was happily released. He sauntered out in search of his uncle. As he approached Wilfred's study he was stopped in his tracks by his uncle's resonant voice.

'How many losses, you say?'

'I'd say about thirteen in all, Sir.'

'That many! What the hell's been going on here behind my back? You getting soft, Albert? All runaways?'

'No, Sir, nine of them died in the fields. We had some trouble with "Boots", so we had to teach him a lesson. Johnson got carried away and whipped the scoundrel to death. It was a bit unpleasant after that. Examples had to be made.'

'Four of them whipped to death?' asked Wilfred rhetorically, without a trace of emotion.

'The example had to be made, Sir.'

'Yes, yes, I suppose so. Sixty pounds in fines to be paid if enquiries are made. You and Johnson will have to be less conscientious in your chastisement, next time. Can't afford so many losses at one blow. I hope the same situation does not pertain at Jeremiah, or I'll be ruined by my short absence.'

'We did our best, Sir.'

'All right, all right. We'll speak no more about it. Now, what's this about a woman who's been stealing?'

'I have her outside, Sir.'

'Bring her in then!' Wilfred commanded.

Barry saw a black woman forcibly propelled forward. Hands tied behind her back, face contorted with fear, she collapsed on the carpeted floor. Cringing on her knees, she sobbed loudly. 'Mercy, Massa, mercy! Is the baby I do it for! Mercy, Lord Jesus, mercy! I no do 'gain, Massa, please, p . . . lease Massa, I beg, I beg!' she blubbered.

Albert strode towards her, jerked her head up roughly and administered a resounding slap to her face. 'Shut up, you black bitch! Have respect for the master!' he bellowed.

'That's enough, Albert,' cautioned Wilfred. 'Now, Mara, that's your name, isn't it? You've been caught stealing food supplies from the mistress's kitchen here in the big house. Red-handed. No one's told lies about you. You've just admitted it so you have no defence.'

'For the baby, Massa. It be hungry. I dry up, Massa, baby goin' die.'

'All right. Enough! Albert, take the baby and carry it to Jeremiah . . .'

'No . . o!' screamed the slave hysterically. 'Don't take 'way the baby! No, Massa, no, Massa . . .'

Without pause Wilfred continued, 'There's a lot of nursing mothers over there. Give it to one of them. Tell Justine to see to its welfare. Now take her out, put her in the stocks for twenty-four hours.'

'No, Massa, I beg you, leave the baby with me!' pleaded the slave, trying frantically to creep towards Wilfred on her knees.

Albert roughly hauled her to her feet. Wilfred spoke again in his dry voice, addressing the distraught woman. 'Go now. Next time you won't get off so easily.'

Just then he turned, realising that Barry had been standing in the doorway. He said pleasantly, 'There you are at last, Barry, m'boy! Come in, come in. How's your first day? Marta treating you well? Very hospitable folk over here, you know. Give you the shirt off their backs!'

Barry stood unresponsively, overcome by the horror and injustice of the previous scene. His eyes glared fiercely at his uncle. His fists were clenched. Without a word, he turned and strode from the room. He marched out of the house and walked swiftly down the driveway. Not knowing where he was going, he was simply intent on putting distance between himself and his great-uncle.

Mercifully, he was stopped in his tracks by Fred. 'Where in blazes are you going at that pace, Wingate? I was just coming up to call on you!' The signs of distress on Barry's flushed faced cautioned Fred, and he continued in a softened manner, 'Let's go to the beach and take it easy for a while, and you can tell me all about what's upsetting you.'

The invigorating sea-bath finally restored Barry's calm, and he was able to relate the upsetting incident to his friend and receive his none-too-comforting counsel. 'Muster up some cynicism, old chap. You simply can't go around raging at every injustice. My, what you saw was mild, I might add. What the hell did you expect, anyway?'

The soothing waters, healing breezes and cheerful blue skies eventually dulled the sharp edge of ugliness that had gripped Barry's mind. Seeing his friend more relaxed, Fred spoke again.

'Barry, you're really in no position to do anything about the system here. It might console you to know that there are other people who feel as you do, who are in better positions to effect change.'

'Yes, through my grandmother I'm familiar with the abolitionist movement, and the heroic efforts of Pitt and Wilberforce', responded Barry. 'But I do know that since the French explosion and the resultant fear of republicanism, the movement has lost momentum. Anyway, it's just a personal revulsion, I don't think I can change the world.'

'That you can't, old chap. Me, I try to view it all philosophically. But I admire your passion. It renews my faith in our race. When it comes down to it, only planters, merchants, slavers or else those suffering poor whites here in the colonies will defend this system. Any objective person can see it's a barbaric business. The average Londoner, for instance, lives contentedly with the free blacks, grateful to them for keeping the city clean, or they ought to be, anyway.' Fred sat up and arranged his

clothing. 'So my advice is cynicism. And look,' he added sympathetically, 'wait until I get back with Kathy. We've friends here and their
system isn't so harsh.'

Fred left the next day for the war-torn island of Grenada and Barry
spent the succeeding days chatting with Marta, bathing in the sea, and
staying away from things that were unpleasant. Fred returned days later
and proceeded to tell Barry of his adventures.

'I've got Kathy out. She and about twenty slaves. She was fairly safe.
Stayed most of the time with friends in the capital, St Georges, held by
us. Her plantation is ruined, of course, burnt, and many of her slaves
have fled into the hills with the rebels. A lot of bungling's been going on
out there. Our forces have been moving too slowly.'

'Tell me what happened. Who is the rebel leader?' asked Barry.

'Julien Fédon, a coloured man, educated in England they say.
Apparently, Victor Hugues made him the Commandant General of
operations in Grenada. Gave him arms and the rest so Fédon stirred up
his people and eventually launched an attack last March. He surprised
the little town of Grenville where he massacred large numbers. He took
about fifty English prisoners and went up to his camp in the hills. It's
quite a mountainous island, you know. He was able to capture the
hapless British Governor, who was betrayed by a slave.

'Oh, the conceit of our people! Thought he could discuss their
business in front of a slave. Well, it cost him his life. He was executed
along with the other prisoners. In those early stages, everybody moved
too slowly, it seems. No help came. Eventually some Spanish soldiers
arrived from Trinidad and then some from our forces in Martinique and
since then from Barbados. That insurrection will drag on until the rebels
can't hold out any longer.'

'So you and Kathy are returning to England soon?'

'Not at all!' Fred sighed wearily. 'I don't know what to make of it, but
she is determined not to go home. Says her husband was monster
enough, she's not going back to her father. Despite the loss of so much,
she *will* stay on in the West Indies and start all over again.' Fred shook
his head dispairingly. 'Wait, before you rejoice, her plans are not for this
island. No, she wants to go to Trinidad.'

'Trinidad? But that's not British – Spanish, I thought.'

'That's right, siestas and all!'

'How will she be able to emigrate there?'

'Oh, that's easy. Under the terms of their *Cedula*, she is eligible as a
Catholic.'

'Ah!'

'She's asked me to go over and make the arrangements. Look over the place and so on. Come with me. Spain is neutral in the war now and slavery is much more humane under the Spanish. Lots of free blacks are allowed to be citizens. They practise a liberal slave code too. When I was there – oh, some seven years ago – an accused murderer, a slave mind you, was awaiting torture in prison. Spanish law, you know, but law or no, no one was prepared to torture him so they simply let him escape. Of course, in the first place, the alleged murder was committed in the wee hours at a wake, which turned into a party.' Fred laughed. 'It's still slavery, but nothing like it is here. A different atmosphere. A fascinating island really. There you can relax a bit. By the way, do you speak French or Spanish?'

'Had a French nanny since the day I was born. My Spanish is only fair.

'Good! French will suffice.'

'In a Spanish island?' asked Barry with a puzzled frown.

'Oh yes, in a Spanish island!' laughed the knowledgeable Fred.

# CHAPTER SIX

## I

Seeing that everyone in the colonies rose at what Barry called an ungodly hour of the morning, very early the day after their nocturnal arrival in Port of Spain Fred rose, dressed, and left their guest house to get about the business of negotiations with Don Chacon.

As usual, the night before they had sat up late, talking and drinking rum. But this morning a sense of excitement kept Barry from further sleep. Not long after Fred left, he roused himself, washed, and dressed in front of a small tarnished mirror.

Six feet tall and of an excellent, athletic build, his fine form was used to expertly cut coats and pantaloons and shiny hessians. The vision before him now though was more one of tidiness than of fashion. Barry smiled wryly to himself. His blond locks were not carefully brushed into the look of studied disorder that he had so recently been cultivating. As for his neckcloth, it was not vaguely close to the starched muslins with their ridiculous convolutions on which he had prided himself in London.

'My goodness! What would Ruggie think of me now?' he exclaimed. There was no rancour in his thoughts, though, for with the flexibility of youth in which the Dowager had put her trust, Barry had quite thrown off the vanities of former days.

Fred had arranged for their landlady, a willing, middle-aged mulattress of fading beauty, who ran the Guest House of the Royal Palms, to provide them with meals. She now tapped lightly on Barry's door.

With his unhesitating command of French, he answered the summons, opened the door and stepped out. 'Ready, Madame, and ravenous!' he said with a mock salute. He accompanied the blushing mulattress to the small courtyard where a table had been set for him.

Eating everything she offered with the voracious appetite of youth, he looked around him, taking in the delightful sights of his yet unfamiliar surroundings. Nowhere but in the tropics did the early morning feel so still, he thought. It was almost an uncanny stillness, for it was not at all silent, as Barry realised when he consciously listened. A profusion of birdsong filled the air.

He spoke to the landlady. 'Is that a macaw making that racket in those trees?'

'Yes, Monsieur, two macaws on the Royal Palms. They travel along in pairs, and come every morning to fly from tree to tree around here. It is remarkable. I suspect that they mate for life, Monsieur, for they never come or leave without their partner.'

'That's not just remarkable, but admirable – a civilised creature!' Barry replied. 'I'll remember that bird as a symbol of constancy.'

'Which is more than most men have, Monsieur,' returned the woman.

'What's this? Do I hear the voice of an experienced lady of the world? A lady with a broken heart, perhaps? Show me the scoundrel, Madame, and I'll call him out, fight him to the death, and defend your honour!' said Barry, swaggering in feigned combat, gesturing wildly with an imaginary sword.

'No, no, no, Monsieur!' The woman laughed. The light comical banter between them made her relax her servile guard. 'You are too funny! Are all Englishmen as happy-go-lucky as you are, Monsieur?'

'Can't vouch for that, Madame, I've only had eyes for the English ladies, that is, until I set eyes on you.' He approached her menacingly, and she, pretending terror, ran laughing from him.

Barry was in remarkably good spirits. Coming to Trinidad was like inhaling a breath of fresh air. The mere act of leaving Barbados released his spirits from their numbing bonds. He was young and wanted to be happy, frivolous even. He could sense that this island held some promise of freedom – or was it something waiting in the wings, waiting to spring into life? Some enticing secret was whispered on the wind that wafted around him as he sat under a large tree in the courtyard of the little guest house. He felt light-hearted and gay. His heartbeat quickened and seemed to resound in his ears, so that his eyes flew open, startled. 'What is it?' he called to the landlady.

'What, Monsieur? The drums? Pay no attention. Slaves. Why they're at it this early, I can't say. Taking a chance, maybe. Don't look so startled, Monsieur!' she laughed. 'It's nothing.'

'Nothing? I thought it was my heartbeat!'

'Maybe it is, Monsieur. Who knows? Or maybe it's a beat to quicken your heart, or the drums and your heart are having a conversation.' Her laughter tinkled as she walked away.

With the landlady's directions, Barry hired a horse. The animal being satisfactory, he reserved a second horse for Fred, and set off for a reconnaissance of the small town that was Port of Spain in the year 1796.

The magnificent hills of the Northern Range greeted him before he could get very far. He stopped and stared. The mountains were everywhere in the distance, surrounding the town with their purple valleys, lush green peaks and serrated edges vying for pre-eminence. So different, he thought, from Barbados. He gazed his full and eventually moved on, his horse trotting slowly through the streets.

Port of Spain was obviously carefully designed. Although very small, it was laid out on the grid plan. It consisted of not much more than ten streets running from north to south, intersecting with three or four more in the opposite direction. Their names rolled off his tongue: Calle Neuva, Rue de Sainte Anne, Rue de la Place, Calle Principe, Calle Infante. The French influence in architecture was everywhere apparent, especially in the lavish embellishments of fretted patterns, their frilly, lacy charm matching Barry's present light-hearted mood. Tradesmen's and artisans' shops, some obviously run by mulattos, were now opening up for the day. There were signs indicating the various languages spoken within.

The sound of human noises drew his attention. He set off up the street and came abruptly upon the profusion of activity, colour and sound that was the market. 'What language! Distorted but vibrant, rhythmic, musical, sensuous and expressive,' thought Barry. His senses stirred to the sway and swagger of moving hips and limbs so unconsciously alluring – the undeniable animation of the African – as vendors arranged their exotic wares, unfamiliar fruits, strange wild meats, and delicacies wrapped in banana leaves. Colourfully costumed brown and black women in saffron-painted headwraps that told stories of their own, and stately mulattresses, bejewelled on ears, neck and hands, even here in the market-place, made Barry catch his breath. Eventually, he moved on and approached the watery edge of the town.   He passed a Spanish-style building, with its typical high exterior wall and well-hidden central courtyard, and suspected that it was the Casa Real, and that Fred might be found within, awaiting the Governor, but he did not stop. Keeping his horse at a slow walk, he continued his survey. Black men and women sauntered through the streets calling merrily to each other in their lilting patois. If they were slaves, they showed no signs of it. At the edge of the town, away from the mole and small fortifications and past the black mudflats, was a mirage of green lawns that for a moment reminded Barry of his grandmother's garden at Grenmill. 'Swamp!' he exclaimed in surprise as he drew nearer to the large pools of stagnant, shallow water. Further on, past that mossy carpet, was an area of remarkably stark trees stretching out black, beckoning limbs from the murky pools, their nakedness contrasting with the lush mangrove growing thick and close nearby. That mangrove, Barry sensed, was concealing a colony of birds.

An early-morning hunter approached, and then a loud noise ripped through the stillness. Like magic, the sky went red, painted with the wings of the most vividly scarlet creatures he had ever seen. 'Ibises!' he murmured in satisfaction, letting out a low whistle.

Completely enchanted with all that he had seen, he hummed happily to himself as he trotted eastwards, and came upon a large man-made water course – the 'Dry River', an impressive feat of engineering. Then he met the Laventille Hills and the Royal Road leading to the east. Satisfied that he had seen everything, he turned and retraced his path through Port of Spain. He decided to ride out towards the northwest, away from the town limits, ready for a fast gallop. He was longing for the sheer invigoration of speed and the thrill, always special to him, of wind in his hair.

The town had begun to come to life in earnest, but the way ahead was clear except for a stationary carriage. He began to anticipate the ride. He was excited and happy. Without thinking, he spurred his horse to an increased pace. Just then a woman stepped from the carriage into his path. With quick reflexes, he swerved his horse into the drain that ran down the centre of the paved street and managed to avoid a collision, but the poor woman had been startled and had dropped all the contents of her basket. Cursing himself, Barry dismounted and went to her assistance.

He was profusely apologetic and immediately bent to help her retrieve her belongings. 'Madame, I am so sorry, I don't know what got

45

into me. I'm an awful fool to be racing through a town like that. I really didn't see anyone about. Would you forgive me? I do sincerely apologise. Here, there's one more item. You think we have them all now? There . . . do forgive me, I *am* so sorry. I hope you've suffered no discomfort. I do apologise.'

They had both been bending to pick up the fallen articles, and all being finally restored to the basket, they straightened up and their eyes met.

Barry, who in his light-hearted way had been keeping up that lively chatter of apologies and self-recriminations while they were refilling the basket, suddenly found himself unable to utter another word . . . he was speechless. There, before him, on that dusty street, in such an unlikely country, stood the most stunningly beautiful creature he had ever laid eyes upon. Barry had come face to face with Eléna.

Nearly as tall as Barry himself, her height alone gave her an elegance that was immediately remarkable. Slim and perfectly proportioned, with full round breasts, she was clothed in a sparkling white, heavily handworked gown of remarkable good taste. This was not what Barry saw, though, for at that close range he was as yet unaware of the many attractions of her figure. It was her exquisite face that arrested his attention and took his breath away.

For centuries there have been poems, book and letters praising the beauty of women with skins as white as the driven snow, eyes as blue as the cloudless skies, and lips like rosebuds. History has scant record of the equally dazzling beauty of black women, and metaphors and similes come less readily to mind. Suffice it to say, however, that the bud of Eléna's beauty that Don Chacon had recognised and which had been slow in opening after the terrible experience when she was seventeen, had certainly opened up by her nineteenth year.

The very olive brown of her flawless skin gave her a special radiance which was rivalled only by the lustre in her large round eyes whose pupils were as black and as bottomless as the night. The nose, which she had obviously inherited from that unknown white father, was straight, and turned up slightly at the tip. But it was her lips that stole Barry's heart. Her full lips tilted up at the corners and could not help but smile. When they did so in earnest, her face lit up with a blushing glow that made Barry's heart do a violent somersault. He found that he could not look at her without experiencing that physical sensation.

The slight accident had disturbed her headscarf, and her glossy, luxuriant black tresses cascaded down her back in beautiful waves, framing her face. One arm was slung through the handle of the basket, and with the other she brushed her hair away, collecting it at the side of her head, bringing all forward over her shoulder. Those movements were so graceful and innocent of their sensuality that they suggested an unawareness, a lack of self-consciousness, that was in itself attractive.

'No harm's been done, Monsieur,' Eléna said, smiling, completely unaware of what havoc that smile was causing. 'If you will excuse me.' She turned to leave.

'No . . . wait, Mademoiselle!'

Shé had already stepped out of hearing range and merely looked back amusedly, saying, 'I thank you, Monsieur, but I am all right.'

Barry stumbled away and collected the reins of his horse. He thought nothing of her race, her colour or her nationality. His only thought, as he finally rode away was . . .

'Velvet . . . her skin is like velvet!'

He recovered his bearings eventually and continued his ride. Finally, sufficiently invigorated after a lively gallop through the uninhabited clearings outside the town, he retraced his path, deciding to see if Fred had concluded his business. He met his friend outside the guest house.

'Hold up there, Whiteways! What say you, any success?'

'Don't you believe it! I'm told I can go and look for the Governor at the house of Don Diego de Las Flores at Santa Clara in Maracas, some few miles east of here. No one is sure when he'll return, so I plan to act on that advice. Would you care to come with me?'

'Well, let me see. I was planning to visit one of the elegant gentlemen's clubs and catch a game of faro or whist, but if you insist . . .' answered Barry mischievously.

## II

The still curtain of morning had risen on a setting of dazzling light which sent lacy, sparkling shadows on the surface of the dusty road as the sun shone through the trees overhead. Fred was in a chatty mood.

'Have you noticed how stark everything seems in the tropics, Barry? All distinct outlines.'

'Yes. Everything is mercilessly and clearly defined. Black and white,' replied Barry, observing a band of slaves trekking through the fields with their white overseer.

'Good God, Wingate! I thought I was the poet and philosopher!'

47

Having missed the sight, Fred had not caught the implication. 'Don't start copying me now, I won't be able to stand two of us.'

'I can't help being philosophical in lands like these, Fred,' Barry countered. 'Philosophical and cynical, what else can one hold on to, to quote a good friend of mine.'

'*Touché!* Seriously, though, I love the visual effect of the absolutely brilliant sun, even if I don't like the effect on my skin,' continued Fred. 'It's not just the clear outlines, but the accentuated vividness of the colours. Aren't these the same colours we see in England? But here they are so much brighter, yet they don't strike one as being gaudy or vulgar, simply clearer and more vibrant. Vibrant! That's the word. They lack the hypocritical subtlety of English colours. Yet they are soft and sensuous.'

'Yes . . . like velvet!' sighed Barry.


At the entrance to the home of the La Flores they were met by a black servant who requested them to wait while he announced their presence. Finally, a long-legged man who appeared to match Fred in age emerged. It was José, now a mature gentleman, dark hair falling over his romantic brown eyes.

The Englishmen explained their mission, but unfortunately both Don Chacon and Don Diego had already left Santa Clara. As was the custom of the islands, however, José invited them to join his family at their midday meal.

At first José, Juanita and Carmen were wary of being too relaxed in the presence of Englishmen, but they were soon put at ease. For neither Fred nor Barry was typical of their class or race. Fred was the born philosopher. As he himself claimed, 'I, like Addison, live in the world rather as a spectator than one of the species.' In Barry's case, having accepted without question the easy life into which he was born and having never had to struggle to maintain it, he was less concerned for the systems that underlay it than for people, and what he thought of as 'humanistic common sense'. His recent propulsion into the arms of barbaric slave society had crystallised this approach.

So, almost naturally, the two Englishmen found themselves befriended by the Santa Clara family. Conversation at table ranged from the English way of life to the present world unrest. The young people remained talking long after the meal was over, retiring to the open veranda.

When the afternoon was well advanced, M. Louis, who had been in the fields all of that day, approached the house. Spotting the young people in the veranda he attempted to avoid them by changing his path. José called to him, however, 'Monsieur, do come and meet our new English friends!'

Louis responded apologetically. 'Very pleased to make your acquaintance gentlemen, but do forgive me, I'm in no condition to join you.' He indicated his soiled working clothes.

Louis made his escape, not even pausing to learn the Englishmen's names, nor to observe the looks and blushes passing between one of the Englishmen and Juanita, not even to observe the fact that Carmen hung on José's every word.

At length the Englishmen took their leave, but not before securing an invitation from José to return for Juanita's twenty-first birthday party in two days' time. José explained that there would be music and dancing and that M. Louis had promised to teach everyone the waltz, a dance that he had recently learnt from some German friends.

'Velvet! . . . I think you're right, Barry. That's an apt symbol of the tropics,' mused Fred as they rode home. 'Look at how softly and suddenly the night is descending, look at how . . .'

'Oh stop it, you frustrated poet! You're getting on my nerves! You'll have me thinking like you in earnest if you keep on like that.'

'But this is a fine how-de-do! You're the one who introduced the image to me, my good fellow!' protested Fred.

'Yes . . . but I was thinking of a girl . . . the most remarkable woman I've ever seen, with skin like velvet and eyes like a wild deer. She came across my path this morning.'

A carriage passed them at a brisk pace, heading eastwards. It was Eléna returning home. She had been later than she ought and had instructed her driver to make haste, fearing the wrath of Yei, or even worse, of M. Louis. For ever since the attempted rape, he had kept a close, protective eye on her.

## III

The carriage finally pulled up in front of the house and three women came rushing out, two of them speaking at the same time, expressing their concern at Eléna's lateness and exclaiming in delight as Eléna apologised and handed out a lively, brown puppy.

49

'That's quite enough, *muchachas*. Eléna, get inside now,' interjected a stern, more mature voice that was heavily accented.

'Yes, Yei, oh don't be cross with me. I will explain all.'

Once inside and changed, Eléna joined the others in the dining-room. She listened to Juanita gush on about the two handsome Englishmen and finally told her eager listeners about her day. At André's request she had been to visit Yvette, not just in her medical capacity (for Eléna was already known for her medical skill) but simply because the young girl had been confined to bed and needed cheering up. Mme Fontainebleau had insisted on cooking her dinner, that is what had made her late.

The pup had been a gift from Yvette's suitor, a wealthy mulatto from the south. Mme Fontainebleau, terrified of the creature herself, had begged Eléna to look after him until Yvette was well enough to do so.

'But I thought you hated dogs, after the time you saw . . .' remarked the ever-earnest Carmen.

'Oh, for a while perhaps, but eventually I came to realise that it was the men I hated, not the animals,' responded Eléna.

The conversation then turned to the prospect of the party. It was a pleasant, cheerful chatter that met Don Diego on his arrival home.

Don Diego was a weary man that night. He ate his meal in silence, hearing but not listening to the merry chatter of the girls. He stopped Yei from silencing them.

After dinner, he sat on the veranda with M. Louis and José. The veranda was graced by elegant chairs from Paris, for which Don Diego had bartered with a shrewd French merchant. Yei's native hammock was there too, swinging sedately from a neat corner. Diego chose to lounge in it.

The velvet night was peaceful. Soft cool breezes fanned the three gentlemen as they sat. A 'lady of the night' bush that Yei had planted was in full bloom and its intoxicating scent filled the night air. Fireflies twinkled over the expansive lawns, reflecting the glow of the myriad stars that adorn tropical skies on dark nights.

Don Diego sighed. He listened to the crickets and the droning, monotonous noises of the night. He said, 'Spain is being pulled into the war. News came today. Chacon is beside himself! We spent the better part of the day composing letters to Madrid detailing the vulnerability of our situation, and begging for Spanish warships to patrol the Gulf. We took pains to explain the weaknesses of our garrison, the lack of fortifications, prisons, ammunition.' Diego paused pensively, studying the stars. He continued. 'We tried to explain our fears about this unruly and divided population of questionable loyalty. Ever since the aborted mulatto uprising in the south, and the one in Port of Spain recently, it's become clear that Chacon's hold on the population is very tenuous.'

'His popularity hasn't been helped by his open support of the British when Spain was allied with them against France, and they were in control of Guadeloupe and St Lucia.'

'Quite so, Louis.'

'It's a very frightening situation,' added José. 'Even now, although we are neutral, we can't stop the French privateers from coming into the Gulf of Paria to be refitted, nor can we stop the British from following and attacking them. If the French don't succeed in seizing Trinidad, the British will. With Spain entering the war, we will be open to direct British attack. Something ought to have been done before now!'

'Chacon has tried. I was with him when Admiral Aristizábal passed through on his way to Santo Domingo to retrieve the body of Cristobal Colón. He begged him to stay and patrol these waters.'

'And yet he rejected the aid offered by Jean François and his black fighters, even though François is a damned royalist. Is it because he is coloured?'

'It was the *cabildo* that rejected the black fighter's offer. They see a republican in every black man,' sighed Diego, shaking his head sadly.


# IV

Having no success in meeting the elusive Chacon, the Englishmen spent the next two days visiting the rum shops of Port of Spain or bantering with their landlady. Thursday finally came, however. The two friends prepared for the party. Seeing Fred dress with such meticulous care, Barry itched to tease him but something about this friend's intensity made him desist. As events turned out, this was just as well.

At Santa Clara all preparations for the party were finally over and the girls were dressing. Carmen and Juanita shared a room, but Eléna, since her childhood, had never left Yei's.

Juanita was so excited and nervous that Eléna knew only she could calm her, so she attended to her herself. Juanita was most preoccupied with the possible arrival of the Englishmen. Laughing at her concern, Eléna teased, 'Why are you so anxious? Please don't give your heart to some passing stranger now, not after you've kept it for so long.' It was a standing joke among the twins and Juanita that they had reached the ripe old age of nineteen and now twenty-one respectively, without marrying.

51

With Eléna, it was simply that after her bad experience at the tender age of seventeen any romantic interest in the opposite sex had been rudely aborted. Juanita, on the other hand, not wanting to be parted from Carmen, who was her favourite, nor from Eléna, who was almost like an older sister to her, had refused the few social invitations that had come her way. Carmen, however, because of an apparent reticence towards coloured people, had not, like Eléna, developed a small circle of coloured friends or potential suitors. Her interests appeared to centre solely on Santa Clara. A vague suspicion had begun to develop in her astute sister's mind. It was a suspicion that was to be confirmed that very night.

By the time the first guest arrived Juanita and Carmen were on hand to greet them, while Eléna, delayed by her attentions to Juanita, was late in coming down. The two girls met M. Louis in the living-room setting up the small orchestra. They were on time to greet the arrivals being ushered in by José. André was already there and Fred and Barry were just coming in. Barry offered his felicitations to Juanita, while Fred, drawing her aside, stood talking quietly to her as she blushed demurely. Barry observed them, a sardonic smile curling his lips. Just then a voice broke in on his musings, a vaguely familiar, strangely enchanting voice.

'Monsieur, would you care for some refreshments?'

Turning, the smile froze on his face. There before him again was his 'velvet girl'. The two young people stared at each other in disbelief.

'You're the same . . .' began Eléna and, remembering their first meeting, she smiled, embarrassed. Barry too broke into a wide grin. He noted with wry humour that his heart had made its usual somersault. They spoke. He could not take his eyes away from her. Unlike Juanita she did not lower hers demurely, but stood looking squarely at him, their eyes almost level, speaking in her smiling, husky voice, with her mobile, laughing lips.

'My God,' thought Barry, 'I'm as badly smitten as Fred!'

Throughout the evening he followed her every movement, drinking in the thrilling sensuousness of her graceful gestures and the remarkable perfection and poise of her figure.

The evening was well advanced when dancing finally began. Everyone joined in, attempting to execute some of the popular dances that had been brought to the island by its many immigrants. José called on M. Louis to demonstrate the waltz, announcing it as 'all the rage in France'.

'Not yet in France, you nincompoop! In Germany! But one day it will take France by storm, mark my words,' corrected Louis.

He had rehearsed with the musicians, who, at his instructions struck up the appropriate tune. The Frenchman bowed politely to Juanita's curtsey, the two held each other at arm's length and proceeded to whirl about the floor. The display was an instant success and M. Louis called on the others to follow his example.

This is how it came about, on that festive night, with good cheer and high spirits embracing the company, that José held Carmen, and Barry held Eléna. Barry, who was one step ahead of André, had had the good fortune to capture Eléna. At first she had demurred, but Barry would have none of it, and led her out to the floor encircling her with his arms.

He felt the pull of her body like a magnet, and guided her to a shady corner of the room where the light from the central chandelier did not quite reach. Under cover of the shadows, Barry held her closer than he ought. 'Velvet,' he murmured into her hair.

He felt her body respond, but only for a second. She was wary, and soon drew away. With the dexterity of the skilled dancer that she denied being, she gradually forced him back into the light.

Barry was not the only one to whom that dance was significant. On that fateful night, while dancing with Carmen, José unexpectedly discovered that he was in love. Perhaps it was the intoxication of the music, or of the perfume that Yei had especially made for her daughter, which made him relax his unconscious guard. Or was it the novelty of finding himself holding her, whom he had always forced himself to look on as a sister, in his arms? One way or another, José felt it, a new and different feeling that he had never experienced before. It terrified him, making him leave the dance before it was over. He excused himself abruptly and hastily walked out into the night, leaving Carmen confused and close to tears.

He did not stay away long, however, for suddenly he came running back to the house. He went quickly up to his father, drawing him aside. The dance ended and Diego raised his hands, stopping the musicians. 'I'm sorry, friends, but I must interrupt the celebrations. André and José will have to leave immediately to report to the garrison. I, too, must leave. We've just received a message from His Excellency, informing us that there is to be trouble in our waters.'

Don Diego hastened out of the room, and the small gathering broke up in bewilderment. José came up to Barry and Fred. 'Stay, friends, I've a room downstairs – sleep there. Yei will see to your needs.' He turned to leave.

'Wait! Tell us, what is the threat?'

'It's a British frigate, it's been . . .'

'Which one?'

'The *Alarm*. Apparently its been around all day, with the corvette *Zebra*, blocking the exit from the Gulf and trapping some French privateers in our waters. Chacon's message says that the captain has informed him that he intends to attack them.'

'What would that mean to the island?'

'Would the British come ashore?'

'They have been known to sink privateers before and then make off, but Chacon is taking no chances. M. Louis will come in tomorrow and bring you back word.' José hurried out, leaving the two friends frozen in their consternation.

The La Flores carriage rolled swiftly out, with André and José following closely behind on horseback.

Fred spoke quietly to Juanita. 'I'm so sorry about this. Will you be all right?'

'I am so worried about José.'

'Please don't think of me as your enemy.'

'Oh Fred, I don't, I won't,' whispered Juanita.

Just then, Eléna came to the doorway and called to Juanita. Barry looked at her longingly, wishing he too could say comforting words to her, but she kept her eyes away from him, almost deliberately. When Juanita joined her she turned softly away.

Despite the upset, however, there was one person who was glad for the end of the party. José, at least, was relieved. He was relieved simply to be out of the house. A battle, any action, was better than the war in his heart, for he could not face Carmen's tears, could not deal with his fears, could not even voice them. He was ashamed and embarrassed by his weakness tonight. He cursed, as he bent his head into the wind, and rode ever more rapidly towards Port of Spain.

# CHAPTER SEVEN

## I

The night air was chill. Lacking the warmth of a peaceful mind, José seemed to have no defences against the wind as he stood at his vantage point overlooking the harbour of Port of Spain. In the distance the British frigate and the corvette could be seen ominously drawing closer to the two French privateers. José peered through his telescope at the dots of light in the distance, willing his thoughts away from his private torment and back to the confrontation in the distance. Soon, however, he had no thought to spare for anything but the ensuing conflict.

The explosions that sunk the privateers brought the French citizens of Port of Spain into the streets. They rushed out of their houses hurling curses at the far-off British. No sooner had they decided to return to their beds than another incident occurred. As dawn broke the British frigate came into port. Leaving his sailors at the jetty, Captain Vaughan marched towards the Casa Real with a small group of officers. He held a brief conference with the Governor, then it appeared that they would leave. The small group entered the house of a known British subject. José prayed that the citizens would keep calm until the captain and officers had regained their ship. This was not to be. The people of Port of Spain were determined on confrontation with the British.

The British sailors from the jetty joined the fracas and before long so did the French sailors from the sunken privateers. The British found themselves severely outnumbered and, dragging their wounded, barricaded themselves in a nearby house. The French gleefully prepared to finish them off.

José, with assistance from André, marched his militia to the scene. Finding a vantage point on which to stand, he proceeded to loudly address the crowd, using every persuasive device he knew. Finally he looked at André and received a nodded signal. José stepped down and called his soldiers away. The angry mob rushed the building, breaking down the door, but they were too late. While José had been pleading with the crowd, André had managed to persuade the British captain to leave quietly by the back door and return to his ship.

If the confrontation was over, the crisis was not. The citizens were incensed at being robbed of their revenge. They turned as one mass from the ransacked building and marched through the town singing the *Marseillaise*. They broke into the arsenal and then they became impossible to stop.

It was all the hopelessly outnumbered soldiers could do to prevent a true riot from breaking out. As the day finally waned and sank slowly into night, the mob was like a threatening, ugly carnival of tricolour flags and cockades, roaring through the streets, until slowly anger began to dissipate and Port of Spain regained an uneasy quiet.

José met the Governor briefly. Chacon was tired and severely harrassed by the panicking *cabildo*. After conferring briefly with him, José left to rejoin his men.

Morning came all too soon, for the new day brought no promise of relief to the troubled members of the militia. With the rising sun came a return of Captain Vaughan and his sailors. This time Vaughan brought his full complement of two hundred and fifty enraged, fighting men, ready to retaliate for the humiliations of the previous day.

José rushed to the harbour and met Vaughan as he landed. He tried to point out the folly of this move but the captain was past caring. Brushing the young Spaniard roughly aside, he entered the town where hundreds of Frenchmen, refreshed from their night's sleep, were already awaiting him.

He marched with his drums playing and his colours flying. As he advanced, so too did the French sailors and citizens of Port of Spain, singing lustily and waving their own flags. The British drums boomed out an ominous tattoo, giving voice to the throbbing pulse of the tense town. Vaughan ordered his men to assume battle formation. They quickly arranged themselves along one of the streets. The French, too, were ready for battle. They formed up on the opposite side, leaving only a few small buildings between the two enemy contingents.

The drums stopped. So did the singing. The town became deadly silent, listening, waiting. The noise that broke the quiet was not that of gunfire. It was the sound of marching feet, as Chacon led his militia right between the warring factions.

José and André ordered their men to hold their ground. Then Chacon raised his hands to still the murmur of protest that had arisen at his intervention, and began to speak. He spoke in English, addressing himself to Captain Vaughan and his men. Listening from among the ranks, José could not understand the words, but he knew the import of Chacon's speech. He was full of admiration for the courage displayed by his father's friend. Don Chacon was bedecked in the uniform of an officer of the Royal Spanish Navy. His golden medals and epaulettes shone in the blazing sun, as he wiped the beads of perspiration from his forehead and offered to give up his life in the defence of Spanish neutrality. He did not use threatening language, but his voice was firm.

'Trinidad is Spanish and neutral. Your presence here, and your threat of open warfare on this soil, is a gross violation of international law.'

The tension in the air was tangible. It was also very clear that Chacon's words had begun to unnerve the British. Vaughan stood in agitated discussion with his officers. José held his breath and closed his eyes tightly. He said a prayer even as he cursed the arrogance of the British. When he opened his eyes again, Vaughan was approaching Don Chacon. He saluted with his sword, spun on his heels and marched with his column back to the harbour.

Chacon had won the battle with words, now hoots and jeers

tormented the air as the French citizens of Port of Spain followed mockingly behind the troops, taunting and laughing at their second day of disgrace. The jubilant crowd refused to disband. They continued to roam the streets all afternoon, despite the militia's efforts. They harangued and harassed every known English household, and rioted among themselves. When the long day finally ended, one English-speaking black man was found shot to death. Although José was not aware of it, the humiliation had proved too great for Captain Vaughan. In despair that night, he put a bullet through his head.

## II

M. Louis had departed early on the first day for Port of Spain, leaving Barry and Fred standing helplessly alone on the veranda, uncomfortable and aimless. Even though they were joined by the girls at mealtime, all three were so tense and solemn that the gentlemen could not in good conscience raise any small talk.

The second day came and no news, no messenger came from the town. The hours dragged by for the despondent Englishmen. Restless and uncomfortable, Barry and Fred hardly spoke.

Yei saw to their refreshments and comforts, inviting them to stroll through the garden. Seeing her set off with a basket on her arm, Barry offered to accompany her.

It was the oddest excursion, for although Barry made several attempts at conversation, Yei only smiled in return, so that he stopped trying and merely walked beside her stately figure. It was a pleasant, comfortable silence, however. Occasionally, Yei would offer him a berry to eat, or a flower to smell, and strangely enough Barry knew he had made a friend.

That night, drained and weary, M. Louis returned home, bringing eagerly awaited news of the events in the town. He urged the two Englishmen to stay on one more night before returning to Port of Spain. The following morning, however, with mixed feelings, the two friends prepared to leave. Their two days' stay in the sanctuary of Santa Clara had been tarnished by discomfort, and tainted by a feeling of ignominy, guilt and impotence.

Now ready and about to return to the ransacked town, they lingered, waiting silently on the lawns beneath the tree that Diego had planted so long ago. The poui was now full-grown and magnificently dressed in all its splendour. Forked-trunked, tall and proud, myriad branches spreading wide, it was breathtakingly beautiful, clothed in its Maytime gold.

Finally, Juanita appeared to bid goodbye to Fred, her light step and smiling face speaking her relief at news of her brother's safety. Fred ran quickly up to her, clutching her hands anxiously and speaking in a whisper. Barry, waiting under the poui, had no idea of what they spoke. He strained tortured eyes, hoping to catch some glimpse of Eléna, but with no success. Just then, however, he chanced to look up. There, framed in an upper window of the house, he saw her gazing down at him. She had been there all the while. He grinned and saluted her, his heart suddenly lightening.

'She's not just a "velvet girl", you know, she's a ruddy goddess!' said Fred unexpectedly, as they rode back to town.

'How'd you know it was Eléna?' asked Barry in surprise. 'I never said a word!'

'Well, from your description, there might be two like her in the world, but certainly no two on this small island. She is astonishingly beautiful. Can't have her just like that, you know. Hope you realise it!'

'Oh yes, of course. I know she's very special,' replied Barry. In truth, though, he did not know or understand, until much later.

# III

Because of the many warnings they had received against staying in the troubled town, the two friends left the guest house early the next morning. They intended to explore the south of the island and to look for the port of Point Fortin where the Dutch had invaded some years previously.

'Seems we've caught you two just in time!' called José as the two Englishmen were setting off.

'*Bonjour*,' added André, who had been accompanying him. 'Have you received good hospitality from *ma tante*?'

'You're related to our landlady? How splendid! She's a wonderful hostess and we love her,' answered Fred.

After they had explained their planned adventure and received José's advice on how to proceed, he ended by inviting them back to Santa Clara for the weekend.

'We'll have a picnic after Mass on Sunday morning.'

Cheered by the invitation, the two friends began their journey. The roads were few and badly kept, and before long deteriorated into mere tracks. Their backs to the mountains, they rode south, past forests and cocoa plantations, into the tall grasses of the lowlands. They met several lazy streams, low still, for the rainy season had not begun in earnest. Eventually they came to the large river which Yei's people called the Caroni, and on which the first Europeans had sailed, penetrating the uncharted lands to site their first town at its head. Its banks were now bedecked with a sea of wide-leaved plants, swaying and rippling like waves in the wind. Sparkling reflections glanced off the jewel-like droplets of dew that had settled on them overnight.

Fittingly, to add to the magical effects of the historic river, some Amerindians were fishing here. A young boy exclaimed in delight as he caught a small, primitive black fish in his net. Seeing Barry looking on intently, his father nudged him. The boy wrapped the fish in a large leaf and offered it to Barry. Barry thanked him and placed the unexpected tribute in his saddle bag. He was quite unaware of the legend of the little primitive fish, for of the cascadura it is said that whoever eats it must return to the island to end his days.

For miles in the area around the large river, they rode through low-lying plains and thick grasslands until they once again encountered hilly areas and vast forests as yet uncleared for cultivation. Eventually they could see a majestic peak far away in the distance.

'San Fernando de Naparima!' exclaimed Fred. 'We're in the south now. At the base of that hill is the settlement of San Fernando. Let's go.'

The plains gave way to low rolling hills on which it seemed some giant hand had placed a patchwork shawl. They had reached the neatly laid-out cane-fields of the south. From the foot of the Naparima Hill, they saw the amber-coloured sea with waves ambling up to the shore. They stopped to gaze at a monster of a whale blowing in that gulf and to ask directions of some brown-skinned people. Then they left the tiny town with its few wooden houses around a central square and rode towards the southwest.

They spent the night in the small port of Point Fortin where a friendly innkeeper prepared the cascadura for Barry, laughing as the English-man gingerly removed the scaly carapace. Barry savoured the unusual taste, not caring that Fred refused to try even a morsel of it.

The next day they went to the famous Pitch Lake. They were met by a startling, strangely picturesque sight. Clumps of trees and shrubs grew around and in channels that intersected the expanse of stark blackness. To stand on it for any length of time was to begin sinking into the fathomless depths of the soft pitch.

'It's a veritable wonder of the world, you know,' offered the well-informed Fred, 'the largest lake of its kind in the world, I'll wager. Here history was made, my friend. In the days of the old sea dogs, our famous Raleigh corked his ships here while on his search for El Dorado.'

'Oh, I'm impressed,' responded Barry broodingly. 'It's so full of natural riches, this island, I mean. Its potential frightens me. How long can Spain hang on to it, I wonder?'

Another day passed before the two friends rode away from the land of the rolling hills, and turned their sights once again towards the towering peaks of the north.


# IV

Back in Port of Spain, Fred devoted the next two days to sorting out the final details of Kathy's immigration to the island, while Barry lazed about, cursing time that moved too sluggishly for his impatient heart. It seemed that the weekend would never come. Come it eventually did, however, and even the hour when they set off for Santa Clara.

They were greeted and pleasantly entertained that afternoon by Juanita and Carmen. Eventually, Barry could contain himself no longer and asked after Eléna, only to be told that it was her custom to help the slaves every Saturday. The subject of his thoughts returned home towards evening, but apart from wishing them a good night, she did not stop to talk and went, they assumed, to bed. Barry was nonplussed and fell into a sulky, quiet mood that was only shaken off by the timely arrival of José, which afforded them their first chance to discuss the previous week's disturbances. It was a less than cheerful young man, therefore, who joined Fred in the guest room that night, and fell into a disturbed sleep.

Early on Sunday morning the six young people set off to walk across the fields towards the church of St Joseph. The morning mist rolled off the rugged hills as the small procession made its way. Always to the side of them were the hills of the Northern Range standing like sentinels, benevolently observing their slow progress. Fred and Juanita had immediately fallen into step with each other, while Barry walked next to Eléna. José, bent on ignoring Carmen, purposely joined the former pair, forcing a visibly uncomfortable Carmen to tag doggedly along with her sister. Arranged into two less than comfortable groups, therefore, they proceeded.

Barry found himself edgy with frustration, overwhelmed with the need to talk to Eléna and resentful of her sister's presence. Thus intimidated, he could find only inanities to say until Juanita's voice calling to Carmen came as a blessed relief.

He turned then to Eléna with quite a different tone of voice. 'Eléna,' he sighed, his voice caressing the word. 'I was afraid when you didn't speak to me yesterday that you were avoiding me. You wouldn't do that now, would you, Eléna?'

She looked at him, made as if to answer, hesitated, caught her breath and then said in a forced voice, 'On Saturdays I always go to visit the slaves. I've done so ever since I was a child and they are used to me. I tend to their small woes and illnesses. I am better able to help them than a stranger. Knowing them closely, I can intercede for them if necessary. I . . . I think they trust me, as I do them.'

'How wonderful! You are in a unique position. You are a remarkable woman.'

'No, no, it's not just me. My mother never considers herself too good for them. As for me, they respect anyone who is part of a "magical" twin. To them twins are special.'

'*You* are special, Eléna . . . and I . . . I can't tell you how wonderful it is to know that you are not callous about the circumstances you're forced to live in. You can't imagine how much I appreciate your personal effort. I admire you, I envy you really. I have the feeling we share a common antipathy for this system. It is a sentiment not shared by many people. The situation I am forced to live under in Barbados prevents me from giving any relief. I'm there at the goodwill of my uncle and I'm not in a position to make trouble.'

'I too am in no position to make real changes, but I am determined that Santa Clara's slaves will be spared the horror of some of those other plantations.'

'I wish this moment could last for ever. Just the two of us walking along on such a lovely morning with the birds singing and the mist keeping the earth cool.'

'You have such a lovely way with words. Like my mother, I don't use many.'

'Oh, Eléna, but you've told me so much in this short walk.' Barry smiled at her. 'To see you is to know all that is good and beautiful and words aren't really necessary.'

She glanced at him quickly and looked away. 'She's blushing!' exclaimed Barry inwardly. 'Under that velvet brown skin is a honest-to-goodness blush! Barry wished with all his might that they were truly alone so that he could take her in his arms and cover that velvet skin and smiling, tempting mouth with kisses.

They reached the church and took their places. Barry opted to sit at the back while Carmen slipped away to join the little choir. Barry feasted his eyes on Eléna, taking in her every graceful movement. As the service progressed Carmen's lovely voice sang a plaintive melody that filled the little church with its power. Barry was physically moved and felt his heart expand in salute to her remarkable talent. He caught a glimpse of José at the front and was thoroughly confused, for the young Spaniard was a study in misery, with head bowed in obvious pain.

Eléna too was moved, but by a different music. Every word that Barry had said filled her with a strange excitement and made her dizzy with the joy that only lovers experience. The unfamiliar sensation frightened her, so she prayed harder and harder, forcing thoughts of him out of her mind, and resolving to be more guarded towards him in the future.

That very afternoon, however, sitting on the lawn under the shady flowering poui, Barry's schemes got the better of hers. She was wearing a pale yellow dress, with a long sash of a contrasting deeper yellow. As she sat on the lawn lazily collecting the fallen flowers, the sash lay beside her, like a calligraphic flourish on the golden carpet. Barry picked it up absently and entwined it between his fingers, carressing it gently. His eyes met hers. She looked away. Everyone else was talking and laughing, and under that cover he whispered close to her ear, 'Tell me about your favourite place, Eléna.'

When it seemed she wouldn't answer, he repeated, 'Won't you tell me, so I'd know where to imagine you when I'm far away?'

This made her jerk her head up and look at him questioningly, as if she had forgotten that he was leaving soon. She answered then, slowly, talking of her favourite haunt under the immortelle, near the stream. Then she asked him to tell her of his. 'Oh, that's easy,' he replied, 'being with my grandmother at her fireside in Grenmill.'

'How lovely,' she said, looking up at him once more, her large, bright eyes melting into his soul. 'I mean, to have a place and a person there that you love, to share it with you.'

Before he could respond further, the air became filled with the noisy cackle of birds. He exclaimed; 'Look! Macaws! My symbols of constancy.'

'Constancy? What do you mean?'

'Well, I have been told, and I like to believe it, that they mate for life, and never, ever, leave each other,' he said, looking her straight in the eyes.

Just then, the little pup which she had rescued from André's mother came bounding up to her. She took it up, playfully, in her arms and hid her confusion by allowing it to nuzzle her face. Barry smiled to himself but did not persist with that unnerving trend, although he spoke with her on a great many subjects before they were forced to join in the others' conversation.

The following evening Fred went to make arrangements for their departure. Barry awaited him in a rum shop. While the waitress was fetching the drink he'd ordered, the conversation from a nearby table assailed him.

'Where were you last week when the British were running like dogs? Off under some woman's skirts, I bet!'

'*Bien sûr, mon ami.* Can't help myself in this country.'

'*C'est vrai!* And the best part is you don't have to marry 'em.'

'Hell no!' A round of laughter ensued. 'All she wants, anyway, is a white child, eh?' Even louder laughter followed.

Barry was appalled. 'Misbegotten scoundrels!' he thought. The rum was having its effect on him. He was already sad at the thought of leaving, and slowly his happy mood of the weekend began to grow solemn. He thought about the abuse of black women, of the whole damned rotten mess that was slavery, of Barbados that he was returning to, of Eléna. Thinking of her, he was forced to question himself and his intentions. In the glare of such callousness as he had just heard, he asked himself what really were his intentions towards Eléna.

'God, no. I'm not a brute, I think too highly of her, I'd never do that . . .'

'But can you marry her?' asked his conscience.

Barry sat motionless. In that short minute, with the rum depressing his spirits and his mind in chaos, his dreams had come tumbling down. Gone was the cheerful, ready smile, replaced by a look of sadness. Gone were the bright, smiling eyes, changed into pained reflections of themselves. The nebulous veil of optimism had been removed. Barry saw clearly that there was no way he could have Eléna. Even if he could in all conscience seduce her, he could not get away with it, not with Yei and M. Louis and José and Don Diego there to protect her. Unless they were to marry, he would never have her at all!

How could he marry her? His father had settled a substantial sum on him to cover this sojourn in the West Indies, but that was not enough to get himself up *en famille*. His parents would not approve of a coloured wife, nor would even his liberal grandmother. He remembered hearing how strict she had been on his father's choice of a wife. She too would be against him. All his family would be against him, so would the British aristocracy, unless he had solid financial weight. Where would he get that? But life in England would be a living hell, especially for her, without it.

Barry struggled against the emotions that threatened to strangle him. Of course, here one could make one's own rules. The abolitionists, too, were still active in England and the number of slave uprisings pointed to the imminent demise of slavery, when everybody would be free, and free to marry whomever they pleased. He tried to calm himself.

But no! The problem could not be solved so easily. How could he forsake his grandmother and Grenmill, disappoint and virtually betray all her hopes and dreams? How could he live out of England for ever?

'No! I can't! I can't!' he finally admitted. There was no way out. It was a terrible impasse.

'But can I live without the dream of one day having Eléna?' he wondered, optimism still struggling with reality. It was then that the truth hit him squarely between the eyes, like a well-aimed blow in the manly art of boxing at which he was an expert. That evening in that dirty little rum shop Barry realised clearly that his feelings for Eléna were not casual. This was not just another 'Annabella infatuation', but love, real love.

'No!' screamed Barry in his head. 'No! I refuse to be in such a trap! I refuse to be in love. No, n-oo, no!' He slammed down his glass, threw down his chair and stormed out of the rum shop into the darkened town.

He did not see Eléna again. The next day, all details of travel settled, he sailed with Fred for Barbados.


# CHAPTER EIGHT

## I

Two months later, undaunted by her brother's report of anti-British sentiment in Trinidad, Fred's sister Kathy arrived in the Spanish island. With her came her son, recently returned from Europe, and full retinue, which included Fred himself. Having purchased an abandoned sugar plantation on the western outskirts of the town, Kathy and her clan began to settle in.

Fred therefore had little time to visit Juanita who had quite rapidly captured his heart, but when he did, he asked her to marry him. She was ecstatic. Not so Diego. Fred was unacceptable! Juanita wept, and looked sad and forlorn. Diego reconsidered. True, he was an Englishman, but then he was also an aristocrat; a non-Spaniard, but a Catholic and a wealthy man. It wasn't so unsuitable. It could succeed. Fred was kind and gentle and suited Juanita. Where else could she find such a suitor on this small island? He relented, on condition the Fred did not whisk his daughter away to England too soon.

Overcome with joy, Fred wrote immediately to Barry in Barbaros inviting him to come to the wedding. It would not be before Christmas, he stated, since it was to be a grand one and he had to establish where they would live. There was the prospect, he added, of a house near Kathy's.

'Kathy,' he continued, 'is fairly well settled and is still particularly obsessed about Trinidad. I'll be staying here to help her a while longer but eventually, as the old man's heir, I must return home.'

# II

Eléna sat pensively under the shade of the spreading immortelle tree, the tree that was life itself to the cocoa and was called *madre de coco* by the Spaniards. Its life-giving shade now served to make her favourite spot cool and inviting despite the fiery heat of the day. She sat looking at the little stream winding its merry way. Carefully, she removed the native *alpagatas* with which she was shod and sunk her feet into the inviting cool of the clear topaz water. She gave herself up to thought.

It was beyond all understanding that she should be pining over Barry. She had met him only a very few times, and most of those times she had given him little opening for intimacy, and yet, quite perversely, she felt as if she had known him for an age as if they had shared a special understanding. The simple fact was that she missed him. She missed his quick smile and the sense of humour that matched her own. She missed the messages his beautiful blue eyes sent her and the thrill – yes, she was forced to admit it – the thrill in her blood whenever he spoke so gently to her, as if no one else but herself existed or mattered in the world. It would not do to pine away over a foreigner, and a white Englishman at that, she reprimanded herself, echoing her own teasing words of caution to Juanita. Her head listened, but her heart heard not a word.

She sighed and forced herself to think of something else. 'Juanita is happy enough,' she thought. 'They are so lucky. Fred with his cool, undemanding English manner is the perfect match for the gentle, loving Juanita. Everyone is happy for them. Even M. Louis who was so funny when he heard the news.' She chuckled to herself at the memory. 'Fred? Fred who?' he had asked. 'Oh Monsieur, the Englishman. You know who. You met him once at lunch, and then at my birthday party.' 'Oh yes, the Englishman. Y . . . es, sorry, I forgot. I never caught his name you see. Well fancy that. I'm not at all surprised, come to think of it. Congratulations, my dear. You'll make a lovely bride.'

Eléna mused on in this fashion, the thought of M. Louis's lovable eccentricity and Juanita's happinesss warming her. But suddenly, she shivered and withdrew her feet from the water. A disturbing thought, like the shock of icy fingers on bare skin, invaded her reverie.

'Carmen. It is quite clear that Carmen is not happy.'

Eléna allowed her thoughts to dwell on her sister. In some ways they were so different, Carmen and she, hardly what one would expect of twins.

Carmen was more like Juanita's sister, really. She even looked like her, except for the tell-tale fullness of her mouth and a warming tinge of tan about her skin. But no! appearances aside, that was not exactly true. Carmen had the intensity that only a child of Yei's could have. 'Just look at her singing, how powerful and intense,' Eléna reflected. 'She takes her gift very seriously, never using it for frivolous purposes. It seems she only sings in church. What will become of Carmen? She's a far more complicated person than we realise.'

Eléna had observed the scene on the night of Juanita's party and she knew that her sister was suffering because of her love for José. And José, who had never been known to be cruel, was deliberately, callously, ignoring Carmen.

'Could it be that he does not return her affection, or worse, is he repulsed by her mixed blood? I don't believe it! Not José! I would have sensed that long ago if he were inclined that way. But what else could it be? I must speak to him and get him to tell me, I can't just watch Carmen grow sadder every day.'

Resolved to discover José's hidden motive, she eventually got him to herself one day. They sat in silence in her spot by the stream. José was lazily biting the raw end of a twig, his wayward forelock dangling boyishly over his dark eyes. Eléna sat hugging her knees. She was watching the butterflies.

The island of Trinidad has a wealth of unusual and beautiful butterflies. Today, more than ever, these ornaments of nature seemed to enhance the magical beauty of Eléna's favourite place. She followed the path of one whose wings, blue as Barry's eyes, fluttered with studied grace as it came to rest on a nearby leaf, enchanting her, then suddenly flying away. Gathering her courage, she began.

'This is very hard for me to say, José. It's about Carmen. I want to know what you feel for her.'

After a long, disquieting moment, she glanced at her companion and was shocked at the signs of distress on his face. He was leaning his head back on the trunk of the tree, his eyes pinched, his face distorted with some terrible agony. Eléna rushed over, embraced him and cried solicitiously, 'Oh José, it can't be that bad. Whatever it is, my dear, it can't be that bad. Please tell me and let me help you if I can.'

He hugged her fiercely. 'No one can help us, Eléna,' he ventured after a while, his voice breaking on a sob.

'It's obvious that you love her, José, then what is so bad?'

'Eléna, you don't understand!' he cried, his voice full of the heartache she could see in his eyes.

'Tell me! Is . . . is it because she's not really white?'

'What! You believe that of me?' he said violently, pushing her away and rising abruptly to his feet. 'As if I would care about that! After I have known Carmen since she was born, and Yei is like my own mother!' He stood with his back to her.

'Then what is it?' demanded Eléna, close to tears herself.

'Can't you guess, Eléna?' he asked in a voice filled with anguish. 'It is a forbidden love. Has it never occurred to you to ask who is your father? Has it never occurred to you that it may be Papa Diego, that we may be brother and sister?'

'No! José, you are wrong! I just know you are wrong.'

'I'm not wrong, Eléna.'

'Then find out, José! I will ask Yei myself!' she declared.

'No, Eléna! Please. Don't. You can't broach a subject like that to Yei. She's kept her secret for too long. I will try to find out, but I'll do so by some other means.'


As it turned out, though, the truth found José.

It happened that, like Eléna, M. Louis – not quite the absent-minded old man he claimed to be – was conscious of the tension and unhappiness between José and Carmen. He came to a swift conclusion and decided to have a serious talk with his former charge.

Seated together one day soon after, in Don Diego's study, M. Louis began, 'I know I'm interfering in an area which you may think is none of my concern . . . but I cannot see Carmen suffer so without wanting to help her, not to mention yourself. Are you so repulsed by her black blood that you cannot marry her, son? But wait! Wait before you reply,' Louis held up his bony hand in a restraining gesture.

'Let me tell you that her father was obviously white and your children are hardly likely to be anything but white in appearance. But in a country like this, being coloured is hardly a devastating matter. Not cause enough for this suffering.'

Shaking his head sadly, he continued, 'I cannot believe that I didn't impart to you a little of the sense of liberty, equality and fraternity that was always so dear to my own heart.' He shook his head again and ran both hands carelessly through his hair, leaving the wild, rusty curls with their highlights of silver forming an unruly halo about his keen, expressive face. 'No, don't interrupt me as yet!' he commanded. 'Let me tell you my own story first, for in the telling, maybe you might see how fortunate you are and not be so callous.'

At this point, José decided to refrain from further protest. He sat back in his chair and listened patiently.

'When I was a young man in France, my family was well respected, but very poor. That was years before the revolution, but the ideas of change were growing quietly. I was interested in change. I wanted an education, I wanted to serve the revolution. As it turned out the revolution met me here. Anyway, my efforts were recognised by a great aristocrat of my area. He asked my father to let me go with him to Paris to attend the university there. Don't think it was pure altruism, it was a politic thing to do. It increased his popularity in the village. I went and I learned fast and well, living with his family as a sort of poor relative. Uncomfortable and nervous, I never relaxed until I met an enchanting young girl who was even more so than myself. She was a lovely girl, and naturally, once I had come to know her, I could not help myself. I fell madly in love. Her life in the high aristocratic circles into which she was born had intimidated her. I swore to her that with me she would find only love. I swore I would never leave her or let her go back to her oppressive family. But it was not to be. Our world came tumbling down when my patron, noticing our interest, summoned her parent. My benefactor sent me packing, in disgrace. I didn't know what had happened to her until years afterwards, but the pain of losing her never left me.' Louis paused, his sunken eyes pained with these memories.

'I'm telling you this,' he continued, 'because I think you should see you're making a mistake if you don't grasp your good luck, or you may end up a broken old man like me. I had no choice, but you have one.'

José had found the story even more interesting than the moral it was supposed to pose. He asked, 'Did you ever find her?'

'Yes . . . I did . . . eventually. But it was too late. I followed her halfway across the world with every penny I had – remember, I was not wealthy – but she was already married.'

'Is that why you came to Trinidad, Monsieur?'

'Escaped to Trinidad, you mean!' snorted Louis. 'I had to run from the wrath of her husband. I arrived here a broken, shaken, young man. Your father rescued me . . . but the worst thing was the pain in my heart, the loss of her,' Louis's voice dropped mournfully. 'I've never got over her.

'Do you understand what I'm saying, José? Listen, race is unimportant, all men are equal beneath the sun.'

'M. Louis, I let you talk for so long, mostly because I was interested in your story, and because you would not let me interrupt,' responded José with a wry smile. 'You are wrong however, Monsieur, my apprehension does not concern the question of race, but that of parentage. I am afraid that Carmen may be my sister, and that it would be wrong in the eyes of God to marry and bed her.'

M. Louis rose to his feet, visibly shaken, then he collapsed on the chair, his hands covering his face. 'Get me some water, José,' he croaked.

Having done so, and seeing his former tutor sufficiently restored, José questioned his response. 'You never suspected?'

'No. It's not that . . . but wait . . . would you believe me if I tell you that it is not Diego? Would you trust me and go ahead and marry Carmen on my word?'

José did not reply immediately, but eventually he said, 'No, Monsieur. I must be sure, or I will not be comfortable as her husband. You must understand. Do you know their father?'

'Yes, but it's not that . . . I swore never to reveal . . .'

'Please tell me, Monsieur, I beg of you!'

'Carmen and 'ti Marie are not Don Diego's children,' he whispered so that José had to strain to hear. 'They are mine.'

José was overcome with shock and joy and wonder. He gasped, 'Does my father know this?' Louis shook his head.

'But didn't he suspect?'

'Perhaps he did, but he has never said anything. Everyone assumed that Yei had had a liaison outside Santa Clara . . . in any case, let me explain, we never continued the affair so Diego had no cause to suspect. We were never much alone together.' Louis gulped some water. 'Yei was very young, and very beautiful, and easy to be with. She once took pity on a broken-hearted young man. It was the Indian way of things. She was not very Europeanised then. That was all. She knew I didn't love her and was grieving. Naturally, as is always the case, we didn't plan on the consequences.

'Once it had happened, though, I knew we could never reveal that brief association to Don Diego, for he would not have understood, and he certainly would have thought it scandalous to keep us both in his home. He would never have believed that the affair was over. We would undoubtedly have been dismissed. Where could Yei go? And me? What could I have done without a job in the depressed place Trinidad was then?

'I had no money. Then, we would have had to be physically separated at the time when I could be of the most help to her and the child – children, as it turned out. Understand, she had no regrets. To the Amerindians, children were always a blessing and were welcomed. But seeing my distress and the difficulties which I explained to her would affect our livelihood, she made me swear never to tell anyone, never.' He bit his lip nervously, fighting back a show of emotion. 'Go to Carmen, José,' he whispered. 'Don't waste a minute more.'

Needing no further encouragement, José rushed from the room. Finding the companion of his heart standing on the veranda, looking sadly out at the garden, he came softly up behind her. He embraced her, whispering apologies and words of love, and asking her to marry him. She turned immediately in his embrace and was spared the necessity of replying by the anxious kisses that imprisioned her mouth.

Don Diego had been absent all that day, and José waited expectantly on his father's return to break the happy news to him. The young man allowed himself to be swept up on the wave of exhilaration that had started with Louis's revelations and had passed, like a thrill, from him to Carmen, and to Juanita and Eléna. Thus he never expected the explosion of disapproval that erupted in roaring anger from the depths of Diego's soul.

'Estás loco! Estúpido!' bellowed Diego, his weather-beaten face florid with anger. 'No son of mine, no grandson of a Spanish nobleman, can marry a half-caste girl with no background. Never! This is not like Juanita and the English aristocrat! Do you think that you are some ordinary hidalgo? No, you're descended from Spanish grandees of the highest rank. We pride ourselves on our pure blood. We have resisted the intrusions of the Moors and Africans for centuries. What do you plan to produce? A brood of peons?'

'Papa, you shock me. It is you who allowed the twins to live here among us. How can you raise such objections?'

'Living with us is one thing. They are good girls. I say nothing against their virtue. They are good for Juanita. For Jaunita! Not for you. You're a man. You don't need companions. Find someone suitable, outside Santa Clara, outside the island if necessary!'

'Papa, but I love her!' protested José.

'I will not have it, I tell you! I will have nothing further to do with you if you marry this girl!'

'Are you banishing us from Santa Clara? But Papa, it's Carmen! Little sweet Carmen whom you yourself love!'

'Not for a daughter-in-law!' thundered Diego, roaring like a mad bull as he stamped out of his study and marched into the kitchen yelling for Yei to attend him.

On hearing the outburst, Eléna had hustled Carmen and Juanita up to their room. She herself went nervously to bed where she lay wide awake, shaken by her kind benefactor's sudden change of face. She wondered as the hours dragged on and her mother made no appearance. What indignity was she being subjected to downstairs? Would they all be cast out with nothing, nowhere to go? Never was Don Diego so angry.

After several hours lying awake in the dark, she got out of bed and softly paced the small room, stopping occasionally to look out of the window at the dark, gloomy world outside, a world that now seemed to offer no quarter. The question of racial inferiority had never struck her with such force before, but after hearing Diego bellow out the words tonight – half-caste, negro, peon, mulatto, miscegenation – she suddenly questioned her way of life, her very existence. Arms folded high on her chest, hugging herself, she paced the room, despairingly.

Quietly, the door opened and Yei entered. Eléna turned expectantly to her, her heart in her mouth. Yei's ageless face was composed and unruffled. She ignored her daughter's look of anxious enquiry, and proceeded to change for bed. Eléna could not believe her eyes. She rushed over and grabbed her mother's arm.

'Aren't you going to tell me what happened?' she cried.

'*Calmate*, Eléna. Everything is all right.'

'We are not to be sent away?'

'Sent away?' chuckled the older woman, '*Claro que no!*'

'And José and Carmen?'

'The marriage will take place, everything is all right.'

'How did you do it, Yei? What did you say?'

'Nothing much. I reasoned. He is a good man at heart.'

'And you're not angry with him?'

'Oh no. These noblemen have strange notions about race. I merely pointed out a few facts to him, including that I too can be considered a noblewoman of my people. It was foolishness on his part. All will be well, go to sleep now.'

With that, Yei got into bed and blew out the lamp. She shifted to her

71

side and fell soundly asleep, leaving Eléna, wondering and not much wiser, in the engulfing darkness.

Wanting nothing more than to be finally and peacefully together, José and Carmen were married quietly one morning in the little church in St Joseph, long before Fred and Juanita's planned wedding. Carmen's voice was missed from the choir that day, but downstairs in front of the altar she was joyously singing in her heart.

Since the wedding itself was very quiet, it was agreed that a small celebration would be held afterwards. On the following Sunday, therefore, the young people and Yei made all preparations and received their guests with high spirits. Conditions on the island were too uncertain for Don Chacon or André to come, but particularly welcomed was Fred's sister Kathy and her son Mark, especially since this was their first meeting with the La Flores family.

Kathy turned out to be a petite lady, short and inclined to plumpness, and obviously not in her first bloom. She had an unmistakable charm, with her short-sighted grey eyes set in a face that showed signs of a life of some strain. Her voice was kind and soft. Her son was a tall young man who, being an artist, went almost immediately to gaze at the landscape of Santa Clara. He seemed strangely familiar to Eléna.

The party was very much a family occasion, except for the absence of M. Louis who had been seeing to some urgent matter with Miguel in the cocoa. M. Louis had become a planter to the extent that he and Diego sometimes laughed at the thought of the young Louis.

Those days and that nervous, uncomfortable person had long disappeared, however. When the children grew up he had drifted into agriculture, making short shift of that science, and before long took over the running of Santa Clara. This was particularly opportune since José had then become preoccupied with his militia duties, while Don Diego increasingly devoted more and more time to Don Chacon and the problems of state, and Miguel, the overseer, was beginning seriously to decline in age.

A more unlikely planter would be hard to imagine. His intense, almost choleric eyes, unruly greying hair, and long bony frame gave him a look of controlled wildness that would be commonplace in the halls of a university, or in some bohemian artists' colony, but was a rare sight to be found plodding through a cocoa estate. However, like an alchemist conducting an experiment, he welcomed the opportunity to grapple directly with the enigmas of his life: slavery, bigotry, political ideology and humanism in general.

Many and heated were his arguments with Diego over the lot of the slaves, and even though he often failed to move the Spaniard, there was no doubt that the slaves at Santa Clara fared better for his involvement.

The little wedding celebration proceeded pleasantly. Eventually José asked Carmen to sing something for the company. She was hesitant, but he had only to turn his eloquent Spanish eyes on his bride and her resistance gave way: '*Bueno, querido*, but it will be a hymn, I warn you.'

'*Perfecto preciosa*, start with the Ave Maria.'

Once Carmen started singing, everyone grew silent. It was a silence not just of good manners, but of awe. Her voice cast a spell over all who heard its unexpected power and rich timbre. Busying herself in the kitchen, Yei listened and smiled to herself. She remembered the source of that gift – a powerful, black Mandingo who had sung to his daughter.

Before Carmen had reached the end of her repertoire, Louis came in. He too listened lovingly as he washed and changed his field clothes. Ready now, he entered the room amid Carmen's well-deserved, loud applause. He shook hands with Fred who proceeded to take him over to meet his sister. As Fred drew near Kathy, Eléna noticed that the little Englishwoman had gone deathly pale.

'*Sal volitaire!* Quickly, Juanita!' she ordered.

'What is it, Kathy?' Fred asked anxiously, as he reached her in one long stride. To everyone's surprise, the unintroduced M. Louis rushed up and clutched Kathy's hands.

In a hoarse whisper, he said; 'Is it really you, Katherine? This is not possible. Is it really you, my love?'

José quietly nudged Fred and the others, motioning them to the veranda. No one therefore intruded upon the lovers' tender words of reconciliation, nor listened to their exclamations of delight, to the questions asked and answered, nor saw the tears of happiness they shed.

Out on the veranda, Fred and José discussed their surprise, Fred declaring that he now understood Kathy's insistence on coming to Trinidad.

'Oh, and I am ecstatic for my Monsieur! cried José. How absolutely perfect!'

The old lovers emerged eventually from the living-room. A blushing M. Louis attempted to explain that he had met Kathy in his youth in Paris where she had been on holiday. Oddly, Fred had never been properly introduced to him. After their first meeting everyone assumed they knew each other and as a friend of the young people, the matter of a name had been of no importance to Louis.

Just then Mark came in and Eléna suddenly realised why he had seemed so familiar. He was clearly a young version of her Monsieur. The grating sounds of two macaws ripped through the air and she looked up immediately and sighed.

# CHAPTER NINE

## I

It was just as well that Carmen and José married without undue delay. Since the conflict in May, unrest had grown increasingly frequent. Don Chacon found himself in an unenviable position: a representative of the ineffectual Spanish Crown, governing a virtual French colony, with threat of foreign invasion and no means of resistance. Spain may have been neutral, but Trinidad was hardly considered as such by the British. The French citizens of the island were quarrelling among themselves and appeared to be united in only one thing: their dislike of the Spanish Governor. Chacon's admiration for the British had not gone unnoticed.

Diego and Don Chacon were constantly together discussing the many problems.

'I suspect that the attempted defiance of our neutrality by the British in May will force Spain back into the war,' said Chacon to his friend one day. 'If only I had not sent such a detailed report of it to Spain. Between the British and the French republicans I would prefer the British, but I am a Spaniard. I assure you, I would not enjoy seeing this strategic island fall into British hands permanently. The situation here is so bad now . . . Diego, do you realise how many near rebellions we've put down recently, or how many runaways into the interior we've had? *Santissima!* Isn't it better to let the British take the cursed island?'

'We desperately need help,' supplied Diego sympathetically.

'Yes, but when I finally persuade Spain to send an engineer and cannon from Venezuela, what happens? The British navy gets to them first. And again, when that corvette was sent from Puerto Rico with money and arms – captured by the British!'

'Fortifications are important, without them no ships will have protection in our waters and we need warships.'

'That's why I have drawn up the plans for the fort. But you know, Diego, even that is a problem. Our beautiful, landlocked harbour at Chaguaramas, near to the town, is safe for ships against nature, but a perfect trap for them against invaders. Even with a fort, which we don't have as yet, in the event of a blockade at sea our ships will be trapped, no?'

'Oh yes,' sighed Diego.' But *amigo*, let us first worry about where we are going to get ships.'


As chance would have it, five ships came their way. Five Spanish warships sailed into Port of Spain, with fighting men, under the command of Admiral Apodaca.

Don Chacon and Don Diego wasted no time in greeting the Admiral. Chacon put the problem squarely to him, elaborating on the value of the island, its strategic location and its virgin soil. He explained its vulnerability and then bluntly asked him to allow his ships to stray and to let his soldiers help build the fort. Apodaca's agreement was not long in coming, for he had seen the need himself.

The construction of the fort was doomed from the start, however. Apodaca's young Spanish soldiers succumbed very soon to the climate and, what was worse, they were attacked by an epidemic of yellow fever. Those few who survived that onslaught were ill for weeks and the building barely progressed.

## II

Barry received Fred's letter one day when he was busy supervising and assisting with repairs to part of Wilfred's Great House. Several days before, a mysterious fire had occurred. If the slaves had in fact been the arsonists, Barry could not help but admire their daring spirit. But that little lifting of his spirits was totally crushed by the spurt of whippings and torturings that succeeded that one desperate act.

To Barry it was unbearable. 'Can't you show some human compassion!' he stormed, only to receive his uncle's benign smile.

'Barry, m'boy, if I don't retaliate, what will happen next time? All of us killed in our sleep! Your Aunt Marta lying dead, what!' laughed Wilfred, walking away from Barry's further protestations.

Before the incident, Barry had succeeded in containing his frustrations. He had attempted to find a way to live in the pervasive atmosphere of oppression, accented by the frequent displays of military might, drills and parades every time he turned around. Immediately on his return, he had tried to befriend Fred's acquaintances. But that had not worked, for even though they did not display some of the senseless carousing, sexual excesses and general banality of the average planter, their conservatism and racial arrogance were enough to repulse him. With the emotional pain and torment in his own heart after that visit to Trinidad, he withdrew, steeling himself and growing sullen and morose.

He took to riding out to the fields where the slaves were working and attempted to shame the overseers with concise, well-timed remarks into a semblance of reasonable behaviour. But mostly he was too overcome with frustration to even try and he would stay indoors brooding and drinking, or participate, as he did today, in physical work.

Fred's letter from the Spanish island came as a salve to ease his torment. He would go to the wedding. He was in control now, he could leave Eléna alone, and by this time she would have forgotten him. He sat reading the letter in the shade of a large breadfruit tree and for a moment he was transported to Eléna's side under the poui. He fell into a pleasant reverie.

Suddenly he heard screams of anguish rending the air. He sat huddled in the foetal position, covering his ears with his hands, like a little lost boy.

Two weeks later, just as the thought of returning to Trinidad for Fred's approaching wedding had begun to cheer him, he heard that Spain was at war with England. He realised to his despair that short of sneaking into the country illegally, he could no longer go to Trinidad.

Christmas came and with it Juanita's and Fred's long-awaited wedding.

A grand affair now seemed incongruous in the face of the two-month-old declaration of war. The presence of Apodaca's fleet afforded only a tenuous security, for the soldiers were still weak and decimated by their illness and the fort was far from complete. But Don Chacon would not allow Diego to cancel the celebrations.

On the eve of the wedding, therefore, while all manner of fuss and preparations were going on around him, Don Diego sat in an easy chair in the living-room, and relaxed as he had not done for weeks. He gave himself up to thoughts of the dear baby Juanita, of his gratitude to Yei, and of his beloved Clara.

He relived that terrible time in his life when he had fled Spain, running from the terror of the moribund Inquisition that had already incarcerated his two elder brothers and reduced his sister to a sickly, shrivelled little woman.

On her deathbed, his sister had begged Diego to take what little he could and flee Spain. 'I beg you to forget your inheritance and save your life. Do this for my sake. Swear it!' Diego had sworn and had fled the country.

He should never have agreed to bring Clara with him, though. Never. But he was young and they were so much in love. 'Ah well, that's all in the past now. Here's little Juanita all safely grown up.' Sighing contendedly, Diego drifted into a light sleep. He dreamed of his beautiful Clara, who had never had a wedding gown because they were married hastily, without ceremony, on the run.

Juanita's gown, carefully appliquéd and embroidered by Eléna, was however the most beautiful that the parishoners of St Joseph and the many wedding guests had ever seen. Indeed, Juanita and Fred's wedding was the grandest affair ever held at Santa Clara. Everyone of note on the island had been invited. Festivities went on into the night, and many guests stayed carousing until the dawn of the next day. The lawns had been decorated with lanterns, and the house with wild flowers and palm leaves. A tent had been erected at the rear of the house for the slaves, where they too were fêted. The air was filled with the *parang* and its plaintive melodies, the *aguinaldos*, or Christmas gifts of song.

Not to be outdone by the French-owned slaves, with their *bèlè* and *pique*, these residents of Santa Clara were expert at the African limbo and the Spanish joropo – dances which would in time be much-loved folk culture of the island.

Indeed, from these humble beginnings the cultural expression of Trinidad would in time be renowned for its uniqueness in dance, music and song. In the future sons of slaves would even invent the only new musical instrument of the Twentieth Century – the steel pan – and give to the world the steel orchestra, the *parang*, calypso and limbo.

An atmosphere of uneasy calm and tense expectation had prevailed in the island since the declaration of war. Now on the morning of 16 February 1797 the alarm was sounded. British ships could be seen in the channel.

The fort was still incomplete. Admiral Apodaca had the option of getting his ships out of the landlocked harbour, out of the Gulf of Paria and through the Boca (the Dragon's Mouth) before the British got close enough, or of staying to attack the transports that would bring the soldiers inland. Doing the latter, he could lose his ships but he would delay the invasion. He felt, however, that his crew was too weak and unreliable to put up a proper fight, and so he procrastinated.

Indecision proved his undoing. As predicted, his ships became trapped in the landlocked harbour, trapped by eighteen British war-ships. The soldiers at the fort could not even fire past the Admiral's ships at the British.

Watching on in despair, Chacon seemed to lose all emotion. He merely started packing up his records and instructed Diego to hide them in a safe place in the east until they could be sent to Venezuela. Looking at him, Diego thought that this was not the man he had known for the last thirteen years, but a living ghost, the mere detritus of that vibrant reformer and organiser of the island.

No sooner had Diego escaped with the precious boxes than crowds of Frenchmen descended upon the Governor demanding that he supply them with arms. Confused and frustrated beyond argument, Chacon took them to the arsenal and began the distribution of five thousand muskets.

It had already begun to grow dark as the last of the munitions were handed out. Soon the night descended in earnest and the lights from the ships in battle formation out in the Gulf could be seen from every hilltop.

At about two o'clock in the morning, loud tearing explosions penetrated the air. Looking out from the fort, Chacon saw that the Spanish ships were ablaze. Apodaca had burnt his own ships.

'Well, that's one way of preventing his own humiliation,' sighed the hapless Governor. Seeing an officer approach, he shouted, 'Is the militia ready for battle?' But the answer brought no consolation. The soldiers had panicked and fled into the bushes. 'Then collect the armed citizens who are still to be found, and prepare for battle,' ordered Chacon.

By the morning of 17 February most of the Spanish soldiers had also deserted, and the citizens whom Chacon had armed had disappeared as well. Chacon had only one stronghold left.

'We will make for the two redoubts in the Laventille Hills,' he called to José.

It was therefore a pitiful band of men led by José and André who accompanied the Governor.

As the day progressed, heavy sounds of cannon filled the air for the British had started shelling the hills. José volunteered to organise some field patrols to investigate the progress of the invaders, and report back to the Governor. At about midday he returned to Chacon in a state of great excitement.

'Sir, the British have landed, but in a most disadvantageous spot, in the Mucarapo swamps. If we move with haste, we can defeat them before they reach dry land. We have the advantage, if we hurry. Any resistance would cripple them now.'

'It is hopeless, José, too late, too late.'

'Excellency, I implore you, the swamp extends far out into the sea there, and their boats cannot come close to the shore. The soldiers are knee deep in the marshes. There are only the guns of the corvette to protect them and that is way off from the shore. Please reconsider!'

'No. I have already spoken, your orders are to assist me here.'

Chacon walked away, leaving a bewildered José staring after him in disbelief.

For the rest of the day, intermittent shots were exchanged with the British, a token of resistance, a mere pretence on Chacon's part. Towards nightfall, a lone British soldier bearing a white flag was brought into Chacon's presence.

'Speak up, man!' commanded the Governor. 'I understand English.'

'I have a message from General Abercrombie, Your Excellency,' said the soldier hesitantly. 'He bids me tell you . . .' He fumbled with a piece of paper in his hand. Seeing that the soldier's instructions were written on it, Chacon demanded the missive. The nervous ensign willingly released it.

After detailing the hopelessness of Chacon's forces, it read, 'I offer him an honourable capitulation on such terms as are due to good and faithful soldiers.'

Chacon conferred briefly with his officers and Admiral Apodaca. 'It is a generous offer,' he said at length, 'and I have no choice, I will go now and meet Abercrombie.'

# BOOK TWO

## *Corbeaux*

## CHAPTER TEN

### I

In an attempt to still the growing ennui that had been overtaking him, and to clear his head of his daily bouts of solitary drinking, Barry had gone for a brisk ride that morning. On his way back, he decided to pass through the fields where the canes were being harvested. He brought his horse to a slow walk and finally stopped alongside Albert, who was busy bellowing out orders to his gang of slaves, freely using the whip any time one stepped out of line.

'I always get the impression that they tend to slow down after a sound whipping,' said Barry, resorting to his lazy London drawl which always caused Albert to feel slightly chagrined, so that he would leave off his latest victim. On this occasion, true to form, Albert strode up to Barry. The two men then carried on a desultory conversation. Barry asked disinterestedly, 'How long is it before the rains, Albert?' Getting his answer he chose another topic. 'Around this time of year they celebrate carnival in Trinidad. Did you know that, Albert?'

Barry was determined on keeping up a friendly front so that he could surreptitiously continue his sabotage of the overseer's cruelties.

'Carnival, Sir? I don't think so,' responded Albert. 'Not this year, Sir!' His eyes gleamed with malicious joy.

'Out with it then! What can stop those Frenchies from celebrating?' asked Barry complacently.

'The British, Sir.'

'The British, in Trinidad?'

'Oh yes, Sir. Heard we captured her, and without any resistance. Fact is their Governor cap . . . what's the word, Sir?'

'Capitulated?'

'That's it, Sir.'

Barry's face turned the colour of chalk. He cursed himself for those

81

days of drunken stupor. There had, in fact, been talk of an unduly large contingent of soldiers on the island, but Barbados was virtually a military state and fleets were always pulling in and out of the harbour. He had paid them no mind. With a hasty excuse, he wheeled his horse around and made for the big house.

In the hall that ran through the length of the first floor, he met Wilfred just going into his study and asked him if he had heard any such news.

'Why yes, of course. Our forces left here for that island some time ago. Where have you been, m'boy? In fact, just yesterday I was chatting with the old smuggler, Carty, who operates a boat to the islands. A young fellah named Picton's boss over there now. No more freeloading for the French émigrés. No more . . .'

But Barry had left.

He knew all the taverns in Bridgetown. He had found them some small escape when his solitary drinking became especially unbearable. He would carouse drunkenly with the ne'erdowell sailors and other disreputable men. If he sometimes found solace there with female companions, it meant little more to him than a break from the pressures of life on the plantation. 'Who,' he would say in his maudling stages of drunkenness,' could have the height, the colouring, the eyes, or the lips, the tempting luscious lips of my velvet girl?'

Today, however, he was not in a carousing mood. The ladies of the taverns who approached him temptingly met blue eyes, fierce and cold. Did they know Carty? He had been seeking him everywhere. His schooner, the *Jezebel*, was a squalid mess and stank, but he hadn't been aboard. 'What does he look like?'

'Well, sweetie, if you takes one o'em dry coconuts and puts a white beard on it and a pipe in 'is mouth, that's Carty.'

After calling at the fifth tavern, he beheld a man that, to his amazement and silent amusement, fitted the description exactly. Pulling up a chair, Barry turned it around and sat astride with his arms hugging the chairback. He said, 'I take it you're Carty?'

'Tell me, Gov, what good wind brung you askin' after me?'

'Why don't I buy us a round of drinks?' drawled Barry with pretended ease, as he motioned to the waiter. 'I hear you've just come from Trinidad . . . ' Barry took a sip from his drink '. . . I'm curious to know what's going on down there.'

'Ooh . . . ooh, plenty, plenty, m'boy. We got the Spanish runnin' down there.'

'So Chacon, the Governor, has surrendered?'

'Needs must, m'boy. We 'ad 'im outnumbered, surrounded, and defeated before 'e could say *Attention* to them Indians with bows and arrows that 'e 'ad there, Sir. Yes, Sir!'

'Who's in charge now?' asked Barry soberly.

'Well, way I 'eard it, Abercrombie took off and left this Picton in charge because 'e speaks the lingo. 'E's a mean cove, bad, bad, bad!'

'You mean he's very strict?'

'Strict? Strict?' laughed Carty, throwing back his head. 'You could say that, Guv. I 'ear 'e's 'angin' people left an' right, throwin' out the damned Frenchies and 'ooever don't like to submit to our glorious, raving King George the Third. I'd call that strict 'nough. Yes. Mark my words, 'e's changin' all them easy, soft, slave laws and puttin' them mulattos in their place once an' for all. Too upperty by far they been down there. 'E's 'untin' down runaways, everything . . . 'Ear this one, Guv, this is the best! 'E's put up a gallows outside a church, in the very yard. You know them Spanish people used to get what they call "sanctuary" in the church, but Picton says "no more". People down there don' know what 'it 'em yet. Long live the King, I say! It's 'ats off to us! The British don' play no games with them niggers, them mulattos, and them warmongering Frenchies!'

Barry took a long pull on his drink. Then he asked, 'So what's it like there now? Has it changed?'

'Well, I wouldn't say it's changed any fer the worse . . . Niggers stickin' more to their places, an' that ain't bad. Frenchies, too, an' that's even better,' laughed Carty as he continued. "Cause you see Piction started – no that's not the word, 'e brought back – torture. Soldiers getting flogged daily, slaves, anybody and everybody's got to mind their p's and q's. Better that way, I say. More challenge to blokes like me,' he concluded, laughing heartily.

'Unless he closes down the drinking shops, and outlaws what we're doing now,' countered Barry, putting down his glass.

'Impossible!' shouted Carty, rising to his feet in consternation, only to laugh uproariously again as he looked at Barry's grinning face. He sat down promptly.

## II

Barry needed to think. He desperately needed a place where he could be alone with his thoughts. Arriving at the big house, he quickly changed his clothes and headed for the beach. He submerged himself in the water as if to wash away the horror of what Carty had said, or to clear his mind of its own torment. Then he sat silently on the gleaming white sand for a long while.

The waves of the crystal waters lapped gently at his feet. He leaned back and looked up at the branches of an overhanging palm tree. The latticed strands of the palm branches above his golden tanned body made his retreat seem secure and protected.

If only half of what Carty had said was true, it was a lot to descend on that poor, unprepared island. What about all his friends there? Dear God, what of Eléna? Clammy fingers of panic clutched at his heart. His eyes stared but saw only Eléna's face, her large obsidian eyes, fearful under the threat of some terror against which he was too far away to lend assistance.

He was not consoled by the fact that the invaders were British; he'd seen too much of British law and British injustice in Barbados. 'I've got to go! I've got to go soon to Trinidad to see for myself,' he decided. 'I'll make arrangements straight away. At least now I can go in, I'm as English as they come?' A perverse drizzle began to fall, playing the palm fronds like the ivories of a piano, sprinkling Barry and exposing the false protection of his latticed roof.

He was resolved. He got up and made his way back to the house, but he had not reckoned with his Aunt Marta's plans.

When he informed his aunt and uncle at dinner that evening of his decision to leave soon, he received a much stronger objection to his plans than he expected.

'You can't leave now, Barry dear,' protested Marta, close to tears. 'You've forgotten my ball that I've been planning for so long, and it's all for you to meet everyone in Barbados and help you out of your sulks. I've had to set back the date a little bit since I got the wonderful news that my sister, her husband and my niece are coming on a visit from Jamaica. They will be so disappointed not to meet you. I couldn't abide it if you left now!'

Nothing Barry said could make them see reason. Even the normally benign Wilfred displayed his first signs of anger. He almost accused his great-nephew of ingratitude – he had rescued him, taken him in in his hour of need, and now . . .

At this point, Barry's anger mounted. Looking at Wilfred disdainfully, he was about to mouth some stinging expletives when he suddenly swallowed the words. Wilfred had in fact, rescued him, and had housed and treated him with the greatest hospitality. Upsetting Marta, that poor, misplaced, childless woman, was no way to repay him, barbaric slave torturer that he was.

While Barry was seething with frustration at his inability to leave Barbados, the household at Santa Clara was slowly adjusting to the political and social changes in their lives.

With Fred's influence, Picton agreed that once the local officers took the oath of allegiance willingly, they would be able to stay, so that the threat of José being deported was averted. José, unlike others of the militia, was also forthwith exempted from military obligation. The young Spaniard plunged headlong into work on the estate, devoting himself to Santa Clara.

There had been some tense moments regarding Don Diego as well. When the initial amiability between Don Chacon and the new military government turned sour, the ex-Governor and many of the more educated Spaniards were deported. But Fred intervened once more and Diego was left alone.

Fred himself was settling down to married life. He had purchased an adequate house just west of Port of Spain, which, by good fortune, was almost next door to Kathy's small plantation. The location was good, being on the outskirts of the town, far enough away from the swampy lands near which Port of Spain was situated to present a more 'healthy atmosphere in which to raise a family', as Fred put it. This statement made Juanita blush furiously, but filled Eléna with amusement. The latter was no ignorant young lady. While the débutantes in the ballrooms of London were being kept away from the mysteries of reproductive mechanisms and child-bearing, she had been her mother's companion on many excursions of midwifery, and was fully knowledgeable on all matters of sex, barring that most important one, of the experience itself.

The task of setting up the newly wed couple in their first home was fully shared by everyone, except for Carmen, who had recently revealed the happy news that she was with child. M. Louis, glad for any excuse to be near his Kathy and confident of José's capable handling of the estate, went often supposedly to help, but it was Yei, and especially Eléna, who were the cornerstones of the whole enterprise.

All this happy activity did not, of course, mean that the change in government had not affected the family at all. The spate of hangings and executions had risen alarmingly in a short time. The number of deportations and departures created a sense of unease and insecurity. The introduction of severe beatings (three men accused of rape were each given fifteen hundred lashes), the persecution of runaways and the scant respect now being shown to the free people of colour did not auger well for a comfortable passage from Spanish to British rule, for a family as liberal and easy-going as that of Santa Clara.

Nevertheless, almost every day Eléna went to help Juanita decorate and arrange her new home, which was called Millefleurs. Many times she stayed overnight if Yei or M. Louis was not there to accompany her on the journey back home.

On one such journey to Millefleurs, Eléna and Yei sat in the carriage while their driver made some small adjustment to his parcels. Eléna heard a low, moaning sound and turned to watch a group of three approach.

A young black girl, arms tied in front of her, was being dragged along by a mulatto, an overseer from his dress. Another man walked behind, determinedly applying a whip to the girl's back. The sight of her face, distorted with anguish, arrested Eléna's attention. Impulsively she called out to the overseer. Ignoring her mother's cautioning words and restraining hand, she got out and spoke to the man, inquiring about the slave girl.

'She's a runaway, Miss. She hasn't begun to receive her punishment as yet. Removal of an ear, you know.'

'I like her . . . er . . . build, slim and petite. I could be interested in buying her, that is, if she's for sale?' offered Eléna unexpectedly.

'I've a feeling the master'd be right glad to get rid of her for the proper price. She's in love with a slave who's run away to the interior. She can't be trusted to stay put. Your hard luck though, if you want her.'

There and then, Eléna arranged for the overseer to approach his master concerning her purchase of the girl, whose name was given as Tessa. Of course, she had first laid down the condition that all further punishment to her be ceased forthwith.

Yei was furious. 'Why, Eléna? You of all people wanting to own a slave? This . . . this is not a propitious thing to do. How can you pay for her anyway?' she asked peevishly.

'Oh, Yei, did you see her eyes, her face? She is so tiny, so appealing. Do you know what they would do to her for running away? I could not bear the thought. Besides, I have an idea. I will ask Juanita to buy her. She still needs staff for her household. This Tessa might be just right.'

'How do you know if she's properly trained for the house?' persisted Yei perversely, in spite of remembering when she too was in a similar position.

'She can learn. Perhaps we can keep her for a while and we could both train her at Santa Clara first. Oh, do say you agree, Yei. Anyway, I could not just pass her by. I could not. Why do you object so, Yei? This is not like you.'

'Just a feeling. But, *que sera, sera,*' she sighed.


Juanita was not displeased with the idea, while Fred was too recent a bridegroom to deny his wife anything. Two days later, therefore, Eléna, accompanied by M. Louis, completed the purchase and drove home with Tessa.

The young girl kept her head bent and her eyes down, huddling in a corner of the carriage. Eléna sat opposite her and had ample time to examine her closely. She was extremely small for a sixteen-year-old, for that was her given age. Less than five feet in height, only as tall as a child, really, thought Eléna. Her skin was as black and as smooth as polished ebony. Her prominent cheekbones and heavy features held a strange interest. They reminded Eléna of a sad African mask she had once seen in one of M. Louis's books, with its blunt, almost triangular nose and wide, perfectly carved mouth, now firmly shut. She sat clutching a ragged bundle, her body moving to the bounce of the carriage wheels.

Eventually Eléna spoke reassuringly and coaxingly to her. The young girl covered her face with her hands and started crying in earnest. Eléna reached over and rested her long, sensuous fingers on Tessa's knee, saying softly, 'What can I say to make you calm down, Tessa? There is no more need for tears. Aren't you glad to be spared your punishment? You must trust me. We must trust each other. If you are quick, you will learn many useful things. There, that's better now. Dry your eyes and look at me. See, I'm not going the hurt you.'

Tessa stopped crying and looked up. Eléna, straining forward, heard her almost inaudible gasp. 'What is it, Tessa? Is anything wrong?'

'Oh Madame, you is so beautiful,' the young slave whispered, her mouth still agape. 'And your voice like music. I ain't know you was black. I' thinking you one o' them white ladies.'

'Oh, it's only that!' Eléna chuckled and winked at Louis in relief.


Having overcome her initial resistance, Tessa soon settled down to a period of pleasant if strenuous activities. Her tiny form could be seen dashing in and out of the house at Santa Clara, her once sad face often lit with a bright, cheerful smile. She had done some domestic work before,

'But it making only two months now since I start as lady's maid,' she said.

One day, not long afterwards, Eléna was sitting on a low stool under the shady tree on the lawn, busying her hands with her needlework while Tessa watched in fascination.

'On that subject, Tessa,' said Eléna, picking up the threads of that earlier conversation, 'don't you think it's time you told me why you had run away?'

Tessa turned away in obvious embarrassment, hanging her head down as was her former custom, and wringing her hands.

'Come now, Tessa! You're not still afraid of me, I know that,' coaxed Eléna in her husky, musical voice as she bit a thread and knotted it in preparation for a new stitch. 'Here, thread this needle for me, and I'll show you how to sew on this scrap of cloth. Won't you like that?'

Tessa certainly would. Shortly after, keeping an amused eye on her pupil's unsteady progress, Eléna continued her sewing until finally Tessa volunteered, 'Madame, you know what happened. I been working the field with mi mudder when the white lady send for me an' send me to live in Esperanza by she family and I start to work in the house. But them people treat me real bad so after I couldn't take it no more, I run way to go back by mi mudder.'

'What about your mother?' asked Eléna.

'She dead, Mistress. When you find me, I was running way again because I couldn't bear it, she get wok to death.'

'How awful! I'm so sorry, Tessa.'

'No, Mistress, at first I was sorry for so, but then I was glad for she. She couldn'ta take no more wok.'

'And what of the talk of your having a young man in the interior?' asked Eléna.

This question caused Tessa some discomfort. She started fidgeting.

'Are you in love, Tessa?'

'Love, Madame? I don't know. I uses to frend with him and he ran way. When the overseer did catch me he say I was running to find him but I don't know nothing 'bout love, Mistress Eléna. The way we does live they don't let you love, a girl lucky to get a decent man, and not be force to take one onliest to make children.' She paused and the two women remained thoughtful for a time. Then she continued, 'You in love, Mistress Eléna?'

'Why do you ask that?' responded Eléna, looking up quickly, quite taken aback by the question.

'Oh, 'cause I wants for you to be happy like Mistress Juanita, and to make a baby like Mistress Carmen doing. You look sad sometimes, and I feel you far, far away sometimes, and I says to miself, my beautiful mistress need a good man to make she smile more. I thinks maybe you have one, and he not here. You too beautiful not to have a suitor. All them ladies in Esperanza was always talking 'bout this suitor, and that suitor.'

'Oh Tessa, you're so funny and far too clever, now let's see you use some of that quick brain on this needlework,' returned Eléna laughing, but the happy mood had however become clouded with thoughts of a six-foot blond man with smiling blue eyes who spoke intimately to her but did not commit himself and then left, never to be heard from again.

## IV

The screams and uproar coming from the slave quarters made Barry put down his pen and look up. It always indicated some unrest when sounds from the slaves penetrated the peace of the big house, for it was not by chance that its designer had located it a considerable distance away. Barry had been in the act of composing a letter to his grandmother. He tried whenever his depression lifted sufficiently to send a few lines affirming that he was well and had not forgotten her, not expressing his ideas about the horrors of the island and distresses of slavery, and always ending with the promise to return as soon as possible.

Hearing the disturbance, Barry decided that he could not, in good conscience, ignore it. Sealing his letter, he put it away, reached for his boots and walked out of the house, down the pathway that led past the stables to the slave quarters.

It was not immediately clear what was happening. Several slaves were huddled together and were being soundly whipped by Johnson, while Albert and his mulatto assistant were tying up a strapping young man, securing him to an old tree stump known as the 'whipping tree'.

The black youth being tied was a remarkably handsome African. Tall, topping Barry by at least two inches, with a muscular build, his every limb seemed to reflect in its tenseness the defiance that Barry read in his eyes.

Barry sauntered up to Albert and asked in his usual, deceptively disinterested voice, 'What's this, Albert? Damned slave deserves a whipping, does he?'

'Yes, Sir. That he does. He's too smart for his breeches. Objects to every task he's given. All beneath him. Thinks he's a free man, he does. Been making trouble. Fighting with the mulatto. These others were trying to hide him, Sir. If we allow them to get away with that, the next time they'll help one escape!'

'What's his name?' asked Barry.

'Christopher, Sir.'

'Christopher? After Columbus or what?' laughed Barry. 'Quite an unlikely name for such a specimen. Likes to fight, does he? Is he any good?'

'Didn't stop to look, Sir,' replied Albert, flexing his whip.

'Are you any good with your fists, Christopher?' Barry came round and stood in front of the bound man.

'I could beat anybody, Sir, you too!' came the daring reply.

'Hmm, throwing caution to the wind, are you?' said Barry. He was intrigued by the unexpected confidence of the slave and with a gesture stopped Albert reacting to the challenging retort.

'What's happening here?' Wilfred's voice broke in, interrupting Barry's next words.

'There you are, Uncle. Was just about to issue a challenge to our young black fighter. I'll beat him for you with my fists while I get my much needed practice.'

Wilfred was not amused, but Barry was not easily dissuaded.

'I think he's game. What say you, Uncle? How long since you've had some good masculine sport? Say yes, and we'll give you an interesting display. What about placing some bets on us, Albert? What say you, Uncle? What are you going to offer the winner? Must give Christopher here an incentive, or he may resist beating a white man. What do you say to granting him his freedom if he wins? Then you're sure he will put his all into the fight. If I win, what can I get? Oh, I know. Give him to me as my own personal slave, to be my . . . er . . . valet. That's it! If I win, I acquire a valet,' laughed Barry.

'Are you mad? Do you think I can just lose a valuable, ablebodied slave like that?'

'Oh Uncle, I've money enough. I'll stand the cost either way, you have my word. Is it agreed, then?'

'You can't expect me to agree to have you humiliate yourself and all of us white men by being beaten by a nigger! This is madness,' spluttered Wilfred.

'Oh, but I'll not lose, Uncle.'

It took considerable further coaxing, but eventually Wilfred gave in, warning Albert to protect his nephew.

Albert untied the slave and used a twig to draw a ring on the dry earth, indicating the fighting arena. Barry stripped off his jacket and waistcoat, all the while glaring menacingly at his opponent. The slave returned his gaze with equal ferocity. 'That's good,' thought Barry, 'he's getting angry enough to lose his head.'

The challengers took up their poses. With arms raised and fists clenched, they began by circling and sizing up each other. At length the fight began in earnest. Barry soon realised that Christopher was as powerful as he looked. He was not worried, though, because he knew that skill and speed could overcome power if he was cautious. For a while they continued sparring in a restrained fashion, delivering very economical volleys. Suddenly Barry gave a quick flurry of blows to Christopher's head and, catching him on the chin, sent him sprawling.

Barry began to feel the sense of exhilaration that a good fight always aroused. It was no lie that he had missed this form of exercise since his arrival on the island. He had practised the art of boxing since his schooldays, and had been trained by several famous exponents of the sport. He was forced to resort to all that training now, as in retaliation the slave came at him with all his might, wearing Barry down with deceptively small punches of tremendous power. Thinking he had had enough of that, Barry countered with a brisk rally of blows to which Christopher reacted by punching him on his head, a blow which caught him in the eye and sent him stumbling backwards.

Recovering just before he fell, Barry shook his head as if to gather his senses, and plunged again into the fray. Time to stop all this flourishing, he thought. He's too good – if I keep this up for long, he'll win by sheer stamina. Barry's face was bleeding and he could feel his eye beginning to close. He threw all his weight behind his next blow and landed a resounding uppercut on the slave's chin, knocking him out.

The fight had been a short one by normal standards, but it had caused as much excitement among the slaves in the yard as it would have in any wrestling parlour in London.

Barry called for some water. Sprinkling some on Christopher's face, he roused him, took his hand, and lifted him upright. Barry then warmly shook the slave's uncertain hand. 'No hard feelings?' he asked, smiling.

'You the boss now, Massa,' came the shaky reply.

'Oh yes! Uncle, he's mine now, isn't he?'

'Yes,' replied his uncle with a look of respect, as he proceeded to congratulate him and expound on the invincibility of white power.

'Ah well, can't have it every way,' thought the hero. 'Anyway, I've won Christopher, now what on earth am I to do with him?'

The next day, nursing his almost classical black eye, the exhilaration of the fight still adding a certain buoyancy to his mood, Barry was faced with the prospect of dealing with his acquisition.

Perhaps it was a testimony to the similarity of their dispositions, but as it turned out both Eléna and Barry unwittingly acquired a slave at about the same time. They were both about to change for ever the lives of these two human souls.

'What have you to say for yourself, Christopher?' Barry accosted the slave as he stood before him the next day. 'We two need not bother with too many formalities. I would require a modicum of respect. Anyway, I intend to grant you your freedom. If you wish to stay with me, it's all up to you. I have no friends here, and a fighting companion is a good thing to have. So if you wish, you could have the post of valet. I'll pay you. Don't be afraid to speak your mind!'

'Afore I takes the job, Sir, I wants two things.'

'Out with it then! What are they?'

'First, I don't want nobody call mi Christopher no more, and if I's to be free, I wants the paper sayin' I's free.'

Barry succumbed to a paroxysm of mirth. '*Touché!* You're a shrewd businessman.'

'If I gets them two things, I stay for a while and do the job,' concluded the slave. 'Except that I don't know nothing 'bout this valet job.'

'Oh, that you'll soon learn. My uncle's man and the maids here will teach you. Now, about this name . . . that's a hard problem. What name do you want?'

'I wants a fighting name, Sir.'

'Oh, like Hannibal. You know, he was a great ancient general, an African too,' suggested Barry.

'No, Sir, I doh know nothing 'bout he. The name I wants is a real fighting name that when I hears it, I thinks of power and a good fight.'

'Damned if I know of any such name,' said Barry thoughtfully. 'Well, what about if we call you "Cuff"? No! No! That's no good! Or how about "Fist"? Yes, how do you like that?'

The slave broke into a broad smile, and brandishing his clenched fist, he answered, 'Yes, Sir, I likes that one! "Fist" is a good name for me.'


Content with his new name, the ex-slave happily served Barry, learning to look after his clothes and possessions and accompanying him on many excursions. His natural dignity at first made him formal and reserved, but as he grew to understand his master he began to show real fondness for him. Barry too, out of sorts with his milieu, made him more of a companion than a servant. Barry taught him how to ride a horse, and eventually bought one for him to ride. As they rode about the island people would stop and stare, for nowhere could one find two more favourable or impressive examples of black and white manhood.

## V

As well as Tessa, there was another person who soon came to be of considerable interest and growing importance to Eléna. That person was Kathy's son Mark, who proved to be an easy-going fellow whose artistic talents were much appreciated by the ladies. Eléna invited him to come with his paints to Santa Clara. When he did so, she took him to find a likely spot of interest.

They walked through the neatly shorn lawns towards the flowerbeds. Here Mark paused to admire Yei's unusual garden. The decorative caladiums and the windflower lilies of delicate pinks and yellows formed a subtle, understated background to the more dramatic statement of the native bromeliads, the ornamental pineapples of fiery red that shot out their striking, variegated waxed leaves. Then there were the wild orchids and the heliconias, almost oriental in the perfection of each tapered cup. Mark paused too, to breathe in the fragrant air, perfumed by the native frangipani, and to wonder at the profusion of red flowers of the flaming immortelles.

Moving down to the cool, shady glades of the cocoa, Mark selected a site under a spreading immortelle. Eléna sat down and took out her sewing. The brilliance of the red flowers contrasted with the white of her simple morning dress. On the banks of the stream that flowed nearby were large jungle ferns attracted to the shade and the dampness.

They spoke of many things, especially of his interest in landscape painting and of his visit to Europe where he had gone to see the works of famous landscape artists.

'But Eléna, another time when I come to Santa Clara, I would like to capture your beauty. Would you consider sitting for me?' he asked.

'Certainly, if I can sit still for that long,' Eléna replied, laughing.

Mark sketched, Eléna sewed. An amiable silence prevailed, broken eventually when Eléna asked hesitantly about his feelings for M. Louis.

Mark's reply expressed his confusion. 'I . . . I know he is my father, Eléna. Heaven knows I'm relieved not to be the offspring of my mother's late husband but I'm not sure I like having a new father thrust unceremoniously on me.'

After a while Tessa came running up, sewing-basket slung on her arm, tiny feet crunching the fallen leaves and flowers. She explained that she had been delayed by having to clean up after Eléna's dog and was sorry to have left her mistress so long unchaperoned.

Much to Eléna's amusement, Tessa had become very protective of her. Whenever free of chores she would follow Eléna around and soon became her acknowledged shadow. She had shown a natural aptitude for needlework and the two women could often be seen sitting near each other, sewing and conversing softly. Eléna had become very fond of Tessa's simple, open personality and her obvious intelligence. She vowed to interest Juanita in teaching her and perhaps even in granting her freedom if a suitable young man came her way.

'You know, Mark, I think it's time I returned that pup. He has grown into quite a large dog, and Yvette is better now. But they never seem to want me to leave, once I get there.'

'I'll go with you on the visit, if you like. Tomorrow?'

'Oh, would you? That would be splendid! They must allow me to leave them, but not tomorrow. I'm going to take Tessa to her new home then.' Eléna looked sadly at the young slave and patted her knees comfortingly. 'I would like to give Tessa some time to settle in before I go back to town though, so I can use the opportunity to visit her as well. Would a week from Tuesday suit you instead?'

# VI

Eléna, accompanied by the pup, arrived at Millefleurs on the appointed Tuesday. Mark was already there awaiting her.

As the carriage turned into the yard a joyous Tessa, now resident there, came bounding out to greet them. She collected the pup from Eléna, cuddling it in her arms and crying out in mock protest as it covered her smiling black face with its wet kisses.

Eléna sat with Juanita, listening with concern to her complaints of Tessa's running off to sightsee in the town. Then she administered a liberal scolding to Tessa, before leaving with Mark for Yvette's.

Whenever she saw the Fontainebleaus' town house, with its many-jalousied bay windows, generous high balcony and frivolous, detailed fretwork edging an elaborate, almost turreted, gabled roof, Eléna was always reminded of her first visit. She almost expected on this occasion to see a jaunty clown dance down the stairs, and as always was struck by the atmosphere of staid respectability that existed in these less festive times.

They were met by the effusive Madame Fontainebleau, who escorted them to the backyard where Yvette was found busy supervising a young black boy high up on a tree picking guavas and throwing them down to her.

'That not 'nough yet, Miss?' came the weary voice of the boy.

'No, no, there's a laden branch to your right, Manuel. *Not* that right, your other right! Foolish boy!' she muttered under her breath as, with hands on hips, she craned her neck upwards.

Mark bit back a smile and Eléna called out to her. Blushing in surprise, she came up, greeting them and reaching out for the dog.

In a gown of fine pink muslin, her feet shod in typically flat *alpagatas*, Yvette came only to Mark's shoulder. She was light of colouring, with rusty brown, almost red hair that curled profusely, and a pair of sparkling brown eyes. Stubby, flared nostrils and full, well-shaped lips gave her face a piquant look. Her colouring and her features were a glowing testimony to her mixed race. She instantly bewitched her young male visitor, and with her mock-serious face and witty repartee kept them amused until André came in.

As he entered the room, André was instantly overcome by a racking cough.

'There, you see, you *are* ill!' cried Eléna.

'Oh, it's nothing. Got caught in the rain this morning while seeing to a minor slave disturbance over at La Rose's place. Damn those royalists! Picton is allowing them to do as they please with the slaves.'

'André, I have brought you a medicine for that cough, a syrup from the *bois canno* leaf which Yei swears by. Promise me you'll take it!' pleaded Eléna, handing him a small container from her basket.

'You worry too much, Eléna, but to please you, I will.' André continued with his topic. 'Do you know, Eléna, that soon your slaves at Santa Clara too will be banned from working their own fields or selling their crops at weekends?'

'No! That is not possible! The Code Noir . . .'

'The French barons have already stopped it on their holdings,' he interrupted.

'I cannot believe it,' protested Eléna.

'There are a great many hard things that you haven't yet begun to hear of, Eléna,' he concluded as he rose to leave, 'and I pray to God that you are spared them.'

It was late when Eléna was finally able to drag Mark away.

'Mark, you're not to be trusted. There you were, quite content to spend the entire day,' she chided as they left.

'Oh, but Eléna, you ought to have warned me that your Yvette was so utterly beguiling,' he answered, airily.

## VII

With Fist as his constant companion, Barry found life in Barbados almost tolerable. It was not that the oppression around him had diminished, or that his loathing of the unnecessary cruelties had lessened, but somehow the new companionship acted as a buffer to the worst of it. They hardly ever spoke openly of these things, but they shared a common antipathy to the system in which they were both forced to exist. It was an unorthodox partnership, to say the least, but with every passing day the bond between the two men strengthened.

Barry was waiting patiently for the coming ball which, once it took place, would release him from his obligatory stay in the wretched island. In the meantime, during the day he sparred with Fist, improving the ex-slave's technique by sharing his expertise with him, or the two men would ride about the island. At night Barry took to roaming the taverns and grog shops, often having to be physically rescued by Fist and forcibly taken home, undressed and put to bed, while he openly proclaimed his heartaches, dreams and desires which, more usually than not, pertained to a mysterious enchantress with eyes like a deer and skin as smooth as velvet. Fist came to know a great deal about that bewitching woman.

Marta's plans for the ball were, however, proceeding apace. Finally her long-delayed relatives arrived. Marta's sister and her husband were typical colonials. They fawned on the very eligible Barry, but their daughter Agnes stirred no tender sentiments in the young man's heart. This became especially so when she declared that Fist ought to be wearing his badge – the blue cross – on his right shoulder like the free blacks of Jamaica, or, when commenting on the wealth of free coloureds in Trinidad, she expressed the hope that the British would soon curtail that, 'for not even a mulatto in Jamaica could inherit over two thousand pounds.'

Every encounter with her enraged Barry further. He would ride himself to exhaustion and then sit staring distractedly at the sea, until one day Fist enquired, 'Why you take on so, Barry?' With his master's permission, he now used this familiar form of address when they were alone together.

'Prejudice, Fist. I can't stand the senseless prejudice, not from the lips of such an innocent dab of a thing.'

'I never understand you. Why you so different 'bout niggers than other white men is? White men don't care 'bout black people. Why you take on so?'

'Oh, I'm bewitched, Fist,' sighed Barry. 'I've been bewitched from childhood by an old woman, and now . . . by a young one. How can I escape? It's my destiny to be a rebel, I suppose.'

'But it tearing you in pieces, Barry. You never happy, and you drink too much rum. The young woman with the deer eyes, you want her?' asked Fist. Not waiting for a reply, he continued, 'Why not take her, then?'

Barry made no sign of replying, but stayed silent, watching the scene in the lively harbour below until he said sadly, 'Can't have her, Fist. I'm not rebel enough for that!'


The sun shone brilliantly in the heavens. Birdsong filled the air, and the lawns and flower gardens of Wilfred's plantation never looked so immaculate and enchanting as they did on the day of Marta's ball.

After breakfast Barry went to his quarters where Fist was tending his wardrobe. The two men conversed in a relaxed manner.

'Would you come with me to Trinidad, Fist?' asked Barry, stretching his long legs out in front of him as he reclined in an easy chair, watching the black man do his work.

'I tell you I could talk Spanish, nah?'

'No need to. I know you can speak French patois. You came from Grenada.'

'Yes, well I onliest come here after Massa Wingate sell he plantation over there and ship us niggers to Barbados.'

'So? Coming to Trinidad?'

'What over there for me, Sir?' came the reply.

'Lots of beautiful women for one thing. Do you know that Trinidad is famous for its magnificent mulatto women?'

'Now, why would they look at a big ugly nigger like me?' laughed Fist, turning around to face Barry with his hands on his hips, and a wry expression glowing on his face that made his employer grin in response.

'Seriously though, it's a very interesting island. It has Spanish laws, French inhabitants, and is now ruled by the British. We ought to go and see how that combination is working out,' rejoined Barry, still grinning.

'You laughing, Barry, but I get the feeling you just acting. You worried 'bout that island or 'bout a certain person there.'

'You're far too astute, my man. Let's just say I'm anxious to see what the British are doing down there. Remember I'm the son of an English peer, and as such come from a long line of British rulers. Just curious.'

'I ain't have nothing to do, Sir. I could go anywhere you wants. Who knows, maybe my destiny down there too, like yours . . .' They stared at each other in unspeaking, unackowledged understanding until Barry turned his eyes away and changed the subject.

'How about a sea-bath? We have five hours at least before I begin dressing.'

'No Sir! You go. I have to get all these clothes ready 'cause I wants you to look good tonight. Leave me be and go by yourself.'

'All right, all right, no need to push and shove! I'm off! See you later, then.'

He was in no particular hurry and enjoyed the scenery as he went. He stopped to look at a humming bird those tail feathers flapped with frenzied gaiety, so fast that they made him dizzy. It danced from flower to flower, its fluorescent colours forming colourful arcs in the air, its cheerful purposefulness matching his bright spirits.

Indeed, he was happy and unhurried. The very sun, the trees and flowers seemed to be humming, 'Soon you can leave! Soon you can leave!'

Further down the road a cloud of dust attracted him. A rider was approaching.

'What, a guest this soon?' he wondered as he prepared to step aside.

Suddenly, his heart skipped a beat. For a moment something about the rider seemed familiar.

'No, it can't be,' he cautioned himself, only to see the approaching figure take off his hat and start waving it furiously in the air.

'By all that's holy!' cried Barry, hurrying forward, shouting joyously, 'Fred! Fred! It is you!'

A more joyous reunion could not be imagined between two young men who normally would be less demonstrative of their mutual affection. They hugged each other, slapped each other on the back, and there and then decided to head for the beach together.

# VIII

'Now tell me everything,' demanded Barry when they were finally out of the water.

'Nothing in Trinidad can surpass the waters of Barbados,' parried Fred, ignoring his friend's urgency for news. 'Wait, let me catch my breath, my good fellow,' he laughed.

'What is really happening in Trinidad? I've heard such horror stories! Is everyone all right? All our friends at . . .'

'Eléna?'

'Yes. Eléna too,' Barry swallowed nervously. 'Is she all right?' He looked anxiously at his friend.

'She's well, Barry. Once we'd got over the scare of deportation for José and Diego, the family settled down to near normality. Of course, my wife has moved to our house in town,' added Fred, for maximum effect.

'Oh, forgive me for forgetting. Congratulations! How is married life?'

'Wonderful! I highly recommend it!' Fred looked slyly at Barry who refused to fall for the bait, asking instead, 'Are all those rumours of atrocities, killings and tortures really true?'

''Fraid so. I've some acquaintance with the man, Picton. I can tell you he's ruthless. Faced with the problems of that less than welcoming population, he's decided to deal with a very firm hand. He is dispensing harsh punishments, but indiscriminately, mind you. Hanged a white man for attempted rape on a free black. Hanged fourteen German mercenaries from his invading force, who deserted because they weren't paid. Threatened and subdued those self-seeking white republicans, like the man Begorrat, until now they are his willing minions.'

Shaking the water from his hair, he continued, 'You know, before, with the Spanish law, they couldn't hang or execute a man without due process and final permission from Caracas, but not so with Picton! His justice is swift and deadly. He has activated the laws on torture, which the Spaniards themselves had let slide. Remember that story of François, the slave?'

'All the Spanish laws do still apply? The Code Noir too?'

'Yes, but what's the good of that when the spirit of the law is not there? Let me put it this way,' Fred snorted cynically. 'It's quite clear that Picton's emphasis is on the rights of the slave-owner, not the slave. He has become a slave-owner himself, you know. Yes, he has a plantation of his own now. Incidentally, unlike Chacon, he's already famous for tracking runaways. I hear the new punishment for them is the loss of an ear!' Fred lifted his eyebrows sympathetically as he saw Barry's look of horror. ''Fraid I can no longer recommend the place to you as an escape from the rigours of slavery, as I once did.

'Well, once the Navy left, the Spanish and French privateers came back into the Gulf of Paria. You see, with no navy and an unreliable garrison, he chose to get tough, prevent anyone getting ideas . . .'

'All I can think of is how hard it must be for those people who lived under the kind Spanish Governor, who aren't used to British ways.'

'Yes, my friend,' answered Fred thoughtfully. 'But the royalists and the reformed white republicans like it. They ignore the Code Noir with impunity. I'm sure Picton will officially rewrite it for them soon. His friends are already denying their slaves use of land or time to plant their own crops, much less to sell their produce.'

'And his attitude to the free coloureds?' asked Barry.

'A lot of them fled the island. He has subdued those that remained. He lumps them all as republicans and troublemakers. Of course, you know the biggest irony of all is that just like Chacon, Picton had a mulatto mistress.'

The two friends laughed humourlessly. Fred continued, 'It never was really a perfect place, but it certainly is no longer the pleasant little haven it used to be. Picton intends to prevent a second Grenada and make a great name for himself back home.'

'I wonder about that. People at home may not approve of his methods. And what about yourself?'

'Doesn't affect me, really.' Fred stretched lazily. 'But I'm not sure about Kathy. I suspect she would have packed it in by now if it wasn't for her Monsieur.'

'Her Monsieur?' asked Barry, puzzled.

'Good heavens, Barry! You mean you don't know about Kathy and M. Louis? Well, it was like this . . .'

The conversation between the two friends went on for hours until Barry suddenly realised that they would have to hurry to be in time for the ball, for naturally he had invited Fred to attend, promising to have Fist provide him with suitable clothes.


Fred had come to Barbados after visiting Grenada where the British were once more in complete control, although at the cost of seven thousand lives. All rebels had now been routed, with Fédon escaping into legend. Fred had gone to settle some minor matters left unfinished at Kathy's departure. But in fact, he had been especially interested in visiting Barry about whose state of mind he had been rather curious. Fred knew that Barry had been unhappy when he left Trinidad and yet he had refused to return there with him.

Seeing him now, Fred was able to observe the subtle changes that had taken place in the young man. There were unfamiliar signs of strain on his youthful face. Nothing very specific – a hollowing-out of his cheeks, a drawn, almost haggard look that was new to Fred. Or was it a hint of melancholy about the once-smiling blue eyes? Then too, Fred had observed a more deep-rooted seriousness in Barry, a seriousness born of maturity, or deep deeling, or pain.

He debated with himself for a moment and ventured, 'Are you going to avoid coming to Trinidad because of Eléna?'

'How could you ask that?' responded Barry, defensively, his blue eyes flashing. 'Do you think I don't want to see her again?'

'I get the impression you've decided to fight the feeling. Am I wrong?'

'You're seldom wrong, Fred.' Barry turned away and fiddled with his cravat in the mirror. 'But look, let's not speak any more of serious matters. I'm so happy to see you, and there's to be lots of music and laughter and good food, and especially good drink tonight. My gaol term ends at midnight, and I'm free! And contrary to your suspicions, I will be accompanying you to Trinidad. Yes, my friend, we'll return together, with Fist here, of course, isn't that so, Fist?'

'Yes, Sir, we goin' south!' came the reply.


# CHAPTER ELEVEN

## I

Juanita, with Tessa in attendance, spent the days of Fred's absence at Santa Clara. One afternoon the three young women sat on the breezy veranda, Eléna at her needlework, Carmen swinging lazily in Yei's hammock. Juanita relaxed in an easy chair. She was happy to be here. She caught a glimpse of young Tessa skipping about the lawns and dashing in and out of the house like a hummingbird. She smiled and turned her attention to Eléna's dextrous fingers.

How industrious and talented, she is! she mused. Carmen is settled, already expecting her first baby. Soon, too soon, I will be leaving everyone here to follow Fred to his strange country. What's to become of Eléna? So much beauty and talent and no clear future ahead.

'Eléna, do you ever intend to accept André?' she ventured impulsively.

Surprised at the pointedness of the question, Eléna at first looked blankly at Juanita.

'Aren't you ever, Eléna?' added Carmen.

'Won't you discuss it with us? He has certainly been unwavering in his interest for the past – how long is it now, Carmen?'

'Three years.'

'You're forgetting he has not asked me,' responded Eléna.

'But that's a mere technicality. He's simply waiting for a sign from you, you know it.'

'I'm afraid you two are embarrassing me,' smiled Eléna.

'Embarrassing? But it's only us girls! Dear Eléna, you can't blame us for being curious, and for wishing you to share in the happiness we ourselves know,' persisted Juanita.

Eléna stopped sewing, raised her head on her long, swan-like neck, and looked absently out across the lawn. Her mind turned to André. He was very eligible, very handsome with his beautiful colouring: his skin a light brown, darker than Yvette's but lighter than her own. He had an intense face, his wavy black hair forming an attractive widow's peak on his forehead, a straight nose that flared at the nostrils, and wide, well-shaped lips with an immaculate moustache. He was not quite as tall as herself, but not so short that it mattered. In any case that didn't disturb her. He was indeed a true and faithful friend, always at hand, never wavering in his devotion to her, and now so humiliated under the British, stripped of his rank, and certainly not in the best of health. Her heart went out to him. So why could she not love him? He is infinitely more suitable than some white foreigner, she thought. It is madness to think of a girl as obviously coloured as myself married to a man as obviously white as . . . Why did he have to be white anyway, with blond hair and blue eyes? It's too much! Worst of all, why does he have to be British?

She rose abruptly and walked to the railing, clutching it tightly, tears filling her eyes.

'What is it, Eléna?' cried Carmen.

'Eléna, darling, have we upset you?' Juanita rose swiftly and joined her at the rail. 'It was an innocent question. We meant no harm. Why does this talk make you sad?'

'We simply wanted to share your emotions . . . but is there something worse? Is it because he is ill?' asked the ever-intense Carmen, her voice filled with sudden fear.

'No, no, Carmen. It's not because he is ill. It's . . . it's just that . . . it's just that . . . I don't love him.'

'Is there someone else? Someone we don't know about?' added Juanita, with sudden insight.

'Yes,' whispered Eléna, as she covered her face with her hands and sobbed quietly, so that she did not see the quizzical look that passed between her two companions.

Chastened by Eléna's reaction, Juanita and Carmen made a special effort to avoid any reference to the upset.

For her own part, Eléna was doubly distressed. Distressed not just by her weakness that day, but especially by the fact that now she was no longer deceived as to what Barry meant to her. 'Thank God, at least he is far away and in time I must forget him,' she told herself.

The girls spent the long sunny days after Eléna's outburst vying in their efforts at cheerfulness. In the end their efforts proved successful. Their pretended gaiety did cheer them and by the end of the week, when Kathy and Mark visited Santa Clara, they were back to normal again.

With Tessa in tow, Eléna went with Mark to see the dancing of the cocoa. As they walked, Eléna described the process of cocoa production.

'After it is reaped and shelled, the beans are left to ferment in a sweat box, then they are spread out in the cocoa house to dry. Afterwards they are danced by the workers.'

'What fun!' exclaimed Mark, 'I never paid attention to these things in Grenada. This will add to my education. I've become quite . . . ahem . . . interested in education, you see . . .' Eléna looked enquiringly at her escort. He continued; 'Yes . . . ahem . . . that is, Yvette did express an interest in learning English.'

'Oh Mark, be careful! You haven't been seeing more of Yvette! You do know that her parents have already chosen a suitable partner for her?'

Mark laughed mischievously, forcing Eléna to join in his dubious high spirits. Soon after they came upon the festivities in the cocoa, and joined in merrily. Mark urged Tessa to take off her sandals, and like him, to join the dance, while Eléna was content to keep rhythm with her hands as she watched on in amusement.

That night, however, Tessa suffered the consequences of her excesses. Administering a warm herbal footbath to her, Eléna listened to Tessa prattle on about how funny Mark was and what an excellent prospect for her mistress, far better than a secret lover.

'Don't think I don't know you love someone, Mistress. One day I go find out who he be.'

'Ah, how will you do that, my prying little miss?' teased Eléna.

'Oh, I go know, Mistress. You can't hide that from your little Tessa. I very smart. I go see it in your eyes.'

Eléna laughed, thinking that Tessa would never get such an opportunity. She was wrong, however, for even then the object of Tessa's curiosity was on his way to enter Eléna's life once more.

# II

No one at Santa Clara was expecting them, so when they arrived at the house all was quiet. A young boy cutting the lawn looked up briefly as they approached, and continued his task. The three men dismounted and led their horses to the stables. Leaving Fist to see to them, Fred and Barry strode over to the house, entering by way of the veranda and into the living-room where they came upon the three ladies.

'Hello there,' greeted Fred. All three women looked at the doorway in surprise. Juanita jumped up and rushed to her husband, hugging him passionately as he covered her face with kisses. Eléna's eyes were fixed on the unexpected visitor at the door.

Barry kept his unwavering gaze on her, smiling broadly, unable to conceal his delight at seeing her again or to ingore the unexpected joy reflected in her face. His arrival had caught her unawares and, unprepared as she was, she could not prevent what she felt in her heart from displaying itself in the warmth of her smile.

With their eyes locked in a trance of their own, Barry approached her. Taking both her hands in his, he raised them alternatively to his lips. He would have spoken but José came in, slapping him on the back, exclaiming in surprise at his presence and the spontaneity of the moment was lost.

That moment had told him a great deal, though. Without affectation, without thought and without embarrassment, she had shown him her heart. He realised now that it was one thing to be resolved to subdue his own feelings, but quite another to have the strength to reject reciprocal feelings from her.

Much discussion and explanation followed, and for a long while everyone was absorbed in listening to Fred's account of his trip and to Barry's adventures in Barbados. Towards afternoon when they had eaten and the animation of the discussions had subsided, the company broke up.

Carmen had just returned indoors after her post-luncheon walk. Tessa was sitting under a shady tree busily sewing. Eléna was about to join the young slave when Barry approached.

'It is really so good to be here again,' he began guardedly. 'How were the pouis this year? I'm still haunted by their beauty.'

In spite of himself, his words seemed to hold a double meaning. Eléna fell into step with him and they walked softly on the golden offerings. The tree itself was bereft of blossoms.

'So much has happened since I was last here. How have you fared? Are you still able to continue your Saturdays with the slaves?'

'Oh yes. I still go. But the feeling now is that soon Picton will make a law punishing owners who do not force the slaves to work on Saturdays,' replied Eléna in the husky, musical voice that had filled Barry's dreams so often in Barbados.

'I'm deeply saddened that my countrymen are the cause of all this, Eléna.' He looked uncomfortably away from the magnetism of her eyes. 'You must hate the British . . .' He fidgeted before continuing. 'Please let me say this . . . under the British, Trinidad might just prove to be the place where the continuation of slavery is challenged. Believe me, in England there are people who will oppose the cruelties and extremes of Picton.'

They walked aimlessly in pregnant silence until he continued, 'You do know that in England there is a movement afoot to end the slave trade . . . and that . . .'

'I know of it, Barry, and I know the movement is dying and the slave trade is growing,' interrupted Eléna, speaking passionately. 'Look at the French, they say they have abolished slavery but are they only trying to use black men to fight their battles of revolution? When the war is over, will black men still be free? And . . . and, look what is happening meanwhile. The royalists are simply coming here with their slaves.

'Barry, the trade must be stopped, but it's not just the trade, it's slavery, the whole rotten thing! It's bad, bad in every way! Here at Santa Clara the horrors don't touch us, but to own people is still wrong. They are not brainless animals. The Spanish law at least admitted that, but these barbarian English . . .'

Eléna had become quite agitated. It was all Barry could do to resist comforting her in his arms. He kept his eyes down.

They reached a frangipani tree. Eléna leaned her arm along a low, flowering branch. When Barry turned to her, she presented a lovely picture, framed as it were by the frangipani. Some of the fragrant white flowers had fallen on her hair, and absently he reached over to remove them. It was an unconsciously intimate gesture. He found himself entrapped by her nearness and aroused by the intoxicating scent of the frangipani. An unseen force seemed to pull them closer. Eléna showed no sign of resisting. She closed her eyes in delicious anticipation of the fulfilment of an unspoken longing.

That moment of ecstasy was not to be.

'Barry, where have you got to?' came Fred's voice, shattering the stillness, breaking the silken thread of commitment.

That night as Eléna was preparing for bed, Tessa came up to her room skipping from bedpost to bedpost, and spinning her tiny body like a little dancing doll. 'Oh Mistress,' she crooned, 'You see him? You see him? He handsome, eh? Oh Mistress, he handsome, eh?'

'All right, Tessa, I agree. Now off to bed? I won't have you tease me tonight!'

Tessa ran off, leaving the already distressed Eléna thinking how annoyingly astute the little slave was. The fact was that Tessa had paid cursory attention to Barry, however, and was really in transports over someone quite different, a tall, strapping African going by the formidable fighting name of 'Fist'.

## III

The visitors to Santa Clara left the next afternoon, José opting to accompany them. The four men were on horseback while Juanita travelled in the carriage, amusedly observing Tessa's flirtatious antics towards the striking African valet.

Arriving at Millefleurs, and all parties finally refreshed and settled, the three gentlemen sat in Fred's cosy sitting-room armed with several bottles of rum and large jugs of lime juice or water. They relaxed and slowly began their discussion. Barry spoke first.

'Seeing you all so unchanged and unharmed, I can finally put my fears to rest.'

'Don't depend on it though, Barry. In this situation one doesn't know what can happen from day to day.'

'Tell me everything from the beginning. I want to understand exactly what happened. First, you're no longer in the militia, José?'

'No, and thank God for that, but I assure you Picton has every store clerk, white indentured labourer from England, every able-bodied mulatto, you name it, in his regiment.'

'He drills them every Sunday morning, sun or rain. Strict discipline, whipping and torturing's commonplace now,' added Fred.

'Damnation! I find that so reprehensible, the reintroduction of torture,' interjected Barry.

'Reintroduction's not the word. It was always the law.'

'I explained to him, José, that Spanish legal systems are very complex, checked and double-checked by Caracas and so on. Its complexity, Barry, was its safeguard.'

'You see, Barry,' added José, 'although we appear to be lax, we Spaniards are very strict about the law. Our laws have now been retained, under the pretext of not disturbing the island's way of life, but in Picton's ruthless hands and without our safeguards, the law is a mockery. Picton will keep what aspects of our law that he chooses, and dispense with what he does not like. It's a dangerous situation. He has also deported all the Spanish lawyers, so it's law according to him.'

'But José, how did he succeed so well? I can understand how Chacon capitulated so readily, but . . .'

'Do you? I was there and I'm not sure I do. There was a point when . . . oh well, I have no wish to be heroic, so I ought to thank Chacon for not engaging in battle.' A rueful laugh escaped José's lips. 'But were I in his place, *amigo* . . . He wasn't himself that day. My father says the spirit had gone out of him.'

'I rather think he wanted to do like that Dutch Governor of Guiana who also capitulated,' suggested Fred as he lounged on a cushioned divan. 'But it is rumoured that he was bribed by our . . . ahem . . . side.'

'It's well known that he preferred the British to the French. In fact, Barry, when he rejected Victor Hugues's offer of help, he sent to tell him that he would rather succumb to a worthy enemy than a dangerous ally.'

'Didn't he change his mind at some point, and try to recapture the island? Was he free to do that?'

'Why yes. After the changeover, he wasn't imprisoned or anything. He was the happiest of men. He was actually able to get back some of his runaways, and sell them.'

'I think he was relieved at that point, don't you, José?' added Fred. 'He became very garrulous about the republicans, so much so that the very next day, loads of alleged republicans were ordered out of Trinidad.'

'But tell me, how did Chacon come to change his tune?'

'That was extraordinary!' exclaimed José. 'It got many notable Spaniards deported, endangered my father as well . . .'

'But I heard a great deal of Spanish on the streets,' said a puzzled Barry.

'Indeed,' replied José, 'there are Spanish-speaking troublemakers in town, men of no quality, but it's French you'll hear on all the plantations.'

'Port of Spain is awash with new immigrants,' added Fred. 'A lot of Englishmen too, hanging around playing billiards, Spanish, English, French, loads of them, drinking rum, molesting the women.'

'But to answer your question, I suspect Chacon got wind of Picton's attempts at stirring up unrest in Venezuela, and began to see that the British were serious about making war on all of Spain's New World territories. I mean, Picton had started issuing pamphlets promising freedoms and liberties, using Trinidad as the base of operations for his intrusion into South America,' explained José.

'That's right,' agreed Fred. 'It was then that Chacon realised just how strategically important Trinidad was to South America. He became very concerned that the British would never release Trinidad in any treaty, which had apparently been his private hope, as I daresay it still is the hope of many people. You know, Barry, the war isn't going that well for Britain. We've lost our allies in Europe. Pitt might be in no position to demand Trinidad in a settlement.' Fred paused and refilled their glasses. Barry spoke again.

'What has happened to Chacon?'

'He and Admiral Apodaca are probably still awaiting trial in Cadiz, poor fellows! Chacon was a good man . . . in the terms of the surrender, he insisted on a commitment from Abercrombie safeguarding the rights of the free people of colour.'

'Although it is clear already that said commitment is not being respected. Fontainebleau had lost his commission, eh?' interjected Fred dryly.

'What of your father, José, how is he?' asked Barry.

'He's never been the same since the British came,' answered José, his voice dropping as if he were loath to express his fears. 'He hasn't been very well. He suffered a mild heart attack soon afterwards and Yei and the girls have been trying to keep him quiet but that isn't easy to do. He insists on marching around the estate. It's worrying.'

'He went off and bought himself a regal piece of equipage recently,' added Fred, attempting to distract José from his fears.

'Oh yes,' smiled José, 'a great bargain, he claimed.'

'It's an ornate European carriage, Barry. What we know as a brougham. Can you imagine such a piece in this rustic setting?'

They all laughed and their spirits lifted for a moment, then Barry once again brought the conversation around to Picton.

'So how has the man been managing the island, how is the economy and so on?'

'Never been better!' answered Fred. 'Bumper crops and all that. He's done his job well. He has subdued the people, is terrorising the slaves, keeping his enemies at bay and pressing forward with road repairs and so on, and he's building the economy. Can the Crown ask for more?' he ended sarcastically.

Barry absorbed the information and then said slowly, 'So now he is probably preparing for slave revolts, unrest in the other islands must be scaring him too.'

'Certainly,' responded José, 'putting down revolts is one of the purposes of the increased militia and indeed of the growing number of commandants of quarters. Officially, of course, they function as in Chacon's time, to ensure that planters don't abuse their slaves . . .'

'As well as to carry out many civic and judicial tasks ranging from examining passports – they're very strict about these things now, Barry – to performing autopsies,' interjected Fred.

'His fears of unrest can be discerned in his many new schemes and experiments for punishment of defaulters. He is the law. What can be more extreme than erecting a gallows in front of his residence?'

'Not to mention Vallot, the gaoler, and Payne, the hangman, who are also in his schemes, or the *cachots brûlants*, the torture chambers of the gaol. Vallot was always a bastard, even in Chacon's time, but now he's in conspiracy with the royalists. They pay him a fee for incarcerating, flogging or torturing their negroes. The fact is, Barry, the gaol has become a centre of punishment for negro miscreants and, believe me, it will get worse,' said José.

'Good God! And London is allowing Picton free reign!' exclaimed Barry.

'It's wartime and he is only the military Governor. We are really living in a state of martial law that's not exactly constitutional. Picton's position is not officially confirmed as yet so that makes him more determined to prove his worthiness.'

Fred paused to savour his drink. 'I fear, Barry, he isn't going to let up. Of course one does call one's fears on oneself. I mean, the harsher the laws, the greater the frequency of revolt.'

'Yes, that's the irony of it. I used to try using some of that ironic logic on Wilfred's foreman in Barbados,' smiled Barry wryly, and he swung into a discourse of his experiences with Albert and Johnson.

The conversation drifted on to reminiscences and different bits of masculine gossip of which young gentlemen are wont to speak when they are well supplied with drink, in good company and seated in a pleasant atmosphere.

# CHAPTER TWELVE

## I

That Tessa was badly smitten, there was no doubt. But, clever girl that she was, she had no intention of revealing this to the young man who now filled her thoughts and participated in her dreams. First she would determine if her interest was genuinely reciprocated, then . . . but then what? She was totally unaware of what rules would apply to her in such eventualities. She was not after all, her own woman, but valuable Whiteways property.

One day she was passing near the stables when Fist happened to catch a glimpse of her. Leaving his task of grooming Barry's horse, he sauntered to the doorway and stood leaning against the wall with his arms folded and a mischievous smirk on his face. As she passed, he said meaningfully, '*Doux, doux*, darling . . . Humm, humm, Lord save me! Girl, you ain't playing you nice nah!'

Tessa cast him a withering look of disapproval and flounced off, holding her head majestically high, only to become convulsed with giggles as soon as he was out of sight.

A few days passed in which she kept a discrete distance from Fist, only spying on him occasionally from the safety of the window in her sleeping quarters. She loved to see him at his tasks in the stables. He enjoyed working with the horses, and took pride in dismissing Fred's stable boy and attending to them himself. He would strip off his shirt, exposing his excellent physique and powerful limbs to the air, singing to himself in his deep, resonant voice, while his muscles rippled as he stroked the animals with brush or comb.

Gazing at this magnificent spectacle of manhood from the concealment of her room, Tessa would sigh wistfully and think contradictory, disturbing and frustrating thoughts. She would have to be cautious, she realised, and keep her distance as far as humanly possible. That was not easy, however, given the circumstances of a relatively small household and the fact that no one else was aware of her plan.

Occasions therefore did arise when she was forced to assist in serving Fist his meals, or handing him Barry's clean linen or things of that sort. Such duties she performed always in the protective company of others, and in a most serious and disinterested manner, even if her heart was pounding in her tiny chest. But Fist always took the opportunity to ensure that his hands did not only receive the proffered item. They would linger to caress those of the giver, while he watched amusedly at the disturbance he was causing on the face of his silent victim.

Fist had decided to bide his time for soon enough, he was sure, the little temptress was bound to fall into his grasp.

The inevitable happened one day some weeks later, when Juanita, wanting to find out Barry's plans for the day and unable to locate him, sent Tessa to the stables to enquire of his valet. Afraid to reveal too much by protesting against the order, Tessa took her courage in her hands and approached the stables cautiously. She stood hesitantly outside and called to him. Fist was cleverer than she had bargained for. Wise to her plan, he chose to ignore the calls, forcing her to enter in search of him.

As she stepped into the shed, he grabbed her playfully.

'Oh you big beast! Put me down, you hear!' she cried, not wanting to raise her voice, and suddenly no longer afraid of him, for he was holding her very tenderly, lifting her in his arms and playfully bouncing her around, like a baby.

He said, 'So why you hiding from me all the time, child? You 'fraid me or what?'

'Leave me alone, Fist. I doing my work. You go get me in trouble, man.'

'You ain't go get in no trouble. Them people like you too much. Think I can't see, nah. Why you hiding so? You don't know I like you real bad?' He brought her down now and leaned her gently against the wall. Pressing only a fraction of his weight on her, and cradling her in his arms, he covered her face with tender urgent kisses.

'Oh Fist, not now! Not here! I must go back with the message. The Madame waiting on me.' Her voice grew weaker as she succumbed to the intoxication of his embrace.

With his lips on her ear, he said, 'If I let you go, when I go see you again? You go promise to meet me here tomorrow?'

'No, no! Oh leh me go nah, Fist,' she pleaded earnestly, for she had suddenly become frightened by the intensity of her response. She knew that without a special effort all her resolve would soon disappear. 'Leh me go this time, or I go get in trouble and . . . and I go meet you as soon as I can. Please . . . please!'

'Tell me you love me, first,' he teased her.

'Anything, anything, just let me go now!'

'You ain't say it, yet.'

'Oh Fist, you too bad. You mean an' cruel. Leh me go nah. All right, all right. I love you,' she whispered and he released her. She dashed out the door, only to stop and turn back, 'Oh God, I forget the message. You know where Mr Barry gone?'

# II

After his initial visit to Santa Clara, Barry had dealt very harshly with himself. There was no question of his leaving the island this time. No. As before, he was very much happier here. For many reasons he cared deeply for Trinidad. Everything about it intrigued and fascinated him, but at the same time he knew that unless he was careful, there was the acute danger of becoming entangled in the hopeless if alluring web of romance with Eléna. There was but one solution. Harsh as it may be, he had to avoid meeting her, to cut her off from his life, even if she lingered in his thoughts.

He was sure he was succeeding. He occupied himself with Fred and Juanita, or with Fist. With Fist, he took to hiking in the mountains around Port of Spain, going on long treks, or conversing. They would sit on some vantage point sharing experiences, and looking out at Port of Spain's breathtaking scenery . . . Barry's passion for the dark beauty of Santa Clara was being tamed, but he had not counted on Juanita's interference.

In the midst of her agreeable social activities, Juanita's one regret was that neither Carmen nor Eléna could accompany her. The white society of Port of Spain would not have found them acceptable. So with the excuse of José and Carmen's first wedding anniversary, Juanita was delighted to throw a party for the family and close friends.


When Juanita announced her convivial plans to Barry, however, he was naturally a little shaken and quite perversely amused at how immediately his new-found confidence deserted him. The mere thought of seeing Eléna had started a rhythmic pulse pounding in his head. He smiled ironically but resigned himself to the inevitable.

He made a point of not being on hand to greet the Santa Clara clan when they arrived, as was expected, before sundown. He had taken every precaution, and was in effect throughly convinced that he was well able to face the ordeal.

The gathering proved large and lively enough to satisfy Juanita. Barry came in just in time to take his seat at the table. Juanita had arranged everything carefully. Eléna sat on André's right, while Mark and Yvette were widely separated. Barry took heart in the seating arrangement, but luck was not on his side. He found himself seated obliquely opposite Eléna, and had but to lift his head to encounter her smiling dark eyes.

With no effort, Juanita's dinner was a great success. Food and wine were plentiful, and conversation free and easy.

Barry struggled to concentrate on his meal, gazing at Eléna only when she was not looking his way. Tonight she was stunning indeed. Her dark hair was piled high behind a Spanish comb that was adorned with one perfect wild orchid of the palest magenta, the colour chosen to highlight her dress of the same rosy hue. Her tight-fitting bodice was cut low, but the delicate French lace that enfolded it from waist to throat was discretion itself, showing the merest tantilising hint of full, pale brown breasts.

It was the first time he had seen her in such finery and in such a formal setting. She who had blended so well against the wild mountains of Santa Clara, or sitting amid the fallen flowers of the poui, or framed against the native frangipani, was never more beautiful than here under Juanita's crystal chandelier. Amid the silver and gilt-edged plates of Fred's aristocratic household, her beauty throbbed, paling into insignificance Juanita's petite charms and Carmen's near-perfect features. Such towering elegance could easily outshine anyone he had ever seen at Carlton House, and make the very Prince of Wales stand agape. A lively conversation was proceeding around him, but he paid it no heed . . .

'So now we can expect a British Constitution in the island?'

'Not until the peace is signed, André. Trinidad may yet return to Spain.'

'Don't count on it, *mon ami*. This island is too valuable.'

'But M. Louis, if we remain in British hands, then surely Britain will allow a local assembly?'

'I trust your question stems from curiosity and not optimism, for surely you know they will not allow coloured men into their government, André.'

'Nor Frenchmen for that matter, I regret to say, Louis. Government here of only Englishmen would be a poor representation however. As you would say, Louis, the British have not read Rousseau, they don't know anything about proper representation!' A burst of laughter ensued.

'But the clamour in France was always for a constitution like the British. If that had been granted, there would have been no revolution at all.'

'I won't go as far as that, André, although there's truth there. But, André, you think the British Government will want to give power to a local body that would exclude the majority of the propertied population, and that population they already consider hostile? Do you think they want trouble? What's more, would they grant power when they are already regretting such power in the hands of the other island bodies?'

'Louis, I must look at you with greater respect. How do you know what is disturbing the British Government so well?'

'Oh, Monsieur Whiteways, my learned one, don't think because I am a humble farmer that I don't know what is going on in the world. When the French citizens of Grenada, with the sanction of the British Government, wanted to be admitted to the assembly there, that assembly was quick to declare its constitutional autonomy from Britain. There are several examples of assemblies going their own way.'

'You are perfectly right, Louis. But worse, now in wartime the local assemblies are throwing many obstacles in the path of the War Office. The Secretary of War wants black troops to defend the islands, but do you think the assemblies of Barbados and Jamaica will hear of it? Not at all! Haven't you heard of that latest turn of events, Barry? . . . Barry?'

Barry jerked his head around, gaped for a moment and then grinned sheepishly at Fred. 'Excuse me, everyone, my mind was far away. I'm afraid I was not quite attending. What did you say, Fred?'

'Do you think Parliament will grant Trinidad a local assembly once the peace is signed?'

'I don't know. I'm not at all sure I'd like that, though. Trinidad is so new and relatively undeveloped. To grant an assembly would mean relegating this island to following the path of all the others. That would be unbearable. Just think of the number of slaves that would have to be imported to facilitate an assembly's idea of development! It's a hard decision to make. Which is worse, to be subjected to the ruthless planters, like the rest of the West Indies, or to be subjected to governors like Picton? Aye, there's the rub! Well, perhaps something different should be attempted.'

'Something different? Like what, you dreamer?'

'I don't know . . . some new system, but whatever it is, I hope it will be a system that would recognise the ruling of '92, that the slave trade should be gradually abolished. In spite of everything, Trinidad has such a legacy of human freedom. It could perhaps become an experimental colony where free labour is encouraged, for instance. I don't know, but I'd hate to see this island turned into another Barbados. That would make my heart bleed. I couldn't bear it.' He turned his eyes and encountered those of Eléna. For a full second, they gazed openly, lovingly, at each other, then, reprimanding himself, he turned quickly away.

In the days that followed, disturbed by that momentary lapse, he kept

114

himself particularly busy. Forsaking even Fist's more relaxed company, he chose to accompany Fred and Juanita on their hectic social rounds, or to go with Fred on hunting parties. He did anything that in his opinion would lessen the occasions for reflective thought or undue brooding.

## III

It was difficult for Tessa to meet Fist privately. Unsure of what Juanita's attitude towards her involvement with Fist would be, and knowing only the taunts of her former master's overseer on the mere suspicion of a similar attachment, she lived in dread of being discovered. So on each occasion when Fist approached her she shied away, cautioning him. 'Oh God, Fist, I can't come now. It just ain't have nowhere we could meet without somebody here seeing.'

After a few weeks, Fist solved the problem. He informed her that he had rented the upstairs room of a mulatto's shop in the town, and surreptitiously slipped her the key. She agreed, reluctantly, to meet him during the next siesta.

Ignoring Juanita's scolding, she had occasionally run off on her own to see the sights of the town, so she could do it again.

The following afternoon, therefore, she slipped quietly out of Mille-fleurs and arrived at the shop Fist had indicated. At the side of the building she found the steps that led upstairs, mounted them and, turning the key in the lock, let herself in. Fist was there before her.

'You find the place easy?' he asked, reaching for her.

'Yes, easy enough,' she replied, slipping out of his grip. 'It all right. I could fix it up real good with some nice curtains and thing if it was mine.'

'Everthing I have is yours, woman,' said Fist, reaching out and embracing her once again. She half turned away. He started nibbling at her earlobes, then at her neck and, turning her around, kissed her full on the lips, taking her breath away. When she finally struggled out of his embrace, she walked to the end of the small room and sat on a stool.

'I shoulda never come here, you know. 'Cause you might get the wrong idea. I shoulda never start this thing with you in the first place,' she pouted.

'How you coulda escape that, girl?'

'What kind o' question is that?'

'That's what Barry calls a "rhetorical question". It don't need no answer 'cause I did done plan for you so long, there ain't no way you coulda escape.'

'Well, you must be feel I easy to get, and I go let you have me so easy. I onliest come here to discuss this with you. You have to promise me you ain't go try nothing!'

'What kinda man you take me for? How I could be so close to you in a room by weself, and I ain't go try nothing? You crazy or what?' He approached her menacingly.

'Fist, behave yourself,' she laughed, slipping out of his grasp once again. 'I serious! I onliest come to talk!'

'We could talk, too. There ain't no law saying we can't talk and make love at the same time.'

'Fist, I go get vex for true, you know, 'cause you not listening to me,' insisted Tessa seriously.

'All right *doux*, *doux*, you talk, I listening, I listening.' He lay back on the bed, which apart from a small table and the stool on which Tessa was sitting constituted the only furniture in the small room. With his hands behind his head he kept quiet, looking up at the ceiling.

Now that he was silent, she found it difficult to get the ideas out. She reflected for a long while before she said, 'The thing is, Fist, that I ain't just a ordinary slave. I has what they calls "obligations" to keep the good name of Mistress Eléna. I can't just go and jump in a thing with you just so. Suppose I start making baby? It go kill Mistress Eléna.'

'The black mistress in Santa Clara?'

'Yes, sheself.'

'What she mean to you?'

'Is she who save me when I did run 'way, and they catch me. She real nice to me. Ii'l run 'way ain't nothing but if I do anything bad is like is she fault. I can't do she that. Why you asking all that?'

'Is all right, go on. I listening,' was Fist's noncommittal reply.

'I don't know what you think I is, but I is what they call a "virgin",' continued Tessa, hanging her head down as if embarrassed or ashamed by the revelation. When Fist made no reply, she asked, 'You know what that is?'

'Yes I know,' he replied soberly and was quiet again, until almost at the point when Tessa could not stand the silence any longer, he ventured, 'Tessa, tell me serious, you love me? You like to be with me all the time?'

She was moved by the sincerity in his voice. She got up and came to the bed. She leaned over him, and touched him gently. 'Oh yes, Fist. I think I love you, and like to be with you for always . . . but how to do that, I don't know.'

'You leave it to me . . . I go fix up that part. Now come here, woman, and don't talk no more foolishness 'bout virgin and thing – we ain't have so much more time to waste today.'


# IV

Monsieur Louis was walking up and down the veranda, stopping now and then to stare distractedly into space. Sitting with her sewing at the side of the garden, Eléna observed these unusual antics and was puzzled. Packing up her things, she walked over to her old tutor. 'What is it, Monsieur? You seem so troubled. Can I help?'

Some minutes later, having coaxed him to accompany her, they sat under the immortelle at her special place by the stream.

Eléna waited patiently for Louis to speak. She gazed at the weeds growing nearby. Just common weeds, pests really. But their flowers were as beautiful as any in the garden, she thought, looking at the bright red, hook-shaped but poisonous flower of the *Crêpe Coq* and the sharp thorns that protected the tiny powder-puff flowers of the ti Marie bush. Common, but alluring, and dangerous and to be shunned. Just like Barry has to beware of me, I suppose, thought Eléna. The number of weeks without a visit from him was no ground for optimism.

'Monsieur Louis, what's wrong? Is it Kathy?' asked Eléna, turning away from her silent musing. M. Louis took a deep breath. 'To tell the truth, I don't know why I'm so silly about this . . .'

'Don't stop now, Monsieur. You have me on tenterhooks,' urged Eléna, as she tickled the sensitive plant at her feet. ''ti Marie, 'ti Marie, close your door, policemen're coming to find you,' she repeated to herself, feeling somehow today those words were significant. She shuddered and looked up as Louis spoke again.

'Kathy and I want to get married.'

'Monsieur, you're so disturbed about that? Only that?' Eléna laughed. 'Oh Monsieur, I'm so happy for you.' She went up to him, throwing her arms about his neck impulsively.

M. Louis clutched her, holding her close for a minute. 'Then you don't find it hilarious or embarrassing?' he asked incredulously. Eléna did not. 'I have your permission then, to break the news to Don Diego and the others?' he asked jokingly. 'You think he's well enough for the shock?'

'Of course, Monsieur. Now, tell me all the details about the wedding.'

'That's just it, Eléna. We haven't settled everything as yet. You see, it's sort of a whim of Kathy's. You already know our history and it is obvious that Mark is my son . . .'

'Yes, Monsieur, although neither of you has told us officially.'

'It is awkward. The situation between us is strained. The fact is, we don't know each other. He never allows me to approach him. Well, as you know, I was as shocked as everyone else at his existence. I was forced out of Grenada twenty years ago, and I think you're old enough for me to say this. I was caught in the compromising act that probably led to Mark's existence.'

Louis remained reflective, picking at the weeds at his feet. He continued, 'Kathy has been estranged from her father since he separated us. Now in declining health, he is begging her to come for a reconciliation. In the face of our present happiness, she doesn't want to appear heartless. Yet she is loath to face him alone, afraid that he will separate us again. She has decided that we should marry first, and then go to England to face her father.'

'Both of you together?' asked Eléna, suddenly realising how empty Santa Clara would be without her kind Monsieur. 'I know you can speak English, but as a Frenchman, will you be allowed into Britain? Will you be safe there? You, a republican?'

'*Mais oui*, 'ti Marie,' Louis chuckled dismissively. 'Kathy wants to reach a compromise with her father, but she also wants to prove her point,' he added.

They said nothing for long moments after that. Then Eléna said with determination, 'I admire her spirit and I support her position. I have no patience with dictators and people who feel they could control the lives of others because they are powerful or influential or in authority. Although I sympathise with the sick old man and I know he must be forgiven, he too must be taught a lesson . . . the lesson that human beings must be judged on their merit, and that love goes beyond the barriers of class . . . or race,' she added softly.

Louis looked at her, his eyes with their crow's-feet lines full of admiration. She was the child he was most proud of, the one that best combined his own intelligence and spirit with her mother's natural wisdom. His heart cried out to acknowledge her as his own. Her words now testified to an astuteness that came from some hidden experience.

'Kathy will be so glad that she has a champion in you.'

'Then let us plan, Monsieur. We will have a lot of preparations to make. Will the wedding be a grand one, like Juanita's?' Eléna's voice brightened determinedly.

118

'I have the suspicion that Kathy might like it to be.'

'I think so too, and you two who have been so faithful to your love for so long deserve every extravagance now.'

'She hopes it will be in only three weeks' time. She's about to break the news to Fred today.'

'Then we'd better ask Yei to start the preparations soon.'

'Oh, Eléna, you're such a joy!' M. Louis rose to his feet and assisted Eléna to hers. They linked arms once more and walked back to the house, chatting animatedly.

When they came within sight of the building a sudden peal of thunder, like an ominous warning, broke into their gaiety, sending them running indoors.

Once changed out of her wet clothes, Eléna went down to the living-room in search of Carmen. One glance sent her screaming to the door. She had spotted Diego collapsed on the veranda floor. Her cries brought the family rushing to his assistance. He was placed on the sofa and given a restorative by Yei. When he came to, vociferously insisting that he was all right, Yei took Louis aside. 'Monsieur, I think we must send for Juanita – she is the only one who can persuade him to rest,' she whispered.

# V

Fist had worked it all out in his mind. He knew that Barry would be glad to help him, but it was an added bonus that Tessa was linked to the black mistress of Santa Clara. Fist had become genuinely enthralled by the tiny woman. What had started off as a mere flirtatious lark had slowly changed into interest, and fascination. He was now totally captivated.

In spite of his humorous denials to Barry, he was not unaware of his strong attractiveness to women, but the life of a slave did not permit one the luxury of love. In fact the less sentiment or emotion one felt, the easier it was to tolerate that form of servile, powerless existence, as Fist well knew. Just look at where his display of anger at the mulatto would have led him, had Barry not intervened that day.

It was true that Fist was a natural fighter. His strength and his physical build in itself suggested power. He would not, however, have reached the ripe old age of twenty-two had he ever before been foolish enough to challenge an overseer. On the day in question, Fist had finally decided to end his torment and die, rather than live another day with his tormentor.

Although he knew that mulattos were notoriously the most cruel oversees and drivers, he never did understand what had motivated the man to single him out for his particular persecution. He never did until later, when he had told Barry of the series of trials suffered under the man. Barry casually volunteered the opinion that the mulatto was simply jealous of him. To Fist's protestations against such an idea, Barry added; 'Ever looked in a mirror, my good man? Not many such fine specimens as you around. Notice how the ladies turn to look at you? Even the white ones?'

Barry had laughed at Fist's consternation. 'You proved a contradiction to his ideas of white, and brown, supremacy.'

'But . . . but a nigger slave lower than a snake!' protested Fist.

'Yes, they could make you feel like that, but they couldn't take away the haughty way you walk or the defiance and pride in your eyes, could they, now?'

Fist had learnt something from that casual observation. For the rest of his life he was to remember it, and trade on it when his confidence threatened to desert him.

'Tell me more about yourself, Fist,' Barry had asked on that very occasion. 'What became of your parents?'

'I never know mi father, but I did know mi mother. I live with she till I was seven or eight. Can't remember age and thing. Then they sell mi mother and keep me. I was big anyway, always was big. After that, they put me in the fields, then they send me in the sugar factory, never know what to do with me. Then I was to apprentice to the blacksmith but just so he sell a group o' we to this English one and we went to Barbados. We didn't know the reason or nothing. That mulatto in Barbados say I only good for the fields. That man!'

'Hell of a life!' commented Barry sympathetically. 'How do you feel, now that you're a free man, Fist?'

'Well, can't say it ain't plenty better. But strange thing, Barry, inside me, I was always free like . . .'

Now that Fist was really free, and fortunate enough to be in a secure position with Barry who had become more of a friend than a master, he was certainly more receptive to developing stronger attachments, and to indulging stronger emotions. Coming at such a time in his life, therefore, the little wisp of a girl, with her innocently seductive ways, her naturally high spirits, lively antics and obvious intelligence, could not help but attract him. Firmly caught, therefore, he awaited only an opportunity to speak to Barry.

This was the period, however, when Barry had kept himself especially busy so Fist had seen little of him. Determined to capture Barry's attention, Fist ventured on the first opportunity that presented itself. 'Barry. I . . . I want to talk to you serious.'

Barry felt a twinge of guilt. He had paid Fist but scant attention for the past weeks. 'What's up, Fist? You sound worried, or is it nervous? Something's wrong? They're not treating you well here, is that it?'

'No, Sir. Just wants to talk 'bout something personal.'

Barry looked at him with aroused interest. It would be really enjoyable to spend a night chatting with him like he used to. Here was not the place for that, though. 'Well, you have me intrigued. Can it wait until later?'

Fist nodded.

'Then, tell you what. I'm on my way out with Whiteways now . . . what if we meet . . . you know where, at my old landlady's, in the town. Meet me there at six, and here,' said Barry giving Fist some coins, 'buy us two bottles of rum. See you later then.'

In spite of a sudden downpour of rain, Fist was in good spirits. He was looking forward to a happy result of that night's meeting. Finishing his chores, he spotted Tessa passing in the distance and whistled softly to her. In the seclusion of the stables, she nuzzled close to him.

'What you calling me for, man?' she began teasingly. 'You ain't get enough o' me the other day, or what?'

'I could ever get enough o' you? Small as you is, it have plenty more there for me.'

'Well, I have to go back now.' She pulled away.

'I go have news for you after tonight.'

'What news? Tell me, nah!'

'Behave yourself, girl. Wait till tomorrow. I go see you tomorrow.'

'You sure? Don't make me fret up miself for nothing nah!' Tessa allowed him to kiss her long and lovingly.


As the evening approached, Fist changed into his street clothes and strolled out of Millefleurs, slowly making his way to the town. He walked with a jaunty spring in his step and a lively song on his lips. He went first to his room and then down to the shop below to buy the rum.

As he was paying for the bottles, a scuffle started among two white customers of the shop. One was apparently Spanish, and the other a timid-looking Frenchman. Fist watched in amusement, quite entertained by the spectacle of white misbehaviour. Such encounters were not uncommon among the riff-raff of the town. But his amusement did not last long. A third man, a swarthy mulatto, entered, and interfered with the odds in the fight.

He held the Frenchman fast, so that the Spaniard, a wiry little man, could punch away without resistance. Fist called out to the mulatto to desist, only to receive a string of obscenities in reply and a command to leave his brother's shop.

Unamused now, Fist could not comply. He intervened. Pushing away the mulatto, he freed the Frenchman, then he grabbed the Spaniard, saying forcefully, 'You can't beat the man just so! That ain't fair, man!'

'Let me go, nigger! This is none of your business. You'll regret this! I warn you, you'll regret this!'

Ignoring these threats, Fist easily lifted the man, a mere feather-weight compared to him, and threw him out into the street. The Spaniard quickly righted himself and continued to hurl profanities and threats. Fist was not the least unnerved. He simply dusted off his hands, returned to the shop, collected his two bottles and, after seeing the Frenchman scurry safely away, left for his rendezvous with Barry. He spared not a thought more for the slight skirmish, never dreaming that those few seconds of interference were to prove such a significant turning point in his life.

Some twenty minutes after Fist had arrived at the guest house, Barry strolled in. 'Sorry to be late, Fist, but we got caught up in a gripping discussion on the state of the islands. At least, I did, Whiteways went home hours ago.'

Barry greeted his landlady, hugging her enthusiastically, their relationship long one of close camaraderie. Then he sat down and poured himself a drink and waited for Fist to begin the discussion.

The earlier showers of rain had cooled the earth. The night was pleasant as they sat in the open courtyard, with the spreading branches of the sapodilla tree overhead. A shy silver moon peeped through the clusters of leaves, casting into silhouette bunches of small brown fruit, whose rough, unattractive skins concealed the exotic delights of one of Barry's favourite fruits.

After clearing his throat meaningfully, Fist began. 'The thing is, Barry, that I have a problem onliest you can help me with.'

Barry looked at him enquiringly.

'I is really not the kind o' fellah to do things just so. But . . . I . . . well

'. . . I find miself . . . I is . . . well . . . what I wants to say is . . . the best thing to do now . . .'

'Are you trying to tell me you want to stop working for me? You want to go away?' asked Barry, seriously concerned.

'Nah! Is nothing so. Not so serious, 'least, I don't think I bound to do that yet.'

'Well, come on. This suspense is killing me, Fist!'

'You ain't go laugh now?'

'Of course, not!'

'I wants to get married!' Fist blurted out.

'What!' shouted Barry in surprise that was instantly transformed into laughter. He roared aloud, throwing his head back and rocking dangerously on the landlady's chair.

'Sorry, old chap. I did promise not to laugh, but I couldn't help it. It's the shock, you see,' apologised Barry, finally containing himself. 'Tell me all about it. Who, pray, is the lucky miss?'

After Fist had revealed all to Barry, and was assured of his willingness to intercede on Tessa's behalf, Barry expressed his satisfaction at Fist's good fortune and proposed a toast to his friend's continued happiness. One toast led to another until both men were well on their way to drunkenness.

'Barry, so when you and your girl go fix up?' asked Fist, alcohol overcoming his normal restraints.

'Aye!' sighed Barry. 'Fist, that's one subject we'd better not get started on,' he cautioned. He bent his head and swished the liquid in his glass. When he spoke again, however, it was of the same subject. 'I love that lady, Fist, but ain't no way I can ever have her. You . . .'

'There you are, Barry!' Fred's voice preceded him into the courtyard, interrupting Barry's drunken discourse. 'Thought I'd find you here. Couldn't wait for you to get home, I'm simply bursting with the piece of news I just heard. Hello there . . . er, Fist . . . er . . . mind if I join you two?'

Fred could not be said to be on a friendly level with Barry's servant. One could not, however, ascribe prejudice to him. It was more a matter of self-assured, gentile indifference. If Barry sat at this secluded table with the African, it didn't particularly disturb him.

'W'ass this about news?' slurred Barry. The rum was taking hold of him.

'You will be pleased to know that Louis and my Kathy have announced their plans to marry.'

'Them too! Oh God!' moaned Barry, holding his head in despair. 'Fist here wants to marry Tessa, Juanita's maid. Tell him you'll give her her freedom so they can be happy?' commanded Barry without looking up. 'I'll pay you for her, if you want.'

'Tessa? The little girl Eléna brought us?'

'Yes, Sir,' Fist's dark eyes were apprehensive, his breathing stifled.

'No need for payment. Why, only recently m'wife was telling me she hoped we'd find her a good match. Why, Fist, you're as good a match as any. I don't see why not. She's all yours. It must be a legal and sanctified marriage, or m'wife won't agree!'

'Yes, Sir! Yes, Sir!' Fist grinned from ear to ear.

'L'esh have a drink for that!' lisped Barry, thoroughly inebriated now. 'Tha'sh right! A toast to Fist and Tessa, and another to Louis and Kathy . . . None to me, though. Can't have none to me . . . never, never, never!' he slurred. 'Know what, Fred? I'll never get her, Fred . . . and you know what?' he continued, while his two companions eyed each other in embarrassed silence. 'Know what's the hardest part, Fred? What's the biggest joke, Fred? She wants me too, me, not Fontainebleau! Ha! Isn't that funny? Hilarious? Doesn't run from me, you know. My woman ain't no silly miss from a London ballroom. No teaser. A real flesh and blood woman. A true blue, a . . .' his voice tailed off, till gathering his wits again, he demanded, 'What would you do, Fist? If you were me, what would you do?'

'I tell you long time to take the woman if you wants her.'

'That's a man of action, Fred. A man after my own heart. A man who . . .' Barry went on in this fashion until Fred was able, with Fist's help, to lift him onto his horse. Fist, sobered now in the face of Barry's genuine sadness, mounted behind his master and held him in strong arms. With Fred riding alongside, they slowly trotted home. Once at Millefleurs, Fist did what was necessary, put Barry to bed, curled up on a rug on the floor and fell soundly asleep.

The quantity of alcohol that Fist had consumed did have some effect on him, however, for the next morning he was unable to rise at his usual early hour. So he missed the sight of Tessa, hopping from one foot to the other, wringing her hands, and darting her eyes about in search of him. For the night before, the message had come that Don Diego had taken ill, and Juanita had decided to leave for the estate at first light. When Fist came out, bursting with excitement to find Tessa, and tell her the good news, she had already left with her mistress for Santa Clara, several hours before.

124

# VI

With Juanita's calming presence and constant attention, Diego responded rapidly. Thus after a short while Louis was able to set his wedding date for two weeks hence, announcing that the reception would be held at Kathy's plantation.

During this period everyone at Santa Clara was so preoccupied, first with Don Diego and then with the plans for Louis's wedding, that no one noticed that Tessa was not in her usual high spirits. The fact was that Tessa was anxious about the situation with herself and Fist, but, even worse, she was harbouring other more private fears.

'Tessa, what are you thinking of? You've not said a word for the last hour and that's not like you,' Eléna remarked one day as they sat in their old manner, busily sewing a special gown for Carmen to wear to the wedding. For, despite her pregnancy, Carmen was determined to sing for M. Louis on his grand day.

The sky was slightly overcast and the day exceptionally cool. Eléna looked upwards, searching the sky. She saw no sign of immediate rain. 'Is anything the matter, Tessa?' she repeated.

'No, Mistress Eléna.'

'Well, if I didn't know better, I'd say that you look so pensive and sad sometimes, and . . . what was it you once told me? You have that faraway look, that I could swear you're in love.' Eléna made a mocking flourish with her hand.

Tessa jerked her head up. With gaping mouth, she studied her mistress. Before Eléna could continue, though, she heard her mother calling to her. Quietly gathering her things, she set off to see what Yei wanted.

'I've just come from seeing Rosa,' said Yei.

Rosa was a young unmarried slave, expecting her first baby within the next few weeks. She was in melancholy spirits and poor health. It was a difficult pregnancy. The rules governing movement of Santa Clara's slaves being very relaxed, Rosa had contracted a liaison with a male from another plantation. In an attempt to allow them to marry, M. Louis had approached the man's owner, but to no avail. Adamant in his refusal, he even forbade contact between them. Yei had been tending Rosa continuously for some months.

'She was in false labour. I left the woman Tina to look after her, she knows about deliveries,' continued Yei.

'Why didn't you call me to come with you, Yei?'

'No . . . no. I will deal with this child, don't get involved in this delivery. Only a few weeks more and yet it is not in the birth position. I must be here for the delivery, and with the wedding so soon I did not want to turn the baby in case it hastens the time. It may yet right itself.'

Eléna returned to her sewing, engrossed in thoughts of the broken-hearted Rosa, having completely forgotten her interrupted conversation with young Tessa.

Freed from her nursing duties, and taking advantage of a rare sunny afternoon some days later, Juanita invited Eléna to accompany her on a stroll about the estate.

The mountainous hills that kept their unwavering guard on Santa Clara stood regally in the distance with their thick coats of green foliage. Their shapes of endless variety were always a source of fascination and comfort to Eléna.

The two young women followed the small stream, walking gingerly on low rocky banks, and stepping here and there on large river boulders. The scenery was wild and virtually untouched. Large clumps of bamboo towered overhead, bending and bowing long limbs, forming almost gothic arches that shaded the river. The atmosphere was cool and peaceful. Eléna and Juanita made their way to a huge boulder, laughing happily at their adventures in this virtual wildneress, which despite its seeming isolation was within the boundaries of Santa Clara.

They sat in companionable silence. There were so many changes occurring now in their lives, thought Eléna. Juanita married and gone to her own home, and now M. Louis. Don Diego was not in reliable health. Carmen would soon be occupied with the new baby, and so would Yei. What am I still doing here? she asked herself.

As if reading her thoughts, Juanita spoke. 'What will the household be without M. Louis, I wonder? Strange how we always took his presence for granted. I'm afraid our world is breaking apart, Eléna . . .' She stopped, gathering her thoughts. 'It is a shame that M. Louis refused to teach us English, because now I have to learn it anyway. I've already started. I believe that Fred may have to return to his country soon.'

'How soon?' The frown instantly marring Eléna's face indicated an anxiety that she was loath to voice.

'I'm not sure, Eléna, but it's going to happen. Fred and Kathy's father is failing in health.'

'You're really making me apprehensive, now. How do you feel about going away?'

'I would never leave if it wasn't for Fred, but he is his father's heir. He must go to take charge of the estates in England and Ireland. Once Kathy returns from this trip, he won't be needed any longer.' Juanita paused and arranged the folds of her wide skirt.

'It's . . . it's good that you've started preparing yourself.'

'Oh Eléna, you like to make us feel you're so strong. Look at what you're saying. That's not what you're thinking.' Juanita reached over and rested her hand on her companion's arm. 'It's hard that the family is breaking up, admit it!'

'You're right.' Eléna steeled herself for the coming conversation.

'You got so upset the last time we tried to probe into your plans, that I am reluctant now to try again, except that . . . I . . .'

'Don't be afraid, Juanita, I won't break down this time.' Eléna bent her head, staring at the peaceful clear waters of the stream. Here and there small fishes darted about merrily, free for the moment from any predators. She looked up. On the opposite bank, a small paw-paw tree clung tenaciously to the very edge of a low muddy cliff, hanging on despite the inevitability of its collapse into the waters below.

'I know you will not have André because you are in love with Barry. No, don't be shocked. I worked it out by myself. I will not betray your secret. But I must talk to you about it, because I don't want you to be hurt.'

'There is nothing to talk about. I did not choose to love somebody like that. I don't think a white man is suitable for me either, nor I for him.'

'Why not? I see no reason why you can't love whomever you wish. Any man would be lucky to win you, Eléna. So it's not that. It's just that hopes in Barry's direction are . . .'

'Foolhardy?' Eléna supplied the word, smiling grimly.

'Oh Eléna,' cried Juanita, putting her arm around her. 'Has he ever told you his feelings?'

Eléna shook her head. 'Not in so many words, no.'

'Eléna, I am afraid for you because no matter what you say about unsuitability, I feel you might yet be harbouring some dreams and hopes.'

'Why are you afraid for me, Juanita? If it's not because he is white, then what is it?'

In a gentle voice, Juanita began, 'Don't you know that Barry is obligated, just like Fred, to return to England?'

'But he is a fourth son. He does not stand to inherit that much responsibility,' protested Eléna.

'He may not be inheriting a title, Eléna, but he stands to inherit a great deal, particularly from his grandmother.'

'His grandmother?' Eléna knew something of Barry's love for that lady. A feeling of panic threatened to overtake her, and she wanted to get up and run away from the information that Juanita was volunteering – information that she knew would put an end to her private, foolhardy, but tenacious hopes.

'Yes, his grandmother,' continued Juanita. 'She has property of her own which is to go to Barry. She is an eccentric old lady, and a radical of sorts, and will not divide her fortune among his other brothers.'

'Barry has told you all this?' asked Eléna softly.

'No, Fred did.' Juanita looked worriedly at Eléna, at the droop of her shoulders and the grimness of her once smiling lips. Mustering her courage, she continued, 'But it is not just a matter of the fortune. It's his love for the old lady that will force him to return. She is depending on him. Do you understand what that means, Eléna? The hardest part is that I feel he does love you.'

Eléna's eyes were filled with questions she would not ask. 'And I know,' continued Juanita, 'because he is a man of honour, he cannot build false hopes in you.' Seeing that Eléna made no response, Juanita continued gently. 'In English aristocratic society, a man is not as free as here, where everyone has a coloured wife or . . . mistress. According to Fred, they are very strict, Eléna. A coloured wife could mean ruin for the man, and untold humiliation for the wife.'

Eléna looked again at the paw-paw tree and stared absently for a long time, fighting back the rushing tide of tears. Finally, she blew her nose forcefully into her handkerchief.

'Then there is no hope for us,' she whispered.


If Eléna had never examined her heart thoroughly before, she did so now in the days that followed. Had she done anything to encourage these feelings? 'No! This love has been inflicted on me,' she reasoned.

Then she would rage against Barry, her heart full of resentment. He had deliberately singled her out from the first, and had attracted her with his tender words and intimate, caring glances. His smiling blue eyes, which seemed to hold a special message for her, had ensnared her. 'Oh I hate him!' she screamed inwardly. Only to chide herself again the next moment and grow even more sad by the realisation that she could take no refuge in hate.

She knew it was not their fault. They naturally had much in common. Their spirits blended so well. They were not to blame. She calmed herself. Her heart became filled with pity for them both. Except for the thought that Fred himself, despite what Juanita had said, did not seem to discourage her feelings for Barry, she did not question Juanita's pronouncements and was fully convinced that there was no hope. Barry's present distancing of himself, too, was proof enough.

That night she cried silently into her pillow. Lying next to her in the darkness, Yei heard, and was in a quandary. Unable to apply any of her usual balms, she kept silent, never revealing that she knew of Eléna's misery.


Two days later, completely reassured of her father's recovery, and of Eléna's revived spirits, Juanita decided to return home to Millefleurs. Seeing how involved Tessa had become in the sewing of Carmen's maternity gown for the wedding, she generously volunteered to leave her behind, telling M. Louis to bring her along with him when he would be coming to prepare for the wedding. She kissed the family, and even waved Tessa a cheery goodbye as she climbed into the carriage, totally unaware, of course, of the distress into which her young slave had been thrown.


# CHAPTER THIRTEEN

## I

Fist was seething with frustration. He had the best news in the world, and no one to give it to. Every day he thought of running off to Santa Clara to find Tessa, but he knew her master would not have spared a second thought on the matter of a mere slave's marriage. He was sure that the family there had not been informed by Fred of either his interest or his intentions. Forcing himself upon them precipitately might undermine his good fortune. He harboured some hopes that Barry would propose an outing to visit the estate so that he could accompany him, but his master seemed bent on staying clear of the velvet lady there.

When the carriage bearing Juanita did return to Millefleurs, he came rushing out with pounding heart, only to have his hopes dashed. She had not come.

Despondent and restless that evening, he decided to take a stroll through the town.

The evening was advancing as Fist set off, his stride and his gait in marked contrast to those of a former walk along the same pathways, when his hopes were high and his heart was light. Reaching the town, he sauntered through, passing groups of Africans sitting idly on doorsteps, smoking or gossiping as was their custom at this hour.

He walked aimlessly. As he was passing a half-erected building, the sound of bawdy laughter accosted him. A female voice said saucily: 'But is where you going, nigger? Looking so high and mighty! Like you own Trinidad or what?'

Fist stopped. In the semi-gloom he discerned the creased face of a black woman. Although she looked old, Fist knew that she could not have been more than twenty-five or thirty years of age, for hardly any African in those days lived to celebrate their thirty-first birthday.

'You talking to me, woman?' enquired Fist.

'Come nah, look, I have some rum here,' came the reply. Fist hesitated, then he joined the reprobate.

'What you doing here, woman? You ain't living nowhere or what?'

'I does live anywhere, pretty boy. I's free.'

'You mean you get kick out,' laughed Fist humourlessly, well aware that many of the old slave-owners punished their female slaves by casting them out and leaving them destitute. Some of them, unable to fend for themselves, ended up with the *mal d'estomac* from eating dirt.

'What you care?' she replied. Fist laughed again and joined her, squatting down on the rough floor. She handed him the bottle. Between them there soon developed the quick, if short-lived, camaraderie that alcohol engenders. The woman offered him some tobacco, he took it willingly. They sat puffing as the sunset gun was heard, attesting to the day's end.

'I does see you passing sometimes. You ain't have a room above the mulatto shop? I see a little child go there the other day. Is dolly you like or what? You ain't want a real woman?'

'Yes, but the one I wants ain't here right now,' he replied pointedly.

'Eh, eh, but you choosy in true. Look that is Picton there,' she changed the subject suddenly. 'Going for he walk. He does walk so every day. See he tall like you and so he bad. You bad so nah?' She crept up to Fist seductively.

Pushing her away gently, Fist commented. 'I ain't have so long here, but I hear they say he cruel for so.'

'Oh God, he and he turnkey! They does do all kind o' thing to nigger people.' She became silent, her black face wrinkled even more in the act of pulling on the pipe she was smoking. A policeman passed by. As he moved out of earshot, she spat contemptuously on the floor and exclaimed, '*Gardez corbeau lá!* Look at the *corbeau*.'

130

Fist knew that the six or so black *alguaziles* or policemen of Port of Spain were much hated by the people of colour. They considered them the lowest specimens on the island and with good cause, for they took delight in harassing their own kind.

'They does take money for carrying niggers,' mouthed the woman angrily.

'Runaways to the gaol, you mean?'

'Nah, you ain't know what they does do to runaways or what? They cutting off they ears these days.' She puffed on the tobacco. 'Nah, just any nigger who ain't go home early, nah,' she finally answered, puffing again furiously. Then without provocation, she laughed loudly. 'But I hear some o' them smart niggers does give themself to them, and does get some o' the money for theyself.'

'But money ain't all. What 'bout the licks from they massa?'

'*Mais oui* . . . but what is a little licks when you have money? Nigger ain't, 'fraid licks.' She laughed and changed the subject once more. 'Eh, eh, so what do you the other day when you throw out the *'piol*, the Spanish man nah, from the shop?'

'But woman, like you watching everything I do or what?'

'Heh, heh,' she smirked, 'You feel you big 'n' bad, you ain't know he have it in for you now. That fellah stink, you hear! Take warning, stay out o' he way, *doux*, *doux*.' She wagged her finger in his face.

Fist looked at her. In the darkness, crouched on the dirt floor, with her bony, wrinkled hands holding the pipe to her toothless lips, she looked like some creature from a nightmare, a ghoul predicting doom. Fist shivered involuntarily and turned his eyes away.

'Look, Picton passing back, he done walk,' he observed.

'Leh we go in your room, nah?'

'Nah woman, it getting late, I better go now.'

'*Qui sait qui faire?* Ahh, go on! go on! You have your candle, nah?' she added. 'You ain't know they holding niggers for walking without lights?'

'But I ain't no slave,' objected Fist.

'That don't count, ain't you black like La Brea pitch?' she laughed.

'Well, I go be careful.' Fist rose to his feet.

'That right, that right. Don't say I ain't warn you. I did warn you good. Beware the *corbeaux* and them!'

## II

Eléna was very occupied with plans for the wedding on the coming Sunday. With only a few days left, Carmen's gown – a creation elaborate enough to counteract her gloom over the loss of her figure – was yet to be completed.

On Tuesday of the wedding week, Eléna and Tessa were sewing indoors on the veranda, a heavy downpour having forced them inside. They saw a lone rider approach in the distance, silhouetted against the hazy outline of the mountains. Eléna had paused in her work and was gazing at the puffs of mist occasioned by the cooling effect of heavy rains on the warm mountains, when she spotted the rider. Her heart began to race. Tessa too, looking up just then, caught sight of the visitor's approach and experienced a similar excitement in her heart.

Both women were due for a disappointment. It was neither Barry nor Fist but Kathy's son Mark who came riding up, soaked to the bone, and calling out to Eléna for rescue from his watery predicament.

Shortly after, having changed and partaken of one of Yei's specially brewed warming beverages, Mark joined Eléna on the veranda. Tessa, at Eléna's bidding, went to stretch her legs for the rain had stopped falling.

Mark and Eléna began to speak of the approaching marriage of Louis and Kathy.

'Well, I can't avoid it now. I . . . I was determined not be become involved with a man who had abandoned Mother and me to that dreadful stepfather of mine. That man hated my artistic interests, you know. He frustrated me at every turn, so I countered by becoming frivolous. You don't know me or my reputation really well, Eléna, I'm frivolous and irresponsible.'

'I don't think you are as frivolous as you believe,' responded Eléna. 'You're just very sensitive, Mark. I think you've done very well. You have survived a harsh childhood and escaped with your sense of humour intact. You claim to be irresponsible and yet you never adandoned your mother, not really. You could have stayed in England and never returned to a life you hated. Why didn't you? A reason to show responsibility has never arisen. Even now, your uncle is here helping your mother.' Eléna picked up her needlework and resumed her sewing. 'And about M. Louis, he did not desert you, Mark. He would not have abandoned you if he knew you existed, for he was nothing to Carmen and me and he treated us with such care and devotion.' Eléna became suddenly thoughtful. Mark looked at her patiently. She continued, 'He was always like a true father.' She shook her head, dismissing a nagging thought, and added, 'Please open your heart to him.'

The bright colours of the landscape were subdued now by the grey, moody skies. Rain flies darted about, flying for short distances in crazy circles then losing their fluorescent wings to the wind, becoming mundane worms without them and crawling away to attack the woodwork beginning the serious work of their species.

'I will,' answered Mark, 'and thank you, Eléna.'

'Thank you, Mark,' she sighed to herself, and remained a long time staring into space. Eventually, shaking herself, she cried, 'Good Lord, what am I doing? Only four more days and this gown is far from finished . . . Tessa! Tessa! Where are you? Oh there you are. What are you looking at? Tessa, is something wrong?'

Eléna got up and went out into the wet grass. Tessa was standing transfixed, with a look of terror on her face. 'What is it, child?' called Eléna as she reached the young slave, caught her by the shoulders and shook her gently.

Tessa pointed, 'Oh, *corbeaux*, there must be a dead animal near here. I'll have it removed. Why are you so frightened? Are you afraid of *corbeaux*? But they are always around, everywhere. They're scavengers. They clear away rotting flesh. They are supposed to be good, useful creatures.'

'I see them eat a man once, Mistress. A slave in the field.'

'That's awful, Tessa, but he must have been dead already. They don't attack living things. Come on now, let's go and finish our work.'

Eléna led Tessa towards the house, but the young girl kept straining her eyes backwards as if hypnotised by the black, circling creatures.

By Friday Carmen's gown was almost completed. Armed with her cooking accoutrements, Yei prepared to leave for Millefleurs. Louis, too, had decided to spend the last few days there so as to ensure no delays or mishaps on the big day. Tessa, bouncing and skipping with joy, was to accompany them. She was finally being sent home.

# III

Millefleurs was in as much a state of excitement and preparation as if it were the wedding house. Juanita's kitchen was the scene of much anticipation with all counters and equipment sparkling clean and laid out in readiness for Yei, who was going to cook there to avoid overcrowding Kathy's kitchen.

The arrival of the carriage from Santa Clara bringing the great lady, not to mention the bridegroom himself, was therefore a special event. There was one person, though, who cared not a fig for either of those worthy personalities, and whose eyes searched only for a tiny little wisp of a girl. Seeing her peering excitedly about he broke into a wide grin.

133

Controlling the urge to run up and embrace her, he forced himself to attend to the business of helping with the disposal of the baggage and packages of the arrivals.

Juanita had been in the process of making decorations for the wedding reception when the carriage arrived, and she immediately commanded Tessa to assist her with that task, allowing her no opportunity for a proper word with Fist. It was all the lovers could do to briefly arrange to run away the following afternoon and meet at Fist's room in the town. Tessa whispered to Fist that if she succeeded in getting away, she would draw the curtains in her room, a ploy that they had used before, as an indication that she was on her way.

Activity proceeded apace for all of Friday and Saturday morning. Towards noon on Saturday Juanita decided to involve Barry in the preparations, sending him to look for some fine sago palm leaves for her decorations. He asked Fist to help him, and the two men rode off, relieved to get away from the frenetic activity associated with the wedding for a few hours.

Overcome with exhaustion, Juanita took to her bed after lunch, charitably advising Tessa to do the same. Naturally Tessa was very quick to agree. Drawing the curtains hastily as the sign to Fist, she picked up her small basket and headed out. Passing by the kitchen, she slipped in and nabbed a couple of Yei's leaf-wrapped corn and meat preparations and put them into her basket, before hurrying out of the door.

She saw no sign of Fist, but cautioned herself against loitering, in case someone found her another chore. It was just as well that she did, or so she thought, for no sooner had she gone a few yards out of the gate when she heard Yei calling to her. She hid behind some tall grass that grew nearby until she was sure that Yei had given up trying to find her.

As she rose to leave, her last view of Millefleurs was one of Yei's tall – and now well-rounded – form moving in its stately way back into the house. The filigreed shapes of the decorative fence, with its pattern of a circle within an elongated oval, appeared to segment Yei's wide back into a number of staring eyes. 'I feel that woman could see me still, *oui*,' she muttered to herself as she ran quickly towards Port of Spain, trying to outdistance the threatening rain.

She arrived in town during the siesta, and the mulatto's shop was closed to customers. One of the shop's wide doors was slightly ajar, however. Tessa was about to make her way up the staircase at the side of the shop when the shop door creaked open and a white man emerged. Seeing Tessa, he immediately accosted her.

'Let me pass, please, Monsieur, I ha' me business to do,' began Tessa sternly.

'What kind of business *doux*, *doux*? You too small for business. I'm sure you don't even have a man as yet,' he teased.

From the doorway, a swarthy mulatto who bore some resemblance to the shop owner observed with an amused grin on his face, 'She have man, *oui*. You know she man too.' He laughed. 'Is the big nigger fellah who throw you out o' here the other day.'

'What! That interfering scoundrel is your man?' he demanded. The pupils of his shifty eyes widened menacingly. 'We'll see about that. I wonder how he will like some damaged goods?'

'Lef me alone!' screamed Tessa, her fear mounting. She looked around to see if anyone was in sight. It being the resting period of the day, the streets were empty. In her rising panic, she did not observe an old woman crouched under a house on the opposite side of the road, but that old woman would have been of questionable use to her, being at that time in a drunken stupor.

Tessa started to scream, 'Fist! Fist!' hoping against hope that he was upstairs, or on his way just around a corner, and would hear her and come quickly. Her luck was out. The man began to drag her into the closed shop. She had no doubt of his evil intentions. In her frenzy she started kicking and clawing at him. In retaliation, he delivered a resounding slap to her face.

Struggling fiercely, she was able to retard his progress towards the door. Sinking her teeth ferociously into his arm, she bit with all her might and bent her knee sharply, ramming it into his crotch.

Unprepared for such a reaction, he howled in pain, and released his hold just long enough for her to escape. She ran down the side of the shop and across the narrow alley.

She dashed into a partially erected building and crouched behind a stack of boards, desperately trying to quieten her rasping breath and her pounding heart.

At first the man searched determinedly for her, and then he just walked agitatedly up and down the alley. As chance would have it, an *alguazil* came along, making his normal round. Tessa's molester ran up to him and said excitedly, 'Help me catch the little bitch. What you getting pay for, anyway?'

'What happen?' enquired the policeman.

'Pedro's brother was just closing up the shop when the little whore who visits the big black man with the room upstairs, came into the shop. As I turned my back, she snatched my purse from the counter. When I

135

saw her making off with it, I held on to her, but she fought me off and look, look at the bite she gave me.' He showed the officer his bleeding limb.'

'Where she went?'

'She ran somewhere . . . somewhere nearby, but I can't find her, the thieving little bitch!'

The *alguazil* had led the man unnervingly close to where Tessa was hiding, and she heard every word with growing terror. Listening intently, she heard the mulatto's voice now and stifled a cry of despair as he said; 'Don't worry, nah. You ain't go have no trouble finding she. I know where to look, she always 'round by the Millefleurs house in St Clair.'

'Robbery real serious. She get away with the money?' asked the *alguazil*.

Crouching in her tiny hiding place, Tessa was numbed with fear. Tears poured unheeded down her black face. 'Ay! Ay! Blessed Virgin, Mother of God,' she prayed. 'What to do? What to do?' She hugged herself in an attempt to steady her trembling shoulders.

Finally she realised that no more sounds were coming from her pursuers. She stopped praying and listened attentively, straining her ears for the slightest noise. Other people were passing in the street now. Normal sounds of human conversation reached her. She waited. Her tears poured freely, mixing with the sweat beaded on her face from her confinement in the narrow hot space.

'Where Fist?' she wondered, desperately hoping that he might pass by and somehow rescue her. In despair, she wondered if he, too, was now in danger. Would he be arrested himself? Where was he now? Why hadn't he come? Had he come since she was hiding, and gone to the room? Was he right nearby, totally unaware of her predicament? If he was, she could not find out because she dared not venture near the shop. 'Oh God, what to do?' she repeated again and again to herself. 'I have to think. I have to think real good. I can't go back home 'cause they go catch me there. They go be looking for me on the way home, too,' she reasoned. 'Oh God! Oh God! Is onliest one place else I could go now, I go have to walk and find Mistress Eléna, she go help me, she always know what to do. She does help everybody. How long it go take me to reach so far? I better go quick, real quick, *oui.*'

She listened quietly for a moment longer. Luckily, despite the fracas, she had held on to her basket even if she had lost her headcovering. Gathering her courage, she slithered out of the tight corner and edged her way out of the building. She ran quickly to the next street, looking back continuously to ensure that she was not being followed. She began to make her way eastwards over the Dry River bridge, up the low Laventille Hills towards the Maracas Valley and the sanctuary of Santa Clara.

'Oh God, I have to go fast! Soon it go be dark, dark, and then what I will do, m'Lord? Me alone in the dark and then tomorrow is wedding. Everybody in Santa Clara coming to town so I have to reach there today, today self,' she sobbed.

At about the time that Tessa's travail began, Fist returned to Millefleurs with Barry. Each man was carrying a load of the decorative palm branches tied to his saddle.

'That ought to satisfy the mistress,' joked Barry.

'Having deposited the palms, Fist went immediately to look at the window of the room in which Tessa slept, hoping to see the expected sign. The curtains were wide open, however. He concluded that his little love had had no opportunity to escape her mistress. He had no way of knowing, of course, that another servant, escaping the excessive work and knowing that no one would seek her in Tessa's room, had retreated there, opening the curtains in an effort to let in more air. The mistress was over at the wedding house and poor Tessa with her, thought Fist. She would probably make a night of it. He resigned himself to waiting another day. In any case, the sky was ominously cloudy. There will be a better day, he concluded.

# IV

Tessa was making her way as fast as she could along the roughly paved road that led eastwards. Still very scared of being pursued, she kept a keen lookout for anyone approaching from behind. Even the sight of a traveller from the opposite direction sent her scurrying into the bushes to hide, afraid that someone spotting her, could give a clue concerning her whereabouts to the *alguazil*.

'I too easy to remember, small as I is,' she muttered.

Her passage was thus greatly delayed by having to stop several times and wait while a traveller moved out of sight. She kept a wary eye on the sky as well, for it still looked threatening.

Within a short while the rain started pelting down upon her.

'God ain't having no mercy on me today,' she cried to herself, 'a place like Trinidad that does have so much sun every day, and today when I needs it, is onliest dark, dark sky and now rain,' she complained.

She thought of braving the wet but the rain came harder, forcing her to take shelter beneath a tree.

Eventually the rain stopped and she resumed her walk, keeping to the edge of the road and trying to avoid the heavy woodland on either side of her. The sky, already darkened by the sunless day, soon showed signs of growing dark in earnest. This being the latter part of the year, the tropical sun would set quite early.

'Oh God, look how dark it getting! Everything, everything against me!' Tessa quickened her pace, stopping only to remove the *alpagatas* that were retarding her progress through the mud.

After a while she tried walking on the grassy edge, but soon found that her feet were covered with fine cuts from the abundant razor grass growing everywhere. Her feet were bruised too, and painful. But Tessa would not stop. Just then she heard the sound of a carriage approaching. She darted off into the undergrowth, in her haste tripping over a tree root, becoming entangled in dangling creepers.

Flat on her front, she looked to the road, only to see that the vehicle from which she had run was none other than a buggy from Santa Clara, driven by Don Diego's coachman. It was filled with servants that she recognised, on their way she knew to help at the wedding.

'Oh no! Blessed Virgin, I shoulda stay on the road,' she sobbed, burying her head in the grass. There was no time to spend weeping. Darkness would begin to fall soon and she must hurry onwards.

Tessa's face was streaked with tears, her woolly hair rumpled and partly covered with mud from her fall. Her simple white shift was dirty and soaked from the rain. She mumbled her prayers in a frenzied, repetitive fashion, as if she were chanting some magical mantra.

The fates were really against her that evening. The sun deserted the sky. Mist obliterated the watchful, comforting mountains. The trees hovered like ghosts through the haze. A storm threatened, and rain and darkness fell with the rapidity that is typical of the tropics.

She waded across the swollen San Juan river, sneaking past the small village of San Juan, making sure that no one saw her. Then she could go no further. Without a light, she could hardly see more than a few inches in front of her, and the sounds of the night already began to startle her as she pressed forward. It was an impossible task. After stumbling over a branch or a rut in the road and almost losing her basket, she realised that she had to admit defeat for that night at least. Exhausted and panic-stricken, she peered around her.

Through the gloom she discerned a large tree near the side of the road, and made her way cautiously to it. Sinking down on the ground, she placed her small body between the buttresses of its roots, laying her head back. Remembering the food in her basket, she groped for it gratefully, tears returning as she acknowledged this as the only stroke of luck she had had all day.

'Mother of God, anyt'ing could happen to me here!' she thought, closing her eyes to shut out the gloomy world around her. In the space of a few seconds, she was mercifully in a state past caring.


# V

Tessa was not the only person having a difficult time. After spending the Saturday in her usual way, seeing to the needs of the slaves, Eléna had been about the happy task of organising her gown for the morning nuptials, in preparation for an early start the next day, when a message came from the slave quarters that Rosa had gone into labour.

'Heavens no!' thought Eléna, 'Yei is not here.'

Eléna had stayed at Santa Clara principally to travel with Carmen, who was already in her eighth month. Also, she had considered it wiser to stay far away from Millefleurs just then, and avoid unnecessary contact with a certain gentleman.

She glanced out of the window. Seeing signs of imminent rain, she picked up an old cloak and reached for a sturdy hat. Then she spoke briefly to Carmen before making her way downstairs. She instructed the sole servant to keep an eye on Carmen and Don Diego.

She could hear Rosa's screams even before she reached the hut. She grew even more apprehensive, for she was not at all as confident as she looked. She said a little prayer and entered.

Much later, having examined the expectant mother and supervised Tina's tidying-up of the small room, she spoke soothingly to her patient. 'No more screaming, Rosa. Take a deep breath, like this. Everyone is entitled to be born with dignity. Don't let your lovely baby come into the world in such a sorrowful manner.'

The rain came pouring down, forcing the women to close the narrow window of the shack. The heat and humidity of the room increased until they were almost unbearable. Eléna sighed, and pondered on the conditions of life to which even those privileged slaves of Santa Clara were subjected.

While Eléna tended the expectant mother, suffocating in the oppressive hut, and Tessa was impatiently sheltering under the dubious protection of a tree, André rode up to the house at Santa Clara.

In contravention of Article Twelve of the Articles of the Capitulation, he had been stripped of his rank. The militia now had only white officers. André felt the humiliation acutely, seeing his demotion as a sign of the erosion of the rights of the free coloureds. He knew that their future was as gloomy as the weather today. He was not on official duty, but something had made him uneasy and concerned for his friends in Maracas. An expression he had overheard in the streets: '*Dormez l'est*'.

The old servant greeted him at the door, explained the whereabouts of the family and offered him a warm beverage. He drained his cup, consoling himself that he would see Eléna tomorrow at the wedding, handed the cup to the servant and took his leave, coughing heavily as he strode out to his horse.

Eléna sat breathing in exaggerated breaths, urging Rosa on. It was late now, almost midnight. Several hours before, she had turned the foetus with deceptively steady hands. Rosa had screamed mercilessly, but Eléna had been firm. It had to be done. She had expected that the baby would come soon after such rough interference, but the labour had gone on and on, endlessly. Eléna was exhausted, longing for nothing so much as her soft bed and some clean, fresh air, but she held on, reprimanding herself for selfish thoughts when Rosa was suffering such agony.

Finally the moment of birth seemed to be near. She talked soothingly to Rosa, trying to allay her expressed fear of death.

'Come now, Rosa, I won't allow you to give up, you must live, and your son must live and his sons, too, until one day everyone will be free and happy. Every child is important, every child represents hope for a better future.'

Eléna went on in this fashion, the slave understanding only that her words were kind and comforting.

The baby boy was born just after midnight. An exhausted Eléna left the slave in Tina's hands and made her way back home. She climbed the stairs wearily, and sank into her bed fully clothed, thinking that she had only a few more hours before it was time to leave for Port of Spain.

Suddenly she was awake and trying to run towards a screaming Tessa, but her legs could not move.

'Tessa! Tessa! What is it?' she cried as the young slave came into view. She was screaming, carrying a baby in her arms, and under vicious attack by large black *corbeaux*.

'Eléna! Eléna! Wake up!' said Carmen's voice. 'It's time to get ready.'

Eléna looked blankly at her sister, then embraced her, breathing heavily. 'My God, Carmen, I was having such an awful nightmare.'

'That's what comes from going to sleep in a state of exhaustion,' smiled Carmen.

Eléna laughed in relief and, shaking herself out of that hauntingly sinister world, proceeded to dress for the wedding.


# VI

Tessa had slept peacefully in her rough sanctuary and did not awaken until dawn. Jumping awake suddenly, she uttered a startled cry, 'Oh God, I fall asleep. Is foreday morning already! Lord, if I ain't hurry, I go miss Mistress Eléna. They go leave early for so.'

Getting to her feet, she screamed in horror and hastily crossed herself, realising that she had slept in the protective buttress roots of the native silk cotton or kapok tree, dreaded by the slaves and about which local folklore attached much superstition. She shuddered, grabbed her basket, dusted off her skirt and hastened forward.


'Is everyone ready now?' asked Don Diego, rising at the approach of the ladies. 'José is outside already, bringing the carriage around. *Mama mía*, you look splendid, Carmen, and you too, Eléna.'

'And you, Señor, today you are the epitome of the grand Spanish gentleman. Don't you think so, Carmen?'

Bantering happily in this manner, they left the house and climbed into the carriage. The coachman was already in Port of Spain, so after ensuring that Carmen and the others were comfortable, José sat in the driver's seat of Diego's much prized, ornate carriage.

A clock in the living-room struck the half hour: five-thirty. They drove off, full of excitement and happy anticipation.

Don Diego was in high spirits. He felt so much better, and his appearance gave no sign of his recent illness. The three occupants of the carriage kept up a lively chatter, speaking nostalgically of their experiences with M. Louis, sharing their feelings of surprise and shock when his love affair was revealed, and gossiping good-naturedly about the romantic twist of fate which had brought the two lovers together. Don Diego began to recall the many instances when Louis played a significant role in his family's life and to assess, as he had never done before, the importance of the Frenchman to his own existence.

'. . . and it was Louis who first introduced Yei to me, you know. Oh yes, he told me of her skill with her medicines when little Juanita was ill, but you know that story already. Now my daughter is a grown woman and has a husband. Ay, time does pass. Tell me again, how long is it before my grandson is born, Carmen?' he asked cheerfully.

Before Carmen could reply, the carriage came to a sudden halt, throwing its passengers forward against each other.

'What is it, José?' cried Eléna, looking out of the window. To her astonishment she saw a crowd of black men appear as if from nowhere. They surrounded the carriage, shouting and gesticulating in a frenzied manner.

'Good Lord, José! José! What is happening?' she screamed.

'Stay inside! All of you! Don't come out,' shouted José.

'Oh my God, Carmen, a slave revolt! What are we to do? Why have they stopped us? Do they think we are their enemies, Papa Diego?'

'I'd better go out and speak to them,' declared Diego, reaching for the door.

'No, no, Papa Diego! Don't, don't.'

Diego ignored her protests, and Eléna crouched down in the carriage with Carmen, listening with horror to the babble of what seemed like thirty or forty black men speaking, screaming, shouting at the same time. She caught a word here and a phrase there, and every word filled her with greater dread. José had apparently taken out a pistol and was threatening to shoot at anyone who came near. Instead of deterring the men, his threats appeared to incense them more.

'Papa, get back, get back!' screamed José as a shot went off.

'Mother of God, what is happening?' whispered Carmen from her position on the floor of the carriage. Eléna could hardly find her voice by then, so petrified had she become, and she clung to her sister, unable to do anything more.

Diego's voice was shouting hoarsely, José was yelling.

Suddenly the carriage started shaking violently, as if the crazed rebels were bent on shattering it to pieces. Eléna tried to cushion the hysterical Carmen from the worst of the movement, praying loudly now.

The carriage overturned, and Carmen fainted.

Running feet . . . screams.

'What is happening out there?'

Stillness.

Tense and shaking with fear, Eléna eased herself out from under her sister. She opened the door above her, and crawled out cautiously, 'José, José, where are you? Papa Diego! Oh my God!' A savage howl escaped from deep inside her. She jumped down from the carriage and raced to the side of the road, where she had spotted Diego.

He was unconscious and clutching at his heart. Eléna's throat constricted with fear. She searched his pockets for a vial of Yei's medicine that he usually carried on him, but found instead a wet spot where the little vial had shattered.

'José, José,' she shouted as she patted Diego's face, easing him to a flat position, chafing his hands and loosening his shirt. But Diego was past recovery. Crying loudly, she looked around for her brother-in-law. 'José, José – oh God, answer me, José.'

No reply came. She turned around and scanned the area but could see nothing. Cradling Diego in her arms, she buried her face in his wide chest, racked with sobs as she realised that his heart had stopped, this time for ever.

After a few moments of complete despair, she raised her head, laid Diego flat on the ground, closed his eyes and went around to the other side of the carriage. A short way off, a large tree trunk blocked the narrow road. She realised immediately why José had had to stop without warning. Then to her horror, she saw him lying at full length as if he had stumbled over the obstacle.

Choking on a scream, she ran to him, her heart drumming a chilling tattoo: 'Not José too, not José too.' He was lying in a rapidly increasing pool of blood. At first she could not be sure where he was wounded. The blood, as well as mud from the road, was all over him. Eléna was beside herself. Tears blurred her vision but her years of experience in tending the sick came to her rescue, even without her bidding. Wiping her eyes resolutely, she began her examination. She forced her trembling hands under his chest and reached for his heart. He was still alive.

His trousers were soaked with blood. She tried to rip his clothes away. Where was he hurt? Blood was everywhere. His legs seemed to have been slashed very badly. Tearing pieces of cloth from her underdress, she began trying to apply bandages, but there seemed to be so many wounds that none of her efforts could stem the flow of blood sufficiently. Her trembling hands served only to retard her efforts. 'I can't do it alone, Carmen! Carmen! Wake up! Come and help me! Somebody help me!' she cried.

It was Sunday. Good Lord, no! Today there was no early Mass at St Joseph, but surely slaves would be taking their produce to market. Somebody must pass by soon. She calmed herself.

Just as she expected, a small group of black men and women rounded the bend. 'Come and help me, please,' she shouted. They looked at her agape, recoiled in horror and started running away, back the way they had come.

'Blood! Blood! Trouble! Trouble! *Dormez l'est*,' they shouted.

'Come back! Come back!' cried Eléna, but they were gone, lost to sight around the bend, fruits and vegetables scattered in their wake. They had not passed her so there was no way they could even spread the news in a direction that would alert the authorities in Port of Spain and bring her help. Perhaps the arbitrary wrath of the British was what they were running from, but Eléna could not then reason. 'Damn you! Damn you!' she screamed, her fears rising to hysteria.

She fumbled on, struggling to stem the flow of José's blood, calling loudly on God to send her a miracle.

# CHAPTER FOURTEEN

## I

Time never moved so slowly. Seconds crept by like hours. Her urgent ministrations seemed slothful and useless as José's blood flowed, and Carmen was still unattended. Eléna fought down her panic. The universe had suddenly become disharmonious with human need, with reason. Accustomed to being resourceful, she felt even more terrified by an overwhelming helplessness. Struggling as in a nightmare, she continued her efforts, cautioning herself, speaking roughly to herself, or calling pitifully on a merciful God to send her help, not to forsake her and her family at this moment. It was then that she saw Tessa running towards her in the distance.

'Tessa? Tessa? It is a miracle! Tessa, come quickly! Come quickly! God himself has sent you to me!' she cried through her renewed sobs.

Through her questions and expressions of horror, Tessa gave Eléna the immediate assistance she needed to tear cloth, apply bandages and tighten tourniquets.

'We can't turn him over, Tessa, but we must keep his face clear so he can breathe properly. He has lost so much blood that I don't think he will regain consciousness fully for a while. The wounds need stitching. What we need is a real doctor, Tessa. First, go to the carriage and see what is happening to Carmen.'

'Oh no! Mistress Carmen there too? Oh God, and she making baby! What we go do?' cried Tessa.

She ran off towards the overturned vehicle. Climbing on the upturned wheels, she gripped the sides of the opened door and lifted her small body to peer inside.

'Mistress Carmen! Mistress Carmen!' she called.

Carmen was slouched in a half-sitting position on the far door of the upturned carriage. The skirt of her lovely peach-coloured gown on which Tessa and Eléna had spent so many hours was soaked through.

'Jesus Lord! Oh God, I 'fraid to touch she!' yelled Tessa. She scampered back down from the carriage, shouting all the while. 'Mistress, Mistress, you sister in blood! Blood! Blood all over she!' It was the young slave's turn to become hysterical.

'No, Tessa, it's just the waters. The baby is coming. We must keep calm. Come with me. Where are the horses?'

Eléna forced her mind to reject the shroud of panic that persisted in creeping up on her. She looked around quickly and instructed Tessa to do the same, but the horses were nowhere to be seen.

'The rebels must have taken them. Let me see! Let me see! We must not panic. With only two of us, we can't right the carriage. What can we do? What? What? Mother of God, why doesn't someone pass by to help us!'

'You want me run to the estate and call a servant? Or to St Joseph for help?' asked Tessa, wringing her hands nervously.

'Yes . . . oh yes . . . but . . . but . . . no! What we need is a doctor, a doctor most of all.' Eléna's head swirled as if caught in a whirlwind. Her brittle hold on hope was about to snap.

'Wait! Listen! Listen, Mistress, something coming. Something coming on the road,' cried Tessa.

The two women ran forward to confront the vehicle that was rounding the bend. It was an open cart driven by an old black man.

'Stop! Stop!' both women shouted in unison, flagging down the cart. The startled, sleepy-eyed driver drew rein, and looked in confusion and horror at the scene of disorder, death and bloodshed before him. After much frantic persuasion, the old slave conceded that he could not incur the wrath of his master by merely giving a lift to a woman up to where he was bound in the Laventille area.

Eléna turned to Tessa. 'Please, Tessa, you go with him back to town. Get Barry or Yei to send us a doctor.'

Tessa backed away, turning her head in jerky little shakes.

'Please, Tessa, please! José or Carmen and her baby may die, they may all die without a doctor. Won't you go? Won't you go and help us?'

Tessa was doomed. How could she refuse that sweet, musical, bewitching voice with its subtle hint of reproof?

'Yes, Mistress. I go go. For you alone, I go go,' answered the young girl finally as she stared hypnotically into Eléna's pitch-black, enchanting round eyes.

'Wait, where are your *alpagatas*?' For the first time Eléna noticed the state Tessa had appeared in. 'What has happened to you? Where is your headwrap? What were you doing here, anyway? Something's wrong?'

'Is all right. Don't worry 'bout that. I go just so. Is all right, Mistress. I do it for you.'

'I onliest going up to here, Miss,' said the driver, stopping about a mile from the entrance to the town.

Thanking him, Tessa jumped off and wasted no time in speeding towards Port of Spain. She ran and ran, using every familiar landmark as a gauge to measure how much distance she had covered. Through the low Laventille Hills she was forced to slacken pace, but once across the Dry River bridge and within the town limits, she got her second wind and moved like a flash of lightning past the buildings. Her small lithe body, youthful and used to exercise, responded now in her time of need. Her body gave of its best, even if her mind was numb with fear and anxiety. What would be the fate of the wounded? What would be her fate if she was caught now? She sped on and spared not a glance for the black figure of the *alguazil*, who, spotting the small, dishevelled runner, took a long, hard look and nodded wisely, a cunning smile spreading on his fat lips, lightening his battered black face with its twisted, broken nose.

Once through the city, she headed westwards towards St Clair. Just as exhaustion threatened to overcome her she saw the gates of Millefleurs in front of her and, rushing up, fell into the arms of Fist.

Breathlessly she explained the plight of the La Flores family to him. He responded to her urgency. Picking her up in his strong arms, he took her to the back yard. Depositing her on a bench near the house, he ran inside and loudly raised the alarm.

## II

The seconds ticked by on the mental clock in Eléna's head. Her distress could find no relief. She tugged at Carmen, trying to revive her, gave up and ran to loosen tourniquets on José's feet, than ran back to Carmen pleading with her to wake up. Eventually she did, only to launch into confused questions and pitiful wailing as labour pains assailed her.

Eléna found herself for the second time in less than twenty-four hours going through the motions of calming an expectant mother, but this time even conditions in the shack were preferable to her present location.

She spent what seemed an eternity, running between José and Carmen. Finally, José groaned and showed signs of regaining consciousness. Eléna bent over him anxiously, afraid that in his agitation he would loosen a bandage. This was how Fist found her as he came galloping up the road, having spotted the overturned carriage some seconds before.

'Mister Barry gone for the doctor, Madame. The others coming right behind me. I come first to help.'

'Thank God you've come. Help me with Señor La Flores, see that he lies still. I'll come back in a minute to check on him, now let me go to my sister in the carriage.'

She comforted Carmen through several more contractions, each growing closer and more intense than the previous one. Then they heard horses approaching and Eléna heard Barry's voice. 'They've come, Carmen. Everything will be all right now!' she exclaimed in relief, the knowledge that Barry was there filling her with inexplicable courage.

It was indeed Barry, and the doctor who he had begged, bullied and finally threatened to accompany him – 'and damned the fact that he had not had his breakfast yet'. Eléna looked out and called to the arrivals, explaining the situation to them. The doctor had already gone to José's aid, and Barry and Fist decided to right the carriage immediately. Calling out to Eléna to prepare her sister against the drop, they did so now.

The carriage rose slowly, then roughly dropped to its correct position. Carmen jolted against Eléna and groaned as she went into another contraction.


Yei had been busy at the wedding house organising the tables and seeing to the arrangements for the breakfast that was to follow the nuptials when M. Louis came rushing over with the news. Face rigid with fear, she followed him back to Millefleurs and waited impatiently as he came around in the wedding carriage for her. She called to a servant to fetch her medicine basket. Receiving it from her, she exclaimed, 'Wait, tell me – who brought the message of the trouble?'

'I think is Tessa,' replied the servant.

'Tessa? But where is she now? Where is Tessa?' She looked around.

'She was here, Mistress. She was just sitting right there on that bench, but like she gone,' came the reply.

Tessa was already far away, and no one knew that after she had sat for a few minutes on the bench she had got up, gone to the vacant kitchen and drunk some water. Feeling better, she had immediately begun to think of her own plight.

Realising that staying where she was would have made it too easy for the police to find her, she got up and ran outside, heading for the gate, unable to formulate a plan but desperate to leave the place. 'Maybe,' she mumbled to herself, 'I could jus' hide in the bush for a while, until Fist come back.'

She had not got very far. No sooner had she stepped out of the gate than a rough hand had grabbed her and dragged her away, screaming, into a carriage. Nobody, nobody, in the almost deserted Millefleurs had heard a sound.

# III

Thrown unceremoniously on to the floor of the carriage, Tessa was soon forced to stop screaming and to desist from any further form of protest. Forewarned of her ability to defend herself, the *alguazil* allowed her no leeway. The carriage stopped in front of the Governor's house. The door was opened by a black servant and Tessa was dragged out and held in an empty hallway. The servant went out of sight, came back and stood looking at her.

After a few minutes, a loud, imperious voice was heard. 'Come in here, man!' it called.

The *alguazil* beckoned to the servant. 'Watch she here fer me.' He stepped forward and paused in the doorway so that Tessa saw only the back of him. A large grotesque shadow of gangling limbs and wide girth loomed out on the empty floor, like a giant about to pounce on the insect that was the *alguazil*.

'What is the meaning of this? Why do you fools disturb me now? Today is Sunday and I am a busy man. What is so urgent?' the shadow bellowed, shifting anxiously, possibly distracted by some unfinished business inside.

'Pardon, Excellency,' mumbled the *alguazil*, doffing his hat hastily, becoming suddenly nervous and obsequious. 'This woman I have out here is the one who the Señor say rob him. I jus' catch she.'

'The woman of some free black from Barbados? Who did she rob, you say? The seaman, Mendoza?' The voice paused. 'I have no time to see

148

into this now.' The shadow turned and Tessa could see the *alguazil* waiting uncomfortably.

'Leave she in the gaol, Sir?' he asked in an unsteady voice.

The shadow disappeared. Its voice was heard calling to someone. It spoke in English and Tessa was unable to understand it.

Just then another door opened slightly and a ruffled servant bowed herself out. Tessa caught a glimpse of a mulatress through the chink in the door. Hands on hips, tapping her foot impatiently, the woman was clothed in what appeared to be a dressing gown, a vision of pink frills and lace. The door closed.

The shadow returned and spoke again in Spanish. Tessa, who only spoke French patois, barely understood. 'Go, all of you, and leave me alone!'

Tessa was hauled outside, shoved into the carriage and driven a considerable distance. Eventually she was dragged out and hustled into a dark room.

She huddled in a corner of the room, trembling with fear, sick with hunger, and terribly apprehensive of what the unseen Picton had discussed with the unseen man. She racked her brain for some piece of hope with which to comfort herself. Would Fist come back and discover where she was? Would he get his master to rescue her? Or would he come and be arrested too. But who would tell Fist? No one had seen her arrest. No one had even seen the altercation between herself and the white man. It had been a mistake to run out of Millefleurs like that. At least, if she had been arrested in the house of her mistress everyone would have known and someone, someone, would surely have tried to help her. But now what? 'Is the tree that I sleep under, *oui*, that evil tree. It ain't have no hope for me now,' she concluded in despair.

The morning advanced. Tessa's bouts of self-pity alternated with thoughts of concern for her mistress. She sighed. She thought of Fist again. 'I wonder what news he had for me? Must have been good or he never woulda smile so. Now I ain't never go know.' This was the hardest cut of all. Unable to control herself any longer, she put her head to the stone wall, and softly cried herself to sleep.

'Get up, you thieving little bitch!'

Tessa found herself rudely shaken. Eyes opening instantly, she focused on a mulatto who now held her by the shoulders.

'The chief ready for you. Come!' She was pushed and dragged along a corridor and down, down, a rough flight of steps, past menacing stalactites to a low, cave-like room with a jagged roof. She saw a table and chairs.

Seated at the table were two white men. One of these she assumed was 'the chief'. She was not to know that the other man was Begorrat, the one whose nefarious activities were to rain terror on many black souls for years to come.

One man spoke. 'What is your name?'

Unable to find her voice, Tessa looked wide-eyed at the man.

'Tell me her name,' he demanded of the *alguazil*.

'We only know she as Tessa, Sir.'

'Tessa, you are accused of stealing the sum of five hundred dollars from Señor Mendoza. We understand that you have an accomplice. Are you ready to confess?'

Still Tessa could say nothing. The white man glared at her from under hooded eyes. His jowls moved menacingly. Tessa started to cry, tears pouring down her face in fast-flowing rivulets. She had experienced many things in her short life, had received harsh punishment and whippings, but she had never felt this degree of panic. Against her best efforts, she was unable to marshal her thoughts or bring a sound to her lips.

The white men conferred. Her inquisitor said, 'This is your last chance. Are you willing to confess, freely?'

Tessa started sobbing loudly, her voice coming in spluttering, indistinguishable sounds. Finally, she was able to say, 'I ain't thief nothing. I ain't thief nothing.'

'If you persist in this denial, you will be making it worse for yourself. There are two witnesses who say you did.' The unnerving, hooded eyes glared at Tessa's trembling figure for a long moment. 'Is the man, Fist, your accomplice?'

'No, no! Not Fist!' cried Tessa, unsure of exactly what the question had meant.

'Payne, take her to the rope!' said the white man, resignedly. 'She is trying to protect the man.'

The *alguazil* came to assist Payne. Virtually lifting her, they took Tessa to the end of the room where a pulley-like contraption was installed on the ceiling. Through the pulley, Tessa could see a length of rope, the ends of which were already tied into nooses. The *alguazil* took Tessa's trembling left hand and placed it in the noose. He pulled it tight. Frightened out of her wits now, Tessa started to make unintelligible, groaning noises which turned into loud screams and pleas for mercy. The two men bent her right leg and tied it behind her back, attaching her foot to her right hand with another piece of rope. One man held the

150

end of the rope that passed through the pulley to which Tessa was bound, and started pulling.

Slowly, Tessa's small body rose off the floor until all her weight was carried by her left hand. She felt as if her wrist would break. The pain rose too in her shoulder, her waist and worst of all in her chest. Involuntarily she cried out for mercy, begging, pleading with the man to let her down. 'I ain't thief nothing,' she screamed, her voice strong and powerful now, with the power of desperation and the fear of death itself.

There was on the floor below her a pointed stake five or six inches in length. To this they now lowered the pleading, choking young woman. Tessa's small black face was covered with sweat and streaked with tears, her nose running profusely. The *alguazil* came close to her and whispered, 'Don't be stupid, girl. Say you thief quick. Say is your man who make you do it. This thing could kill you.'

Unable to comprehend what was about to happen next, unable to tolerate the pain, she instead kept on begging for mercy and pleading her innocence.

Slowly the man lowered Tessa. Inch by inch her weight dropped, until her left foot touched the spike. Tessa screamed hysterically, but they lifted and lowered her over and over again with greater speed each time. She struggled wildly and felt something snap inside her. Suffering now beyond her capacity for endurance, she mercifully passed out.

When she came to, she found herself bound by irons and chained to a wall in the same cave-like room with the low ceiling. She could not move her fingers. Her wrists were badly swollen, and appeared to be broken. Her foot was numb. The pain in her chest and the swelling told her that something inside her was badly damaged. She did not move. She could not move. She continued to slouch motionless in the corner, and felt warm blood oozing out between her legs.

# IV

By mid-morning everyone, including the dead, the injured and Carmen's new-born baby boy, was safely in Santa Clara. Fred and Juanita had come too, Juanita in a state of pitiful hysteria. Before he left the doctor spoke to Barry, 'With good attention, Señor Flores' wounds will heal. One ankle is broken, though, and that will take a few weeks to mend. Of course he has lost a great deal of blood and will be weak. His wife's delivery went well, but she has broken a rib and will need to be careful for a while. I will return tomorrow to check on them. By the way, who is the girl who saved them? The brown one?'

'Eléna?'

'Yes. The La Flores have her to thank this day. Without her presence of mind and good sense in applying and loosening tourniquets, the lad would surely have lost both his feet. A remarkable woman! I have advised her to keep to her bed too. She doesn't realise it but she too is in a state of shock.'

A detachment of the militia, coming straight from their Sunday morning drill, had arrived at the house as well, with gory details of the attempt at burning and pillage on the plantation at which the slaves had rebelled. Some of the rebels were already caught and others had been found dead, poisoned by their own hand. The leader or leaders were however still at large, having apparently escaped on José's horses. The officer seemed confident of their capture and relished the prospect of their punishment. He asked to see José and was reluctantly ushered into the injured man's presence.

With a shaky voice, José spoke of the appearance of fifteen or twenty ferocious black men who demanded his horses. 'I took out my pistol only to scare them, but then Papa came out of the carriage. Seeing him mobbed by those wild men, I . . . I . . . It was hard to know what to do. I fired, I hit the leader. This incensed them. After that I can hardly understand what happened. I must have tried to ride through the mob but they pulled me off. I tried to get up and to run then I felt my feet give way and then . . . then I was here in bed and now Papa is dead and Carmen injured . . . Oh God, damn them!'

Under the best of circumstances, the death of Don Diego would have been a horrific experience for the La Flores household, but with both José and Carmen bedridden and Eléna consigned to rest, the disruption was magnified.

'It's like a *hurucan* hit us, Barry,' whispered Yei, 'Thank God you are here to help.'

The greatest burden seemed to have fallen on Barry. Fred had his hands full with a distraught Juanita. M. Louis was forced to return to town, with the doctor, to make peace with his abandoned betrothed and the many wedding guests. So Barry had volunteered to see to the funeral arrangements.

Don Diego's body could not be kept until the next day for burial. That Sunday had been swelteringly hot without a hint of the rain that had caused Tessa so much distress the afternoon before. Having arranged with the priest to conduct the service in St Joseph's and made all other preparations, Barry had only to arrange the purchase of a casket from the town.

He wanted desperately to see Eléna, however, to talk to her himself and to allay his own fears on her behalf. He could not ask her to leave her bed, though. Seeking out Yei, he asked her to arrange it. Yei agreed and took Barry up the steps. Knocking softly, she ushered Barry in and turned quietly away leaving the door discreetly open.

With some hesitation, Barry entered. Seeing him, Eléna sat up against her pillows. At the sight of the grief and distress on her face, Barry's heart went out to her. He knew at that moment that he could never learn to love some 'lesser mortal' and that he had been a fool to think he could forget Eléna.

'Words are so inadequate at a time like this, Eléna. You have been so very courageous. Would that I could have spared you these awful experiences,' said Barry, as they began to speak of the events of the morning.

Before taking his leave, he told her of his arrangements for Diego's funeral. Her face became contorted as she tried to hold back the tears, and it took all Barry's strength to restrain himself and comfort her with words alone.


Barry set out for the town, accompanied by Fred who had to return to his home to leave instructions and to collect Tessa and Juanita's belongings. Fist too, and the coachman with a cart for the casket, came with them. Fist rode ahead – he had to gather his master's clothes as well, for it was clear that Barry was needed at Santa Clara and would stay there for some time.

'Do you get the feeling that as part of their revolt, these slaves set a trap particularly for Diego's carriage?' began Fred as he rode beside Barry. 'I don't believe they planned to injure the La Flores, though. José's shot must have made them angry. But think, they could have deliberately harmed the women and they didn't.'

'Yes. It smacks of a mystery, Fred, I agree.'

The noon sun seemed to burn with a particularly fiery vexation that day. The heat beat down wickedly on their heads, scorching their backs as they rode. Fred left Barry to rouse the undertaker from his siesta, and headed home.

Having ridden at a spanking pace, Fist was the first to arrive at Millefleurs. A servant immediately came up to him, and to his surprise, asked, 'You see Tessa anywhere? She up there by the Madame or what?'

'Wha' you mean, Tessa ain't here?'

'No, Sir, she left since after you bring her this morning and we ain't see she since then. Yesterday afternoon the mistress was complaining too, but with all the rain she couldn't send to look for her.'

Fist felt a strange constriction in his heart. 'You look in her room?'

'Yes, Mister Fist.'

'Well, go look again, now!' he commanded, his voice stern with apprehension. He waited nervously for the return of the servant, his mind racing with thoughts of what could have become of his beloved. Suddenly he began to remember the way she had looked that morning. He wondered how she had come to know of the attack of the Flores family. What has she been doing up there? He remembered little things: how dishevelled she had been, no sandals, no headwrap as if she had been in the attack herself – but nothing he had heard so far seemed to point to that. The whole idea of Tessa bringing the message, suddenly made no sense. No sense at all.

'She ain't there nah, Mister Fist,' announced the servant when she came back, wringing her hands nervously. 'What you think coulda happened to she?'

'I go look in the yard.'

'She ain't there, I tell you. She ain't nowhere here, Mister Fist.'

Fist argued no more. He jumped on his horse, all thoughts of gathering Barry's necessities forgotten as he raced back into town. He found Barry about to set off with he casket-laden cart for Santa Clara. 'Barry, wait!' he shouted.

'What's wrong?' Barry had turned, and instantly saw the worry stamped on his servant's black face.

'Is Tessa, Sir! She ain't nowhere, she ain't there, Barry. Something happen to she. I just feeling it, Sir, something bad happen to she!' He related to Barry his memory of how she had looked. Barry listened, his eyes reflecting his growing concern. 'Perhaps there's a simple explanation, Fist. Just the same, it does seem strange that you can't find her. Is there anywhere in town that she normally goes?'

'Yes . . . er . . . but she woulda never go there without expecting me to. . .'

'Look here, Fist . . . wait a minute.' Barry went up to the coachman who had gone forward already with the cart. He instructed him to return without him to Santa Clara. 'I'm coming with you, Fist.'


Barry and Fist looked everywhere. Tessa was not in the room above the shop. She was not to be found anywhere in all of Port of Spain.

'Tell you what, Fist. Time's wasting. It's not yet two o'clock. If we

154

hurry, we may just catch Fred on his way back to Maracus. We need his help in this. No, don't argue. Let's go to Millefleurs without further delay.'

Fist did not protest. He urged his horse on and within the space of five minutes the two panting horsemen arrived at the filigreed gates of Fred's house. Fred was still there.

In the absence of Tessa, the task of packing his wife's clothes had fallen to an uninitiated servant and he had been considerably delayed. About to leave, however, with portmanteau strapped to his saddle, he looked up at the sound of horses approaching.

'Fred, we need your help. By now you yourself must have realised that Tessa is missing.'

Fred nodded. 'Caused me a hell of a . . '

'Yes, yes! No time for chatter. The situation might be quite serious. I'm glad I caught you. You have some association with General Picton and I think this disappearance is serious enough for you to apply to him for information or help.'

'You mean you think she could have been taken in? That's impossible!' protested Fred.

'Upon my soul, Fred, you know this wretched country better than I do. Anything can happen here!' exclaimed Barry irritably.

'This won't do at all, Barry. I can't just go off and kick up the devil of a fuss over something we're only guessing about!'

'Fred, you don't seem to understand. There's something mysterious about her disappearance,' rejoined Barry, his impatience mounting.

'Couldn't she just have gone off on a lark?' She's used to doing it. M'wife is always complaining.'

'Hang it, Fred! We've looked everywhere, and furthermore, there's something strange about her doings today. She was the one who brought the news of the attack this morning. She's the one who helped Eléna save José's life. Yet what was she doing up there before six o'clock in the morning? Fist here says she was in a terribly dishevelled state. In his anxiety to help at the scene of the ambush, he paid her no mind but now he has reconsidered. Can't you see? Everything points to something other than a mere escapade . . . or . . . or what have you,' spluttered Barry. 'Deuce take it, Fred, you've a streak of the donkey in you, sometimes! It's . . .'

'Hold on, Barry. You've persuaded me. What do you want me to do?'

'Go to Piction and well . . . at least "enquire" if he's taken in the girl. Perhaps she's broken one of his confounded regulations, or something.

You own the girl. You have the right and the duty to inquire if she's missing.'

'Very well, I'll go straight away.'

The three men returned to the town. Fist said nothing all the while, his face grim and forbidding, his eyes alert and flashing in their intensity.

On reaching the Governor's residence Fred applied within, only to be informed that Picton was at the gaol. Hurrying there, Fred and Barry waited to be seen by the Governor, while Fist waited outside with the horses.

When he finally appeared, the Governor himself began the interview.

'Sir, we are doing all in our power to capture the men who killed your father-in-law. Please accept my condolences,' he began. A seemingly endless conversation on the ambush, the injuries, the escapes, the capture, and the poisonings ensued until Barry unceremoniously butted in.

'Excellency, we've come here on another matter.'

'Oh, excuse me, Excellency. You have met my friend, the Honourable Barry Wingate. He's my guest here, visiting from Barbados.'

'Yes? Well, what concerns you?' drawled Picton ungraciously.

'A young female slave of mine, by name Tessa Villaneuf, has disappeared under somewhat mysterious circumstances. I would like to know if she has been arrested, and if you or your men have any knowledge of her whereabouts.'

'She's very small, under five feet in height, black-skinned,' supplied Barry. 'She has not been seen since early this morning.'

Picton's large frame stiffened. 'Mr Whiteways' she's your slave, you say?'

'Do you know of her?' Fred responded to a faint note of recognition in the Governor's voice.

'Oh no! She's probably run off into the interior.'

'No,' declared Fred. 'There's no reason for her to run away. Apart from the fact that she's to get her freedom as soon as we set the date for her marriage to Wingate's valet, she's a loved and trusted slave. She's the one who helped save my brother-in-law's life. I mean, if anything were to happen to her, my wife and her relatives will be very distraught,' concluded Fred, looking fixedly at Picton.

The Governor did not at first meet Fred's eyes, but he answered firmly, 'I have no one fitting the woman's description here in the gaol. There is nothing more I can say to you. She hasn't been missing long enough for concern, I'd say. In any case, let's give it a while. I am very busy with the business of interrogating the rebels. The slave-owner is up in arms about the attack on his home and his crop, as well as at the suicides. Look at it this way, you've lost one slave. The man in there has lost twenty! I will do the best I can.'

Picton turned abruptly on his heels and called to the guard to show them out, then he marched away and was swallowed up by the dark, forbidding interior of the gaol.

'Damned impudent oaf!' swore Barry. 'Let's get out of here. I wager he knows more than he's let on.'

Once outside, Barry explained the encounter to Fist.

'Oh God, Barry, I ain't know what to do,' groaned Fist. 'We have to find she today.'

'I know . . . what the deuce of a situation to be in! Well, we can't be in two places at the same time,' Barry mumbled to himself. 'Wait here, I'll send Whiteways along and stick with you, something's bound to turn up.'

After a moment he was back, mounted and ready to begin the search once more. At a walking pace, the two friends set off, eyes alert and scanning every doorway, alley, construction site, every hovel, every place of business, drain or rubbish heap. Time was slipping away. Checking everywhere two and three times, the men began to feel they were going around in circles. Then coming again upon the incompleted shed where Fist had once spent part of an evening, a familiar cackle assaulted the black man. Stopping, he dismounted and gave his reins to Barry. 'Hold she here for me. Let me talk to this ol' woman.'

'Eh, eh, young man, long time I ain't see you. How you scarce so?' began the drunken voice.

'Listen, I ain't have time today to ol' talk. You know the girl you was teasing me 'bout, the one you call the little dolly? You ain't see she nowhere?' Fist looked anxiously at the woman crouched on the dirt floor.

Something about the intensity of that look demanded a sober answer.

'To tell you true, Monsieur, I did see she over by Pedro's shop. She was in trouble, but that was since yesterday, oui.'

'What trouble?' demanded Fist, his voice ugly now.

'The same man I did warn you 'bout the 'Piol, he name Mendoza, he try to hold she, but she fight like a Trinidad tiger and run from he. Look, she did drop her kerchief, and I pick it up. Look it here in mi pocket.' She offered the rag to him.

'Where she run to?' asked Fist in a strained voice as he reached

157

tremulously for the precious piece of evidence, the one link to his lost love.

'I ain't know nah, but he ain't ketch she. The *corbeau* did come then but none of them ketch she. I laugh too bad.'

'You think they have she in the gaol?'

'Who knows? This mornin' I was sleeping right here, and I see them carry somebody to Picton, but it was so early, yampie was still in mi eye. I ain't see too good. Coulda been she, but that person ain't go in the gaol you know. Nah, as if I see the carriage ride off so . . . wait, nah, they must be go in the west.'

'The west? Where? Why? What it have there?'

'What? Is not what, but who!'

'Who then? asked Fist irritably.

'You never hear 'bout Begorrat? He is real friend with Massa Picton. He have all kind o' scheme. He living in the west for one thing. I hear them say he carrying out experiment there, but what that is I ain't know.'

'Thank you, woman, thank you,' cried Fist, turning rapidly away.

'Eh, eh, just so you gone?' The woman rose on her haunches and looked to see him. 'Beware the *corbeaux* 'n' them, eh!' she yelled as the horsemen rode out of sight.


'Look, she give me this cloth Tessa does tie she head wit'. Ley we ride to the west. She say she could be by Begorrat.' The words tumbled out of Fist's grim mouth.

'In Diego Martin?'

'Yes, I think is round there. Oh God, Barry, if anything happen to she . . . God help Mendoza? I go kill him with mi bare hands!' snarled Fist.

'Calm down, Fist,' cautioned Barry, breaking in on his companion's violent imprecations. 'At least we have a clue now. It's a long shot, but let's go and snoop around. Somebody else might know something.' Barry's voice was none too confident, negating his attempt at optimism. 'The strange thing is, while you were talking with the woman, a rider left the gaol in a great hurry heading up this very street. I wonder . . . Oh well, idle speculation can't help us at all.'

But Barry's intuition was more accurate than he imagined. Despite Picton's denial and blustering dismissal of his countrymen, he had been shaken by a strange suspicion that the girl he had been too busy to question that morning, and had dismissively handed over to Payne and Begorrat for questioning, was the much prized slave of the influential Englishman. If so, he had been badly misinformed. He had thought the

158

girl merely the woman-friend of a free black from Barbados, a person of no consequence. Now it could well be that she was actually promised to this free black, who was in fact Wingate's servant from Barbados. 'Christ! What rotten luck!'

It had seemed such an open and shut case. Had he been less distracted this morning, the misunderstanding would never have occurred. The role of governor left one no time for lapses. He silently cursed the tempting, demanding mulattress and the equally demanding Sunday military drill, which were both in need of attention that morning.

Well, no real harm had been done. With luck Begorrat hadn't been too zealous in his interrogation. He would instruct him to release the woman straight away. It would be her word against his. All would be put right.

He wasted no time. He penned a hasty note and dispatched a messenger with instructions to ride 'hell for leather' to Begorrat's. The note instructed the Frenchman to rid himself of the prisoner immediately. He wished no further investigation of the charge against her. True, torture was within the ambit of the law, but he had no wish to come up against the will of Fred Whiteways.

The messenger arrived in record time. The note was received. In less than a minute, Tessa's limp and swollen body was hauled into the yard, flung on to a horse and carried half a mile away. There she was wantonly dumped in an open field covered with weeds, whose long blade-like leaves bowed sadly and swayed mournfully over her prostrate body.


When Barry and Fist arrived at the Begorrat estate in the Diego Martin valley they were met by a mulatto overseer, who looked at them contemptuously and responded unco-operatively to their enquiries. Seething with rage, Fist was about to pounce on the man, but Barry drew him away. 'We can't get anything out of him, Fist, we're just wasting precious minutes. Come on!'

'I just know that man hiding something from we, I just feel it in mi bones, Barry.' Fist cast a menacing glance backwards. They rode slowly away. 'What we go do now? Where we could go? I still feel she is there, man.'

'She can't be there, Fist. No, they're not mad enough to hide the property of a man like Whiteways. For such a thing, against a man of his influence, Picton could be recalled. No, she's not there, but she may be somewhere nearby, somewhere where no one can connect her with this place, so it will be only her word against Picton's or Begorrat's.' As Barry spoke, the seed of suspicion that had started growing earlier suddenly reached maturity and blossomed out. 'Let's just look around, and enquire in this area.'

The two men rode slowly through the narrow cart tracks that constituted the roadways in Diego Martin. They cast searching eyes everywhere. There was nothing, no one. Eventually they saw some shacks in the distance. No, no one there had seen any young girl. 'Not by here, Massa,' answered the harassed woman with children swarming around her like little sugar flies. Then, after riding further, they came upon a man forlornly mounted on an excuse for a donkey. He paused, allowing them passage on the narrow path. They stopped, enquiring of him if he had seen anything, anything at all – a carriage leaving the Begorrat estate, a rider, a young woman without a headwrap, or in a badly rumpled condition.

'Well . . . no, Massa, no . . . I can't say I see nothing . . . no . . .' He studied them thoughtfully, stroking his straggling goatee. 'But something . . .' He paused again. '. . . No, it ain't nothing.'

'What? Please, please. If you know anything, please tell we,' begged Fist, in a pitiful, supplicating voice.

'I don't think is nothing . . . but I seeing a set o' *corbeaux* over so . . .' The two men looked up simultaneously.

'Look, Fist, there they are! Vultures circling! Let's go and investigate!' shouted Barry abruptly. He spurred his horse forward, riding through tall grass. They had forgotten the man to whom they were speaking, absorbed now with their gnawing fears, hearts throbbing with apprehension.

'Jesus Lord, *corbeaux*! "Beware the *corbeaux* 'n' them", the woman did warn me! Oh no, God no!' cried Fist as he followed rapidly behind Barry. Then his horse came to a skidding stop as he reined in suddenly. Leaping to the ground, he uttered a bloodchilling cry that came from the depths of his soul. He had found Tessa lying still, like a broken doll in the tall grass, with black *corbeaux* circling over her and bloodstains on her skirt and legs.

Cradling her in his trembling arms, he sobbed loudly, so that Barry, in spite of his sympathy, was forced to shake him roughly, insisting that they get her quickly to a warm bed and a doctor. For, vultures or no, Tessa was still alive.

Very gently, Fist and Barry propped her on one horse, Barry holding her, while Fist mounted behind and enfolded her unconscious body in his arms. They rode away, Barry instructing Fist to make directly for Millefleurs.

For the second time that day, Barry went for the doctor.


# V

At Millefleurs, Fist laid Tessa gently on her own bed. The servants wiped the dust and mud from her tiny face and applied burnt feathers under her nose in a vain attempt to revive her. Fist sat on a stool at the side of her bed, his eyes glued to Tessa's ashen face and swollen body. He reached over every so often to reassure himself that her heart was still beating. He muttered impatiently for the doctor.

Just at his patience was running out, he heard Barry come in with the physician. Relinquishing his place at Tessa's bedside, he stepped into the shadows, his eyes on the still figure of the tiny girl on the small bed.

The doctor examined her, listening to her heart and lungs. He shook his head and asked all but a female servant to leave the room. In greater privacy, he conducted further examinations. Finally, stepping out, he said to Barry, 'I'm afraid she's in a bad way. Whatever happened to the child? She's barely alive.' Standing in the shadows, Fist jumped involuntarily, 'You the man involved?' He turned to Fist.

'Yes, Sir.'

'Yes, he's bethrothed to her. They are to marry soon,' added Barry.

'Sorry about it . . .' The doctor hesitated. '. . . She must have gone through some terrible accident . . . or . . .'

'Torture?' supplied Barry.

The doctor pursed his lips and nodded slowly. 'That might explain it, the dislocated wrist, internal rupture, vaginal bleeding, damaged foot. Who would do such a thing?'

'What's going to happen to her? Will she recover?' asked Barry, ignoring the unanswerable question.

The doctor shook his head. He drew Barry away, out of Fist's earshot. 'I'm sorry, it's obvious that the woman means a great deal to your man, and perhaps to you too, but chances of recovery are slim. She is bleeding internally. There is nothing anyone can do.'

'Will she regain consciousness?'

'She might. One never knows, or she may go straight into a coma from which she won't recover. One way or the other, she won't last another day.'

'Good God! Not this, not this!' Barry's voice hissed through his clenched teeth. 'There's nothing, nothing we can do?'

The doctor laid a kindly hand on Barry's shoulder. 'Let's walk out into the yard, and we'll talk about it further.'

Seeing the slump of Barry's shoulders and sensing that the prognosis for Tessa would be bad, Fist stood motionless in the shadows. He hung his head down and breathed heavily. His own dear precious little doll, his gay, happy, miniature lady. All his dreams and hopes crushed. 'Now ain't no time to grieve. I must go back to she. I go have the rest of mi life to grieve,' he philosophised with a resignation born of a life of slavery and constant exposure to cruelties beyond normal human endurance; a resignation that concealed but could not diminish his pain or his growing anger.

Calmer now, he went back to Tessa's bedside and took up his former position. Hands on his forehead, shoulders hunched, he presented a sorrowful picture to Barry's tired eyes as he returned to the room.

Fist looked up at his friend and benefactor, and simply asked, 'He say it have anything we could do for she?' Barry shook his head. Fist, deceptively calm, turned back to look at Tessa. He held his head in his hands. After a while he covered his eyes and sucked in his breath, and Barry knew his friend was weeping.

# V

After Diego's funeral, it was a silent and cheerless group that made their way back to the house at Santa Clara as the sun sank in the west, going out today without its usual blaze of glory. The guests from Port of Spain went directly home. André offered to come back to the house with Eléna, but she advised him that that was not necessary, since she was going straight to bed. It was just the members of the family, therefore, who returned to the house.

Once there, Eléna headed for the stairs intent on going directly to her room. It was Mark who stopped her.

'Stay a moment, Eléna,' he said seriously. 'I might be wrong in telling you this, but I have shared many hours with you and Tessa, and I know of your fondness for her. You ought to know that she was missing this afternoon.'

# VI

'I thinking you never woulda come,' said a voice close to Fist.

'Tessa? You wake? All you , she wake up!' he announced excitedly.

162

'How you feeling, *doux*, *doux*?' Fist's heart beat a joyous tattoo. Only a minute ago he was despairing that she would ever recover.

'Don't ask that, Fist, I wake up to hear the news you have for me. Tell me now, nah, I can't go without hearing. So long I waiting to hear it.'

'Oh, Tessa, you worried 'bout that? Is good news. Your master say he go free you, and we could get married any time.'

Tessa smiled broadly. 'I so glad. Onliest, the news come too late for we.'

'Don't say that *doux*, *doux*. It ain't too late yet. What happen, Tessa? Who do this to you? Is Begorrat?'

'Forget that, Fist. It done do already. Forget them. I ain't know who they was anyway. I never see none o' them before. I ain't know they name or nothing. I did try mi best, Fist, but everything was against me. Is like I blight in true.' She lapsed into a troubled silence. Fist mopped her brow and spoke soothingly to her. Presently, she spoke again, 'What happen to the Mistress 'n' them? They safe now?'

'Yes, we was in time. Mister Barry bring the doctor in time.'

'An' she sister, she make the baby?'

'Yes, a boy.'

'I mighta make a boy, too, but now that gone . . .'

'How you mean? You think you was . . ?'

'I did only suspect. Maybe I was just wishing, but that gone, you ain't see the blood? But is for the best. Don't grieve, eh, Fist, you carry on for we. You'se a fighting man . . .'

'I sorry Tessa. I real sorry. I shoulda never make you . . .'

'How you could say that? You ain't see how hard black people life is? Anything could always happen to we, but the chance to love, we lucky to get that. That didn't have nothing to do with no massa and I never could be sorry for that.' Her voice was growing weaker and her eyes held a glazed, unfocused look.

'Tessa, is there anything you want? Anything we could get for you?' asked Barry, who had been all the while standing in the background.

Tessa looked at him.

'Your eyes so blue like the sky on a pretty, pretty clear day . . . and they does talk like . . . my mistress have talking eyes too . . . No. I don't want nothing. I onliest sorry I ain't go ever see my black mistress again.'

'Eléna?'

'Yes. It hard to go without seein' she. I leave she in so much trouble this morning.'

'You don't have to worry. You ain't know Mister Barry like she bad. He go look after she, for you.'

'Is you then? So was you all the time? I did never guess.' Tessa tried to laugh, but the effort was too much for her. 'Don't break she heart, you hear!' She closed her eyes. Fist spoke tenderly to her. Her eyes suddenly shot open and she cried out: 'Oh God, Fist, the *corbeaux* coming for me, Fist! Oh God, they so big 'n' ugly, Fist. Fist, hold me, hold me, hold me tight!' Her voice trailed off, and the room became silent.

Holding her awkwardly in his arms, Fist gently rocked the frail, lifeless body from side to side. A low moan escaped his lips and large glistening drops ran down his distorted black face.

Barry rushed out of the room and ran off into the night, his eyes blinded with unshed tears. He reached the fence and clutched the filigreed shapes until they cut into his palms. His stomach heaved and he retched, but he had not eaten all day so after a few minutes the spasm subsided, and he hung on, breathing heavily.

## VII

The carriage moved so slowly that Eléna felt it would have been better if she had walked. To her fevered mind, the road to Port of Spain was never so long at it was that night, when not even the moon deigned to show its face. The journey was as frustrating as had been her attempt to get information about Tessa from Fréd. And then to have learnt so much and so little. Tessa had been promised in marriage to Barry's man! Fred had never told them. So easy to forget about a slave. Oh, that man!

After an eternity they could see the lights of the town, and then they were past the lights and out of Port of Spain, heading westwards. Finally, they arrived at Millefleurs and turned into the yard. The gates, usually closed at this hour, were still wide open. Eléna jumped out of the carriage without assistance. She had seen Barry leaning dejectedly on the fence.

'Eléna!' He gave a startled cry as she ran up to him. 'How did you know to come? Tessa is . . . Tessa is . . .'

'What? What has happened to her? Have you found her?'

Barry reached out with both hands and held Eléna at arms' length. 'It is very bad, Eléna, I wish . . . look, there is no way I can soften this for you. She was probably tortured, but we won't be able to prove it, we . . .'

'Where is she, Barry?' interrupted Eléna, her eyes in the darkness wide and round like two black balls of fear.

'She's inside in the servant's room, with Fist.'

'Mother of God! Oh, Mother of God!' cried Eléna as she lifted her long skirts and flew into the house, brushing rudely past Mark and Louis, and bursting into the servant's room. 'Tessa! Tessa!' she called. Then she saw the tiny, waxen figure on the bed where Fist had just laid her.

'No use, Miss. She done gone. You too late. We was all too late to save she.'

'It can't be! It can't be! Tessa, oh Tessa! Why? Why? Barry, help me! Help me!' she screamed. Barry came up behind her, having followed her into the house. She turned and collapsed in his arms, in a fit of wild sobbing.

He lifted her like a baby and took her out into the yard, away from the concerned looks of the others. Placing her gently on an old wooden bench under a tree, he hugged her tightly while she poured out her sorrow; her tears soaking into his sleeve and her grief into his heart.

They stayed locked in each others's arms like this for a long time until Barry was sure she had regained some control of herself. Then he spoke gently to her and led her slowly back to the house. Asking a servant to show him to a suitable bedroom, he led her in and directed her to the bed, insisting that she lie down quietly, talking soothingly all the while.

At her request, he told her all that he knew of the circumstances surrounding Tessa's troubles, of her involvement with Fist, and her running off to meet him, her encounter with the Spaniard, and the possible sequence of events after that. Finally, he said, 'You must rest now, Eléna. You've experienced a lifetime of calamities in this one short day. It's too much to ask of anyone.' He rose to leave.

'Don't go! Don't leave me, Barry,' she whispered. He stayed. 'Tell me . . . were there . . . were there any . . . *corbeaux*?'

'Why yes, how did you know?'

'Don't leave me, Barry!' she grimaced. Tears rolled down her cheeks, past her fiercely shut eyes. 'Don't leave me alone in this nightmare.'

# BOOK THREE

## Immortelles

# CHAPTER FIFTEEN

## I

The funeral was over. The events that precipitated it left those involved in an unsteady state, but the world plodded on steadfastly. Life continued.

With respect to Barry's suspicions, the doctor had advised him to apply to the Commandant of Quarters, who was also a coroner, for an autopsy. But mindful of his own comfort, he was prepared to take the matter no further. Not so with Barry. With a reluctant Fred in tow, he had faced the Governor.

It was no use. Short of beating the truth out of him, there was nothing the two friends could do. Frustration and anger overcame Barry. With a reckless impetuosity, he warned the Governor that he would not forget the fate of the dead slave. He guaranteed him that the day would come when such activities as those perpetrated on Tessa would be brought before the British public. It was all Fred could do to drag his friend out of Picton's house.

Even the next day, after the funeral, Barry's anger was unabated. He raved not only against Picton but all the perpetrators of the rotten system.

'Barry, you're looking at it from the wrong side of the fence, from that of the slave, the free coloured, not that of the planter,' consoled Fred.

'Damn them all, then!' expostulated Barry. 'I'm ashamed to be of their class, to . . . to be British, even! I may not kick up a fuss every day, but I'm acutely aware of the atrocities of . . . of the commandants of quarters and their henchmen, the *alguaziles*. Of their excessive punishment of slaves, even despite the protests of some owners. Look at the torture of that slave in San Fernando who was placed naked on a nest of stinging ants! Or that of the runaway woman who was hanged

167

immediately, before her owner could come to claim her.' Barry had worked himself up to a frenzy.

Fred searched for some palliative and could find none.

Barry continued, 'And now Tessa! Oh my God! The commandant could not be found to perform the autopsy. We can't get any information anywhere. But we must persist in asking. I want to see just how much covering up that man is prepared to do.'

'Yes, I agree. We must try further. Tell you what, let's go see if we can find the man, Mendoza. He's our only lead.'

Going first to the mulatto's shop, they got little assistance from the owner and his brother but they did learn that he was a seaman, so they made their way to the wharves. They met the Spaniard as he was preparing to leave on a trip to Tobago (the island to the north, just twenty-six miles from Trinidad). Unable, after the experiences earlier, to trust his emotionally charged friend to conduct this investigation calmly, Fred undertook to interrogate the man.

Mendoza stuck to his story of being robbed. 'What did the little bitch tell you?' he demanded.

'Didn't say a word.'

'Well? So why you coming to me? Who told you I had something to do with her? She is the one who wronged me, and nobody wasn't even there to see when she stole my purse, and bit my arm.'

'That's what you think. Of course you didn't see the old woman near by, but she saw you. If I were you, I'd get a lawyer because, as I'm an Englishman, there's such a thing as justice, and it's going to be done in this case. The girl was my slave and now she's been murdered. We know you have something to do with it and you aren't going to get away with this.'

The Spaniard was visibly shocked by what he heard, but he reacted with loud expletives, denying any knowledge of any murder, protesting that he had never seen the woman after she ran from him, and declaring that he suspected she had been arrested for the robbery. They should go and see the *alguazil*.

'Which *alguazil*?' asked Fred, still keeping Barry at bay.

'I don't know his name. The one with the broken nose. An ugly nigger just like all the rest, but his nose is different, it's twisted like.'

'Very well then,' replied Fred, still holding Barry off. 'Be assured that on your return from Tobago, you'll be hearing from us again.' Fred pulled Barry away, allowing him no means of reaching the Spaniard. 'Calm yourself, man, we'll get to the bottom of this yet and without having to resort to fisticuffs. Let's go and find the *alguazil*.'

'Hey there, young Wingate!'

Hearing his name, Barry turned and saw the old seafearing man from Barbados. 'Carty. What a surprise to see you of all people,' remarked Barry, his state of mind subduing his normal enthusiasm.

'Damned glad I found you so easy like, Guv. 'Ere, I was about to burst me brains findin' you an' like the good Lord brings you straight to me.'

'What ! You're looking for me? Is there a message from my uncle?' enquired Barry with aroused interest.

'That's right.' Carty searched in his pockets and brought out a crumpled paper. 'I reckon it's more likely from yer ol' man 'imself, comes from the great country, this 'ere letter does,' he answered, handing over the much abused missive to Barry.

Barry put the letter safely away in his pocket, intending to read it at his leisure in a calmer frame of mind.

'How are things in Barbados?' he asked Carty with no real interest.

The older man answered cheerfully, but Barry's distracted expression gave no encouragement to Carty's natural volubility, so without further exchange, they parted.

Barry and Fred moved off and Carty stood looking at them sucking on his pipe, his hands on his hips. Presently, Mendoza came surreptitiously up to him and proceeded to question him closely on the identity of the Englishmen he had been speaking to. Then the sailor walked thoughtfully away, heading into Port of Spain.

He went directly to Pedro's shop and spoke quietly to the owner's brother. He was very worried. He didn't like this turn of events. Picton had been known to execute a white man for an attempted rape before and without much proof. Mendoza felt for the small dagger he had tucked into his waist.

He spent the next few hours walking about the streets of Port of Spain as if looking for something, then he turned into a billiards parlour. He tried his hand at the game which the immigrant English were so enthusiastic about. At the sound of the sunset gun, he went into a rum shop and had a few drinks. He sat in the shop for a long time. Suddenly, he gulped down his drink and sauntered out into the moonless night. The rum had had a bracing effect on him, and he walked confidently, looking straight ahead, quite sure of his destination. He never looked back, or he may have noticed that there was a shadow following him silently, always a few hundred feet away.

He made straight for a half-completed, unlit building. Within a few minutes he had done the deed, and stepped out. He had not moved a few paces, however, when a firm hand grabbed him from behind, and clutched at his throat. He felt himself being pushed back into the shed. Struggling fiercely, he unsheathed his dagger and swung wildly.

His assailant, a stronger and larger man, eventually caught hold of his hand, twisting it as the Spaniard lurched forward. The dagger plunged into the owner's chest. The other man released his hand. Mendoza fell with a thud to the floor, writhed in agony for a few minutes, then lay still.

The other man groped in the darkness for something. Feeling the prostrate body of the woman, he touched her, searching for some sign of life. Then he drew back hastily. His fingers had encountered the unmistakable feel of thick, warm blood. He shook his head sadly. Without pausing to wipe his hands he made a hasty retreat, leaving without a second glance.

## II

Barry and Fred persisted determinedly in their investigations, but day after day brought them no success. The news of the murder of Mendoza and the woman came only to baffle them in their efforts. Eventually, therefore, they had to turn their attention to the pressing problems of Kathy and Louis. Kathy still had to leave soon for England but, with José laid up, Louis could not abandon Santa Clara. Try as he might, Barry could find no immediate solution for the distraught Monsieur.

A solution did come, however, but from an unexpected quarter. Mark had opted to accompany Fred and Barry to Santa Clara that evening. Once there, he suggested that he should undertake the running of the estate. Barry too, offered to help and Louis was finally persuaded to start showing the two gentlemen the ropes.

Matters being thus settled, the discussion broke up, and everyone started making their way to bed. Louis lingered pensively at the veranda rail. Barry approached him.

'You're not really happy with the plan for Mark and myself to help, Monsieur?'

'No Barry, it's not that . . . I was actually thinking of something quite different.' Barry waited, so Louis continued, 'André was here today.'

'Oh, with the militia?'

'Yes. He was part of the detail that came this time. After announcing that they had caught the leader, the officer went to speak to José. I was able to talk to André, quietly. He told me the leader's name – François. He reminded me that I knew him, that I had in fact tried to buy him once. I can't believe he'd set upon members of this family.'

Barry listened silently, and made no comment. He was thinking that there was yet another mystery to add to those he was still trying to solve.

# III

Barry held the letter from his father firmly between his fingers, stretching his hands out into the wind and watching as the leaves of paper struggled to fly out of his grasp. The wind was powerful here on the hill where he had come to wait for Fist. He was earlier than the appointed time, but that was intentional. He needed to think quietly by himself. Here he was sure to be undisturbed.

His father had written to say that he was free to come home. The charges against him had been dropped. His efforts on his son's behalf had been greatly aided by the openly acknowledged collapse of the Claymore sugar plantations and the declared bankruptcy of that family. 'We are expecting you back any day now. The sooner the better.'

The letter had been dated several months before. There was no doubt about it, he was free to go home.

Barry leaned into the wind. He felt the burning sun on his face and, looking out, saw the clear outlines around him. 'Hell,' he thought, 'there's no way one could blind oneself to the realities here.' Fred had been right − under the brilliance of the tropical sun, subtleties evaporated. To be replaced, however, Barry now thought, by stark and glaring contradictions.

It was one thing if a man like Wilfred was attacked, but for Don Diego of all people, so liberal a slave-owner, meeting his death as the result of slave rebellion! A rebellion provoked, no doubt, by forces he had surely been against. Then Tessa, she who had belonged to the kindest, most generous owner. Tessa's life should have been simple, uncomplicated. Fist loved her. Fred would have freed her. All of us would have wished them happy, and given them a good start in life. Yet she too had to be caught in the vicious arbitrariness of the times. It was one thing to rage against Picton, but it was more than just him, Barry realised. It's as if no one can escape. None of us can escape. The all-embracing tentacles of slave society reach us wherever we are. Picton, he knew, was just the local arbiter of a pernicious, cancerous system that had tainted man. And man? Man was not much better than the animals, so utterly primitive and cruel.

Barry thought about the prospect of returning home. He reviewed what his new consciousness had taught him. He was painfully aware that the refinements of London came as a result of wealth accumulated on the backs of these islands, at the expense of people like Fist and Tessa, at the hands of ruthless governors like Picton, overseers like Albert, owners like Wilfred. These he knew, were probably not even the worst of the lot.

His father's letter could not be ignored. The prospect of returning was now very, very serious. What would it be like back home? he wondered. He could not project himself into a future there so he thought about the past, about his former life in England, about his grandmother and Grenmill, the Rovers and Ruggie, Annabella and Clifford. He wondered if he was the same person who had moved on that alien stage so many aeons ago. Would anybody he knew then recognise him now? Was he in fact the same person? Was it just under two years ago that he had left the glittering halls of London's ballrooms, the staid mausoleum of White's, the gay fireworks of Vauxhall Gardens? He had harboured so much resentment against this enforced exile, thinking then how primitive, boring and futureless life in the West Indies would be, how much he would miss civilisation. Now was the time of reckoning. Had he really missed England?

He had met the most civilized person he knew here in this wild, primitive island. What was civilisation anyway, when men, Englishmen – rulers – were so far from human? he asked himself. Mere trappings, a sham when one saw what engendered it. A sham glossed over by form, manners and culture. What was all that manners and polite behaviour? What but hyprocrisy? he ruminated.

'Christ! Why am I attacking my own kind? I could have lived happily in England, I could have if I'd never been here, never met Fist and Tessa, never learned to love Eléna . . . or could I? What had my life been, anyway? A series of silly, mindless rebellions, looking for and inventing adventures and challenges. What was that all about, anyway? What forces was I reacting to . . . or against? At least life here is a real challenge. No one here has to go looking for danger. Ha! It's everywhere. Do I really care anything about balls in London, or kicking my heels in a life of gay dissipation for the next ten years – for surely Grandmama has a solid ten years still to go – ten years without Eléna. That future doesn't seem so appealing. Faith, I'd be a poor lover, indeed, to leave her now in distress, in her disturbed state of mind.

'The truth is I really have no life in England to resume. I'd have to start afresh anyway, learn to conform properly, to stay out of trouble. Even if I did learn to play the part, could I ever really forget Eléna, or fully accept the fact that the only reason she could not be my wife was because of her colour? She's as refined and well bred as any highborn lady I've ever met or I'm every likely to meet in England, and infinitely more sensible and attractive. Colour just doesn't seem to be a good enough reason against marrying her. Christ, what's happened to my traditional upbringing? All my status-preserving instincts? I don't know. In the end, all of that is just damned hypocrisy, mere play-acting. Every white man here has a black or mulatto mistress hidden away somewhere, most not concealed at all. It's clear that relations between black and white are harmonious in the bedrooms of Trinidad. I just happened to find a black woman who could fulfil more than bedroom needs.'

He thought now of how his love for Eléna had grown from a mere fascination with her beauty, to being captivated by the beauty of her soul and her spirit. Enumerating her perfections could not blind him to the fact that he could not have both Eléna and Grenmill, however, and that he had finally to make a serious and binding decision, and soon. For here was his father's letter forcing the decision on him.

In his mind he relived the events since that fateful Sunday, less than a week ago . . .

He could see now the sad, small funeral, everyone numb with grief. Eléna hardly able to bear up, and Fist unnaturally unemotional, his face an impassive mask – stern and forbidding. Tessa had been buried on the Monday morning.

No sooner was the burial over than the mask that was Fist turned to Barry and spoke without animation or noticeable emotion, 'Thanks, Barry. Thanks for everything. I hope you ain't mind, but I can't work right now.'

'What are you going to do, Fist?'

'I just want some days to miself. I can't talk now. I going up in Morvant, up the mountain. If you wants me, meet me any afternoon . . . 'bout a li'l way up from the top o' the spring. You know the place, on the look-out like. We went there once when we first come. I go leave some sign for you, three white stones in a triangle.'

'But where will you sleep? I understand this is still the rainy season, even if we've had sun for these two days.'

'Barry, a li'l rain ain't nothing to me. Nothing can't worry me now.'

'Fist, it isn't safe for a black man to be roaming any part of this country on his own, with no fixed dwelling. Don't forget the new regulation ordering all coloureds to keep the nine-thirty curfew, and you must carry your papers now. Slaves found on the streets must show their passes. You might be mistaken for a slave.'

'I go be careful.'

'Fist, I . . .' Barry checked himself. Instead, he reached out and clasped his friend on the shoulder.

'It ain't have nothing nobody could say, Barry, so don't try. We was in it together, and I done know how you feel. Just let me go now.'

'I'll come on Friday at about three o'clock.'

Waiting for Fist to appear, Barry pondered on whether Fist had deciphered what had happened to Tessa and whether Eléna had too. He knew that she blamed herself in some unreasonable way for not having paid sufficient attention to Tessa in the recent past, and especially on the day of her death. He wished he could reassure her. But now, back at Santa Clara, she had completely withdrawn. What could he offer her anyway? Only his love. He wasn't even sure of his decision. Busy as he had been with the investigation, and now on the estate, he had really needed to find time to think everything through. Today had been the first real opportunity for private thought. Soon he knew, he would reach an irrevocable decision.

'How long you waiting?' Fist's deep baritone broke into Barry's thoughts.

'There you are. I didn't even hear you come up,' responded Barry.

'I does move quiet-like these days,' said Fist. 'Leh we sit down nah.' He led the way to a fallen tree trunk. Barry followed, asking him how he had been. The two men sat down and lit up some tobacco. Barry looked at the black man and saw in his face that he was still consumed with grief.

It was like old times in Barbados, just the two of them. Strange, mused Barry, that he should look with nostalgia to a time he had so hated. But wasn't that the way of all men? Barry smiled wryly to himself. Barbados could not match the grandeur of this scenery, though. He gazed about him at the sheer cliffs running down to the flat lands and the steep slopes rolling gently far, far down to the toy town that was Port of Spain. The blue waters of the Gulf glittered with toy ships anchored offshore in the harbour and in the harbour of Chaguaramas. In the distance too, Barry thought he could detect the faint outline of Venezuela. He drew his eyes away and looked instead at his friend, waiting for him to speak.

'Well, I all right up here,' ventured Fist, as if there had been no lapse between the question and this answer. 'At least, I ain't have to see nobody I don't want to see, and make no stupid ol' talk, when I ain't feeling to talk.'

'In that case, I'll try to make this meeting brief,' smiled Barry.

'No, I ain't mean you!' Fist returned the smile.

The easy repartee between them never ceased to amaze and comfort Barry. Despite the differences in their stations, Fist was able to be so at ease with him. It wasn't a matter of insolence, the question didn't arise. Barry shared the same ease with the black man. They were brothers of the soul. With Fist, no frills, no pretences were necessary. Their backgrounds could not be more dissimilar, their prospects and roles in life more divergent. Yet they were bound together in common under-standing, so that words were sometimes hardly necessary between them. Barry thought now of how much he admired the black man, not, as he smiled to himself, in the glorified way of the abolitionist poets who romanticised the 'exotic savage', but he had come to know the essential man within. Perhaps Fist was unique, but somehow, rather than abstract him from his race Barry saw in him the intrinsic dignity and worth of all black men.

'You've heard that they caught the leader of the rebellion? Won't be long before they execute him and the others, I suppose,' ventured Barry.

Then he cleared his throat and changed the subject. 'You've heard of the murder of Mendoza and the old woman?' he asked, watching his friend intently. 'Would I be correct in assuming that you weren't involved?'

Fist lowered his eyes. 'Why you ask, Barry? You hear some talk? They suspect is me or what?'

'No. No talk. Not even talk of an investigation, which in itself is strange. Seems to me the Governor isn't about to open any inquiry that could lead to any revelation on Tessa's death. It's all connected, the unavailability of the Commandant, the missing *alguazil* . . .'

'Which *alguazil*?'

'One called Joe, the one with the twisted nose. You should know him, he patrols the town. I was told he's the one that arrested Tessa. He's been missing. You don't happen to know anything about him, now, do you?'

'You was checking things out or what?'

'Yes. Whiteways and myself, but we didn't get anywhere. So?'

'Nah, I ain't know nothing 'bout no *alguazil*. At least not yet.'

'Whatever that means! Well, have it your own way, but remember I'm your friend. I care about you. I will help if you're in trouble. By the way,' he added, 'I almost forgot, I brought you a pair of strong boots and a bottle of rum. They're in my saddlebag at the foot of the hill. I know you won't be able to buy rum now with the new regulations.'

'Sure right, ain't no way I could buy five gallons to tote up here,' responded Fist, referring to Picton's new decree that no alcohol under five gallons in quantity was to be sold to blacks. 'Well leh we go for it, nah. Leh we take a drink. By the way, you mightn't find me here next time.'

'But why? Where are you going?'

'Are you going to tell me about it, or am I to be kept in the dark about this too?'

Fist laughed, 'Come on, leh we get the bottle and forget all the rest.'


# IV

Barry had assured himself that Fist was managing to survive. He was alive and in good health, even if his state of mind, plans and present activities were shrouded in disquieting mystery. He turned all his efforts now to his apprenticeship with the good Monsieur. Being an experienced teacher, M. Louis soon had Mark and Barry growing in understanding and confidence of what the work entailed.

On the second day of their foray as novice farmers, heavy morning rains drove them back to the house. Mark went inside to visit José, while Barry and M. Louis sat on the varanda, looking out at the drenched earth. They watched the mountains disappear behind their veil of mist, and waited calmly for their midday meal.

Lulled by the soothing monotony of the rain, they remained absorbed in their own thoughts. Barry's lingered on Eléna. It was so ironic. Now that he wanted so much to see her – for he was no longer trying to subdue his feelings – now that he was residing at her home, he saw nothing of her. He never even heard her voice. He felt cut off, and helpless. He knew it was foolish to feel that way, but how else was he to respond when the object of his dreams was just a flight of steps away – fifteen feet that may well have been fifteen miles.

There were times when he could not bear it. In the mornings, before he left for the fields, when the dawn lingered softly like a lover's kiss, stirring his desires, or in the evenings, when his self-control, his decorous good sense and patient understanding were weakened by the urgent sensuousness of the tropical night. Or on a day like this one, enticed by the drone of the rain. At these times he would succumb to the languorous mood that gnawed away at his restraints. Then he would gaze at the tempting, offending stairs with a dangerous glint in his eyes.

'Doesn't she ever leave her room, Yei?' he had asked, 'It's been almost a week now. Does she eat?'

'Don't worry, Barry, she'll soon come round, it's necessary to mourn. She . . . oh nothing.'

'What is it?' He waited. 'Are you more worried than you'd like to admit?' he coaxed.

'No. It's not that . . . although I can see that you are very concerned about her, maybe too much so . . .' The woman of unshakable dignity looked at him with steady eyes as if she saw through to his soul. 'But no. I was only thinking of my premonitions from the first day I saw that child and again on the day she ran off.'

'Would that you could have changed those events!' sighed Barry.

'I don't know. My intervention might have made it worse. Fate knows best.'

'Anyway, it's all over now, nothing worse can happen,' Barry sighed, looking at her for a confirmation that was unnervingly unforthcoming.

The letter from Barry's father was still unanswered, but there was no longer anything to debate. No, he had not forgotten his grandmother's hopes, but he couldn't live just for that hazy future. Eléna's need was more urgent, his need, was more urgent. He could not ignore his temptestuous feelings, nor the bond of shared experience and shared sorrow, not to mention shared love.

He would make his life here. They would live modestly. He needed only to see Eléna and he would declare himself, profess his love and claim her as his own. Yei was right, just a few days more and she would come round. I sincerely hope so, thought Barry. If not just for my sake, at least for Louis Sauvage's.

That Frenchman of aggressive name and contrasting disposition was obviously very disturbed, particularly by Eléna's indisposition. Unspecified guilt, at having opened a Pandora's box by his decision to marry and leave, was seriously troubling him. The veil of unhappiness that hung over the house only added to his patent unease.

Indeed the house was a very changed place. Carmen was still bedridden, and so was José, while Juanita – who had temporarily taken up residence there – was a subdued version of herself. She had returned with Fred to Millefleurs to arrange things there.

These thoughts raced each other through Barry's mind as he sat on the veranda, looking out at the now lightening rain. He savoured the pungent smell of the damp earth and watched uninterested as the pestilential black grackle birds emerged from the trees, shook the rain drops off their wings and darted aggressively about, clucking tunelessly. They swooped menacingly at the stable boy's head as he crossed the lawn. The black youth aimed a pebble expertly at them, sending the birds screaming in mad circles. Above the uproar came a sudden, equally unpleasant clamour of human noises defiling the morning's peace.

The two gentlemen looked up in unison, jumped to their feet and hurried out onto the soaking lawn to see what the commotion was about.

'Mistress Eléna, Mistress Eléna! Oh God, where she? Mis-tre-ss!' came the importunate wail.

Eléna looked out of her window, and called, 'What is it, Tina?'

'Oh God, Mistress, please come, please come!' the woman shouted, her face a study of distress, her hands raised in supplication. 'I beg yer, Mistress, see if yer could help Rosa, do.'

Eléna appeared at the kitchen door. Barry started at the sight of her. In the few days since he had seen her, Eléna had become drawn and almost emaciated. Her cheekbones were more pronounced, a pained, dull expression had possession of her eyes. Her lovely hair, given perfunctory attention, was pulled severely back on her head, leaving her beautiful face stark and vulnerable.

'Tina, what is wrong with Rosa? Is it the baby?'

'Don't take it too hard, Mistress, I beg you I had to call you.'

'Say what is wrong, woman,' commanded Louis.

'Please tell me what has happened, Tina.' Eléna's voice held a dangerous hint of hysteria.

Barry, listening with the intimate knowledge of a lover, noted it with growing apprehension. He would have intervened, but the slave woman began her explanation.

'Mistress, the slave they holding for attacking you all is the same man – Rosa child-father. They have him in the gaol to hang today. Rosa onliest find out that this morning.'

'But why? Why would he attack us?'

Barry saw the wild look in Eléna's eyes. With determination he marched up to the little group and interrupted. 'Please, Eléna, you must go back inside. Let us handle this.'

'No, no, Barry. I'm all right. I want to hear the true story from Rosa's own lips. She could not have known before hand. Poor Rosa!' Eléna pushed her way through the small throng of slaves. Barry and Louis stuck close to her.

'Why did Rosa's man attack the La Flores?' interjected Barry.

'Massa, Rosa onliest crying but she have something to do with it, 'cause is she who tell him about you all being in the last carriage to the wedding.'

'Wait a minute,' exclaimed Louis. 'You mean our Rosa colluded with her man, François? You remember I mentioned him to you, Barry? I tried to arrange for him to be with Rosa but his master refused, the royalist dog!'

'So François decided to take matters into his own hands, is that it, Tina?' Barry asked, steadying Eléna over a rut in the path, and noting how very shaky she was.

'Massa, all I know is they planning to hang him today and Rosa feel the Mistress like the child so much and do so much for he to born that she ain't go let them hang he father.'

'I'm afraid it's too late to save him,' interjected M. Louis. 'I've already made enquiries. Picton isn't going to be persuaded this time. François is scheduled to be executed at noon today – my God, about this time too.'

Eléna gasped, and Barry felt her weight rest heavily on him. He wished she would not go on this mission. He searched for a way to caution her, but could find none. He kept silent, supporting her with the strength of his arm.

The procession finally arrived at the slaves' huts, nearing the one in which Eléna had spent a long, tiring night just one week ago. Like that Saturday, the air was filled with the disturbing wail of Rosa's strident voice, made worse today as it combined with the breathless screams of the child.

'Let me speak to Rosa alone,' insisted Eléna, pulling out of Barry's grasp.

'No, I'm coming with you.' Barry's manner brooked no argument.

The crying increased as Rosa saw Eléna, and started bemoaning her fate. Barry stood protectively behind, tense with apprehension.

'Oh Mistress! Mistress!' The slave was seated on the bed with the baby in the crook of her arm. She rocked her body uncontrollably. Her short hair was wild and uncombed and added to her look of frenzy. 'Please help him, Mistress. He did get shot. He couldn'ta come for me. I now find out . . .'

'So it's true! I didn't believe it. I couldn't believe it. *You*, Rosa . . .'

'I beg you, Mistress. He never mean to harm you all . . .'

'You, Rosa, you of all people . . .'

'No-oo, Mistress, he onliest want the horses to take me with mi big belly. Them did done plan they thing long time. I couldn't tell . . .'

'To plot and conspire against us!' continued Eléna. Her voice rose and fell in jerky, emotional spurts, her movements were becoming disjointed. She passed her hands over her eyes, she brushed back her perfectly neat hair, sucking in her breath in choking sobs.

'I couldn't tell nobody, oh God, Mistress!' continued Rosa, crying in anguish, hanging her head, covering her face with her free hand. The baby, but for its persistent wail, was lost in the folds of the confused garments and beddings that enveloped her.

Barry took hold of Eléna and led her outside, ignoring the protests of the woman. 'Monsieur, let us go back home,' he called to M. Louis.

'Yes, yes. You take 'ti Marie home right away. I will deal with the woman now.' Louis marched determinedly through Rosa's doorway. Outside, Barry tried to lead his charge back down the pathway but the sound of Rosa's screaming seemed to shake Eléna once more. 'Let's sit down, Barry. Let me catch my breath. Here on this bench.' They did so. Eléna began to speak, all the while glancing nervously back to Rosa's door.

'I don't know what to make of it, Barry. To think that Rosa, Rosa would . . . What did we do wrong? I can't even understand why Tessa had to die. Everything is happening in the wrong way. Nothing makes sense, nothing . . .'

'Eléna, you're not thinking clearly. It seems illogical, but that is the tragedy of the . . . of the times. You're forgetting that this is a slave society. As much as some of us try, we are part of it. Those people are slaves, they cannot all have the loyalties of a Tessa or the loyalties we expect of free men. It's not just the guilty that suffer when the sores of this rotten system erupt. Anyone can suffer, the more innocent, the more vulnerable. Only the heartless remain unscathed.'

'But it's too hard, too hard!' cried Eléna, averting her face.

M. Louis appeared, walking sadly away from Rosa's door and down towards them. The Frenchman lifted his hands in a gesture of helplessness, saying, 'I had to tell her it was hopeless, that the deed was already done and she had better look to herself and her child. She has quieted down now. Come, 'ti Marie, you've enough sorrows without adding this one to them. Let's go back to the . . .'

A blood-chilling wail rented the air.

'What? What now?'

'Good Lord, that Tina again!'

'Wait here, Eléna. We will go and see.'

'No! I'm coming too!' Eléna raced after the gentlemen. 'What, what is it, Barry? Monsieur, what is wrong now?' She pushed her way past the men, and saw Rosa prostrate on the bed with the baby apparently feeding at her breast. 'She's fainted! Take her out of here! Let her get some air!'

'Woman, stop that noise! Eléna, take the baby,' commanded Barry.

Tina would not stop her hysteria. 'Mistress, she season, Mistress! Tell she nah, Massa!' she cried, appealing to M. Louis and Barry in turn.

Barry ignored her ravings. He manoeuvred the woman out of the door. As she picked up the baby, Eléna's mind seemed to register on Tina's words.

'Tina, speak plainly! What do you mean?' she cried.

'She done gone, Mistress. She season sheself.'

'No, no! Barry, is she alive?' Eléna called, understanding finally dawning.

'Don't come any closer, Eléna. It's too late. She's dead already – examine the baby,' answered Barry.

Eléna looked down at the perfectly still child in her arms. She fumbled frantically with it, feeling for a heartbeat, trying to prise its mouth open and make it vomit the poison. It was too late. Eyes wild and half-crazed, she persisted in her attempts and then, turning helplessly to Barry, she crumpled like a piece of paper and fell to the ground. Barry snatched the lifeless child from her arms and handed it hastily to Louis, and lifting Eléna easily in his arms he walked swiftly back to the house.

She lay unconscious in his arms. She had finally succumbed to the repeated violation of her sensitive mind. Her spirit appeared to struggle no more.

As they neared the house, a small cry was heard. Yei, dropping her basket of herbs, hastened towards her daughter, terror imprinted on her face.

Long moments of confusion followed. It seemed to Barry that the air became thick and suffused with panic and chaos. Hasty movements seemed dream-like and ineffective, as if a stupor of paralysis had overcome everyone. Louis managed to direct Barry to the couch in the living-room. He explained to Yei what had happened while she, with trembling hands, succeeded in reviving Eléna, who eventually opened her eyes. Those large, round eyes, once opened, were glazed and unseeing, and stared absently with the distrait gaze of an unfocused mind.

With Barry's help, Yei was able to get a warm liquid down her throat. At length Eléna closed her eyes again. Barry lifted her up the stairs to her room, and laid her on her bed. Yei thanked him, and ushered him out. He left, walking dazedly down the stairs, leaving Yei to see to her daughter's comforts.

'In a little while she will be back to her old self. Give her time to heal,' said Yei the next day.

Barry nodded, afraid of the emotion that would show in his voice, but his face already spoke volumes to the strange and wise woman. She saw the grim set of his mouth, the tension around his piercingly blue eyes and the involuntary throbbing in his temples.

'Listen, my son, when she is better, promise me you will not discuss anything emotional with her . . . not for a while. Do you understand? The deaths are not the only concerns of the heart she has, you see.'

Barry's eyes widened questioningly, but he still did not speak. He thrust his hands in his trouser pockets, mumbled an incoherent assent and strode out of Yei's presence into the grounds. He went to the garden shed and collected a cutlass, which he used to clear pathways for himself through the bushes. He proceeded to walk aimlessly for a long time, like a lost soul.

He climbed one of the hills surrounding the estate and sat for hours. Then he used his cutlass to pick a bunch of small red, berry-like fruits off a native palm tree whose trunk was as thorny as life now seemed to him. There in the shade he ate the scant meat of the tiny gris gris nuts. Eventually his mind turned from thoughts of Eléna and flashed to those of his black counterpart Fist. He sighed heavily. He missed Fist, and wondered what he was up to in his own misery and self-enforced solitude.

# CHAPTER SIXTEEN

## I

Fist ran quickly up the steep slope, a crooked stick in one hand and a razor-sharp cutlass in the other. He was thankful for the sturdy boots that Barry had given him. True, his feet were as tough as leather, but this was jungle, real rain forest, hard to see under foot – and worse, this was Trinidad, land of snakes.

Just a bit further, he surmised. He plodded on, until finally the scent of cooking wafted on the wind. He quickened his footsteps, moving soundlessly on the padded carpet of thick undergrowth. A large mahogany tree loomed overhead, and beneath it now was a small clearing, and there, at last, the Amerindian camp.

'Welcome,' said the cacique, speaking in Spanish. Fist answered hesitantly, his Spanish none too good. The man gestured to Fist to join him.

'You learn anything more? You decided on anything?'

Fist leaned back against a tree and spoke slowly. 'I find out they send him in the south.'

'You're going to look for him, then?'

'Soon. First I want to learn how to use the weapon.'

The man called out and a strapping youth emerged, from the nearby *ajoupa*, his golden-brown skin smooth and glistening in the sunlight, his straight black hair with its rounded cut sitting like an overturned bowl on his well-shaped head.

'This is my son,' the man said, 'he is very good with the bow. He will be your teacher.'

'Your business finish here?' asked Fist.

The man nodded. 'Yes, we leave in a short while, after we have eaten, to return to Quinam. We go down to the marshes, then by piragua on the sea to the south.'

'Is a large village?'

'No.' The man laughed ruefully. 'No more of those. No more people, just my small tribe, a handful of us. We hide from the white man. But for how long, eh?' The question caused him some thought. For a few moments he stared into the distance.

'I surprise you still surviving so,' commented Fist. 'You real lucky they ain't pack you in a mission.'

'Not luck, brains.' The man grinned, his face breaking into a thousand wrinkles, like a dried fruit or the fallen *bois canno* leaves that wrinkled in curious patterns and were to be found all over the forest floor.

The meal ready, they ate in silence, affording Fist a chance to reflect on his timely meeting with the Amerindian. They had unexpectedly chanced upon each other, scaring each other half to death. Both had been shunning the company of other men by camping far up on the forested hills around Port of Spain. They had bristled like frightened animals, tense, suspicious of the other's next move.

Fist had been the first to speak. He had ventured a few words in his French patois but the Indian answered in Spanish. Thankfully, Fist had caught the meaning of the words. Afterwards they relaxed, and shared their reasons for seeking isolation. They had parted friends. Another chance meeting, days later, had improved their acquaintance.

The Amerindian had been hunting. Fist stayed with him as he moved stealthily towards a brilliantly green reptile. It was the first time Fist had ever seen an iguana. But for the keen eye of the Amerindian, he would have missed the spectacle, so well camouflaged it had been among the leaves.

The man took careful aim with his bow and the reptile was killed.

'We will eat well today,' said the cacique, pleased with himself. It was then that Fist decided to ask him for the lessons.

Fist was looking forward to the experience. The last few weeks had been filled with his persistent personal grief, and worse, with the horror of the treatment of those rebellious slaves. They had been kept in the stifling heat of the *cachots brûlants* and then tortured even more deliberately by that Begorrat, before their execution.

It was said that in the art of torture, the royalist Martiniquans could rival the devil himself in cruelty. Fist had seen the truth of that statement. The reality of those executions clung to his mind, lingering in his nostrils and in his ears, and combined with the pain in his aching heart to make the black man unable to think of anything but his hatred for the General and his sinister friend.

'Come, friend, we are ready,' said the cacique. They dismantled the *ajoupa*, cleared away all evidence of their stay and, gathering their few belongings, set off down the mountain.

## II

The days blended into weeks. The raw edge of revulsion and horror at Picton's atrocities towards Rosa's ill-fated lover and his cohorts began to grow dull in the minds of the population. Christmas came and went uneventfully, and the new year dawned.

The dark fog of uncertainty that enshrouded the house at Santa Clara, like black funeral curtains, lingered on. Then, imperceptibly, the curtain stirred. A new breeze was finally beginning to blow. Occasionally, laughter could once more be heard, or the less familiar exclamations of loving young motherhood, for Carmen was much improved. True, Juanita looked wan and tired, and her small oval face was pale from lack of sun, but she had held up beyond everyone's expectations to the demands of the crisis.

Then there was Yei, never daunted, even in the face of this landslide of travail. She was busily alert, keeping the house alive with her persistent hope, fervour and deceptively unruffled energy.

And Eléna had begun to improve. She had tottered precariously on the brink of a deep pool of mindlessness, and knocked at the entrance to a region where mind and body parted company at the door, but her inner strength and natural resilience had forced her back. She had slipped, but she had not fallen.

Sensing that the death of the baby had been like the loss of hope to her, her family was very protective of her. Carmen and Juanita felt she was not well enough to resume normal life but when they appealed to Yei, she merely shook her head sadly saying noncommittally, 'Who can stop Eléna? *Que sera, sera, muchachas.*'

As expected, the three women were not able to confine Eléna for much longer, and the day finally came when she descended the stairs. When Barry returned home for his midday meal on the said day, therefore, he was beside himself with happiness to see his velvet lady once more, the first time in weeks.

Barry, M. Louis, Mark, Juanita, Eléna and Carmen sat at the luncheon table. Even José and the new baby were present. It was a meeting of pure joy for Barry and Eléna. In the midst of the large company, Barry could say or do little to express his delight. He reached out with his smile and beamed warmth and welcome on the pale and still shaky figure of his beloved. She basked in the sunshine of that smile, and responded with a timorous one of her own.

That meal marked a watershed in their lives, and Barry was always to remember it as a brief golden moment when the world was benevolent, and all cares were forgotten in the comfort he felt at seeing Eléna well once more. He felt the harmony between them. They were encased in a private, iridescent bubble, too beautiful and delicate perhaps to withstand the rough treatment of the world, but strong enough to bind by its sheer beauty, and powerful enough to give them strength for any trials ahead.

It was a grand reunion. They were all together for the first time in weeks. To add to the perfection of that halcyon hour, Fred also arrived. Warm and hearty were the greetings and exclamations, the hugs and handshakes. The conversation and general palaver were like music, punctuated by the dulcet gurgles of the happy infant in their midst.

Barry said little and, like Eléna, was content to respond with smiles and pleasant agreements as they savoured the wonder of the hour.

At length the meal was over, and the gathering broke up. Barry lingered, and drew Eléna aside. Eyes sparkling with suppressed emotion, he ventured, 'Could we sit a while on the veranda, perhaps? For just a minute?' He smiled encouragingly.

'For just a minute,' she agreed, returning the smile. He led her out and saw that she was comfortably seated before he spoke.

'Oh, Eléna,' he began drawing out the words, turning her name into a sigh. 'You don't know how good it is to see you, just to see you, after so long.'

'Did you miss me that much?' she laughed, a tinkling, bell-like laugh that was music to his ear.

He stared at her, lips pursed in satisfaction, and rocked his head in wonderment. 'I've done nothing but pray for this moment. How *are* you?'

'I'm afraid I gave you rather a scare. But I am fully recovered now. It was . . .'

'No, you don't have to talk about it. Let's not think about it even, not yet perhaps.'

'No, Barry. It's all right. No one wants to talk about my collapse. No one but me.' She chuckled ironically. 'So talking about it is a relief, not a burden. You at least should understand that.'

He nodded. 'You are amazing, Eléna. Yes. I do understand. I admire you so much . . . I've felt so helpless, so useless these past few weeks, unable to do anything to help you.'

'Oh no. Let me tell you, you were the biggest help of all and I don't mean by the flowers you sent up to me every day or . . .'

'How then?'

'You know it was my stubbornness, my arrogance, that caused the collapse . . .'

'Your innocence, Eléna. Only that I may concede.'

'Well, you are kind . . .' She lowered her eyes in momentary embarrassment.

'Listen, dear lady, please don't feel badly, you've nothing to . . .'

'Barry, let me finish before I lose the nerve. That . . . that day, when I collapsed and for a few days after, my mind seemed unable to deal with the tragedies, the . . . the finalities of so many deaths. Don Diego, the death of my little Tessa, the little baby . . . In my arrogance – or innocence, as you so kindly suggest – I felt almost responsible on the one hand, and on the other, the whole thing, everything, was incomprehensible, intolerable.

'There was nothing to ease my torment, no salve. It seemed I alone felt the crushing blow of the deaths and the betrayal. I . . . I don't know if what I'm saying is making sense, but I felt guilty of scolding Rosa, of not listening to Tessa, of not stopping Papa Diego. I felt betrayed too . . . betrayed and alone. And I felt no one could understand or comfort me. Most of all, I could not understand and I could not make it better. It was as if my mind had been assaulted or thrown suddenly into a strange, unknown world.

'Then I thought of you, and I remembered your words to me that day, and I knew you did not see the events like everyone else, that you understood more deeply; not philosophically like Yei, or politically, like M. Louis, but with emotion. I held on to you . . . oh . . . to that thought, and to your words. Hard as it was, I began to see that there was logic in all the awful things that had happened, and that the universe had not suddenly gone berserk, but that I had not been living in the real world. That innocence that you spoke of is a useless quality in this society, perhaps not for everyone, but it certainly is a liability for someone like me, whose place and role isn't prescribed.'

'Eléna, you shouldn't be hard on yourself. The reality is harsh, but you have been sheltered and protected, in a way, all your life, haven't you?'

She smiled ruefully. 'Yes. But I didn't know it. For years I have been investigating this reality, discussing burning questions with anyone who would take me seriously. I thought I understood . . . and more, I thought that reality would never touch Santa Clara! Ha! In my arrogance, I thought I could prevent it. My type of logic is for a different time and place. I finally understand. I know that I'm not going to break down again. I have to live. I have to take my own advice to Rosa. I have to survive and I thank you. For yours was the one clear voice that penetrated my nightmare.'

'My God,' whispered Barry in a voice filled with awe. He reached for her. His hand on her arm, he continued tenderly, 'You are wonderful. I understand you so well. You are perfection itself, dear, beautiful lady. I have so much to say to you.'

'I knew you would understand. But let's not talk any more today. There is my mother waving at me from the living-room. I fear she is thinking I'm over exerting myself. She is probably right.'

His eyes pleaded with her but, conceding, he squeezed her arm meaningfully and released her. He stood looking lovingly at her retreating figure.

Yei spoke briefly to her daughter as she passed her, on the way up to her bedroom, then she turned and approached Barry. 'My son,' she began soberly, 'she looks well, but I want to remind you not to forget your promise. Do not tempt her. Oblige me in this.'

'But I would never say anything to harm Eléna. I . . . I may do her more harm by not declaring my . . . Yei, we . . . we . . .'

'Patience, Barry.'

'But Yei, you know. You know how I feel . . .'

'There is what I know, there is what I sense. Trust me.'

He lowered his head and turned away. The older woman moved off in dignified silence. Barry cursed under his breath and smote the veranda rail with his palm. He had tacitly promised her that day, weeks ago and he would have to abide by that commitment. His face set grimly, he marched out of the house and headed towards the plantation.

# III

Fist eased himself into the dull topaz waters and swam gracefully out into the ocean. His long black limbs cut lazily at the surface, then he turned on his back and kept himself afloat with slow back strokes as he gazed dreamily up at the aquamarine sky.

Not a day had passed when he did not think, as he did now, about his gay, playful little lady, and the tragic end to which she had come. But he had been happy here with the Indians. True, they could not be said to live in luxury, as they claimed their ancestors did, but they caught plenty of fish, even had a small corral where they kept a ready stock, and there was always cassava. They were good, hospitable people, generous enough even to offer him a woman, somebody's wife! But his grief would not allow him to accept.

He looked up at the azure sky. He was saying farewell to these few weeks of peace. His tortured mind welcomed the rough days ahead. He was prepared to go forth like a willing bridegroom to his fate. Death was no threat, no deterrent, but failure would be.

He turned and swam back to shore, shook the water from his hair and sat on the beach looking out at the horizon. His black back, still faintly scarred by some forgotten whip, glistening in the rising sun. The tide was coming in. A wave sped up on the brown sand. Fist smiled, looking at a little bird running from the menacing tide. The water soon reached him too, licking at his bare toes, nudging him away. He sighed, rose, and made his way back to the camp. He dressed and packed his few belongings in his old sack, and slung the bow over his shoulder.

Fist had said goodbye to the old Amerindian, smoking one last *bois canno* pipe with him and listening to his cautioning words. 'Don't look for death, my son. Retribution is an illusion, only time will ease the pain.' He had left the jungle hours ago, bypassing the mission village of Siparia. He walked until he was in full view of the Naparima Hill. Once in the small town of San Fernando, he immediately started making discreet enquiries.

It wasn't very long before he located who he wanted. He watched him from a distance for a few days. He noted where he spent his nights. On the third day, Fist set his plan in motion.

He squatted patiently in the bushes, watching the track carefully. All around the jungle encroached. There were no houses near by, but he could see lights flickering in the distance on the hillsides. Now he could hear the rustle of feet above the drone of the crickets and frogs. No, it was no one, maybe an animal. Fist kept very still. A nocturnal agouti, eyes gleaming in the faint moonlight, met his gaze briefly, before scurrying away in fright.

Fist waited. He wished he could light up some tobacco to help while away the time, but he could not risk alerting the man to his presence. He stood up slowly, easing his cramped limbs. Then he saw a light drawing near. Crouching once more, he smiled knowingly. The light shone on the man's face just long enough for him to be sure that it was the person he sought.

He allowed the man to pass, then he moved stealthily down, coming up behind him. He pounced. The man did not know what hit him. Acting with great power and speed, Fist gripped him around the neck. He pinioned one of his hands behind his back. In the same instant he swung him to the right, slamming him hard against an embankment. In shock and surprise, the man could not struggle. Fist unrelentingly slammed him again and again until finally he stopped and dragged him off into the woods. Despite the darkness, for the man's flambeau had long since fallen and spluttered out, Fist knew his way. He stopped finally and tied his unconscious victim securely to a tree trunk. Only then did he sit down. He leaned his head back and waited for the dawn.

# IV

Eléna had to admit that it was her fault. She was the one who had stopped Barry from talking the first day. Now it was a week later, and he had said nothing. Nothing that she wanted to hear, at least, nothing that she longed to hear, or that she had secretly expected. She was sadly disappointed and disturbed. She knew he loved her. The way he looked at her, the tenderness in his voice, his every small gesture of concern spoke the words his lips would not utter. They had met every day and talked, and emotion sometimes overwhelmed them, at least it did her. Yet he hesitated, almost as if he were biting back the words.

'I know what it means,' she said to herself, 'he has to leave. That is why. But what do I care? Now that he's here, this is the only time we've got. And he's wasting it. Oh, fie on all honourable men!'

She leaned her forehead on the windowpane, feeling the cool of the glass against her skin, and watched distractedly as her breath caused a slow fog to spread, blurring her view of the outside. With her index finger she idly drew a pattern in the misty glass. Through that one clear spot she saw a lone soldier, like a fairy-tale hero, come riding up. He

189

looked so unreal. Lost in her own melancholy world, she simply stared lazily, enchanted by the picture-book quality of the image. Then, quickly snapping out of her stupor, she wiped the glass clean and realised that André had come calling.

Quickly adjusting her gown and patting her hair in place, she went down and out on the veranda to meet him.

André was extremely glad to see her again and for some time he spoke of nothing but his concern for her. Presently he came to the point.

'Eléna, I'm afraid you have been through a great deal. I wish it could have been avoided. I wish you would allow me to take care of you.'

'Oh André, what am I to say?'

'Seriously, Eléna. You know of my deep feelings for you. You can't imagine how frightened your recent upset had made me, how frightened of losing you.'

'But André, this is not the time or place . . .'

'Then tell me when, Eléna. Tell me when or where?'

She shifted uncomfortably in her chair. 'Please, André, it is no use.'

'Don't say that, Eléna. You haven't given me a chance. You never gave our relationship a fair chance to develop. Ever since that awful day years ago, you've turned away from me. Is it that the cruel touch of those white men turned you against all men?'

'No, no it's not that. Actually, I recovered from the assault very quickly. I never . . . I never thought of them as . . . as men . . . wanting me as a woman. Only as cruel depraved beasts. I don't think they saw me any differently from how they saw the slave they were torturing. I was just another black body on which to commit an atrocity. You don't understand, André.'

'Then explain to me, Eléna. Tell me what it is. Is there someone else? . . . The Englishman, perhaps?'

'André, don't make this difficult for me.'

'Eléna, I . . . this is not the way I planned it. I know this is hardly the proper way to proceed, but I . . . I'd better make a clean breast of it now that I've begun. I love you, Eléna, and I'm asking you to marry me, to become my wife.'

'But André, I can't!'

'It is my fondest hope that you will consider it, and change your mind. You know there is no future for you with a foreigner. At least, please say you will think about it.' He took her hand and held her limp and tremulous fingers in his.

Eléna tried to explain that what he hoped for could never be. But what could she say? That she was bound by a hopeless love for another man, a man whom she suspected returned her regard, but who could not even acknowledge his feelings for her? She could not raise her head to meet his demanding, imploring eyes. Tears threatened her, instead, and to add to her utter misery, the sound of voices and approaching footsteps reached her.

André quickly released her hand and tried to adopt a nonchalant pose, but when Barry and M. Louis entered it was quite obvious to them that they had interrupted an intimate scene. Barry's eyes grew hard, his lips tightened and his breathing became short. He stared at the couple in grim silence. Fortunately, Louis had the presence of mind to take the situation in hand. He greeted the Frenchman heartily and enquired after his health. Barry merely mumbled something incoherent, offered a slight bow, excused himself and made to leave, but not before Eléna raised her lovely head and glanced up at him with pained, accusing eyes. That look touched his soul and forced him to turn abruptly away. His anger was suddenly transformed into a fear as violently disturbing as the paroxysm of coughing that overcame André. Barry made his escape.

Once in his room, he dragged off his working clothes, dressed himself in riding gear and stormed out of the house by the back door. He saddled his horse and rode like a crazed man out of the precincts of Santa Clara.

At length he slackened his pace and trotted into Port of Spain, heading directly for the Guest House of the Royal Palms. He would spend the night here and think carefully of how to approach Yei, and plan to be firm in carrying out this resolution. He could wait no longer, obviously neither could Eléna, nor André. He had to declare himself. First thing in the morning he would do so, by then his plan would be clear to him. The next time he saw Eléna, it would be to put an end, finally, to their mutual suffering.

He entered the gate, gave his horse to the care of a young servant boy and strode into the courtyard.

'M. Barry?' said the landlady, incredulously. 'Speak of the devil! This is so strange. I've just been talking about you. Did you not hear your ears ringing? An old sailor came here to deliver a message to you. Why don't you go and look for him. The shameless man told me he could be found at the 'British Coffee House', that notorious brothel! I'll see you when you come back – you're spending the night?'

'Oh yes, spending the night,' he affirmed distractedly. He opened the gate and stepped out.

In no time at all he had walked to the coffee house and located the old sailor Carty from Barbados. 'How are you, Carty? What is it this time? A note from my uncle?'

'No Guv. 'Tis another from yer honourable father, it is. From 'is Lordship 'imself.'

'Yes?' A frown appeared on Barry's tanned brow and a twinge of guilt pricked his heart, for he had not as yet answered his father's last letter.

'The good man, yer uncle, that is, 'as instructed me to obtain a satisfactory response to this 'ere missive, or else!'

'Let me have it,' demanded Barry, suddenly growing serious.

'Why yes,' chuckled the old sailor, ''Ere I am jawin' on an' on, 'an I ain't even give it you yet.' He handed it over.

In frowning concentration, Barry took the letter from Carty's hand. 'Well, thank you.' He tapped the envelope against his palm and turned to leave, but Carty caught him by the arm. ''Old on there a minute, Guv. I've to speed 'ome to Bridgetown tonight. My instructions are fer you read it right away, and give me a message to take back. I'm to report a *satisfactory response*, to be precise.'

'Very well. Barry's voice came hoarsely from a dry, constricted throat. 'Walk with me over to the guest house – I'll read it there.'

'Lead the way, Guv,' replied the old sailor jauntily and he immediately fell into step with Barry's purposeful stride.

Once there, the landlady offered the sailor a seat in the courtyard, and ushered Barry to the room he had requested for the night. Barry closed the door behind him and leaned back wearily against it. Then with tense fingers he ripped open the envelope and dropped it uncaringly on the floor, as he slowly unfolded two leaves of crossed paper, and read with rapidly increasing heartbeat:

Barry,

This letter follows one I wrote several months ago and to which I have not as yet received a reply.

I pray to God that this one reaches you speedily wherever you are. I have instructed my uncle to read this, and to do everything in his power to ensure that you are aware of its contents, for from his recent letter I gather you are no longer with him.

In my last letter, I informed you that it was now safe for you to return home, that all charges had been dropped. The details, in case you do not know them as yet, can now wait until I see you. The purpose of this letter is far more urgent and important. I expect an immediate response.

Since there is no way to soften the blow, let me state it directly. My mother is extremely ill. Son, your grandmother is dying. She has suffered two serious strokes in rapid succession. The doctors

192

hold out little hope for her. At the time of this writing, there appears to be one slim thread keeping her alive and defying the doctor's most dire predictions. That is the hope, very much alive in her, even before the attacks, of seeing you very soon.

I urge you now to make haste. Take the first ship home. I have faith that she will hold out to see you, for her will is as strong as iron, even if her body is all too frail.

Your name is the only word that leaves her lips, for the stroke affected her speech, and words do not come easily to her. You can well imagine the distress of our entire family. Your presence during this trying time will be an enormous help to us all. I need say no more; I expect you home in the next few weeks.

     Your loving father.

Barry threw back his head and groaned. He squeezed his eyes shut and distorted his mouth in a grimace of agony. A moment later, he stumbled over to the bed and sat down heavily, his head cupped in his palms, his breathing harsh and rapid.

Thoughts criss-crossed his mind with frightening rapidity as he fought for an alternative to the terrible summons from his father, and tried to grasp the awful tragedy that had hit his beloved grandmother.

It seemed that the world had suddenly grown dull and infinitely gloomy. Finally he dropped his hands and raised his head. He thought of Yei and how right she had been in forestalling his proposal. He took a deep breath and ran his fingers through his dishevelled hair. He poured some water from a ewer and washed his face. Then with his head high, he opened the door, and walked steadily out to meet Carty.


# V

'Sitting here with you reminds me of that last time. It seems so long ago. So much has happened since.' M. Louis frowned and looked with deep concern at his young companion. 'Ah, 'ti Marie, my sensitive little flower, I worry so about you.'

'There is no need to, Monsieur.' Eléna smiled up at Louis as he sat next to her under the immortelle, by the stream.

He returned the smile, but continued in the same vein. ''ti Marie, my little 'ti Marie!' He sighed. 'You do not know the half of it, the truth of my . . . my.'

'Isn't it time we two brought your secret into the open?'

Louis looked at her in surprise. He said hesitantly, 'You know? How?'

193

'I simply guessed it one day while talking to Mark.'

'Oh my darling!' He hugged her closely. 'It was not possible for us to tell you when you and Carmen were children. It's all so complicated. You must have so many questions. It will be good to make a clean breast of it now, most of all, it will be so good to finally call you daughter.'

'Monsieur, it is not as strange for me as you think. The questions and answers can wait. You have never shirked your responsibility towards Carmen and me. You have been a wonderful father. No. What I want us to talk about is not the past. Let's talk about your marriage, about the future.'

Louis released her and looked questioningly at her beautiful face, observing the signs of her recent indisposition in the slimness of her cheeks and the prominence of her bones.

'My dear, I have another confession to make.' Louis hesitated. Kathy and I have exchanged our vows already, some weeks ago. We did it quietly, never wishing to repeat anything that faintly reminded us of the last aborted wedding plans.'

'Oh Monsieur, I am so glad! That is indeed the best news I've had in a long while.' She squeezed his arm lovingly. 'When will you be leaving then? How soon?'

'Kathy is ready to leave at a moment's notice but I was not sure when I could, not until I had spoken to you, anyway.'

'I knew it! It's all my fault!'

''ti Marie, listen. Not even Kathy means more to me than you . . . and Carmen too, but you are special.'

'Monsieur, I love you so!'

'And I love you, my darling, darling daughter.' They embraced once more and Louis kissed her softly on the forehead.

'Then you will be leaving soon? No more delays now!'

'The political situation in the island is not very easy. I cannot go with an easy mind.'

'I have a question for you on the subject of politics, Monsieur.'

'When did you not have such a question?' teased Louis.

'Did Carmen and I keep you from your revolution, from fighting for republicanism?'

'Oh no, *ma chérie*. Because of you I would have liked to be active, to have helped make the country and the world safer for coloured people, for my precious babies. Had I remained in France or even in Grenada . . . oh well. But conditions here never ripened, never until now. But who can fight Picton? Whatever posterity may say about him, Don

Chacon was a benevolent governor, whose only fault was an exaggerated fear of the spectre of republicanism.

'But what is a revolutionary? I rather hope that I have absorbed the ideology, in such a way that my whole life reflects it. So, my darling,' Louis pinched her chin, 'Perhaps I have only helped to influence four wonderful young minds here at Santa Clara. *Ça suffit, n'est-ce pas?*'

Louis sighed, and Eléna felt there was a note of something less than resignation in that small wistful breath. He continued, "'ti Marie, 'ti Marie, will you keep your door closed from all trouble when I'm away? You are so vulnerable, even like this island.' He regarded his daughter intently, his fiery eyes searching her lovely face. 'When you were seventeen, I was able to save you, but now this . . . this violation of your mind . . . I feel so helpless.'

'No, no, Monsieur, I am stronger and much more realistic now.'

'Realistic yes, but in losing your innocence, don't reject all idealism. Without it one can become bitter and cynical. Remember that.'

'I will, Monsieur. You worry too much,' she laughed.

'*Eh bien!* Then I will go tomorrow and arrange the passages. We will sail on the first available ship.'

## VI

A few days had passed and Barry had not returned. Eléna was convinced that his non-appearance had some connection with her and the encounter with André. She became restless and upset. Then, M. Louis returned from town to announce at the dinner table that he had obtained passage on a ship that would be leaving Port of Spain in a few days' time. He added, to Eléna's consternation, that young Wingate would also be sailing with them.


It had been a hard period for Barry, a period in which he had had to draw on every ounce of the good sense, discipline and maturity that he had acquired during his meagre twenty-one years of existence. He went through the motions of finding a passage, of appraising Fred of his departure and even of making discreet enquiries about Fist, but inside he was torn apart.

On his bed at the Guest House of the Royal Palms, he hugged his weary body and stared sightlessly. Nothing could defeat the searing passion that burnt in his heart at the very sight of Eléna, yet he had fought valiantly to subdue that passion. Always he had done the honourable thing. Emotionally entrapped as he had been, though, he could not protect his naked, vulnerable heart from that closer, more intimate association with her that had been occasioned by the recent events. Eléna was now part of every waking moment, every nocturnal fantasy, part of every breath he took.

True, their actual moments together had, in retrospect, been so few, but it was not the number but the intensity of their interactions that had enslaved him. They were simply soulmates who shared a common psyche, who instinctively understood each other. For what more could a man ask, he wondered, than to find a woman who thrilled his eyes, and stirred his manhood with her sensuous beauty, and companioned his soul by mirroring it with her own?

In such a large and vastly uncaring world, where cruelty against slave and free man, white or black man, was commonplace, and virtually of no account — certainly unworthy of attention by one of his class and breeding — Barry had discovered that his social life had not warped his soul, his essential being. What would a man with a conscience do in this world with the average English aristocratic miss for a wife? he wondered. A man, moreover, who could find nothing attractive in the missish, milksop girls that he knew would be paraded before him in the marriage market awaiting him in England. He was yet young, but it would not be long before his parents insisted that he marry. What would he do then? Could he learn to settle for less than the best? Less than that one perfect, imperfect woman of his choice?

Could he entertain the hope of returning, of eventually settling all matters in England and coming back to Eléna, or coming back for her, to return there with her? Even if these pipedreams were to come to pass, was there really the possibility that she would wait indefinitely? Was he forgetting the interlude with André? He felt now the terror that had struck his heart then. He knew that Eléna might not be able to withstand the pressure from all sources to accede to the less problematic and more acceptable André.

Barry felt almost feverish with frustration. He cursed fate and banged his head soundlessly against the whitewashed wall. Then he remembered when he had felt a similar frustration. That day on the deck of the *Norfolk*. That day he had cursed the fate that was sending him to the West Indies. That one thought made him grow calm; he felt strangely comforted. There was no predicting the future. The fates had not been as unkind as he had expected. To have met a man like Fred, people of such liberal persuasions as the Santa Clara family, to have shared companionship with a man of the princely stamp of Fist . . . no, the fates had not been unkind, he admitted now. He could not reasonably have been granted greater good fortune, yet he had been. For the greatest good fortune of all was in meeting the woman who matched his heart.

For such good fortune a man must pay. This separation was the price demanded of him. And it was fitting. He owed his grandmother so much. She had been the one clear light in his life. Her influence was much, much more than he could ever calculate. His own mother had been an insubstantial figure in his life, he had not had sisters, or female relatives. Without the Dowager, he would have had no model of womanhood. Always he had found forceful, capable women attractive, and he suddenly realised why. Even Annabella, in her warped way, fell into this category. And now Eléna! There was a similarity between her and the Dowager. Suddenly everything made the merest bit of sense. Suddenly he felt better.

Tomorrow he would rise early and seek out Eléna. He would see her for the last time before he sailed. He would see her in the morning. Perhaps she would walk with him in the gardens, her natural element, the perfect backdrop for this last scene. She would be like a wild flower, a precious gift of nature, and he would savour her beauty and her sensuous fragrance for the last time. Then, playing his part well, he would say goodbye.

# CHAPTER SEVENTEEN

## I

It was very early, too early to awake when the day held only growing despair and disappointment or inevitable sadness and heartbreak. A noise, the drumming of horse's hooves or some knocking at her brain, had awakened her. She opened her eyes and stared at the ceiling.

It was no good indulging herself in pointless longing, she thought. There was only one more day and he would be gone. She would have to snap herself out of these doldrums.

The way to begin was to get out of bed now, busy herself and put a stop to those distressing ruminations. She would take a basket and go off and collect some herbs. It would be pleasant out in the early dawn, and the sun would be up soon. Eléna rose and dressed quietly, not wishing to disturb her mother who was still asleep. Then she tiptoed downstairs, collected her basket from a rack in the kitchen and went into the yard.

The world was just shrugging off the sombre cloak of night, and the day beginning to emerge like a drowsy butterfly from its sleepy cocoon. A fresh new light shimmered delicately on the horizon and seemed to touch Santa Clara with a magical wand, bequeathing to the precious land an aura of gold. Eléna stared in awed silence. She felt herself transported out of the normal pale of her existence, to some mystical time and place where all problems disappeared and all prayers were answered. She made a silent wish and smiled, in spite of her heartache. Chiding herself for her foolishness, she started to walk and before long the sun rose in earnest, diffusing the gold.

She went into the fields and bushes collecting her herbs, and gathering a pretty array of wild flowers. At length, with one arm slung through the handle of her basket and a large bouquet of wild flowers in the same hand, she approached the little stream and walked towards her favourite spot which was hidden just beyond a thick grove of trees. She planned to sit for a while and sort out her medicinal harvest. As she drew near, however, an unexpected sound startled her, and soon an equally unexpected sight greeted her eyes.

The sound was made by a horse grazing lazily nearby, and the sight was the one for which she had longed all week. His back towards her, Barry stood leaning against a tree. His tall, manly form, the muscles rippling beneath skintight riding breeches and neat, close-fitting cutaway jacket, sent her pulses racing. She stood motionless for a moment and feasted her eyes hungrily. Then she clutched her bouquet tightly, took a deep breath and walked up to him.

'Barry, whatever are you doing here this early?' she asked by way of announcing her presence.

He turned in surprise and saw her. 'Eléna!' he half-whispered. He sprang forward and took her free hand.

Eléna gazed unashamedly up at him, thinking that the magic of the morning had not left the earth, for it lingered now in Barry's golden hair and sparkled in his brilliant blue eyes.

'What brings you out so early? I never expected to meet you here,' said Barry.

'Nor me, you. What brings you here?' responded Eléna. She withdrew her hand and turned slightly away.

He kept looking wistfully at her, and replied. 'I . . . I simply wanted to see the place that you liked the best, before . . .'

Eléna turned her back to Barry. She wandered a little way off. She came to the tree under which she had sat to hear so many confidences and she leaned dejectedly against its noble – and to the French immortal – trunk. Unconsciously twisting the stem of a flower from her bouquet, she found herself fighting emotions that seemed intent on surfacing and embarrassing her.

Barry studied her melancholy figure for a long, unnerving moment as if he were also struggling not to betray himself. Then he ventured in a soft, almost tender voice, 'I came this early so I could . . . could tell you of my . . . I believe you have heard that I must return to England?'

Eléna quickly wiped away a disobedient tear, took a deep breath, and turned to face him. 'Yes, M. Louis told us. It is good that you both should sail together, n'est-ce pas?'

Barry gazed at her with a weary eye, suspicious of her too sparkling reply, her too high-pitched voice. 'Yes,' he replied, regarding her keenly with bitter, inexpressible regret in his eyes. 'I came to see you so that . . . so that I could explain, and say goodbye.'

'I have known for a long time that you had to return, Barry. So then this is adieu.' She extended her hand to him bravely in a formal gesture. Barry did not miss the slight tremor in her voice or the unruly quiver of her lower lip.

He took her hand in his but did not shake it as she expected. Instead, he also reached for the hand with the flowers, and stood holding both her hands. He looked unflinchingly at her as if imprinting her features on his mind. Then he threw his head backwards, and looked up at the familiar tropical trees, at the riot of red on the branches of the immortelle and the startlingly blue sky. His chest heaved. He shut his eyes tightly in obvious agony, and spoke. 'Eléna, I must leave, and I cannot, cannot say . . . what I would like to. It . . . it would be no good now. Oh Eléna, I . . . I . . .'

'No!' Eléna snatched her hands away and shouted with an intensity that seemed to arise from some primal source within her. 'No! Why can't you speak? Do you think I am some delicate English lady that I cannot face reality? Look around you. Look at this primitive place! I too am as wild, as warm, as real! Wake up! See me as I am! I can stand it!'

'But Eléna . . .'

'I, too, am struggling against feelings for you, an Englishman! A white man! Words cannot hurt me more than your leaving me without my ever knowing them.'

'But Eléna . . .'

'No! Who can hear you but me?' she continued in her frenzied pace, without pause, even as she choked on her sobs and flailed her hands about wildly. 'Who? These bushes? This immortelle? This stream? The water won't talk. If you tell me in plain words, who will repeat it?'

'Eléna . . .'

199

'Are you to go without true words ever passing between us? Never! We may never meet again. You may never return, and even if you do, where or what will I be, then? Where or when will we ever be alone like this again? Oh Barry, oh Barry, forgive me! Forgive me! I presume too much.' Her hand went to her mouth, and her body shook with anguish. Giving the startled Barry no time to respond, she drew away and rushed off into the undergrowth, flowers and herbs scattered in her wake. She ran in a vain attempt at getting away from him, and hiding her shame. Sheer frustration at his reticence, when he was about to say all the words she so longed to hear, had forced her to divulge more than she ever intended, and certainly more than was ladylike.

She could not escape. Moved by the very emotion that had made her speak out, stimulated by the wonderful implications of her fiery denouncement, Barry shot off after her. He reached her almost immediately and grasped her arm. She struggled blindly, still bent on escape. Both stumbled and fell together on the warm earth.

Any vestige of resolve or resistance that lingered in the mind of either melted as they landed, and the struggle passed without noticeable change into a frenzied clinging of wildly aroused bodies. His lips sought and clung to hers with an intensity that was as akin to an act of violence as it was to one of desperate, hopeless love. Eléna made no protest, but returned his embrace willingly, and Barry knew at that moment that she had cast all caution to the wind and would not reject his advances. It was he who tried to break off. 'Eléna,' he groaned, his voice hoarse with emotion. 'Only say the word, and I will stop. Stop me, Eléna!'

'Don't stop, Barry,' she answered, whispering in his ear.

Eléna was his. With her own free will she gave him her body, and he took her now skilfully, tenderly without further hesitation. Their passion soared, engulfing and transporting them to a private world where nothing and no one else mattered but their united bodies.

Eventually she lay in the crook of his arm, contentedly, and listened to the words of love and of explanation and apology for his recent reticence – words that were food to her starved spirits. But Barry's euphoria soon ended and he grew serious, his voice sad and emotional. He held her close.

'Eléna, I never intended this. How can I leave you now? Oh my darling, I love you so much.' He pressed his lips to her scented hair, his strangled breathing telling more than his words ever could.

When he finally grew calm, he translated his father's letter for her. She listened with increasing seriousness, every word sinking her hopes further but stirring her sympathy for the unknown woman and for the young man who loved her.

'She may be dead already, Eléna and I may be leaving you for nothing.'

'No. Don't think it. Fate cannot be that cruel.' She touched his face tenderly. 'Barry, you'll never forgive yourself if you don't go.'

He drew her against him, embracing her and covering her face with urgent kisses. She responded to his rekindled passion as if drawn by an invisible magnet. The shared passion served only to increase the feeling of desperation in Barry, and once the moment of ecstasy was over, he began again to curse his fate.

It was Eléna who reminded him of Grenmill, asking him to tell her more about the place.

Barry suppressed a sob. He described the beauty of his grandmother's estate, but all he could think of was whether Eléna would ever be able to go there. He clung still to the thought that even in the rules of society there was room for exceptions, even though he knew that those who controlled his destiny would have much to say against his having a coloured wife.

'You describe it with such love. If you are to inherit it, you must go, or you will always regret it.'

'I know you are right, my love, but apart from leaving you, there is so much unfinished here. It goes against the grain to let Tessa's murderers get off so freely. And you have to live on this island too, and feel safe here. How can you, with such atrocities going unchallenged?

'Eléna, listen to me.' He turned her to face him directly. Staring earnestly into her dark eyes, he continued, 'Picton had already proclaimed restrictions on the freedom of blacks and coloured people like yourself. There are the restrictions on the sale of alcohol, and the early curfew. It is a frightening situation. Worse may be still to come. He will use any excuse, particularly that of republican unrest, to clamp down further on your freedom.

'He has no mercy for slaves. Rosa's lover met a horrible death. I feel the horrors are just beginning. Only recently a runaway dropped dead as his ear was removed. I know Picton's attitude is no different towards the free coloureds. He is also allowing the importation of vast numbers of slaves, even though in Britain men are clamouring for the reduction and end of the slave trade. With his unbridled power, and no direct intervention from London, he can do anything. He is bent on turning this country into another Barbados, a so-called thriving plantation society.

'My love, will you be very, very careful? You may not know it, but since Christmas he has stepped up the visibility of the militia. He has been steadily increasing his forces. It's an army now, not just a little militia. He has declared martial law, and now it's the carnival season he is bent on deterring anyone from using the licence of carnival to ferment unrest. Eléna, do you plan to participate in the masquerade in any way?'

'Oh no, my darling. Don't worry. I will be here at Santa Clara.'

'How I hate to leave you at such a time and with M. Louis leaving as well. And to leave without seeing Fist. We came to this island together. I feel like I'm abandoning him. But nobody knows where he is. He has vanished into thin air.'

'There's nothing you can do about these things, Barry. Don't torture yourself so.'

He sat up and gripped her by the shoulders, looking with frightened eyes down at her.

'Keep my father's letter. It has our address. If anything happens write to me immediately in England so that I can come to you as fast as possible.'

'Of course, Barry, don't worry so.'

The morning had passed imperceptibly into afternoon, and suddenly they discovered it was late and that Eléna could not stay out very much longer. They got to their feet but hesitated to say the words of parting. They leaned heavily against each other, voicing silly, random thoughts. Barry's voice was strained as he murmured in her hair, 'There are so many things I wanted to say, to ask . . .'

'Like what, my darling?'

'Foolish little things, like why does Louis call you 'ti Marie.'

'It's because as a child I liked the sensitive plant – the mimosa – and the verse about it – " 'ti Marie, 'ti Marie, close your door, policemen're coming to find you". And, as you know, my full name is Maria Eléna or Marie Hélène.'

'It's a beautiful name, like music in itself. Do you know that I, too, have a pet name for you, a secret name?'

'What is it?'

'Velvet.' He smiled and rubbed his cheek against hers.

'What does it mean?'

'It means your skin is so smooth. It means this man loves you and you must never forget it.'

'Velvet,' she repeated, trying to copy his English accent.

He laughed and held her closer. 'Eléna, it's been the happiest and saddest day of my life, and you are the most wonderful woman in the whole wor—' His words became lost as the sound of migrating parrots, screaming their presence, cut through the quiet.

'Look, Eléna, that makes it perfect! Macaws! Now I know I shall return to you!' He looked down at her and tilted her chin up with his fingertips, so that he could gaze directly into her beautiful dark eyes. 'Don't ever forget, Eléna that I will not rest until the day that you're truly mine. What has happened between us today is only the beginning, the commitment. I don't know how, but one day I'll come back for you.'

They clung together, protective of their last moments, savouring the lingering solace of each other's arms. Then she tore herself away and left, running off through the trees, the tears streaming down her face.

Barry stood a long while in the afternoon sunshine. At length he found his horse, mounted and rode away from Santa Clara, leaving the stately immortelle to carry his passion without comment into eternity, and the lonely little stream to murmur softly on its ceaseless journey to the sea. Perhaps it spoke tonight of the stately brown woman who had grimaced in distress on seeing the saddled horse, and had turned hastily away in confusion. If it did, only the immortelle heard, for no one had lingered to listen.

## II

It was not a long list, and it was not written down anywhere for he could not read or write. The names were indelibly etched on his soul, and Fist was determined to deal with the owner of each name.

He had thought long and hard before he had decided on how to obtain that list. He had laid careful plans. Now, looking back on it, it seemed so easy. Joe, the *alguazil*, had been in no position to deny him any information after having been subjected to a night and a day of terror, tied to a tree trunk in the forests outside San Fernando. Perhaps he had spared the hapless *alguazil*'s life, or perhaps not. He hadn't killed him outright, but he had left him tied in such an isolated spot that only God or luck could free him. 'I let one go, the rest can't escape,' he vowed.

He knew there was no justice in the island. He was a free man now. How could he, as a free man, live with himself and see Tessa's murderers go unchallenged? 'Never!' he swore.

He was a fighting man, but this was no time for heroics. Face to face, they were sure to beat him. Power was on their side. What did it matter how he beat them? Justice was the issue, not honour.

He shifted his weight carefully, and adjusted the bow on his shoulder. Up here, crouched in the mamie apple tree, like a vulture, he was well hidden from view. The shiny dark green leaves were thick and plentiful. He had an excellent view of the roadway too, and had but to stretch his head to see beyond the tall bushes and into the interior of Begorrat's yard. To add to his good fortune, he was well supplied with food. Although the rough, brown skin of the mamie apples was as ugly as the task before him, their insides were as yellow and sweet as revenge. He was prepared to wait.

It was early yet. He had come to Diego Martin on foot during the night. He had not loitered in Port of Spain once he had arrived there, this time making the return journey from San Fernando by the ferry that travelled on the coastal waters. He had skirted the town, stopping only to buy a drink of mauby from a roadside vendor, the bitterness of the drink steeling him for the task ahead. He had remembered the location of Begorrat's estate well. A sob escaped his lips, even now, as he thought of that last day he had been here, and had found Tessa like a discarded plaything cast out for the circling *corbeaux*. And she so afraid of the creatures. 'Well, I is the *corbeau* today, waiting to pounce.'

Dawn had broken some time ago and the sun was rising. His ears caught a sound, and he jerked his head to attention. Every muscle in his body tensed. Yes, there was a rider climbing the hill. A white man with heavy jowls, visible even from up in the tree, he fitted Joe's description. Fist couldn't believe his luck. 'And that was the one man I didn't know how to find,' he smiled. His smile was cold and mirthless. He watched keenly as the man entered Begorrat's gate. The mulatto foreman greeted him by name. They were speaking. If Fist strained his ears and concentrated, he knew he could hear what they were saying. It seemed that Begorrat had stayed the night in Port of Spain to be there for today's parade. The visitor took a drink of water and left.

Fist unslung his bow. He reached for an arrow. Then, at the precise moment, he let the arrow fly. It found its mark. Tessa's inquisitor never knew what hit him. The horse went speeding ahead even as he fell, killed instantly by the cacique's deadly poison.

Fist wasted no time. He had got a bonus prize, but it was Begorrat himself that he wanted, Begorrat and the General, and they were in Port of Spain at a parade. He forced his weapons into the waiting sack, making an awkward parcel. He silently slid down the tree and made his way cautiously through the tall grass. He was going to head for the town.

Breathing heavily from his exertions, he finally arrived in Port of Spain. From the lack of people on the western streets, he guessed that the attraction of the parade was as yet unabated on the other side of the town, towards the hills, on the parade ground. He entered the town slowly, eyes alert, face intense. He had to think quickly but decisively.

Cheers and hurrahs greeted him as he neared the parade ground. The crowd was thick here. The carnival season was approaching, and Picton clearly intended to display his intimidating military might.

No longer was Port of Spain protected by a miserly little militia as it was when José had been a commissioned officer under Don Chacon. Now Picton had a substantial army of light dragoons, hussars, artillery men, battalions and companies. It was an impressive array of uniforms. The dark-green coats of the infantry vied with the red of the dragoons, as the parade passed before Fist's eyes. Those eyes saw only the large shape of the Governor. He was dressed in full regalia, his huge frame astride a magnificent, proud animal. Next to him, in civilian clothes, was his close friend, the infamous Begorrat. Around them were several white officers of Picton's army.

Fist edged his way forward, pushing against the crowd. The parade was heading south along the broad roadway which was separated by a row of buildings and a narrow alley from Pedro's shop. Fist needed a vantage point from which to see his victims. He could not aim wildly in such a large crowd. 'Where? Where?' he asked himself frenziedly. 'There!' Across the narrow alley was a new construction site. The scaffolding was still up. He stumbled over a mound of dried leaves and twigs that was used for binding with clay to form the *tapia* of which most local walls were made. His heart was pounding.

It was no mean feat to attempt an assassination when the streets were full of soldiers. He would not easily escape. 'I ain't go mind dying though, not if I could take them two dogs with me,' he said resignedly. The time had come, he moved quickly, heedless now of witnesses. He mounted the very stairs that would have saved Tessa's life had she been able to reach them before Mendoza had grabbed her. Then he scaled the railing, jumping onto the nearby scaffolding — unaware that this structure had once protected Tessa. He worked his large frame around the narrow boards and finally found himself in full view of the approaching spectacle. He crouched behind an unfinished wall and withdrew his bow from the parcel.

Slowly, the lines of marching men crept up the street. The drummers rolled their steady beat. The crowds cheered. Picton and Begorrat came into view. Fist removed an arrow carefully and set it to the bow.

He took aim. He fired.

In that split second while Fist still held his breath and his every nerve was alert and taut as the string of the bow, in the very second that the arrow was released, a man ran out in front of the General, screaming a warning, his arm upraised.

The arrow, with a heavy thud, split that arm in two.

There was a moment of confusion before all eyes turned upward to the unfinished building. Fist used that moment well. He never hesitated. Running the length of the board, he leapt with all his strength on to the roof below and, with the same power, hurled himself like a bullet on to the pile of dried leaves and twigs at the far end of the lot. Then he scrambled to his feet, heedless of his bruises and ran like the wind.

## III

It was a sad morning for Barry, his last day on the same soil as his beloved. He had stayed the night in the Guest House of the Royal Palms. He spent most of the night chatting with the ever wakeful landlady. In the small hours he had taken to his bed. But, too filled with emotion, he had hardly slept.

Now it was just past eight. He strolled down to the harbour paying scant attention to the lively crowds hurrying to see the parade. His few belongings were in a small portmanteau, carried by the servant boy from the guest house.

At the waterfront he met M. Louis, Kathy, Fred and Mark. Juanita, Fred explained, had been too upset to come. They shook hands and delivered their baggage to the ship's agent. Barry tipped the servant boy and saw him leave. M. Louis and Kathy took the first lighter out to the large vessel, but Barry opted to wait for the next, wanting a few minutes yet with his friend.

'So this is goodbye,' said Fred, extending his hand.

'And I'm already beginning to feel the melancholy of leaving one place and going to the next,' answered Barry with a twinkle in his eyes, as he took Fred's hand in his.

'The passing of time,' continued Fred.

'A touch of the all-seeing eye,' concluded Barry. The two smiled sadly, remembering the litany of their first meeting.

'You know, Fred, this time the melancholy of departure surpasses anything I felt the last time. I never thought that could be possible.'

'Sentimental fool! You never did develop into a genuine cynic, did you? More's the pity! Never did get the goddess either, eh? Just as well. Couldn't quite present her to the Wingates, I suppose. Would have been interesting to see you try, though.'

'I know. You're not part of the species, only an observer. Well, this is goodbye. I'll miss you. I think I'm already homesick for this wretched place.'

'In no time at all Juanita and I will be back home, looking you up, and before that, there's Kathy and Louis.'

'Listen, don't forget to look out for Fist and give him all my gifts and messages.'

'Will do, old chap, and I'll keep a look out for that *alguazil* as well . . . Oh, there's Mark waiting to speak privately with you. I'll say farewell now. Must hurry home to Juanita. She's terribly upset at your leaving, you know.'

'Give her my love. And Fred, thank you for all your kindnesses.' They embraced, slapped each other on the back and parted. Fred hurried off and Mark came up to Barry.

'Been waiting to get you alone,' he began. 'Here's something for you.' He handed Barry a small parcel from his breast pocket. 'A little gift from the great lady.'

'Eléna?' Barry's heart leapt at the thought of a memento from his loved one, but the sparkle in his eyes turned to surprise when Mark answered.

'No, her mother Yei. She bade me tell you when you were quite alone that she awaits your return, especially now that you've broken some sort of promise and acted in haste. She says you forgot her words.'

Barry blanched visibly, but he ventured no comment. Mark shook hands with him and left.

The lighter was not yet ready. Barry ambled distractedly along the quay, walking like a somnambulist, lost to the reality around him, pondering on Yei's consistent astuteness. It took him a few minutes before he realised that someone was speaking to him.

'Look, Monsieur, that sailor over there is waving to you.'

'What?' responded the dazed Barry.

'Over there, Monsieur, by the small boats, an old sailor waving to you.'

Barry looked in the direction indicated, and to his surprise he saw the familiar battered form of Carty. He ran quickly up to the dock and, cupping his mouth with his hands, shouted a greeting.

'Off today then, Guv?' shouted Carty. 'Back to merry old England?'

'Yes, finally. Did you see my uncle?'

'Indeed! Told 'im the satisfactory response!'

'Now you can confirm that it's done!' laughed Barry. 'Glad I saw you. This is goodbye then!' The old sailor resumed the lifting of his anchor and set off, and Barry went back to board his transport. On the short walk back, however, he was again stopped.

This time it was a timid little Frenchman in dirty white knee breeches. The Frenchman doffed his hat nervously.

'Pardon me, Monsieur. I could not help but recognise you as the gentleman who used to ride with the big black fellow with a strange English name . . .'

'You know Fist?'

'He rescued me once from a sound beating. I thought you'd like to know that there was a terrible scene at the parade a while ago. Your man, Fist, tried to assassinate the Governor, but he got the mulatto, Pedro's brother, instead. Then he headed out towards the hills . . .'

'Last call for all passengers boarding the *Bristol*!' came the voice from the lighter, but Barry had already set off at a brisk pace, all thought of departure forgotten.

He stuffed the little parcel from Yei inside his breast pocket, and picked up his heels. In the confused streets, his own fast-moving figure held little interest. There were only a few soldiers left in the city, the rest were obviously off hunting Fist.

He reached the exit of the city and started climbing the low foothills of the Northern Range before he saw some of the scouts. He hid quickly behind the large tracts of indigo trees that grew profusely here, and waited until the men moved off. He had but one thought in his mind, and that was to find and help the black renegade. With any luck, Fist would head for the area where they had met some months before.


Barry advanced and climbed cautiously. At the sound of approaching soldiers, he crawled on his stomach and squeezed himself between two boulders. The perspiration poured off his face. It was nearing the hottest part of the day. The sun beat down fiercely. He was having difficulty breathing in that narrow space. Now it was time, the sound of the soliders had receded into the distance. He inched out from behind the boulder. There was no one in sight and no movement, not even a rustle from a cooling breeze. Nothing stirred the bushes – brown now for it was the dry season and the hills were parched. He eyed the cliff doubtfully for a moment. Then he set his lips in a firm line, and like a man possessed he scrambled up the steep slope, praying that no one from below would spot him clinging tenaciously to the few small trees and roots hanging out from the rocky surface.

For an agonising moment he dangled dangerously above the faraway town. 'Only a little effort and I'll be safe,' he urged himself. He made the effort, and pulled himself up.

Now on a higher level in the forested areas, he knew he had not only lost the soldiers but gained a considerable distance on them. He began to climb with renewed energy to the area where he had once rendez-voused with Fist. From here on, his eyes kept searching, not just for the red of the soldiers' coats, but searching for something much smaller, something on the ground. Then he saw it and smiled knowingly to himself.

He had found their sign. Three white stones in a triangle. Fist had passed this way and was expecting him. He reached down quickly, collected the stones and proceeded upwards. His clothing was dishe-velled, torn and covered with dust. He pushed himself on and on, walking swiftly now. Again, there was another sign. He kicked the stones away quickly. As he did so, the sound of movement in the bushes startled him. He jumped back and raced for the protection of a tree. He did not make it.

'Halt!' Not another move if you value your life!' came an English voice. There was no chance of escape.

'Shoot on sight, you fool! Out of the way. Let me do it,' came a second voice. A fraction of a second later, a red-coated soldier lurched into view, musket poised for action.

Barry raised his hand in protest, and shouted even as he realised he was breathing his last breath. The gun went off with a thundering bang that screamed a terrible note of finality in Barry's petrified ear.

The noise was all he felt. A second later he was still standing, without injury, his hands raised in protest. Stunned, he stumbled backwards and gasped in momentary disbelief.

Faster than he had could have thought possible, the two soldiers had been felled by an expert at the bow and arrow.

'Fist!' he exclaimed, wheeling around in wonderment.

'Bring the gun. Come, leh we get out o' here quick!' spoke the much-welcomed voice. 'Don't bother with them, they ain't dead, I keeping the poison arrows for the murderers.'

Barry followed his friend with wide-eyed amazement at his words and his subsequent calm efficiency. Fist moved like a seasoned veteran of military campaigns. Impressed or no, however, Barry still berated him for his reckless foolishness. Fist was unrepentant.

'You shoulda never come! I heading out for Toco anyway, the end o' these mountains. Is best we double back over the hill in Laventille first.

They go be swarming by here after that set o' gunfire. Come on,' urged Fist.

They walked for what seemed like hours, pausing only infrequently, making their way through tall, strangling, yellowing bushes, keeping well away from pathways. Once Fist shoved Barry forcibly aside and pointed to the sleeping coil of a large mapepire – the viper whose sting is swift and deadly. Eventually they crossed over and were in the low-lying Laventille Hills, near once more to Port of Spain.

'Fist, let's head for Santa Clara. You can hide there for a while and still take to the hills if you must.'

Fist agreed. It was late now, but the sun in no apparent hurry to turn in for the night still blazed in a blue sky. Suddenly, Fist nudged his friend and made a telling gesture of caution. Barry listened and heard it too, the sound of human feet. They moved on, but with greater care, pausing behind trees, listening, then moving stealthily again. But the soldiers spotted them. Now they came rushing. Barry fell on his stomach, musket in hand. Fist took refuge behind a large immortelle tree.

There were only two soliders. One soldier fired. Fist returned an arrow. A man fell. Fist reached for another. The second soldier was fast, too fast. Before either of the renegades could act, he responded with deadly accuracy. A shot rang out and took Fist in the left shoulder. The black man received the bullet with only a low groan as he sank helplessly to the ground where his blood became indistinguishable from the thick carpet of red immortelle flowers that cushioned his fall.

The soldier, totally unaware that his victim was not alone, ran up to Fist in triumph, bayonet aimed at the black man's chest, prepared to take him back dead rather than alive. Barry had crawled the short distance to his friend, keeping low. He now sprang to life as the soldier drew back his arm and moved in with the thrust. With perfect timing, Barry levelled a stunning blow with the butt of the musket to the back of the Redcoat's head. Then he turned to Fist on the carpet of flowers.

'Don't give up now, old man,' mouthed Barry. 'Can't stay here.' Fist had lost consciousness. Barry had to drag him, leaving bow and quiver behind.

Once out of the immediate area, Barry paused, dragged off his cravat and made a rough pad for Fist's bleeding shoulder. Then he pressed on the pad with the fingers of his left hand, as he half-lifted the large man and carried him forward.

They could not get very far now, Barry knew. There was no way Fist could travel as far as Santa Clara. He could only hope to find a reasonably safe hiding-place. He struggled downhill, counting his blessings with every safe footstep. They were almost off the hill. Soon, very soon, they would be on the flat lands. Barry had a tentative, if unclear, plan in his mind. Just a few more minutes, he consoled himself.'

Then, when he believed them almost home, the sound of voices assailed him.

There was a small company of soldiers in a clearing. He released Fist gently and took a few moments to secure the wound with another rough bandage from their torn clothing. Fist had lost a great deal of blood, but he stirred now and regained consciousness.

'Shh! Don't try to speak. Soldiers in our path. I'm going to see how many. Don't move!' Barry touched his friend encouragingly, cocked his musket, and crept out on his stomach.

A burst of laughter slapped him in the face. The soldiers were obviously relaxed. Perhaps they were waiting to move out. How could he get past them? To circumnavigate this spot would mean having to climb back up the hill, back into the arms of foraging soliders. What could he do? Could he hope to wait long enough until they left this spot? Who was to say that more would not appear by then? Fist was only barely conscious, unable to support himself.

Never had he been in so unyielding a trap. Panic began to assail him. He breathed deeply and willed himself to be calm. He crawled nearer. There was no gainsaying it, there were too many of them, and not enough cover in this spot. He would have to turn back, go up the hill and risk Fist's life.

A lone soldier stood apart from the others, his back towards Barry. He paced the clearing idly. Barry was about to turn back quickly before the soldier came too close, when the lone figure bent his head and coughed violently. Something about that gesture was familiar. 'God, I pray that I'm right,' he murmured. Then, in a loud whisper, he called out a single word. 'André!'

The handsome brown face turned and saw him. He gave an almost imperceptible nod. Boldly suggesting to the officer that it was time to move on, André was able to draw his fellow soldiers away. Barry and his once more unconscious burden were able to sneak past.

Half-lifting, half-dragging Fist, he hustled down the remaining short hill and moved directly to the flat lands and headed like roosting birds straight for the beckoning arms of the mangrove.

Now that they were in the swamps and safe from their pursuers, what was he to do? Fist had lost a great deal of blood. He had struggled to stay alert but his efforts could no more stem the creeping shroud of

211

unconsciousness than they could the fall of night that descended now with amazing rapidity. With the darkness engulfing them, the unfamiliar landscape of the swamp made a frightening refuge.

Barry lifted Fist on to the fork of a mangrove tree and tied him to the trunk, using his tattered jacket. He took off his waistcoat and fashioned a new pad for the wound. The bleeding was less now, or so it seemed, as his exploring fingers gently probed the wound. There was no way to keep it clean, lamented Barry, as he stood in calf-high, watery marshes, and hugged his friend's limp legs. He rested his head on Fist's immobile knee and gave himself up to desperate, despairing thoughts.

Where was he to turn for help? Fred, Mark, everyone would have thought him far away by now, out on the high seas. Fist groaned and twisted restively. Barry stretched up quickly and righted him. He lapsed again into unconsciousness. How could he leave Fist alone here even for an hour? There was no ground on which he could be laid. The murky, filthy waters would prove a ready grave. Should he take him back to dry land and risk meeting soldiers? What was to be the black man's fate? To die ignominiously in the swamps of Port of Spain like a wounded bird? Or to be roasted in the *cachots brûlants* and then executed? Could he put together a raft, a platform, something on which to rest him while he went for help and made proper plans? No. There was no real hope of doing that. He had no tool, no knife, no cutlass. He could not even break a branch from one of the trees without a tool. No. His only recourse was to tie Fist more securely, and leave him there while he tried to reach Fred.

Barry stripped off his shirt, exposing his bare back to the cool night air. With it he tied Fist tightly around the chest, shaking him to ensure that he could not easily fall. Then he turned around, wondering how he was to find his way without a light. Well, he would try. 'Nothing ventured, nothing gained,' he said, as he patted his friend reassuringly on the leg and then set off, hands groping before him, feeling for the trees that were thick everywhere.

He moved on a few paces, splashing in the clammy water, and then he stopped suddenly in his tracks as if hit by a stunning blow. His jaw dropped and his eyes opened wide in horror. His hands fell to his sides. This was the end. After everything, after the heroic struggle, the almost unbelievable escape, they had been caught. Who would have thought that Picton's men would follow them into this morass of a swamp? Who could have expected men of such devotion that they would enter the black, murky, marshland at night, when all they had to do was wait until morning and they could come in at their ease and grab them?

Tears of frustration stung his eyes as he watched the hypnotic light come closer and closer towards them. Only one man came into view, the others were probably near by. Barry did not even have the heart to try to hide or to run back to Fist. He stood his ground, shirtless, filthy with mud and muck. He waited for the expected voice of the arresting officer.

When the voice came, Barry staggered in shock and almost fell. It was the one voice he had never expected, but the sweetest one he'd ever heard.

'That you, Guv?' was all that it said.

'Carty!? You? . . . You? . . . Is that really you? . . . How? Why?

'You alone 'ere Guv? Thought you 'ad a friend with yer, I did.'

'Yes, yes, my friend's back there. He's hurt. Wounded, a hole in his shoulder. In bad shape.'

'Well, best get 'im and' push off fast, Guv. Time's a'wastin'. It waits on no man, yer know.'

'Carty, you're unbelievable! How'd you know to look here for me?' Barry could not disguise the happiness in his voice. He turned and took the light from the old sailor, and led him the few paces back to Fist.

'Started to leave, then I saw when you runs off this mornin', I did. An' ain't I the one 'oo promised yer uncle to "ensure a satisfactory response" to the letter? I's a man o' my word, yer honour. 'Ere I was watchin' you run away liked a frightened rat from said response. I says to myself, something ain't right. So I makes a point to cross examine the Frenchie you was jawin' with. I fell upon a stroke of luck too. Over'eard an officer, 'eard tell yer man was likely shot up, so I made fer the guest 'ouse. Reckoned you'd go there for 'elp. An' what yer think 'appened? Afore m'very eyes, the woman there ups and gets a missive from 'er nephew, tellin' 'er to send to that Whiteways fella to get 'elp fer you, that you done 'eading towards this 'ere swamp. So . . .'

'André, by God!' whispered Barry in disbelief.

'The same. So I says to 'er,' continued the sailor, 'no need to trouble 'im – Whiteways, that is. Let 'im rest easy in 'is bed. I can do a sight better than 'im, anyways, with ole *Jezebel* waitin' in the 'arbour, ready to push off. This way I'd be sure of gettin' the satisfactory response.'

'Carty, I love you!' laughed Barry.

'Watch yerself, Guv. Keep yer distance. I ain't that kinda fellah,' joked the old sailor, as he helped untie Fist and handed Barry his jacket. He released the black man slowly into Barry's arms. He lifted his feet and helped carry him out towards the sea.

Once aboard, they were not quite free from danger, however. There was still the routine inspection by the harbour officials. Carty was not perturbed. 'Ever wondered why this boat kicks up so?' he laughed. 'Take 'im down to the fish bin, Guv. Ain't an official on earth 'oo can bear the stench.'

Barry could barely stand it himself, but he was not about to protest in the face of his good fortune. His trial did not last very long, though, and he was able to remove Fist and himself to a more salubrious location. Now he faced the worry of the black man's condition.

'Can we risk leaving the ball in him until we reach Barbados?' he asked, hoping that Carty would supply some alternative suggestion.

'H'em,' Carty pondered. 'I suspicioned you'd ask that. May'ap you're thinkin' I should pull in at Tobago. Can't say as I disagree with you, Guv. Only trouble is I ain't got no connections there.' He snickered. 'Fact is, I got only disconnections. Tell yer what, though, since this 'ere *Noble Savage* seems so important to yer – what call 'e 'as to be is beyond me. You crazy aristos! But as I was sayin, push come to shove, I'll take the damned ball out meself. I done it afore.'

Barry breathed a sigh of relief and settled Fist into the narrow bunk, thinking the surgery would be performed before long, but nature had other plans. Carty's generous intentions had to be postponed for a considerable time for all his energies were centred on keeping his boat afloat in an unseasonable gale that sprang up.

By the end of the second day, therefore, still without proper attention, Fist developed a raging fever, and Barry was hard pressed to control it. Despite all his efforts, the fever mounted, and Fist became delirious. 'My God, Fist, you cannot die on me. You did fall under an immortelle tree, you know. You can't die now, not now.' Frantically, Barry applied to Carty. The old seaman offered to perform the surgery immediately, but could not find a ready solution to the problem of the fever.

'If you don't get that fever down, 'e's a gonner fer certain, even without the bullet. I don't know what to say, lad. We need some medicine, we . . .'

A startling shout escaped Barry's lips, and he slapped his chest so suddenly that Carty jumped.

'What's bit you, son? What's the trouble?' asked Carty anxiously.

Barry was not listening. Like a crazed man, searching for a stinging insect, he fumbled inside the jacket he had only just put on. He dragged out the package Mark had given him. He rushed over to the light and tore it open. A crumpled immortelle flower fell out like a spurt of blood, or a message of knowledge and of life. Then he saw what he was looking for. Yei, the far-seeing, had come to his rescue. Small flat packages,

214

neatly labelled, tumbled out of the brown wrapping. One was clearly marked: ONE SPOONFUL BOILED AND DRAWN FOR FEVER.

'Incredible!' shouted Barry. 'How on earth could she have foreseen such a need? How could she know?'

'What's that, Guv?'

'Medicine, man, medicine!' was Barry's joyous reply.


The wind fluttered the sails, and the little boat picked up speed. Carty put his razor-sharp blade through a candle's open flame. '"Old 'im down good. This'll be done in a trice.'

No skilled surgeon could have been more efficient. With hardly a fumble, he produced the bullet. 'Pour the rum, plenty of it, Guv. That'll do the trick. Fever's goin' down too . . . See, told you we'd fix 'im up right. Won't be that long afore we reach Barbados. 'E'll make it, Guv, mark my words. 'E'll live to be a bloomin' troublesome nigger yet!' the old sailor guffawed, his face wrinkled in belligerent amusement.

# BOOK FOUR

❦

# *Macaws*

## CHAPTER EIGHTEEN

### I

Tall elms lined the driveway. The barouche emblazoned with the leonine crest of the House of Vantage rolled past the gatehouse and proceeded in dignified ostentation up the stately avenue.

The welcoming elms glided by like the years. Cool spring breezes found their way through the open window, and it was inevitable that the young man seated in the carriage would feel the pinch of nostalgia; a bitter-sweet feeling now, so different, he thought resignedly, from what he once would have expected. Two years ago, how he would have rejoiced that this day had finally come. Now his face showed no hint of excitement or anticipated pleasure.

The soft light of the spring morning illuminated trembling new buds on the trees, and painted the flowers with a delicate pastel blush, imbuing the world with a fairy-tale beauty. This world, as hauntingly familiar as the sight of his own face in a mirror, today seemed alien, and as bewildering as the dull pain in his heart. He smiled briefly. He was remembering a friend's observations as he looked now at Grenmill with the 'omniscient eye' of one who had recently left the stark, primitive beauty of Santa Clara.

The carriage wheels turned monotonously. The driveway was long, the house not yet in sight. He found himself drifting back and reliving the last few weeks . . .

He remembered how Fist had finally awakened to find himself in Barbados in Wilfred's house, still determined to kill Picton. Barry had had to use all his persuasive powers to make him realise the foolhardiness of such thoughts, telling him that the solution lay rather in political action. Then he had announced that he was leaving for England. On the spur of the moment he invited Fist to come with him.

'Come with me, Fist, it won't be that bad. You'll always have a position with me, you're a damned good valet, and by the way, there are thousands of black people in England, you know, and they're all legally free.' That was all the inducement Fist needed.

Without ceremony they had left Barbados, two forlorn figures silent in their private misery. Before his departure, Barry had made sure to communicate his love and fidelity to Eléna by ordering her a special gift and ensuring that Carty would collect and deliver it to her in a few weeks' time.

As Barry had insisted that his valet share his small cabin with him, the two men had many a long night to share experiences. Fist asked many questions about England and Barry told him of its wealth and beauty, or its ugliness, poverty and exploitation, and dispelled many of the black man's fairy-tale illusions of the perfection of that country.

'So much o' misery in England and you does worry so 'bout black man?' asked Fist. Barry was forced to realise that his awareness had started in the West Indies.

'But the slaves, you know, Fist, are in a state of physical bondage, and that does put them in a worse position,' he answered.

Fist asked many questions about Grenmill and about Barry's grandmother and the Wingate family. Since he knew that Barry was the heir to his grandmother's 'little farm', he wondered whether his brothers would be left penniless. Barry laughed at this and attempted to explain the extent of the Wingate fortune.

'Apart from the entailed property, which goes to Lord Templeton – that's Graham, the eldest – there's still the unentailed property and the vast wealth of our mother. That's to be shared between Jeffery – he's the second, a military type, somewhere in India now – and Richard, an otherworldly, intellectual, politician. And, my dear man, Grenmill is no "little farm", the pastures and woodlands alone cover over 200 acres and that's not counting the farm lands, the tenanted lands, and all that.'

Then again, one night, Fist asked, 'If it have all them free black people over there, then they don't hate we over there?'

'I can't say that, Fist,' answered Barry. 'Bigotry exists, but prejudice is possibly less insidious than . . .'

'An' what about Wilbyforce? He going and free the slaves in the islands in true?' countered Fist.

This question stumped Barry, but he tried to explain. 'Wilberforce and his mentor, Mr Pitt, that's the Prime Minister, are dedicated to abolition, but they face strong opposition from West Indian planters in Parliament.'

'So how you go get them to help Trinidad?'

'Well,' answered Barry thoughtfully, 'sugar is noticeably collapsing, the war in Saint-Domingue is going badly and Wilberforce has got an agreement to gradually reduce the slave trade. It's a question of strategy . . .'

'Strategy, eh? And I go never understand it. I can't even read or write.'

It was then that Barry offered to teach Fist, and proceeded to do so through the long days and nights of the voyage.

They had finally reached England. From the bustling port of London, where piled hogsheads of sugar gave testimony to England's link with the lands from which they had just come, they had taken a hackney coach to Vantage House in Mayfair. But the family had not been there. His parents were at Grenmill and his two resident brothers away in the country. His grandmother was still alive. The servants were overjoyed to see him and highly impressed by his black servant.

They had stayed the night in London. One of His Lordships's carriages was immediately made available to him. They had left at the crack of dawn the next day for Grenmill, in distant Somerset.

The carriage halted. The black servant immediately jumped down and opened the door. The young man rose, shared a wide grin with the black man, and stepped out. Footmen, wreathed in smiles, rushed to welcome him. Barry and Fist had arrived at Grenmill.

Barry stepped into the lofty entrance hall and into a loving reacquaintance with his parents, but it was his meeting with the Dowager that was the most touching.

Her once robust body lay like a mere feather on the vast and ornate fourposter bed. Though prepared for the change, Barry was still shocked at the thinness of her face and at the unexpected whiteness of her unpowdered hair.

Her nurse bent over her still form and spoke in a rousing whisper, 'M'lady, your grandson's here. Your boy's home at last.'

'B . . . arry?' came a weak murmur. The Dowager opened watery, unfocused grey eyes that after a moment's disorientation suddenly lit up at the vision before her. She raised a weak, emaciated hand. Barry's heart lurched with pity. He bent and kissed her lovingly on the forehead and on each hollow cheek. Tears welled in his eyes, but he fought them back. He would not give in to sadness or despair. He would always be cheerful in her presence, and furthermore he would not allow her to die.

'I'm here, Grandmama, and here I'll stay until you're better, completely better and full of life again as I love to see you.'

Barry wasted no time in telling his father about his stay in the West Indies. He hastened to express the hope that the issue of Trinidad and Picton's merciless cruelty could be raised in the House.

His father was not optimistic, however. 'We've a war on. In wartime atrocities are commonplace, m'boy, and of course everything depends on whether we retain the island after the war settlements. You're too much like my mother, you know,' he laughed. Then he lasped into parental pedantry, 'What's more important now, is that you have reformed your behaviour. I expect you to see to the running of Grenmill.'

Barry's parents left shortly afterwards for London, his father to attend Parliament and his mother the opening of the London Season. Barry and Fist were forced to adjust to life at Grenmill.

Feigning total unawareness of the unsettling effect he was having on the household below stairs, Fist conducted himself with characteristic poise and confidence. But he was much less at ease than he let on. Only to Barry did he confide his trepidation at having to survive among 'all them set o' white people'.

Barry merely laughed. He knew that Fist had been properly trained by Wilfred's *valet de chambre* for life in a grand household and, moreover, he knew that no one belowstairs would dare upset the servant of the Dowager's beloved grandson.

Slowly and inevitably the servants warmed towards Fist, however, and in a short time he was taken into their fold. Indeed, the parlour maid was heard to say humorously to the footman with whom she was stepping out, 'Every fam'ly's got its black sheep, ain't it? So we're no different, are we?'

Barry's adjustment to English country life was ironically more difficult. A day hardly dawned when the young Englishman did not awaken to think himself back on the island of towering hills and exotic orchids, where wild parrots screeched, and butterflies as blue as his eyes lazed in unconscious grace. But time lessened the acuteness of the pain of separation from Eléna and eventually he fell into the routine of Grenmill. He devoted himself to his grandmother, reading to her or simply sitting in the sickroom when she was asleep, gazing wistfully out of the window. Those hours away from the sickroom he spent with Fist, continuing his reading lessons, or riding through Somerset or tramping through the farmlands.

He was surprised one day by a visit from his eldest brother. Graham had dropped in with a friend to see their grandmother, while visiting in the neighbourhood. To Barry's unaccustomed eyes, Graham seemed quite the dandy.

He wore a violet longcoat highlighted with striped lapels of a deeper purple, the whole contrasted daringly with buff coloured breeches and dazzlingly black pumps. Several fobs and a quizzing glass hung from his attire, while his shirt was a miracle of tucks and lace, not to mention the devastating height of his shirt collar and the intricacy of his cravat. Barry, in his now customary plain linen shirt and dull brown breeches, presented a sharp contrast.

To Barry's polite enquiry about his wife, Juliana, he shook out the ruffles at his wrist, proceeded to take snuff and said languidly, 'How should I know? We meet with tolerable infrequency. Different interests, you see.'

'Interests? Have you taken over some of Father's holdings?'

Graham's friend burst out laughing. 'Believe me,' he interjected, 'your brother's interested only in human flesh, of either sex. Ask him if he isn't now on his way to court your neighbour's daughter.'

'But Lord Wolverton's daughter's only a babe, hardly out of the schoolroom. She comes to visit Grandmama sometimes . . . oh, I see, it's her sister then? The married one . . . ahem . . . I see.'

Clearly, Graham was a bit of a rake – or was it even worse than that? From his appearance one could not be sure. But Graham's friend's words continued to puzzle Barry until his brother happened to catch a glimpse of Fist.

'I say, old chap, is the blackamoor yours?' he exclaimed. 'You're a fine one, Barry, hiding away rusticating down here with such a prime specimen in your pocket. I've been on the lookout for a prize fighter. I can offer your man here a sizeable purse if he's as good a crowd-pleaser as he looks.'

Barry could not believe that his brother was still in the sporting business, but with Fist's consent they agreed that once he had fully recovered from his wound, they would negotiate.


## II

The month of May came and the flowers in Grenmill Park blossomed in all their glory, but though Barry's eyes saw the flowers his mind flew faraway from Grenmill. Their appearance only renewed the ache in his heart, making him remember that in Santa Clara the poui would be in bloom. He had written to Eléna on his arrival, so she would soon receive his letter. He was overcome with an unbearable longing.

His grandmother was improving, though, sitting up every day now, trying to speak. Barry's new strategy was to stimulate her by raising issues she loved to discuss. He would read from Clarkson's essay on the 'Impolicy of the African Slave Trade' or from Cowper's trite if provocative 'Negro's Complaint'. He smiled secretly to see her reaction, but the smile never reached his eyes. These days his eyes remained a melancholy, cold blue.

But apart from entertaining his grandmother, or indulging in the occasional sport in the summer air, little occupation presented itself, for Grenmill was well taken care of by his grandmother's capable steward. Barry faced the prospect of powerless longing, political impotence and numberless long, uneventful days.

## III

Since Graham's visit to the Wolvertons, Jessica Wolverton, the shy unobtrusive youngest daughter of that family, had begun to visit Grenmill with growing frequency, or so it seemed to Barry. She was obviously a favourite of the Dowager. Barry did not find her presence either stimulating or disturbing but he fell into desultory conversation with her occasionally. Mostly, he left the young girl alone to visit his grandmother.

Apart from Jessica visitors to Grenmill were few, but one day the Dowager and Barry received a visit from Barry's brother Richard. The complete foil to the elegant Graham, Richard, with his careless clothes, sloping shoulders and stooped posture, was nevertheless a wealth of information.

Richard had brought mail from London to Barry, leaving him to read it as he visited his grandmother. Barry searched through the small pile with growing dismay. There was none from Trinidad. He almost threw the pile in the fire and then he noticed one of great interest.

The letter was from Fred, detailing his arrival and stay in England, announcing that his father had passed away leaving his Irish estates to Kathy (who had now gone there with Louis). He mentioned that everyone at Santa Clara had been well when last seen (José hopping about, Eléna in excellent beauty as ever). He ended with the news that Juanita and himself were leaving shortly for their castle in Northumberland and that he was sure to see Barry soon.

Barry folded the letter and leaned back wearily in his chair. It was the first news he had had of Eléna. Why hadn't she written herself? he wondered. He felt he would go mad with longing to hear from her. Surely she had got his letter and the gift from Barbados, surely she knew he still loved her.

Entering the room at that moment, Richard saw the pained look on his younger brother's face. 'What's the matter, Barry? Bad news of Trinidad? Father has told me of your preoccupation with that island.'

Barry roused himself and launched into a discourse of the ills of the island.

'I agree that something should be done,' conceded Richard. 'Too soon to know how the war will end, though – last year the French gained a great victory in Italy. The war in Saint-Domingue is killing Britain, you know. Anyway, Nelson's just left with a new ship for the Mediterranean. He's the best we've got although I hear that a formidable fleet sailed from Toulon in May.'

'And what of the man Napoleon?' asked Barry, suddenly impressed by his brother's knowledge.

'He's the man to watch, little brother. At the moment I hear he's riding roughshod over Egypt, but don't worry, Rear Admiral Nelson's *Vanguard* and his twelve sail-of-the-line will soon put a dent in his armour.'

Eventually the two brothers spoke of personal matters. Barry enquired whether Richard had any marriage plans. His brother laughed soundly, declaring that he was content with his books and that he would never marry.

'The women of our class, my boy, are too sophisticated for me. I'd probably be a cuckold within a year. It's up to you and Jeffery to produce heirs,' he concluded.

'And Graham?' questioned Barry.

'Afraid that's unlikely now.'

'What do you mean? I gather he's a dandy and something of a rake, but . . .'

'He's throwing his life away at the gaming tables and the boxing rings, and with trifling with the ladies.'

'It saddens me to hear this. I mean, I never thought I'd hear myself criticise the life I was obviously aiming towards, but I . . . I suppose I grew up in the West Indies.'

'I thought the planters lived a life of extravagant debauchery,' countered Richard.

'That's not far from the truth, especially in Barbados – it's a singularly uncultured society, nothing at all like the golden age of

223

Greece – slavery and culture, I mean. I was forced to become introspective and serious. Tell me, though, about Graham.'

'Waiting for a title is not easy, just look at Prinny. But he has become much worse since Juliana lost the baby. You didn't know about that? It's sort of hush-hush, but you're entitled to know. He accused her of having a liaison and in a fit of rage she took off on her stallion raging through the park. She was thrown and lost the child, the doctor says there's no hope of any more. Since then Graham has virtually abandoned her.'

'And what of his love for her?' asked Barry.

Richard smiled sceptically. 'There's little of that in marriages in their set.'

A movement through the window caught Barry's eye. It was the train of Jessica Wolverton's skirt as she strolled through the park on her way home, but his thoughts were not on her, they were on Eléna and their love. Dropping the subject of his eldest brother, he resumed the political discussion, asking Richard what he knew of the present position of the Abolitionists, and whether Pitt was cooling on the issue of abolition.

Richard snorted almost disdainfully. 'That has become quite obvious, Barry,' he said. 'True, Pitt was all for abolition. But now we can see that his interests were simply economic. He proposed abolition because the British were the largest suppliers of slaves to Saint-Domingue and that island's vast production of sugar began to ruin the British sugar trade. He was merely trying to ruin French commerce. He tried to encourage importation of Indian sugar too, but the West Indian monopolists would not allow the tax on non-West Indian sugar to be lifted, so his plan failed. Had he known that he would be offered the island by the royalists he would have had no need for such humanitarian ideas. You see, now that they have offered it to him, begging him to rescue them, he has been forced to concede the extension of the trade. It's merely that Saint-Domingue equals slaves and he means to possess that island even at the risk of one hundred thousand lives – yes, that many – and at the expense of humanitarian ideals.'

Barry whistled in horror. Richard continued, 'He tries to keep up appearances but he stopped Wilberforce from making his annual motion in '96 and this year he tried to get him to leave the task to the colonial legislatures. Ridiculous, eh? And to add to it all, the slave trade is increasing and we are losing the war in Europe.'

'So there's no hope then of raising the question of Trinidad?' asked Barry dejectedly.

'None at the moment, for to add to Pitt's troubles there is the problem of the Corresponding Societies.'

Barry knew that those associations had been inspired by the promises of the French Revolution and nurtured by harsh, hopeless living conditions.

'The world is desperate for reform,' he said. 'Radicalism is in the very air.'

He did not add that he himself was a radical of sorts, who secretly supported slave rebellion, who wanted equality for all men and even wanted to marry out of his race.

'And, too, there is the constant threat of French invasion,' continued Richard, 'and mutinies in the Navy, and problems in Ireland.'

'I've just heard that some Friends have gone there – tell me about Ireland,' responded Barry.

'Things there couldn't be worse. The country's been in a state of great disorder since Fitzwilliams was recalled in '95. The Orange Society of Ulster is still hard at work, harassing the Catholics, and since the United Irishmen have been plotting with the French, Pitt is determined to crush all resistance. I understand quite a bloodbath's going on over there. Our troops would put your Picton to shame, you know.'

'My God, Louis and Kathy!' was all that Barry could reply.

'My God, the whole world, m'boy,' averred Richard sadly.


# IV

The summer faded but slowly the Dowager's health improved. She smiled more and spoke with growing clarity. Barry's hope grew. Soon, soon he would be released and he would be able to go back and claim the companion of his heart.

During the long, dark, days, however, he succumbed to crippling despair over Eléna's silence. With his grandmother, he had perforce to be cheerful, but cold blue eyes turned on anyone else who attempted to break into his icy, silent mood. During his reading lesson one day, Fist confronted him.

'So you going to grieve away your life, eh? She ain't dead like Tessa, you know! You think the woman forget you or what?'

'Fist, let's get back to your lesson. Use proper English. I never badgered you when you had your troubles.'

'Yes, but you straightened me out, stopped me from playing *corbeau* again, made me see my troubles as more than a personal thing. I talking to you like a friend, man. Forget proper English. What's wrong? Is write

225

she ain't write you or what? Listen, man, you can't see the girl ain't want to write? You know the type o' woman she is. You know she noble, but you could only see it in the way she carry sheself. You forgetting that she black. She have she pride too. She ain't go want to force sheself on you.'

'You don't know what we've shared, Fist. I never told you . . .' began Barry, turning away and facing the window.

'You don't have to tell me, man! I know 'bout love. I could imagine. There was Tessa, remember?' The black man continued in softened tones. 'Them kind o' woman don't give themself so easy, man. She ain't ever go forget you.'

'But why won't she write?'

'How I go know? You have to have faith. You know she loves you, have faith then. Maybe she just want you to feel free to forget a black woman, to please your family, to get a white wife. Maybe she loves you enough to be unselfish.'

Barry spun on his heels and faced Fist. 'I never thought of it that way!' he exclaimed.

'You ain't really know black people, is all,' answered the black man.


The year 1798 was drawing to a close. As Christmas approached the Dowager was sitting up and stoutly discussing her Christmas dinner with the surprised housekeeper. Barry was in a pensive mood. He thought of many things and many people. Fist's left shoulder was back to normal and from their sparring sessions he knew, with a pang of regret, that his black friend was ready for the ring. Then there was Fred. He had written again to say that Juanita preferred life in the country and they were extending their stay there. The year was almost over. This was the year of Nelson's great victory at Aboukir and the year of British defeat in Saint-Domingue, the year of the massacre of Irish Catholics at Vinegar Hill, and the year when some fifty or sixty thousand black souls had been transported to the West Indies.

In the new year Graham came for Fist. Barry knew it was a great opportunity for the black man to make his own way in life, so he concealed his own sadness. Both men pretended that they would soon see each other, but in the end Barry ran after the coach, shouting, 'You will keep in touch, won't you? Don't let us lose each other, Fist!'

'That won't happen, man! You found me when I needed you, I will find you too!' shouted Fist into the wind.

With his black friend gone, life at Grenmill became ever more tedious, but the Dowager was steadily improving and eventually felt she could bear to be alone for a few weeks. She instructed Barry to go to London for at least part of the Season.

'Go, enjoy yourself, fall in love. Then come back to help me with my exercises in the summer. Jessica will be here to keep me company. Go on!'

Once in London Barry tried to fall into the spirit of merriment of the season. He accompanied his mother to her routs and balls, he went out on the town with Graham and his high-flying friends, but he could not erase the memory of his feelings on the mountain that day after Tessa's death, his feelings that the refinements and sophistication of London extracted too great a price. He was also very disappointed at not meeting Fist, for the now acclaimed champion of the ring was away answering a challenge in Scotland. Even Fred was still away in the north.

After the first heady feeling of freedom, all entertainment began to strike him as uniformly dull, lacking the one unattainable ingredient that would have given it life.

There was one occasion, however, when he came fully to life. To accommodate his brother Richard, he had agreed to meet him one day at his club. The prospect of spending an evening with Richard's earnest set was daunting, but once again his brother's mantle of dullness proved to hide a fascinating world of ideas and interest.

Arriving at the club before Richard, he was welcomed by his brother's friends and drawn into the current conversation.

'Is there still doubt about Pitt's turn-about on abolition? If there is, James, let me inform you that in last year's issue of the transporting of slaves to Trinidad and Guiana, all Pitt had to do was issue a simple order in council . . .'

Barry's head jerked up immediately. The speaker continued, 'And even after he was defeated in his attempt to sanction the transportation, by an adamant Wilberforce, he still tried to allow slaves into Trinidad from the older islands. I have it on good authority that Wilberforce had to force him to see that he was actually going to embarrass himself by such a position . . .'

'I've come only last year from the island of Trinidad,' interjected Barry at this point. 'Its welfare is still very much on my mind.'

'Tell us about that island. We understand it's badly in need of slaves for development,' interrupted a stern-faced, greying man.

'It is underpopulated, if that's what you mean, yes,' answered Barry. 'But I fervently hope that in view of the ruling of '92 on the gradual abolition of the trade, the void won't be filled by slaves, that some means of attracting free labour would be arrived at. With the large free-coloured population, that island has all the possibility of being an ideal model of free West Indian society, perfect for the abolitionist's cause.'

'Yes, my lad, it seems you've given the matter much thought', responded the stern-faced gentleman, now softening in his manner. 'You are aware that the society against slavery is now compelled to look for serious issues to bring before Parliament? No longer can they hope to get Pitt's support. In fact, since the opening up of Cuba by Spain, Cuba has become his nemesis! It threatens with its vast potential to overshadow all of Britain's possessions in the Caribbean. So I suspect that Pitt is willing to use new possessions, like your island, as competition to Cuba. He can no longer support the cause. What the Society needs now is concrete issues to raise in Parliament. The settlement of that island can be made into an important issue. With your personal knowledge of it, you should be of help to men like Wilberforce. As soon as we know our position in this war, you should meet the man and discuss your ideas.'

But to Barry it seemed too soon to pursue his ideas. The war was far from over.

# V

That summer the Dowager tried shaky legs on the pathways near Grenmill Hall, aided by an encouraging Barry and an enthusiastic Jessica. Having lost most of her shyness now, the young girl had virtually become part of the small family at Grenmill. Barry had become quite fond of the petite, blonde young woman, but was quite unaware that she had lost her heart to him.

Apart from his grandmother's improvement, his only other source of joy was the occasional letter. True, none came from Eléna, but he did receive one from Fist, in a clear if childish hand. It told of his exploits and of his recent attachment to a young black girl. The other was from Fred, informing him of Juanita's pregnancy and continued stay in Northumberland. 'She had never been happy in London,' he emphasised. There were three words about Louis and Kathy, 'still in Ireland' and, about the Santa Clara clan, he merely confirmed that all were well.

The last year of the eighteenth century came to its close. In the newspapers there were accounts of the total suppression of the Corresponding Societies, news that Lord Nelson was staying with Lord Hamilton in Naples, much news of Napoleon's exploits in Egypt, and much scandal concerning the Prince of Wales and his secret wife Mrs Fitzherbert.

Christmas brought Barry's brother Jeffery, now returned from the Orient and on his way to join the army in Europe. He was dashing in his dress uniform, but his handsome face was marred by the harsh set of his jaw, and by his eyes, as blue as Barry's but of a chilly, unsmiling hue. His years in India had left their stamp on him. He was vociferous against the abolitionists, the Irish, the French and what he called the lazy races of coloured people. Barry kept his distance, grateful that Jeffery would soon be off to the war. He also kept Jeffery far away from Fist who happily spent Christmas that year at Grenmill. Fist told Barry of his many successes in the ring and of his current plans to start a gymnasium of his own in London.

By spring the Dowager was greatly improved, walking now with the aid of a stick. Jessica came less frequently this year, and not at all since turning seventeen in February. She was to be presented in May and was already in London, preparing for the grand affair. Her absence cast a damper on the Dowager's spirits and caused Barry to rethink his decision to leave just then. He had, however, made up his mind that before long he would speak to his grandmother. He was going back to Trinidad to claim Eléna. He would marry and live there. He would not be rich, but he ought to have enough money to start a small cocoa estate somewhere in a cool valley, surrounded by the majestic Northern Range, protected by the lush, wild greenery from the harsh realities of the world. They would employ only paid freemen and he would run it himself. Eléna would be a great help. They would build a lovely, lacy, house with a wide veranda to catch the breezes. They would have children, beautiful, pale brown children who looked half like him and half like her. All he needed was the right moment, and the courage to speak to his grandmother. How would he get the courage?

The Dowager, unhampered by his compunction, caught him quite unprepared therefore with her incisive perspicacity. She broached the subject herself.

They had spent a dull, joyless few days. She was thoughtful and withdrawn, while he was silent and moody. He never realised that his grandmother was quietly observing him.

It was April but a stubborn chill had forced the Dowager to order a roaring fire in Barry's favourite room, where they sat uncommunicatively. The old lady appeared to doze off. Barry watched as the orange glow from the dancing flames caressed her worn features, then he too fell into a reverie.

Without warning, the Dowager's feeble voice broke the silence. 'Was she very beautiful?' the voice asked.

'Who, Grandmama?' Barry's eyes opened wide, questioningly.

'You know who, Barry. The woman in your thoughts.' The Dowager's bony, aristocratic features twitched expectantly.

Barry's face flushed with discomfort, like a little boy caught in an act of mischief.

'Barry, I have watched you . . . seen your sadness. You don't want to leave me. But I am better now, thanks mostly to you. I would welcome a granddaughter-in-law.'

Barry raised his head and met her eyes squarely. The old woman looked into haunted pools of blue, and felt her heart melt at the sight of such patent distress.

'Grandmama.' Barry leaned forward in his chair, his hands clasped together, as expressive of the struggle in him as was his pained eyes or his strangled voice. 'Part of the problem is that you may find the girl unsuitable, and I cannot bear to fight with you over her. I . . . I love you both too much.'

The Dowager looked into the face that she loved above all others. She had always prided herself on being an astute judge of character. How could this young man, whose mind and opinion she knew and respected so well, make a choice that could be reproachable? She had heard of the incident with the Claymore girl. He had shown clearly, even then, that he was not to be fooled by a pretty face or by seductive wiles. Nor did she think him an irresponsible young man. Look at how he had stifled his own desires and unselfishly devoted himself to her for two years. He had done it out of love and generosity of spirit, for surely he knew that his inheritance was assured. How could she repay such generosity?

'Is . . . is she a married woman?' she asked.

'Of course not, Grandmama. Nothing like that,' spluttered Barry.

'Then, go to her.'

'But how?' exclaimed Barry in confusion. 'I tell you, you may not find her suitable. Please wait until I explain.'

'No, Barry. I see in your face how much this woman means to you. You have suffered long enough. Listen to me. If you were the heir to Vantage, I could not be so generous. But I can be generous to you, as generous as you have been to me.

'I'll tell you a secret. All my life I've played at being the radical. As a woman, indeed as an aristocrat, one can only play at it. But now is my chance to resolve that contradiction. So . . . I will respect your choice

. . . no matter what. Grenmill and all I have is yours, always. One condition only. Make this house your home. I long to see your children. This family needs children.'

'Oh, I love you so, Grandmama!' Barry cried passionately. He leapt to his feet and embraced the old woman's frail body in his muscular arms. He knelt by her chair and buried his face in her wrinkled neck. She chuckled merrily and stroked his back.

'Wait for Jessica's ball. Then you can go with my blessings.'

The leaping flames played on the exotic oriental rug at her feet and glowed on her face, transforming her, with their dancing lights of gold and bronze, into a benevolent, Byzantine madonna, as she smiled and caressed her kneeling, worshipful grandson.


# VI

Flowers and glitter: that was how Barry always remembered Jessica's ball. The Wolvertons' magnificent London ballroom, with its twenty-foot ceilings and mirrors that spanned almost that full length, was ablaze with light from crystal chandeliers and aglitter with the reflection of the diamond, ruby and sapphire baubles of their guests.

The shy young girl that Barry had hardly noticed two years before was now full-grown. She possessed a delicate, lithesome beauty. Dressed in the traditional white silk, with her straight blonde hair in a simple loose, style, she was the embodiment of a creation by Botticelli. Her only adornment was a pair of diamond earrings, a gift from Barry to the young girl. Looking at her now, he saw them and smiled uneasily, wondering if she had read more than was intended into the simple avuncular gesture.

For many hours, as the evening progressed, guests continued to arrive. When eventually his brother Graham did so, Barry went to speak to him. Graham spoke first, however. 'There you are, lad, lucky for me. I've brought you a friend. Met him on the way in and happened to be introduced. Said he was dying to see you. Oh bother! Where is the man?' Graham turned languidly. 'There,' he pointed, 'handing his coat to the footman. His back's towards us.'

The two brothers strolled slowly towards the back of a tall, slight gentleman. The lanky form turned and smiled. Barry instantly lengthened his step, hand outstretched in greeting as he exclaimed, 'What the devil! It's Mark! Mark!'

They shook hands warmly, and Graham withdrew.

'No, Mark, come, let's to a private place. You must tell me how you've come to be here.' Barry excitedly drew his friend away from the dazzle of the perfumed, sparkling crowd and the sound of music and chatter.

'It's marvellous to see you in the flesh,' Mark responded. 'How is your man Fist? I heard of your daring rescue of him. Where is he now?'

'Here in London. He has his own gymnasium, and is doing quite well for himself. But wait, we've too much to talk about,' answered Barry as he opened a door and found a vacant sitting-room. 'Ah, let's sit here. Now tell me everything, everything. What brings you to England?'

'That's a long, sad, story, my friend.'

'Then before you begin, tell me about Eléna and my old friends.'

'Eléna and family are fine. Carmen and family as well. Yei too.'

An unbidden pulse began to throb uncontrollably in Barry's temple. The pupils of his blue eyes dilated, and his palms grew suddenly clammy. 'I . . . I didn't follow you. I must not have heard you correctly,' he stammered.

'Oh?' Mark frowned in some consternation. 'Did I say somthing of significance? I'm so absent-minded of late. Wasn't I just telling you about the well-being of Carmen and family and Eléna and . . . family?' Light seemed suddenly to dawn on the young man. 'You didn't know?' he whispered. 'My God, Barry, no one told you? I . . . I'm sorry. I wouldn't have been so casual had I realised, not after what I've just been through. I always suspected you two had a *tendre* for each other, but I didn't know. Forgive me, please, old chap.'

'Tell me plainly then,' Barry forced the words through a constricted throat.

'I'm sorry. Yes, she is married. She married Fontainebleau two years ago. They have a child.'

Barry stared unbelievingly at his companion. His face had grown as white as chalk. He rose abruptly from his chair, unable to utter another word to Mark. His hand rose to indicate that he did not wish to be pursued, and he strode out of the room. Behind him he heard the strains of music, and the words which he knew well went around in his darkened, swirling, brain: 'Begone, dull care, I prithee begone from me!'

# VII

There were long, shadowy, indistinguishable days, and short, iniquitous, phantasmal nights beyond counting, most of them lost to his memory for ever. Only a vague recollection through alcoholic mists lingered on his numbed, bemused brain and penetrated to the light of day. But the light of day hardly met his red-rimmed eyes. The curtains remained drawn in whatever hovel he chose to swelter, and the shadowy minions who supposedly saw to his welfare were vilely denounced if they dared to let in the merest streak of the 'blinding, cursed thing'. His life had virtually become one long, useless, drunken night until one day he awoke to find his jaw shaven clean, the light dazzling him, and a rich, familiar baritone singing the old Somerset air:

> 'Oh Madam since you are so cruel
> And that you do scorn me so
> If I may not be your lover
> Madam will you let me go?'

Barry rose on his elbows and cleared his phlegmy throat. He could not match the African's perfect timbre, so he half-talked the response: 'Oh, no John, no John, no John, no! Appropriate eh?'

Barry blinked at the outline of Fist's bulk against the glare of a window.

'What the hell're you doing here, Fist?' he asked in a rheumy voice. 'She won't let me go you know, the velvet lady, I mean.'

'I know who you mean, man. Don't think about that now. Come on, let's get out of this foul place,' answered the black man.

It had taken months for Fist to find Barry. As Fist explained, 'Mayfair folks thought you in the country, country folks thought you in town.' Fist took Barry home with him to his cosy rooms at the back of his gymnasium and supplied him with wholesome food and no strong drink. Feeling better at the end of a week, Barry generously offered to help out in the gymnsium.

'You're not in Trinidad now, Barry. Here you're quality folks. Can't work in a gym, bad form, you know.'

'I meant to ask, what else goes on here, Fist? I've noticed odd comings and goings. Come on, be frank with me,' demanded Barry.

'I've no secrets from you, Barry, but promise to keep this under your hat, eh? We've a small press here, and we print propaganda.'

'You mean you've a damned corresponding society here under your roof?'

'Ain't no one society as such. Just a group of us who trying to right some wrongs. We print propaganda for the Abolitionists, for the workers' combinations, and so on. I mean to take a jibe at Picton, one of these days.'

'By Jove, Fist! You're a man after my own heart! You've not sat around and done nothing, like me,' added Barry sadly.

'Wasn't it you who told me political action was the answer? You'll make your contribution too. Wasn't it you who taught me to read and write? And through you I got my present position. Any achievement of mine is an achievement of yours, my friend.'

'No. I have things to do, too. Thanks for reminding me.'

There were times too when Barry became melancholy with despair over the loss of Eléna and it was Fist who supplied him with his uncomplicated wisdom and suggestions. 'Mr Mark left town, but why don't you find Mr Whiteways? He can tell you what happened to her. That Mr Whiteways, he was never against you being with a black girl?'

Barry laughed as he answered, 'Mightn't do it himself, but being a liberal, an observer of mankind, he's tolerant of other people's idiosyncracies. I'll consider going to look for him. You are right, Fist, I ought to sort myself out.'


The year 1800 did not find Barry going to look for Fred, however. Vowing to forget all thoughts of Eléna, he returned to Grenmill. His grandmother saw on his face that he had suffered in the interval. There was a degree of hardness about his eyes and a grim set at the corners of his mouth that bespoke a new disillusionment. The hollows in his cheeks too, made him look hard, and much older than a man in his twenty-fourth year. Thus she made no attempt to caution him when he took to a life of gaiety with his eldest brother and his set, a set that now included the young Jessica.

Forcing himself not to think about Eléna or about reality, politics, the war or slavery, he began a giddy round of parties, balls and routs, fox-hunting meetings and general jollification. Barry was Jessica's constant escort, and they soon became an acknowledged pair with everyone expecting the young Wingate to come up to scratch and declare his intentions. Barry's heart was not engaged, but he saw the result as quite inevitable. 'Well, why not? It would make everyone happy,' he decided.

He forced himself to ignore the monumental happenings of the times: Pitt's resignation over the King's veto of religious tolerance towards Irish Catholics in the House; Napoleon's successes, British losses and willingness to have peace on any terms; or the fact that Picton had officially been made Civil Governor of Trinidad with wide powers of administration. For none of these could he spare more than a passing glance, for to think was to remember, and to remember was to feel the pain again, and to reach for the bottle again, and to be lost completely.

It took a tragedy in the family to finally bring the giddy whirl to an end and to force Barry to genuine sobriety.

234

It was clear to everyone that the peace would soon be signed. Most of Europe had already entered into agreements with Napoleon and, apart from their successes at sea, the British were in no position to hold out. France too seemed to want peace. The war went on, but unenthusiastically. Then, when it was almost at an end, the Wingates received news that Jeffery had been killed n Egypt, dying at the feet of Sir John Moore.

The family was thrown into chaos. Lord and Lady Vantage were inconsolable. Jeffery, the least radical, most praiseworthy son had been killed in some useless battle in a declining war. The Dowager journeyed to town for the first time in years. Barry was forced to face reality.

He realised that he had perceived all of his brothers as reflections of what he could be. Jeffery had represented the possibility he most abhorred. Now he saw that by his inaction he had been on the same side as Jeffery. In fact it was worse than that, for he had no principles at all. Didn't all his commitment hinge on the love of a woman? Losing her, hadn't he lost all dedication?

Barry cursed himself as he looked in the mirror and saw the lines of dissipation on his face.He thought of how Fist had put him to shame, and resolved to make an effort. He would get Richard to introduce him to that sharp young politician, Canning, and try to interest him in helping the island. Then he would be free, free to put Trinidad honestly behind him, and free to propose to Jessica.


# VIII

Canning was happy to meet him. Confirming that the Abolitionists needed issues to force the hand of Parliament, he was very interested in Barry's ideas.

'In the war settlement,' began Barry, 'I feel that important possessions like Ceylon and Trinidad will be retained. Then the government ought to issue some order for Trinidad's proper settlement – we can enforce the ruling of '92 and even introduce a new and more equitable system of government for the colonies. Regulations for distribution of agricultural land to new settlers is important. For example, land should be apportioned only relative to the number of slaves already on the island – a clear policy so that lack of adequate labour cannot be made into an issue. And after compiling the statistics and ascertaining just how much labour is needed, a new class of settler can be encouraged. Free labour. Peons from South America, perhaps, or free blacks from the other islands, native Indians or creoles. Since sugar is declining economically, and there are many cocoa plantations already, agriculture on the island can easily be diversified. Then there is the question of the administration of the island.'

'The present Governor has been confirmed in his appointment – I gather you're against the man?' asked Canning.

'Not the man, but his methods. He encountered a situation that could have been controlled, and he unleashed terror, breaking the terms of the capitulation, intimidating the free people of colour, overturning humane attitudes towards the slaves, torturing and killing indiscriminately. What is needed is an investigation of his administration.'

'It may be possible to tackle the settlement issues and start such an investigation at the same time,' ventured Canning, enthusiastically.

'One thing more, though,' added Barry, 'the question of introducing a local assembly. In an island like that where the majority of propertied citizens are coloured, I fear they will be manipulated out of any control over their political lives.'

'Probably, but present indications are that the assembly system is no longer tenable, especially in new territories where the population is alien and possibly hostile. There's no perfect solution, but control by the Crown could give the appearance of equal treatment. It's the most one can hope for. I do sense that the development of Trinidad will be a touchstone in the struggle for abolition and for colonial development, however. It's the very sort of issue we've seen seeking.'


Barry felt a new lightness of spirit after his meeting with Mr Canning. Turning his mind towards the final parting of the ways with Trinidad, he set off one morning in early June for the north and finally reached Northumberland on a crisp, cool summer day. There was no great difficulty in locating the new lord's castle, and as soon as he set eyes on Fred he knew that their friendship could never be destroyed. They embraced fondly and began immediately to get reacquainted, words spilling out of Fred with the old exuberance.

He told him of Juanita's difficult pregnancy and about the new baby. Finally, on a more serious note, he said, 'So, you've heard of Eléna's marriage from Mark?'

'You've seen Mark? Is he here?' Barry was patience itself and digressed without a qualm.

'No. He went directly to Ireland to see his parents. Louis foolishly got involved in the damned revolution there and was shot in a skirmish.'

'No! Louis, at his age!'

'Mark wrote to us though,' continued Fred, 'and sent us a gift of a

236

painting.' He paused. Barry contemplated the carpeted floor of Fred's sitting-room and Fred peered at his friend with uneasy eyes. Eventually, the new lord sighed and said: 'I know you feel I betrayed you by not telling you of Eléna's marriage.'

Barry looked up, blue eyes unrelenting.

'Look, Barry, at first I really didn't know, Juanita kept it hidden from me. When she finally did speak, it was to insist that you not be told. You do understand? It did seem to be for the best.'

Barry nodded wordlessly, thinking that in spite of his liberalism Fred did possess a thin streak of callousness.

'Anyway, I had hoped that you'd forgotten her and with your grandmother so ill, it seemed you'd never to able to return anyway. I . . . well, I just allowed myself to be persuaded of that, I suppose.'

'And what has changed your mind?' asked Barry quietly.

'Mark's letter and his picture.'

Fred got up and led the way to a large room lined with bookshelves. Above an oak desk was the painting. He indicated it and backed away. Barry stepped forward and gasped audibly.

He knew that Mark was considered a landscape painter, and indeed the sweeping bamboo arches which filtered the sunlight, the sparkling stream and the flaming flowers of the immortelle were magnificently rendered. But to Barry, the landscape could hold no candle to the portrait of Eléna in the foreground. Mark had captured her face in repose, slightly turned away from the viewer. Her dark eyes gazed wistfully into the stream, looking ineffably sad. There was an orchid in her raven black hair, and her elegant hands curved towards her breasts. She was so beautiful, so very beautiful. He gazed and gazed at the portrait. Then suddenly he leaned forward, peering more closely, as if something in the picture shone out and spoke to him. He turned abruptly and marched out of the room, calling to Fred. 'Can you tell me when this picture was painted? Was it since her marriage?'

'Oh yes. After she'd been married almost two years. Is something wrong?'

'Something is wrong! Very wrong! Wrong with Eléna and that marriage. Do you know what, Fred? I'm going back. By Jove, I'm going back to the island on the first ship I can get!'

# IX

Having made his decision, Barry steeled himself one morning, rode across Grenmill Park and said goodbye to Jessica. She was supremely

237

suitable and a lovely girl. But her face went blank whenever he mentioned a truly serious thought. She could never argue or struggle with him. She was a Dresden doll to be loved and pampered, while he wanted an equal and he needed someone whose beauty was planted firmly on the earth.

It was the evening before he was to sail. Fist welcomed him with a sombre, haunting expression on his brawny face. They walked outdoors and finally entered a tavern where the ale was reputedly good and Fist was welcomed like the champion he was.

'I remembering so many things,' said Fist.

Barry looked fondly at the black man who had risen from slave, to servant, to independent businessman and radical pamphleteer. His faith in Fist had never been misplaced. The man was made of superior stuff.

'So, you going back then? Don't go and break your heart though, and stay off the bottle. Won't be easy in Trinidad now with Mr Whiteways gone and the other gentlemen too. I get the feeling the island's all folding up like . . .'

'Like the 'ti Marie leaves, eh?' Barry regarded his mug of ale. 'Yes, the island is like her, sensitive, unhappy, threatened.'

'You think she's unhappy?'

'Saw it in the painting I told you about, and she hasn't forgotten me either. I saw that too. We made a commitment to each other, Fist. If she broke it, she had a reason. I can't live with the question any more. Well, what about you and your girl?'

'My question is, which is the bigger commitment, love or marriage?'

'I'll find out about that, won't I?'

'In my case, you know, the girl was just there. She's no trouble. Cooks a decent meal, warms my bed. Now she just start crying, tells me she making a child and that I will just leave her out in the cold like her father left her mother. I didn't say anything to her, but I had to admit slavery do that to black man. Kill family feeling and all. I just use up the girl. If was . . . Tessa, you know . . . that was different, but now?'

'I have no answers. But I can tell you, among my class, marriages are rarely for love. Some of the unions work out. In your case, why shouldn't it? There's no more Tessa, my man. I do wish you happiness.'

'And I you, Barry. How I wish I could come with you just for a day, to feel that burning sun, and climb those mountains and . . .'

Their voices low and unhurried, their heads bent over the table, their hands intermittently guiding mugs of ale to their lips, they continued far into the night. Before dawn broke, the black man accompanied his friend to his stately home in Mayfair and loaded his luggage on the coach. He drove with him to the port, and stood looking out to sea, long after the ship taking Barry back to the West Indies had sailed far out of sight.

# CHAPTER NINETEEN

## I

Clouds sailed in wispy greys, teasing the moon, sifting its shy light and casting speaking shadows on the small group huddled in concentration beneath the sky. The broad, arresting face of the African speaker was briefly illuminated in the eerie light, his cheekbones momentarily cast into high relief as his whispering voice rose resonantly in the semi-gloom.

'You all see for yourself, since the new Code Noir Picton make he done take 'way all we free time. Saturday gone from we. We have to work more hours and he charging the massa fifty dollars if he ain't follow the law. Now he want we to be studs for he like if we is cattle in true. He ain't care nothing 'bout we as people, only to work and make more o' we to work till we dead for them. Aahh . . . and he ain't saying nothing in the whole law 'bout how we could buy we freedom. Nothing. And we can't do nothing now. Even li'l party he banning. Don't talk 'bout we religion, for that he killing you. But all o' we who know the word o' the Loas and serve Ogoun, we must remember he's a warrior, and we he followers, is all warriors in the faith.'

Antoine's bulging eyes gleamed intensely as he paused and stared with maximum effect at his subdued listeners. The lone woman in the group shuddered involuntarily. The man next to her moved protectively closer. The voice with its hectoring tone resumed.

'We all agreed that something must be done. This is the part I want to tell you all. This is between the four o' we alone. You all understand that?' Everyone in the group nodded grimly. He continued, 'The faithful in St Ann's, in the Coblentz estate, and in Diego Martin, decide to make the first move. The word come today. They intend to do for the white devils, for Baron de Montelambert and . . . for Begorrat.'

There was a unanimous gasp in the company as the speaker uttered the name of the dreaded slave-torturer with dramatic emphasis. 'Why? We ain't ready yet. We now start to organise,' protested one voice.

'Yes, but is because o' all this talk 'bout the peace. They figure if we put some fire in they tail now, the English ain't go want to keep the island after the peace and we go go back to Spain and how it was then, even if we ain't succeed in real freedom. And when we make the big move, at least things go be easier for we.'

'But they don't understand Begorrat is the chief magistrate for this year? Now he more powerful and bad than ever!'

'Yes, they know. But they ain't 'fraid. The leaders in Coblentz in agreement with those in Diego Martin. They have they plan. That I can't tell you. You must understand. And we done agree on action. All these months we telling everybody that, so we have to support them now or they go think we was jokers. Is a dangerous plan in my opinion, and I tell them so, but instead o' thinking 'bout waiting, they decide to go ahead. Believe me I 'fraid, I wouldn't lie. I worried in true. Aahhh . . . that is why I call you all here tonight. You see, I myself tell them that the Baron de Montelambert and Begorrat ain't no easy men to take, and if Begorrat catch them, even one o' them, is death or worse than death for all who was in the plan much less for the dauphins, the leaders. They know how we people stop. Once a plan like this fall down you know what they go do. One thing go give them freedom and ruin the massa!'

'Oh God, not seasoning?'

'Yes. I warn them, but you know what they decide. This is the part I 'fraid. The dauphins say, since it might happen anyway to plan for it. They get the nurse Thisbe and she husband Felix to pledge to prepare the seasoning in secret. To serve it. People first, dauphins last.'

'But, oh God, after that time in the same Coblentz some years aback when hundreds o' we do that, I don't see how them leaders could think like that, to do that again! Them mad or what?'

'Yes, they mad. Picton and Begorrat have them mad. We can't do nothing, we can't inform on them. We have to stand with them to the end. We have to try to get everybody ready too, to see if we could make the move together, but if we can't do that, at least we have to keep quiet. Listen what I telling all you. If it come to seasoning in true, I wondering if we can't make some plan o' we own. I was thinking, you, Tina . . .'

'Me?'

'Yes, you, woman! Don't sound so 'fraid. It ain't nothing hard I telling you. The woman you does work for, the one I hear you say who know all 'bout bush medicine . . .'

'Mistress Eléna? But she ain't go be . . .'

'Wait, hear what I saying good first. She must be know all the poison in Trinidad, and all the ways to stop them working. What you must do is to interest yourself in she medicines and thing. Talk to she on the sly like. So it go be natural when you start asking her 'bout the remedy for poisons.'

'But . . . but even so I ain't go know which bush Thisbe have in she mind to use!' protested Tina.

'None o' we ain't know that woman! I go work on that part. You just bring up the talk, casual like, when you get the chance. I working on Thisbe too, but I have to be real careful. In case I ain't get to convince she, your job go be real important. We have time still. They ain't go try for some weeks yet, I think. At least I go try to hold them back. Listen, woman, you call on the strength of Ogoun, and on the cunning of Damballah, the snake heself. If we have some kind o' remedy and the worse happen maybe, just maybe we could stop plenty black people from dying for nothing. You have to do it, girl.'

'Well . . . all right. I go try, but it ain't go be easy! That Madame o' mine real smart for so.'

'The spirits go guide you, woman. But I warning you! You know how you woman like to talk! Shut your mouth 'bout this business. If this talk come out before the day, is you to catch you hear, *crapeau* go smoke your pipe.'

The speaker's protuberant, snake-like eyes stared almost menacingly at Tina and she returned the look with wide-eyed, hypnotised apprehension.

The moon, as if itself intimidated, slid beneath a dark cloud and no light shone on the small group as they rose to their feet. 'Tomorrow night we praying to the god Shango for guidance,' said the speaker as they dispersed. 'If all you can't come, is all right. Pray by yourself, you hear.'

Tina and La Fortune, the man who had sat protectively near her, made their way carefully in the darkness. 'Don't worry to go back home now. It too late and too dark anyway. Stay with me in the shack, eh *doux, doux.*'

The lovers stopped only to exchange passionate kisses. Then, locked in each other's arms, they ran quietly to a hut set well back from the town where lingering lights flickered like fireflies in the night. La Fortune scooped Tina's light body up in his powerful arms and, kicking the door of the hut open, swung her on to the sole bed.

It was well after dawn when Tina shook the sleep from her eyes and rose hastily. Her long white skirt tucked in her belted waist, her shawl making a tight bundle under her thin arms, she ran until she came to the town proper, then she slackened her pace. Stopping once, she bent to pull up the straps of her *alpagatas* and then hurried on. In her haste she bumped into a gentleman who was stepping out of the Guest House of the Royal Palms. 'Pardon, Sir,' she muttered apologetically, lowering her head. She walked on a few paces. Then she stopped short and turned around suddenly, mouth wide open. 'Massa Barry?' she muttered to herself in disbelief. 'Eh, eh! I wonder if Madame know he back here?' A moment later she was off again, hastening towards the gabled roofs of the Fontainebleaus' home.

Gaining the yard, she crept around to the kitchen, passing under the large shady trees. A husky, musical voice rang out.

'Tina? Tina?' The door opened and Eléna stepped out, a bundle of frothy white frills and curly brown hair in her arms.

'There you are, Tina! I've been searching for you. Where have you been?'

Giving her mistress no time to continue her questioning, the slave ran up to her and reached for the warm, sleepy bundle in Eléna's arms. 'I just went for a morning walk is all, Madame.' She snuggled her bony, black face next to the creamy skin of the cherub.

'A walk at this hour of the morning?' asked Eléna with a distinct note of disbelief in her voice.

Evasively, Tina responded. 'You know who I just see, Madame? You never guess in a hundred years. Mister Barry, the Englishman with the yellow, yellow hair who uses to be at Santa Clara long time, you remember he?'

Eléna's brown face turned a chalky hue. 'B . . . Barry? No! You must be mistaken, Tina!'

'But Madame, eh! eh! My eyes good, good. I telling you is heself.'

Seeing her mistress in a state of some bewilderment, Tina took the opportunity to escape. Muttering something about seeing to the welfare of the child, she hurried indoors.

Eléna sank down heavily on the garden bench. Her eyes, glazed and unseeing, stared fixedly at nothing. Her face was a study of shifting emotions. Then her hand reached almost convulsively for her chest as if to still her racing heart, but instead fumbled a moment and slowly withdrew a gold chain that was hidden under her blouse. The pendant sparkled as it caught the sunlight. She held it in her hand and stared at it unblinkingly. Her fingers imperceptibly began to caress the beaten gold forms of two expertly wrought, miniature macaws.

## II

Barry rode the well-remembered roads to Santa Clara in record time. He did not pause, not for a minute, not even to look towards the swamp where the mangrove trees still raised their beckoning arms, nor did he linger reminiscently over any landmark. He knew well that Eléna was not to be found in her old haunts. Suppressing his desire to see her immediately, he chose to go instead to Maracas. He hoped that from there a better rendezvous could be arranged.

Drawing near to the estate, he slowed his hired animal and trotted into Santa Clara. A stable boy ran up to meet him, grinning in recognition. He pointed to Yei in the distance, ensconced on a garden seat under the shade of a tree. Her back was towards them. Barry approached noiselessly, and stood not ten feet from her. He listened as she rocked an as yet invisible infant in her ample arms, and sang a strange haunting chant . . .

'Tumpuna, Tunapuna, Aripo, Arima,
Chaguanas, Chaguaramas, Talparo, Cuaracara,
Piarco, Chacachacare, Cipero, Tucuché,
Nariva, Annaparima, Moruga, Tamana.

Couva, Cuma . . . na . . .'

Suddenly, as if sensing a presence, Yei stopped singing. Without turning, she called out, 'Come, whoever is behind me!'

Lips twitching mischievously, Barry walked towards her. Anchoring his hand along the bole of the tree, he swung in front of her.

'Ah!' cried Yei. 'Barry? Barry? My son, you've come back?'

'It was worth a trick to see you startled, Yei,' he teased, engulfing her in his arms, baby and all. Presently, she pushed him gently from her, and looked deeply into his smiling eyes.

'Let me look at you, my son. What have the years done to you in that cold, sunless country of yours? You are so pale!'

'I'll soon be brown as a berry again. To see your smile makes up for three years of grey skies.'

'Ah, I see you have not changed,' Yei laughed. 'Come, sit with me.'

'Who is the baby?'

'Little José, Joselito we call him. Carmen's third.'

'My word, she's been busy! And the second?'

'Rodrigo.'

'Another boy!' Barry reached playfully for the child's eager hand, and remained with the tiny fingers clutching his. He sat on the grass and looked up at his old friend. 'What was that song you were singing?'

'Oh, that is nothing.' She laughed again. 'When little Diego was a baby, he liked to hear the Amerindian names of Trinidad, so I strung them in a rhyme and made up a silly tune. It's become the children's lullaby.'

'It reminds you of your people.'

'That too!'

For a moment they said nothing more. Then Yei spoke. 'So, you know about Eléna and André. Maybe now you understand my warning.'

Barry sighed in agreement. 'Why did she do it, Yei? Didn't you tell her I would return as you instructed me! I had counted on you to be on my side, you know.'

'I never doubted you, but you must ask her yourself. I can't speak for her. I never could.'

'Could you arrange it? I can't just force myself on the Fontainebleaus' house demanding to see her. I've come this long way in spite of knowing how things stand. I must see her alone. What do you say?'

Yei was slow in replying. Eventually she answered, 'I can't just send for her, Barry. Not to meet an old lover. What kind of mother would I be? However, next week is the second *cumpleaños* of the other child, Rodrigo. We are planning a small party. It's unlikely that André will come, but she will. It could be arranged for you two to wander off alone, for maybe an hour. Would that do?'

# III

August and the rainy season. For five days Barry cursed the weather. His burdened heart, like a leaden weight, pressed on his spirits. His depression was acute. When at last the appointed day came he was a wreck of boiling emotions. Anxiety to get the meeting over, excitement at seeing Eléna again, and a pervasive feeling of despair. Worst of all, he was overcome by a rising, rebellious anger.

He dressed with meticulous care. His face was rigid. His movements were precise and economical, like an automaton. He collected his horse and rode off.

Once at Santa Clara, he sent word to Yei who was busy in the kitchen.

244

He held a brief, disjointed conversation with Carmen who was hurrying to supervise the dressing of her brood. Then he walked out through the garden towards a clump of trees.

He glanced repeatedly at the house. Finally he saw a carriage approach. He stood in the shadows of a tree. The carriage drew up in front of the house. The tall graceful figure of Eléna descended. She bent, reached inside and lifted a sleeping infant in her arms. She walked up the veranda steps and out of sight.

'A girl!' Barry whispered. Strangely, he had never enquired about the sex of her child. He had assumed it was a boy. But a girl! He felt a pang of uncontrollable jealousy. There had been no girls in the Wingate family for generations. What a treasure she would have been! Suddenly, it was immeasureably harder to face Eléna, to face the thought that she had really given herself to another. She had produced a child, a tangible link with another man. He could not face her. There was too much anger in him at that moment. He would bungle any meeting. He turned and walked back a few paces. Then he stopped again and reprimanded himself. It was all too foolish.

Resolutely, he spun on his heels and marched back to the house and entered the veranda. He hesitated at the top step, and then Eléna came out.

No words passed between them for a long moment. Finally, she extended her hand. He reached nervously for it and felt hers tremble in his grasp.

'Let us walk in the garden,' was all that he said.

With Barry holding her limp fingers, they walked out past the poui and the frangipani and the neat beds of flowers. Eventually they stopped. Eléna had carefully avoided walking towards her favourite spot. She approached a tree and half sat against a fork in its trunk. He leaned an extended arm boyishly against it.

'How have you been, Eléna?'

'Very well. And you?'

'As you see.'

'And your grandmother?'

'Greatly recovered. She'll never be exactly her old self, but tolerably well and active again.'

'That's wonderful.'

He glanced at Eléna and saw her downcast eyes and agitated fingers. How nervous she was!

'Eléna, let's talk like we used to, please.'

'Oh, Barry, what you must think of me! I . . . I don't know what to say now or how to explain without. Oh, I never thought you'd come back. Honestly.'

'Why would you think I'd never come back? Didn't I promise to? Didn't you get my letters? Please try to make me understand or I'll go mad with the questions. You know how much I love you, I loved you from the first moment I saw you, if that's possible. Try as I might I couldn't help myself. I thought you knew that. I respected you always as a woman of forthrightness. Why the betrayal, the silence, the evasion now? You knew I had to go back, but I wrote. I sent the gift. I know you got it, I saw it in Mark's painting. I saw that it meant something to you, that's why I came. I thought it would speak for me if doubts set in, and the time grew too long for you to wait. Why didn't you wait or write? At least you could have written to say you couldn't wait.'

Eléna hung her head pitifully and tears ran unchecked down her lovely brown cheeks. 'Please, Barry, no more! No more! My heart is already broken.' She pushed herself out of his reach, sobbing heartrendingly. She attempted to walk away.

Overcome with his own heartache and frustration, with months of doubt, grief and confusion, maddened by the nearness of her undiminished, unattainable beauty, Barry's heart had no room just then for sympathy. He gripped her arm roughly, pulled her around and pushed her none-to-gently against the tree. 'Why, Eléna?' he hissed fiercely, his blue eyes angry and full of an emotion closer to hate than the love he professed.

'Because I didn't want you to ruin your life over me! Because I'd never fit into your world! Because your family would hate me and ruin you, because your grandmother needed you and would never have understood. Because . . !' The words tumbled out.

Barry slammed her hard against the tree, his knuckles white from the pressure with which he grasped her arms. 'For that? For silly, solvable obstacles you did this to me, to us? How do you know what my family or my grandmother would think? Did I ever tell you any such nonsense? Couldn't you have faith in me to solve these problems? Couldn't you have loved me enough to wait, you little fool!' he cried with barbed emphasis.

Eléna was weeping helplessly. Her hair had broken loose from its tight chignon and fell now in waves about her face. It became entangled in her damp skin and stuck to her streaming eyes, blinding her. He did not let her go. He stood inches from her face, glaring unrelentingly at her attempts to avoid his piercing eyes, or to remove the suffocating hair.

'You're mine, you know that! Don't expect me to leave you alone. I have been honourable and restrained long enough. God knows I have no strength left to care about what is right or wrong!'

'I'm married, I tell you!' Eléna cried. 'To an honourable man, a sick man, I can't hurt him, Barry, I can't.' She had begun to struggle with him and forcing her hands up now, she pushed hard against his chest. Tearing free at last, she went running far into the bushes, crying unrestrainedly.

Barry checked himself. As enraged as he was, that was no way to act. He watched her go and made no move to follow. He was breathing heavily, his face flushed and distorted by the excess of passion he had just displayed. He passed his hands over his brow and then sunk down into the fork of the tree Eléna had recently vacated. He cupped his face. Shame and remorse at his cruel conduct flooded through him now. 'What the hell am I becoming?' he asked himself over and over again. 'My God, my God help me. It was ridiculous to expect anything else. What on earth had I expected her to say? She *is* married and to a very honourable man. No doubt she really didn't believe I would return. Why did I return? Why did I come here? What did I expect?'

Taking out his handkerchief, he wiped away unbidden tears. He made an effort to calm himself, straightening his stock and smoothing back his hair. The sound of children playing in the garden invaded his consciousness . . .

'Lors! Where are you?'

'L-o-o-rs!'

'Here, Diego!' came a childish giggle. A tiny little girl with a crown of brown curls and delicately bronzed skin came into view. She started at the unexpected sight of Barry and stood momentarily stunned. And Barry, looking at her, found himself suddenly staring, as if at his own reflection, into a pair of eyes as blue as his own.

'Velours! Where you gone?' bellowed an African voice. Tina appeared and scooped up the child. 'Sorry, Sir,' she muttered.

'Velours?' Barry repeated. 'Velours . . ! Velvet! My God!' He rose immediately and ran through the bushes, along the stream and came as he expected upon Eléna bent over under the immortelle. She was still weeping uncontrollably. He went up to her and embraced her gently, kissing her face and her eyes. Her defences were all shattered. She put up no resistance but clung helplessly to him.

'Why did you try to hide it from me, Eléna? Oh, my love, why didn't you tell me? Why didn't you write as you'd promised? Come, no more tears, we have to speak seriously now. Tell me everything this time.'

She looked at him apprehensively.

247

'I apologise for my rotten behaviour. I am a beast! Please, I promise. See, I won't touch you if you prefer. I'll never treat you roughly again, never again.' He attempted a weak, encouraging smile.

She wiped her eyes with his handkerchief and brushed back her hair, tying it once more into a tight knot. He waited patiently this time and after a few more sobs she recounted to him the sequence of events which had forced her to abandon her love.

'After you left, I was wretched and miserable. Not only because you had left, but miserable too, because in spite of all my brave words the realisation that I was a helpless, useless woman whose efforts to affect slavery had been naïve was affecting me badly. But that's another story. Anyway, the misery inside me seemed to be affecting my health. I really thought so. I was sick every day. It was Yei who first suggested that I was pregnant. By the second month, I knew Yei was right . . .'

'Why didn't you write to me immediately?'

'Oh Barry, I did want to.' Eléna looked away guiltily. She resumed. 'I wrote so many letters and tore them all up. Then when Juanita's first letter came, I knew I could do nothing.'

'Juanita's? What could she say about us?'

'You mustn't blame her, she only meant well. She has always been a true sister to me. She had warned me long before, not to set my heart on you, that you had to go back to England. When she wrote, she said your grandmother was still very ill, that there was almost no hope of recovery, that you had taken on the running of her estate, that she hoped I knew what that meant, that you couldn't return now, even if you wanted to. She said I was not to delude myself, not to make life harder for you by tearing your heart in two when you had to be there. There was more . . . she also spoke of her own misery in England, of how she hated the snobbery of the British aristocracy, that she was having such difficulty with the language and how that class hated foreigners, even white ones. The only use they had for black people was to sweep the streets and clean the filth of London . . . Even mulattos . . . like me and my unborn child, I supposed. She said that she longed to leave and go up to the north, to Fred's castle where she wouldn't have to be in society very much.'

Eléna lapsed into silence and Barry used the moment to gently caress her hair and her face and to point out the misinterpretations in Juanita's pronouncements, before he asked: 'So when André proposed, you accepted?'

'Yes.' Eléna's face twisted convulsively and she began to sob once more.

248

'When you got my gift, the macaws, even that didn't stop you?' Barry's voice held no reproof, his anger was completely replaced by tender empathy.

'Oh Barry! It came on the day before the wedding. Everything was arranged, but still, even then, I was immediately determined to cancel everything, to go back on my word to André, everything. It was such a perfect gift! Oh Barry, it's meant so much to me. I wear it always. That day, you can imagine how poignant the message of your constancy was. I felt such a traitor. I told Yei I could not go through with the marriage. Strangely, she agreed. Maybe if she hadn't . . . anyway, she said she knew you'd return. She said among her people my condition was no disgrace, that white man's censures were inhuman, wrong and caused too much suffering. She was almost anxious for me not to marry. I . . . I don't know, but her support, ironically, sobered me. I understood and agreed with her but I knew she was from a different world, a world of simple practicality, an idealistic world. I had stopped being idealistic since Tessa and Rosa and Papa Diego died, and I realised my petty efforts could not even protect Santa Clara. In this world, this island, my child needed a father. I needed a life, a function. To get out of Carmen's way too, to let her run her own household. Oh, now I wished my Monsieur had been here. But he wasn't. I was alone, and I had to stop dreaming. I decided to go through with it. Yei said I was a poor disillusioned girl, and André . . .'

'Tell me about André. What did he say when he knew you were carrying my child?' asked Barry as he watched Eléna bend her lovely, sad head on its elegant neck, like one of his grandmother's campanulas in the summer garden.

'André was so noble about it. I told him everything, that I was in love with you, that we'd made love that last day because I knew I'd never see you again and I couldn't help myself. André said he'd not allow me to go through the pregnancy unmarried, alone, humiliated. He said he would gladly marry me and give our child his name, because he loved me so well, and had for so long. But there was a condition.

'You were not to be told of the child. This was not just a matter of his own pride, you must believe me. It was for all our sakes, to avoid further heartache and confusion. He said our child would be a Fontainebleau and would inherit all he had.' Eléna fought down a renewed outburst of tears and continued diligently, determined to finish now that she had started telling all. 'He has been very good. He loves Velours as if she were his own, really, Barry. He's a good father. It would kill him to lose her, please understand.'

'Does anyone else know? Carmen? José?'

'No. Yei of course. The others may have guessed, like you.'

'There was no guessing once I heard her name.'

'That was my weakness.'

'Thank heavens for it! Oh Eléna!' Barry held her tightly. 'I couldn't live without knowing the truth. All these months of doubt! And then today, your evasions!'

'Can you live with the truth now?'

'Oh my darling, I don't know. How I want you! How I want my velvet daughter!' He kissed her face passionately then, releasing her, spoke again. 'Let us not decide anything now. I need time to think, to absorb everything. Tell me more, tell me how your life has been.'

'Well, I got married and went to live in Port of Spain and I was pregnant and quite ill. Yei could not come to live at the Fontainebleaus' so she sent Tina with me because she knew about childbearing and Yei trusted her. She's stayed on since. Velours likes her.'

'Now as you say her name, I remember why she looked so familiar. She was the one with Rosa that day, wasn't she?'

'The very same. The first year wasn't so bad, but after that conditions in the island steadily got worse for us coloured people. I can't begin to tell you the indignities! We can't give a ball without seeking permission from the Commandant of Quarters and we have to promise not to admit slaves. Can you imagine how they think of us? Many of us have been forced to take renewed oaths of allegiance and to produce letters of manumission on demand. We are required to walk with a lighted lamp just like the slaves at night. We can't play a musical instrument in any public tavern. If you walk with a stick, even a walking stick, you can be arrested by any white man. The list goes on and on, Barry.'

'That bastard Picton! He'll go too far one day!' exclaimed Barry angrily.

'The worst of all was what they did to André, to the Fontainebleau family. André was never greatly liked by General Picton, I never knew why. Perhaps because of his proud bearing and gentlemanly conduct. Even so, it was a shock when Picton took him from the militia and appointed him an *alguazil*, and even further humiliated him by posting him to guard the house of the Commandant of Quarters.'

'I can't believe it!'

'Yes, Barry. The Fontainebleaus were incensed at the indignity, as you can imagine. It was awful, Barry! The family went mad. His father was like a man possessed, he struggled so hard trying to lobby among

250

Picton's friends that he became ill and declined so rapidly, before our very eyes.'

'He died?'

'Last year. He had aged overnight, you wouldn't believe it. His death was almost a blessing.'

'Oh Eléna! My sweet love, I had no idea.'

'I must tell you about Mark too before I go further. You did know that Mark was in love with Yvette?'

'I merely suspected.'

'Yes. Poor, sensitive Mark. He'd just begun to find himself, to develop a sense of responsibility and confidence, to come to terms with his parentage and everything. He wanted to marry Yvette. Poor boy! The Fontainebleaus, even André, who knew he was my brother – I don't know if you are aware . . . ?'

'That Louis is your father? I'm not surprised, but go on.'

'Even André was adamantly against the match,' she continued. 'No white man was to be allowed in their family – no Englishman! All I tried to say on his behalf was to no avail. They had another man in mind for Yvette. I had known of this for many years now, a rich coloured gentleman from the south. They insisted on an immediate engagement to discourage Mark. Mark would not be discouraged. Oh how I felt for him, Barry, and for poor sweet Yvette who was torn between loyalty to her race and her family, and love of my white brother. Anyway, he challenged Yvette's fiancé to a duel – Mark, an artist, knowing nothing about the sword. His life was spared only because Yvette had rushed to the meeting. To save his life she swore to marry the man and never see Mark again.'

Racking sobs overcame Eléna and Barry could do nothing but hold her in his arms and comfort her gently with soothing words, until she was able to speak again.

'You know, Barry, before the English came you would not have found them so adamant. Now all the races are fighting each other. Mark stayed on for some months afterwards, until he got a proper overseer for Kathy's estate. He used to come here to Santa Clara often. I would come to visit him. That was when he did the painting of me. He had begun to paint again with a vengeance. Eventually he left for England. You know the rest.'

'So much has happened to you and your family, and I . . . I knew nothing, nothing!'

'Oh, but there's more,' continued Eléna through her persistent sobs.

'Go ahead. Tell me everything, my darling.'

'André became ill – the lung sickness, you know. He had been coughing badly for many years, but after his job as an *alguazil* he started coughing up blood, and he was becoming very thin. Picton was forced to release him from duty. I've persuaded him to rest a great deal, and with the help of our herbs we have kept the illness at bay . . . for now. So you see, you have no need to be jealous. He is only half a man . . . and . . . I cannot leave him, Barry. Without me and Velours, he would surely die. His mother too depends on us. She herself has grown thin and is a mere shell of her former self.'

Now that Eléna had finished, she rested her head on Barry's lap, and he stroked her hair lovingly and wiped away the occasional tear. He said nothing. It was all too much to have befallen his lovely lady, and he was utterly helpless to change anything.

At length, she spoke again. 'What will you do now, Barry?'

'I don't know, my darling. Nothing for a while, I think. José has invited me to stay here at Santa Clara, so I'll see if somewhere, somehow, I can find a solution to our problems or to some of yours.'

Silence again and then he added, 'Will you meet me here, again? Could you arrange for me to spend some time with the child?'

'I ought to deny you, but I know I cannnot. Will you promise . . .'

'Listen, I'll do nothing to upset you, or your life or the child. Nothing without your consent.'

'Then I'll send her here to spend a week with Yei so you can visit her.'

'And you?'

'You'll see me when I come to collect her at the end of the week. Yei will tell you when.'


# IV

Eléna was true to her word. She sent Velours for the week. Slowly Barry made friends with the child.

One evening, after Carmen and the children had gone to bed, he got talking to José. Their conversation turned to politics.

José spoke of the rise of racial discrimination that would have shocked his father, of the activities of the government, of the present agitation by the British citizens for a British Constitution, of Begorrat and the French barons. On the latter subject, he elaborated.

'It's no joke at all. The French barons are dangerous men. They are playing a cautious game, currying favour with both the British Governor and the Spanish Court, just in case Spain regains the island when the peace is signed. I've been meaning to tell you about Don Chacon.

'In '98 he was tried at Cadiz, along with Admiral Apodaca, by a council of war. They were acquitted then, but have since been retried. Do you know why? These French barons instigated an investigation of Chacon's conduct – Spain used to require this at the end of a governor's term of office. Picton set up a committee, mostly Frenchmen of course. They noted their compatriots' denunciations of Chacon's surrender, sent their report to Madrid and got the poor man retried. He has been stripped of his rank and sentenced to perpetual banishment with no right of appeal and the constraint of perpetual silence.'

'Good gracious!'

'Indeed! Thank God my father did not live to hear of it! The poor man is in Portugal now, awaiting death – what else?'


The household stirred early the next day. Barry entered the living-room to discover Diego and Velours neatly dressed and sitting like models of good behaviour. On enquiry, he discovered that they were about to set off with their grandmother to see the Indians. He included himself on the trip.

'Where exactly are we going?' he asked Yei, entering the carriage.

'To Arima. It's the feast of Santa Rosa de Arima, patron saint of all Amerindians.'

'Santa Rosa? You mean Santa Rosa de Lima, the first Catholic saint of the Americas? Didn't she have something to do with flowers, and dedicated her life to the Indians and the slaves of Peru?'

'She is of Arima to us. It is said that after her apparition to the Amerindians in Arima, they converted to Christianity.'

'I see. Arima? What does it mean? Do tell me more about your people, Yei.'

'The name Arima came from that of an Amerindian chief, Hyarima. He was a great hero who fought valiantly against the Spaniards. Our history is full of great struggles and great heroes, terrible massacres by the white man and bloody revenge against him. Mass suicides too, many, many times. Oh, it's a very bloody history and over all is the steady advance of the Church to subdue and convert us.'

'Do you believe in Christianity, Yei?'

She shrugged. 'What's not to believe? The only thing I question is the part of man, his rules and regulations, the suffering he sends in the name of God.'

'I can find no fault with that argument,' responded Barry, looking at the older woman with respect, and seeing through her the pride and wisdom of a fallen people.


Flowers, feathers, plants and palms decorated the church. Drums rang through the air, and ornately dressed Indians paraded with the venerated, reputedly miraculous statue of Santa Rosa. After the official services, the small town of Arima took on a bazaar-like atmosphere, with stalls of sweetmeats, local game, fruits and Amerindian delicacies everywhere. The young Indians serenaded and danced for the amusement of the Commandant and all the many visitors. They chose themselves a king and a queen and then participated in sporting competitions, showing their enviable prowess with the bow and arrow.

The four from Santa Clara thoroughly enjoyed the day. Sheltering from a sudden downpour, Barry noticed an old, wrinkled Amerindian man looking fixedly at him with disturbing, seemingly clairvoyant eyes. Yei spoke to the man in their strange, almost latinised tongue. They appeared to be speaking about him.

Later in the carriage on the way home, Barry turned to Yei. 'Did that old man say something about me?'

Yei laughed. 'Nothing worth repeating, a riddle really.'

'A riddle? How strange? Do share it with me, Yei.'

'He told me that your parents had produced four children. The eldest, he said, could not; the second, would not; the third did not; but you will. The last will be the first, and he laughed.'

'Will do what?' asked Barry, his interest aroused.

'I thought you'd be able to work it out. Can't you?'

'I've no idea,' answered Barry with a frown, as he gazed at Yei's enigmatic, Gioconda smile.

They completed the journey home in silence. At Santa Clara Eléna was waiting for them on the veranda. Barry's heart sank. Had something unexpected happened, or had he got the days confused? He had expected her on Monday, tomorrow, the thirty-first. He jumped hastily out, took out the children and walked swiftly up to her. 'Is anything wrong? You've come a day early.'

'No. Nothing's wrong. André merely thought as the weather was fairly good today, I should come now and stay overnight.'

Barry smiled joyfully, his eyes locked into hers. 'Oh, Eléna, how wonderful! We'll have some time together. There's so much I'd like to tell you, all that happened to me over the last three years.'

# CHAPTER TWENTY

## I

In the dry season the poinciana in the Fontainebleaus' backyard flaunted itself in a riot of tangerine, orchid-like flowers, but now it was a sedate green. A few tapering seedpods remained, stretching down from the branches, like wagging tongues. 'Women's tongue', they were sometimes called, remembered Eléna as the wind stirred them and their seeds rattled sibilantly, whispering secrets.

André sat beside her on a bench beneath the tree, his legs propped on a stool, a cushion at his neck. He was still so thin. Beneath his shirt, she knew, his bones stuck out distressingly. But it had been worse a year ago and he would get better, she mused. At least she had persuaded him to accept the need to rest every day. His eyes were closed as she gazed at his handsome, barely tanned face. Though her eyes saw him, her brain focused on the image of Barry. Soon he would be back from Barbados, where he had gone to visit his uncle. It was almost the end of October; he would be back to say his final farewell. How could she face that day? To know that she would never see him again. Where would she get the strength again to let him walk away and not run screaming after him, pleading with him to stay, cursing the fate that had made him of another race. Race was the only thing when all was said and done that had kept them apart. Or was it fate? Fate that all their passion could not change. She had tried so very hard to love André instead. All she could squeeze out of her intractable heart was respect, and admiration for his pride and courage in the face of the collapse of his way of life. No, that spark of deep private communication that she shared with Barry was never there and could not be manufactured. A sob rose in her chest, but she forced it away.

The wind stirred the poinciana again, and the seedpods rattled, joining with a sudden burst of thunder and a distinct and ominous wail of human distress. Eléna had been in the act of waking André and rising at the hint of rain. Now, she recognised Tina's voice and ran over to the servants' quarters.

Eléna entered the annexe and saw her slave, face down on the cot, crying noisily. 'Tina, what is the matter?' she asked. Tina responded with increasing hysteria until Eléna shook her forcibly and she began.

'Madame, all o' them dead. They season just like Rosa do and the medicine you tell me, ain't help at all. The rest in Diego Martin go dead too. Oh God, Madame! I ain't know what to do. Oh God, help me! Help me!'

'Tina, what are you talking about? Who is dead? Who has poisoned themselves? Make sense, girl! Talk plainly!'

'All them slaves in Coblentz, Madame,' Tina cried, renewing her wailing.

'What are you telling me?' Eléna shook the slave. 'Why Tina? Why?'

'They was planning a revolt, Madame, but it gone bad.'

'What is this about Diego Martin?'

'They by Begorrat going and do the same thing now. Remember I was asking yer 'bout this bush to cut poison an' t'ing? Well, it was for them, but it ain't work, I tell you, it ain't work!'

'Tina, when is all this supposed to happen?' demanded Eléna.

'Today, Madame, now. Today. I just come from Coblentz.'

'Jesus Lord!' Eléna let go of Tina, and turned hurriedly, only to bump into André standing fixedly at the door.

'I heard everything,' he said crisply. 'I'll ride right away to Begorrat's and try to stop them. There's nothing else we can do. We cannot trust to send a message – it might make it worse for them.'

'André, you are ill! Let me, please. See, I will take the carriage. I can try to stop them. We can't alert that fiend Begorrat by sending a message but we must do something!'

'This is a man's job, Eléna,' he said firmly, turning away. 'You wait here. I'll come back shortly.'


Eléna waited and waited. Arms folded, she paced the floor, peering anxiously at the unrelenting rain, thankful only that her mother-in-law was at Yvette's in the south. Finally, after the clock struck the third hour, she called in a constricted voice to the yard boy, ordering him to ready her carriage. Throwing a cloak around her shoulders, she purposefully climbed in. The carriage swung out of the wide gates, heading towards Diego Martin.


Tina had cried herself into a frenzy. After three hours she could cry no more. She heard Eléna leaving. That was her chance. Maybe her mistress could stop the poisonings in Diego Martin, but she herself had to know what had happened to La Fortune. Was he safe in his shack, or had he been lingering at the scene in Coblentz?

La Fortune was a contract slave, hired out to do odd jobs by his master. He had plenty of free time and was almost his own boss with his own shack in the Belmont Hills.

Tina hurried through the drenched streets. She climbed the low hills and arrived quickly in sight of the remote hut. She pushed open the door. Immediately she was grabbed by the powerful arms of Antoine. His eyes, naturally protuberant, now seemed to reach out from their sockets, terrifying her.

'What you doing here, woman?' He held her in his iron grip. 'You trying to lead them white people to we or what?'

'Where La Fortune? Where he is?' cried Tina.

'Where the hell you think? What it is you do, woman? I see you head back to town from Coblentz. You went and tell your Madame, nah?'

'No! No!'

Antoine slapped her hard, his palm leaving a white, bloodless mark on her black cheek.

'Tell me the truth! You tell she or what?'

'Yes! Yes! But that ain't nothing. She ain't go do nothing bad, she a good woman.'

'You see how woman crazy! And what happen after that? What happen? She ain't gone to Diego Martin to warn Begorrat?'

'No! Yes! Oh God, where La Fortune?'

'Jesus Christ! All you woman does talk too damn much. Dead people can't talk, but if that woman gone to Begorrat, they go know for sure was a plan. It go be torture for La Fortune and all the rest o' we! Why all you woman so stupid!' He boxed her fiercely on the head. 'You ain't realise she is the same woman who give you the wrong remedy for the poison? Eh? Eh?' He aimed another blow, but Tina shied away.

'Look, you better come with me, *oui*. Me and a few others going up to the temple grounds to hide out. We have to protect not just we self, but we plans for the rest o' the island. If some of we leaders get catch today down in Diego Martin, you ain't see it could be years before we could get this island ready, in true?'

'But I can't come and leave La Fortune. I ain't even know where he is, self. Where he is? Oh God, tell me where he is, nah!'

'He in Diego Martin nah, where else!' Antoine spat out the words like a curse. He threw her from him roughly on the dirt floor, and hurried outside, hunched against the pouring rain.

Tina picked herself up hastily and dashed off back towards the town. Diego Martin was too far away. Her mistress ought to be back by now with news. The rain began to lessen and finally ceased altogether as she raced down the hill.

She reached the Fontainebleaus' house just as Eléna's carriage was swinging into the gate. Tina stopped. Closely following the carriage was a group of soldiers. She turned and ran. A soldier spotted her and shot off in pursuit. He was younger, his legs were longer and his strength greater. In no time she felt a cruel hand grabbing her shoulders.

## II

As soon as Barry stepped back on to the shores of Trinidad, he could sense the tension in the air. He tasted it in the way one could taste the salt in a sea breeze. He had been in Barbados when news came of the signing of the preliminaries to the peace, and of the retention of Trinidad by the British. He felt that trouble was brewing. This settlement would bring no peace to Eléna's island. Suddenly, he had become very afraid for his beloved.

He went directly to the guest house and called to the knowledgeable landlady. Soon she was telling him of the two attempted slave uprisings and the resultant mass suicides. She told of Begorrat's success in trapping the nurse Thisbe into a timely confession. All the leaders except Antoine had subsequently been arrested. They were roasting in the *chacots brûlants*. As an afterthought, she mentioned that among those imprisoned was André's maid, Tina.

Urged on by Barry, she explained how André had ridden in the rain to try to stop the poisonings but that he had arrived too late. 'That Begorrat accused him of duplicity in the business and made him stand in the rain until his wife came and pleaded for him.' André, she explained had as a result become very ill and his poor wife was now fighting to keep him alive. 'Señor Flores tried to help. He interceded on behalf of Tina, but that Picton sent him away with a flea in his ear.'

Barry inhaled deeply and muttered through his teeth, 'I knew it! I knew something was wrong. Thank God I've come back. I'll go and visit them right away.'

## III

Since his return, he had seen Eléna several times but always only briefly, and very formally. Every time he was unaccountably mortally afraid for her. She herself had grown thin and pale from staying so much in the sickroom with André. She was trying very hard to forestall the dreaded final stage, the haemorrhaging. The doctor too visited often, and was not optimistic. André's mother had returned and was of some help, while Velours had been sent to stay with Yei.

258

The poisoning commission that Picton had set up on Begorrat's request, as a result of the mass poisonings, had begun to sit regularly. Seven planters, including Begorrat, made up its members. Anyone remotely connected was being questioned. They were torturing some of the prisoners, trying to get some information on the man Antoine who was still at large. It was possible that Tina, too, was being deliberately tortured, even as Tessa had been. Barry had promised Eléna that he would intervene on her slave's behalf.

Picton was too busy to see him. Apart from the poisoning commission and the disturbances with the English settlers, he had other problems. There had been a large robbery, and he had to attend the investigation of a woman called Louisa Calderon. He could not listen to Mr Wingate unless he had come to supply him with information on any of those matters.

It was almost the end of December and Christmas was fast approaching. A visit to Eléna revealed that André, though still in bed, was greatly improved. She, too, looked better, although the dark, tell-tale circles under her haunted eyes were still there and the house still held a persistent, unhappy atmosphere.

'It's Christmas,' Eléna sighed, 'and Tina is still in that awful prison, perhaps in the torture chambers. Can't we do anything?' Her pleading eyes touched Barry's soul.

The day before Christmas Eve, he tried Picton once more. The General was at his desk. He listened to Barry while he signed papers. Gazing down, Barry inadvertently read the words, '*Appliquez la question à Louisa Calderon.*' Barry knew it was the order awaiting Picton's signature, the order to apply torture to the young girl accused of robbery. He remembered Tessa. This Louisa, a free mulatto he had heard, was about Tessa's age. He knew the robbery charge was trumped up. The man who had supposedly been robbed had the very day after the alleged robbery spent a great deal of money. He would have loved to challenge Picton in this case. But no. He could not pick another quarrel with the man.

Picton signed the order. Barry shook his head in a gesture of resignation and looked away. To both gentlemen, that was indeed the end of that. Little did Barry suspect that he had just witnessed the act that would achieve more than his own best efforts against Picton. Nor did the confident General have the vaguest inkling that in the course of time his simple act of signing was to cause him to stand in the dock in the high court of London to be tried and convicted for torture.

Unburdened by premonitions, he turned to Barry. 'I'm sorry, Wingate. I cannot release the woman now. The commission sits again on Tuesday, the twenty-ninth. She has to be questioned then.'

# VI

There were no drums tonight and no frenzied dancing, but when Antoine called on Legba, the doorkeeper of the Loas, to open the doors and give passage to the spirits of Guinée, the devotees could feel the power of his voice rolling through the stillness of the night almost in imitation of the missing drums.

The ceremony began. A white fowl was sacrificed, and the devotees drank its blood. Hours later, the passion of their worship subdued, they lay in small groups, prostrate with exhaustion. Antoine sat near the low fire.

This month of December was one of the coolest he could remember. 'Living up here in the bush with only a damn carat-roof lean-to, like an Indian, is real ketch-ass,' he said to his companion as he slapped away a mosquito.

'All that suffering going on down there in the *cachot* and soon, soon more go start. When they start to kill we people, all we leaders gone. Thisbe and Felix, La Fortune and Tina, all o' them go get kill too and in the worst way that man or beast could find . . . aahh . . .' He sighed softly in his deep, throaty fashion. 'That blasted mulatto woman! Is she who cause all the leaders to get hold, I know is she. She force Tina to tell her and then she went to warn Begorrat. When Thisbe see that Begorrat done know was a plan, then she panic and confess.'

'But I hear was her husband who went Diego Martin . . .'

'Yes, she send he first, but he didn't talk. Was she we people see talking to Begorrat. Is she I telling you! Is she who cause it!'

'But you know I hear they say she have powers, she and she mother. Tina did say . . .'

'What powers? She ain't have no powers in true, she know a li'l bout bush medicine, everybody know that, but is bad she bad. She ain't have no powers. She just like all them brown-skin devils who second in badness only to the white-skin ones, and sometimes they worse. You listen to me, man, don't ever fool yourself into thinking you could trust a mulatto. Them ain't sure if they standing up or sitting down. They wants to be white like the whites, and they hate the least drop of black blood in they body.' Antoine chewed his fat lips agitatedly and bobbed and turned his head menacingly on the pivot of his thick neck. 'That

260

woman who betray we go pay. Let them kill one, just one o' we, and she breathe she last. I swear it to you!' His bulbous eyes stuck out from this large face like the eyes of a sea crab, their whites gleaming forbiddingly in the firelight. 'We go teach a lesson to all them mulatto bitches!'

# V

Christmas fell on a Friday. Eléna and the elder Madame Fontainebleau, in an attempt at cheerfulness, busied themselves in the kitchen. In spite of her gay conversation, Eléna could not shake off an underlying nauseating whiff of decay, of putrefaction, that seemed to smother her senses.

'What is that awful smell, Eléna?' asked the widow, pulling aside the window curtains to let in more air.

Then Eléna saw it. It was a young grackle bird, camouflaged against the leaves, hooked agonisingly on its back. It was in a state of advanced decay. Neck stretching downwards, its immature beak was pointing like a veritable finger of death into the kitchen.

'Oh *mon Dieu*,' the old lady crossed herself quickly. The pendulous skin of her once fat arms, bared now that her sleeves were rolled up, trembled with the movement. 'It must have fallen from a nest. The breeze has been blowing the scent in on us, like a curse. Oh Lord, it's as if we can't escape death in this house!' Her voice broke on the words. It was all Eléna could do to distract her and put back a note of cheer into the day.

On the Monday after the Christmas weekend, André started coughing with alarming violence and frequency. Eléna ordered him to remain in bed, relenting only by the afternoon at his insistence. They were thus sitting in the living-room, conversing quietly, when a messenger arrived with a note from the chief magistrate. The note read: 'M. Fontainebleau, you are hereby ordered to appear at the hearing tomorrow of the poisoning commission, to present evidence and be questioned.'

'But André, surely Begorrat knows how ill you are! There is no way that I'm going to let you leave this house!' she declared. She penned a hasty note and sent it back to Begorrat, all the while trying to shake the feeling of impending doom that had been clawing at her since the stench of the dead bird had invaded her nostrils.

Nevertheless, her determination was no match for the platoon of soldiers who came on Picton's order the next day to escort André bodily to the hearing. Madame Fontainebleau added her pleas to Eléna's loud protestations, but all in vain. Helplessly they watched him go. Anything could happen to him: the exertion alone could kill him; the slightest drop of rain could bring on the dreaded pneumonia from which she had tried so hard to protect him. Convulsed with frustration, Eléna tore away from her mother-in-law's fearful embrace and flew off towards the Guest House of the Royal Palms.

Barry was not there. He had gone to Santa Clara and would be back soon.

Dazed with disappointment, Eléna turned and walked back home. For the rest of that morning, she was in a state of uneasy apprehension. Several times she sent the servant boy, Manuel, to the gaol to see if he could find out anything.

'Nobody ain't know nothing much, but they passing sentences today, a man tell me,' reported the boy.

'Manuel, go again. Wait around. Come and tell me if anything happens.'

At about two o'clock, the boy returned. Talking excitedly, he informed her that sentences has been passed. The slaves were to be executed on the parade grounds. Some of the prisoners had to be baptised before execution. 'They going to the church now, Madame.'

'*Virgen santisima!*' exclaimed Eléna. 'And the master?'

'I ain't see him, but everybody gone to the church, Madame. You could go too and see if he there.'

A crowd of people was there at the church before her, witnessing as the curate baptised the writhing, manacled slaves. She saw André up near the font, his face unreadable. He coughed distressingly at irregular intervals. She could not get close to him.

At last the ceremony was over. The soldiers took the Africans out forcibly, and led them to the open parade grounds. A scaffold was already up. Groups of government-owned Africans passed through the throng, ominous faggots of sticks and branches in their hands. Eléna tried unsuccessfully to force her way through the crowd to get to André, who was still detained with the official party. She was jostled and pushed by the wave of curious citizens straining to see. It was as if a vice were closing in on her. She looked about hastily, grateful for her superior height. An icy panic was beginning to assail her. Then her searching eyes espied the glint of gold hair forcing its way in her direction. With a quiver of relief she cried, 'Barry! Barry!'

He could not get close to her, but at the top of his voice he admonished her for being there and sent her home, for she was being buffeted around like a piece of flotsam on the surging tide of the crowd. 'Leave André to me, please go home now!' he shouted.

The first African was summarily hanged. The crowd roared. As Barry neared the spot where the officials stood, hemmed in by the protective soldiers, the slave's body was taken down. The head was instantly and savagely severed from the body, and impaled on a spike. Then a group of four were forced to wear shirts that bulged curiously, and led to the heap of sticks and dry branches. They were tied to stakes next to the bloodsoaked, headless corpse, and by the time Barry looked again, all four were engulfed in flames.

Immediately the crowd as a mass drew back, screaming and stumbling away. Barry was sent reeling along with the rushing hordes, fighting for breath. He felt himself suffocating, but not just from the press of the crowd or the expected smoke. It was the smell. The scent of hell itself, the pungent nauseating odour of sulphur and burning flesh. 'Sweet Jesus! They filled their shirts with sulphur!' cried one scandalised voice.

The powerful vortex of curiosity that had drawn the crowd suddenly reversed its magnetism. The choking onlookers swung backwards, as they caught the gusts of wind from the east. They stampeded in waves of panic, fighting to get out of the area. Barry moved with the disbanding masses, and thankfully was soon out of the press. With a small effort, he reached André and broke through the guard of soldiers standing upwind. André was staggering helplessly on shaky legs. With a cutting glance of wordless accusation at the Governor and Begorrat, Barry half-lifted the sick man and drew him away, trying to walk him back to his home. André, gasping for his every breath, was near collapse. Barry saw to his horror that the handkerchief, convulsively pressed to his mouth, was clearly soaked through with blood.

Barry took the Frenchman up bodily and rushed through the streets and into the house, all the while calling loudly for Eléna.

Madame Fontainebleau and the servants ran out and helped him to rest André on the bed.

'Send for the doctor immediately!' Barry ordered. 'Eléna!' he shouted again. 'Where is Eléna? Where is the mistress?'

'But Monsieur, she did not return,' responded a white-faced Madame Fontainebleau. Barry's spirits quailed and for an instant, his face mirrored the widow's with the look of terror that permeated his very soul.

# CHAPTER TWENTY-ONE

## I

No one had seen Eléna. She had simply vanished into thin air like the smoke from the pyres, leaving, unlike the pyres, not even a faint smoulder or a trail of ash. A strong feeling of *déjà-vu* assaulted Barry. Oh no, not another hunt like the search for Tessa! The thought drummed through his head as he ran through the town like a crazed man, eyes darting everywhere, enquiring of everyone with no success.

In defeat he went back to the house, and was instructing Eléna's yard boy to take his master's horse and go with the news to Santa Clara when José appeared.

'Yei sent me. She had been thinking of all you said today and had become very worried about Eléna. She is on her way here as well,' explained José.

Appraised of the situation and assured that the Commandant had been informed, José advised Barry that they should go to the guest house, sit calmly and consider all the possibilities.

A heavy downpour drove them from under the sapodilla tree, to take refuge in the landlady's sitting-room. They examined every possibility over and over again. Finally, the hovering landlady plumped herself down next to them.

'Messieurs,' she began, rapping the table impatiently. 'Listen closely, I have a theory. I feel in my bones that her disappearance has something to do with the events of today. You know the man Antoine is still at large? Let's say he is hiding out near here in the hills. Those Shango people always holding their meetings a little way from the town where the drums can't travel. Suppose, just suppose, he blames her for Tina's arrest . . .'

'Was Tina executed today?' asked José.

'No. No women today, Monsieur.'

'Barry, that reminds me of something Eléna mentioned . . . Did she tell you that Tina told her that her remedy for the poison did not work?' asked José.

'Eléna's remedy? But that's implying that . . . Holy God! José, you go to the Fontainebleaus' and tell them what we've discussed. I'm going to the gaol and demanding to speak with Tina. She is our only . . . our only hope.' He gulped tensely.

264

# II

Barry was determined not only to see Tina but also to obtain her release. He had to question her in privacy, away from the gaol. Steeling himself to face the final battle with Picton, he marched over to the Governor's house.

Picton had just retired to his bedroom after sharing several glasses of Madeira with his friend Begorrat. The impact of the day's executions, and their plans for repeating the exercise (with minor variations) daily, had been discussed. Everything was going well. Picton sat in an easy chair and swung his long, thick, legs easily over the side. A voluptuous mulattress, bare to the waist, climbed on to his lap. Just then Barry's presence was announced by a servant through the closed door. The delay would enrage the mulattress, but enraged she was even more desirable. His moustachioed lips curled in a wanton, teasing, smile. He agreed to see Barry.

Eyes drooping with intoxication and aroused desire, Picton went out to the sitting-room. He regarded Barry playfully.

'Sit yourself down, Wingate,' he said with uncharacteristic affability. Barry almost refused. 'Would you care for a glass of Madeira?' Barry did not. Picton helped himself to one. 'Always so urgent and intense eh, young Wingate? Still after that slave prisoner?'

'Excellency, the woman is innocent. The Fontainebleau family needs her. She is their child's nurse. As you know, the mother in missing. André Fontainebleau is a dying man – consumption, you know. Out of charity for the family, please!' Underlying his humble plea, Barry's voice held a threatening tremor of impatience.

'You can be a dangerous man, young Wingate,' teased Picton as he toyed with his glass. 'What schemes, I wonder, are you planning in that aristocratic head of yours?' He glanced at Barry now with naked hatred, his heavy brows arching like the wings of *corbeaux* in flight.

Barry's gorge rose to choke him but, fighting down his anger, he looked away. 'Excellency,' he continued calmly, 'this matter I have come about is . . .'

'Wingate!' bellowed Picton, silencing Barry. 'I am willing to accommodate you in this request, if . . . if I can have an agreement with you.' He glared intimidatingly for another long moment at Barry. 'Your word that you will use no agencies overtly or covertly, to obstruct my work here.'

'You have it, Excellency,' replied Barry without hesitation, confident that he had already set enough in motion against the man, and knowing that the British citizens of the island were already petitioning the Crown against him.

'I have your word as a gentleman?' He did. 'Then it's agreed, Mr Wingate.'

Picton walked over to his writing desk, scribbled a note and handed it to Barry. Nothing in particular had been proven against the woman. She was of no further use to the commission. 'Take this to Vallot in the gaol, and you have what you want.'

'We both have, Excellency. I bid you goodnight, then,' answered Barry. He made a brief, perfunctory bow and left the Governor.


# III

Limp, swollen, unable to walk, Tina was taken home and laid on her bed. Yei had by then arrived and was on hand to attend her. Finally, she allowed Barry and José to enter the room.

Barry spoke very gently, explaining to Tina the terrible plight they were in, and asking whether she had any reason to believe that the rebels would have interfered with her mistress.

'Yes, Massa,' answered Tina with a loud burst of tears. 'He say he go kill the people who betray we, and I done know he thinking she is one o' them. And he against mulattos real bad. He go "execute" in the same way the white people do it. He go burn she, Massa. Oh God, I try to tell him she not like the rest but . . .'

'Tina, calm yourself,' admonished Yei, the soul of stoical calm herself. 'Tell us, *hermana*, do you know where he would have taken her?'

Overcome with tears, Tina answered with an affirmative nod.


'We will leave before dawn, my sons,' instructed Yei, after the tearful Tina had managed to describe the place to them. 'I will accompany you. Do not protest, Barry. I know these people better than you. I must go. No, the dawn is not too late. They cannot light such a fire in the night and call attention to themselves, and not in this rain.'

Before dawn could lighten the sky, therefore, they were ready. José had wisely brought his pistols with him, and Barry went to borrow André's. Entering the dimmed room, he was alarmed by André's pallor. He bent and explained the situation to the sick man. André could only grip his hand in thanks and look with the sad, glassy eyes of death at Barry's departing figure.

They set off in the pearly dawn light, moving like three determined pilgrims through the almost frosty, mist-covered hills. Barry followed doggedly at the rear as Yei, shimmering in the mother-of-pearl light almost like an angel, led them on.

Barry's eyes took in the beauty of the morning, and his numbed brain thought of the beauty of Eléna, of the beauty of the island, that beauty that masked its savage, heartrending cruelty. No, it was not the island but the people. Those who acted, those who reacted, like the poor runaway plotters they were now seeking, and those caught in the middle, like Eléna. She was always caught in the middle, paying the price for her black blood, and now paying the price for her white blood as well.

They climbed and climbed. Barry's mind was in turmoil. Was this how Eléna's life would end? She, who had been one of the few sane, truly unbigoted persons in the rotten pandemonium of slavery and racial confusion? Was it her destiny to pay the price for those countless mulatto traitors, people who, despicable as they were, were themselves no more than dupes, victims? He remembered Fist and his oppression at the hands of a brown-skinned overseer, and he knew the problem was an old, old one.

Would all his own struggles to come to terms with his unique need for Eléna come to this? What would life be like without knowing that Eléna existed? It would be, he thought now, like returning to find one's home utterly destroyed. Only it would be worse, far worse. Possessions could be replaced, but people never – Eléna, never!

## IV

Eléna knew that she was drugged, but she could not fight it. The stench of the dead nestling came now to stifle her anew. Black grackle birds flew menacingly towards her face, rapaciously aiming for her eyes. She tried to brush them away but her hands, unaccountably, were tied behind her back. She tried to run, but her feet too were tied. She could only jerk her head frenziedly to fend off her attackers. The grackles metamorphosed into the larger black creatures with the wider pinions. She tried to scream. It was Tessa's dreaded *corbeaux*. She could not think clearly. She must try. She would think of something pleasant, she would think of Barry. She must think of Barry.

Then there he was and they were drifting, drifting together on a cloud until she felt deliciously sleepy.

An avalanche of cold water flung in her face awakened her. She opened startled eyes and blinked rapidly, turning her head to look for

267

Barry. He was not there. There was no cloud, no comforting, protective arms. It had all been her imagination, her drugged mind seeking escape from the horror that had assailed her ever since her last clear recollection in the crowd on the parade grounds.

'Why you treating she so, man?' said a voice close to her.

'What it matter how we treat she? Today they burning La Fortune and Tina, and the onliest reason she live to see this day dawn is because we can't light no fire in the night and in the rain.'

Eléna opened her mouth to protest, but no words emerged.

The man with the bulging eyes came closer. He grabbed her by the hands and pulled her to her feet, dragging her from the rough carat shed and out into the open. Then he tied her securely to a pole in the middle of the clearing, and instructed his minions to build the pyre.

'Don't do she all that, nah man. I tell you she have powers.' The other Africans paused at the man's words and listened. He continued. 'Leh we do this thing quick, *oui*, and get out of here.'

'Why you nervous so? You getting everybody frighten. You didn't see how cool Picton and Begorrat was yesterday? Look, we go do it now and done. The sun done up. If she have powers, she better use them fast!'

## V

'Wait. Listen . . .' The three kept silent. 'We are there. Quietly. Let us go in,' said Yei, fully in command of the rescue party. 'Low. Stay low,' she added.

They advanced, almost on all fours. They saw the clearing. Barry uttered a muffled oath of protest. He had spotted Eléna tied in the middle, head sagging forward pitifully, long, black hair falling about her like a veil. His heart drummed in his chest with dread and suspense. Then she moved. She struggled. She was alive, he confirmed to his relief, alive and conscious.

'We stop here,' ordered Yei succintly.

'We have four guns,' said José. 'There are only ten or twelve of them, and we have the advantage of surprise.'

'No! No bloodshed, I must speak to them alone,' insisted Yei. 'Shh, Barry, it will avoid much violence. I don't wish to see these people suffer more than they have already.'

'But Yei, it's dangerous.'

'I've lived more years than most of my people survive under the white man. I'm not afraid of death. But I will be all right. I know what I'm doing. I know these people.'

'Let her try, Barry,' José intervened. Barry acquiesced after assuring Yei that they would come in at the first sign of trouble.

Yei spared a moment to look deep into Barry's frightened, intense blue eyes. She smiled comfortingly, patted his head then she edged away soundlessly and was swallowed up by the bushes.

For a long, agonising moment, she was lost from their sight. Barry unconsciously held his breath. Then she emerged. Even Barry was startled. He stared unblinkingly as the strange woman rose majestically out of the shrubs and seemed to glide effortlessly towards the clearing. The Africans had seen her now, and broke up in disorder at the apparition. There were screams and then a wild babble of confusion. Yei advanced. They drew back, clearly intimidated by her awe-inspiring presence.

Watching her from the bushes, Barry smiled ruefully to himself. Had he not known better, he would have thought her an exponent of the theatrical arts, a rival to the famous Mrs Siddons herself. An aura of calm and confidence and power surrounded her now. Dramatically, she raised her hands, extending them out like portentous wings. Instantly the babble ceased. The black men stood agog with wonder. She turned her head and looked hard at every one in turn, as if meeting each eye individually. Then she spoke.

Her deep, musical voice, so seldom heard in the house or the vast acreage of Santa Clara, rose resonantly, clearly. The slight Amerindian accent that tinged her speech gave her words an added touch of otherworldliness. 'You know who I am?' she asked. No one answered.

'I will tell you.' She spoke slowly, deliberately. 'I am the mother of this girl you have so cruelly stolen and brought here for your mistaken revenge. Who among you is the leader? Let him come out and tell me why my daughter is here against her will.'

Antoine stepped forward, swaggering confidently. The others, cowed, hung behind him. 'What you doing here, Madame? How you come here?' he asked boldly.

'Ain't I tell you she and she mother have powers?' mumbled a shaky voice behind him.

'Why do you have my daughter here?' asked Yei.

'She betray us to the white devils. Like Picton orders does say, she has to be executed.'

'To defeat an enemy, to defeat evil in the white man, you should be careful not to corrupt your soul. You have the wrong prey. My daughter has betrayed no one. It is not in her heart to do so. She has helped your people all her life. Who among you do not know of her skill with the herbs?' Yei's voice rose forcefully. 'Yet you plan to kill this girl, this valuable woman?'

'Not just her,' threatened Antoine, 'but you too, if you put yourself in this.' He advanced on Yei.

'Come no further, Monsieur. I am not afraid of you. One hand on me, and you are the the one who will die this day.'

'She have powers, Antoine! I telling you she have powers,' whispered the voice again.

Yei turned inscrutable eyes fleetingly to the speaker, and continued. 'You, Monsieur, and your followers, have the power to apply good sense and mercy. The girl has suffered enough for whatever it is you imagine she has done. She has a young child who needs her. She has a sick husband. You expect mercy from the white man and you will show none yourself?'

'Look, woman, we don't want to hear you!' bellowed Antoine.

Yei increased the volume of her voice and continued, 'I have come without the soliders who would surely have had you all dead by now. I have come to give you a chance to live, but you must find mercy in your heart and give me my daughter now, or you doom yourself for ever.'

'Don't listen to she!' shouted Antoine to his restless followers. 'We ain't no more doom than Picton and Begorrat. Take the woman, I tell all you. Look, grab she right now. Tie she up with she daughter!' he commanded.

Crouched in the bushes, Barry was becoming exceedingly nervous. Yei wasn't winning the battle of words. 'José, let's go in,' he said tightly.

'No. Wait. Look, she's talking again.'

Yei had raised her hand once more and the Africans were listening. 'You want to be like Picton and Begorrat? Then you have given up the religion of Guinée? If you have not given up your religion, then you must release the girl!'

'What we religion have to do with she?' asked puzzled voices.

'Then you don't know? This man has not told you who this girl is? Or is it that he did not consult the spirits? Is it that he does not know himself?' Yei paused, knowing that she had their complete attention. 'You have never heard of the twins of Santa Clara?' Yei threw her voice out powerfully. 'Everybody knows that this girl is one-half of a twin and that twins are sacred to the people of Guinée.

'Everybody knows that she is of no ordinary twin, but of the black and white twins of Santa Clara. She is the black half. The half that represents you. Her sister is as white as the clouds, everybody knows her, the wife of the son of Don Diego de Las Flores.'

The babble of confusion had begun again, the Africans now discussing the truth of her statements. Yei knew she had them almost convinced but, like a wise strategist, she pressed on, ramming home her advantage. 'And who is the father of the twins? Ahh! That is the question everybody has asked for twenty-four years, but who knows the answer? Are you prepared to take the risk without knowing? Are you prepared to lose the favour of the Loas by destroying this girl? Which of you will light the fire? Which of you will damn your soul? You, the leader, you think your favour with the gods is high enough? You wish to risk it?'

Confusion on the faces of the Africans, excited speech. It was clear that Yei's last words were the master stroke. The men circled Antoine, speaking heatedly. Barry could not distinguish any words clearly. In a short time Antoine broke free of the crowd and went up to Yei. His stance and his voice were menacing.

'You win, woman. You done bring fear and doubt to the minds o' the people. Take your damn daughter and go! Untie the woman!' he shouted to his hovering followers and then turned his back and walked angrily away.

They released Eléna. Yei supported her, half-lifting her out of the clearing. Yei walked slowly, turning briefly to forbid anyone to follow her, then she headed down the hill. Passing Barry and José, she spoke in a low voice. 'Keep down, don't show yourselves, follow behind us.'

# VI

Much, much later, when Eléna was safely at home, Barry spoke to Yei. 'You were magnificent, Yei, so magnificent!'

The older woman shook her head wearily. 'It is so sad, Barry, that there is no justice for the black man and when he tries to make his own, he stumbles, catches the wrong prey, he fights himself, kills himself . . . just like my own people did so many, many times. But you know, it is even more sad that in religion, the soul of what is man, superstition should carry more weight than human mercy.'

'Yei, aren't you yourself superstitious too? I always thought . . .'

'Oh, I believe in a lot of things. I believe the black and white twins of Santa Clara are sacred too, special . . . but then, so are all children, *n'est-ce pas?*'

There was a measure of peace now. The executions were over. La Fortune and the others had met their deaths but Tina at least had been spared and was recovering. Antoine and his followers too lived on, uncaught, surviving to organise their future assaults. André, however, had finally succumbed to his illness. But most of all Eléna was safe.

Yvette had come for André's funeral and had taken her mother back with her to the south. André's estates were to be administered by Yvette's husband. He would hold them in trust – the will had read – for Yvette and for Velours. Eléna had cried and mourned, but she was back home in Santa Clara and in much brighter spirits. Barry had not pressed himself upon her in her grief, he knew that that would only increase her unspoken guilt at not having loved her husband.

It was two months later and Barry had decided it was time. He was waiting for just the right moment. After lunch the family dispersed and Eléna went up to her room. Barry relaxed with José in the veranda, half-listening to the Spaniard's chatter. As José was speaking, a servant came in from Port of Spain with the mail. José opened one of the letters and read it with apparent pleasure. Then Barry playfully snatched it from him and ran without anyone's permission up the steps. He knocked at Eléna's door and went it.

She was lying on the bed, but she was not asleep. 'What do you have there, Barry?' she asked, seeing the letter in his hand. She sat up.

'The answer to that will wait for a moment, my love.' He sat on the bed and leaned over her, covering her face with kisses. She sighed luxuriously and did not discourage him.

'It's time for us to discuss our future, my darling.'

'Now, this minute?' she asked with mock severity.

'Yes, this very minute. Don't look so serious, though,' Barry laughed. 'I'm only asking you, quite formally, to marry me and come to England with me. Ought I to go down on my knees? Come now, say yes quickly or my presence here in your boudoir will be the scandal of the island.'

Eléna laughed in her throaty, musical way that assured Barry she was well again, truly well. 'Barry, are you sure? What would it really be like if we married and lived in England?'

'Surely, Eléna, you're not still concerned about your colour? You must trust me and know that I wouldn't persist if I wasn't positive that life without each other would be worse, far worse than whatever lies ahead of us. You're the woman of my heart, Eléna, my brown-skinned beauty, and I won't have you any other colour and I won't have any other wife.'

'It's not you, Barry, but your family, your . . . er . . . set in England and all that.'

'Do you think that our marriage will be the talk of England?' He laughed. 'I'm sorry to disappoint you, my love, but although I'll be as rich as Croesus, I'll still be just a humble squire from Somerset. We can hardly count on being more than a passing conversation piece.' As he talked, his wayward fingers reached for the buttons of her blouse.

She slapped his hands away playfully. 'Be serious, my love.'

'Listen, darling, they'll all love you. And hey, don't you know it's fashionable nowadays to have a coloured wife? Doesn't even the great Napoleon himself have one?'

'Oh Barry!' she implored. 'Won't you be serious?'

'No, Eléna, you be serious.' He sat up. 'You don't really believe that I'll ever let you go now that I finally have you, do you? Nor can you believe that I am like all the other English gentlemen and must live in the way of others and for the opinion of others. I must ostensibly become a country squire, but that cannot be my life's ambition. I've wasted too much time already. Even my man, Fist, has put me to shame. I've learnt much from his courage and his daring. But I need you at my side. You are living proof in this mad world that I am a sane man. And Eléna, love like ours is not easy to find.'

Eléna could make no immediate response. The eloquence and stirring import of his delivery had moved her deeply. She spoke with her hands and caressed his face gently. His already amorous mood needed no further encouragement. Soon they were lost to any other reality than their own passionate kisses. Their mood again became light and playful and Eléna resumed her questioning.

'And Velours, and our children, have you considered carefully that there'll be coloured heirs to all of your grandmother's property?'

'The property is very large,' he answered lightly, proceeding to nibble at her ear. 'Far too large for Velours alone, she needs brothers and sisters.'

'But what will I do in England? I'll be completely out of my depth. I'll be quite lost.' Though the import of her words were serious, she uttered them now in a yielding tone that was as weak as her limbs at that moment under the intoxicating spell of Barry's caresses.

'Oh no you won't! You'll find life not much different. There'll be a lot for you to do. Ha! Apart from what we'll attempt politically, with your propensity for administering to the unfortunate you'll find plenty of scope even in Somerset. I can see it all now. I'll be hard pressed to get a moment alone with you. Oh, I'd better make the most of this one.' He started again, teasing her neck with warm kisses, working his way down diligently, melting away her last vestiges of resistance. With an effort, she fought her way back to reality and laughingly dragged herself up. She forced her voice to a business-like tone.

'Very well, my darling. You make my fears seem like nothing. But first, I want to speak to Yei, and too, I must find out something about my Monsieur.'

'*Voilà!* That's the clue I was waiting for. See, I can work magic. Here's a letter just come from Louis.'

'Barry! Let me see it quickly!' she exclaimed.

'Read to your heart's content. I've better things to do,' he murmured as he handed over the letter and pressed on with his amorous advances.

'He has done what he could for the revolution and is coming home! Barry, he says . . . oh it should be any day now. He and Kathy. Mark is staying on in Ireland to run Kathy's estate. Oh Barry, isn't it wonderful!

'Hhumm, hhmm,' mumbled Barry, quite distractedly.


Outside, under the trees, in full view of the mountains that stood like guardians of the peace watching benignly over the haven of Santa Clara, Eléna found Yei. She sat down beside her mother. 'He has asked me to marry him, Yei, and go to England. What do you think?'

'What do *I* think? Hadn't you made that choice years ago?'

'But to leave Trinidad! Yei . . . I'm part of this island, like a piece of vegetation, like a tree – no, a weed. Like the 'ti Marie bush. I will be exiled in England without the sun or the mountains or the poui, always wondering if I'll return. It is so hard to go and . . . what of you, Yei? It will be terrible to have to leave you and go far, far away. Won't you miss me and Velours? Won't you be sad to see us go?'

'I've learnt to sleep in the bed without you, you know,' smiled the older woman. Then she leaned over and touched Eléna and said more gently, 'Go, child of my heart. I will endure, I will. Don't throw away your gift of caring. With him you may end your disillusionment, you may do more than you know, for our people and our island. He needs your strength.' Yei paused, continuing to pick leaves off the stalk of one of her medicinal plants. Then she spoke again, 'My people, the Amerindians, were once great travellers. It is the destiny of island people.'

Yei seemed to have said all that she wanted to, and then unexpectedly she resumed speaking. 'My only question to you is, are you prepared to be the mother of British peers?'

'There's no chance of that, Yei. Don't worry. Barry is only the fourth son, neither he nor his children will inherit the title.'

'Ahh! . . . ' responded Yei, guardedly, but her mind focused on the shaman in Arima. She at least had deciphered the riddle, but it was better that her daughter remained in ignorance of it, she decided. '*Que sera, sera muchacha,*' she said with a sigh.

'Oh Yei,' Eléna laughed, 'You and that, again!'


# VII

The marriage had taken place quietly one day, soon after the still untamed Louis and his Kathy had returned. Eléna had begun to learn English. She was so happy at this task and so happy to be with her Monsieur, that Barry had not the heart to hasten their departure.

The poui had flowered and spread its carpet of gold and the rains had come. Eléna had grown remarkably competent in English. Barry knew it was time to leave. Yet they lingered. They lingered as if waiting for something, as if hesitant to abandon the island to an uncertain future. Something wonderful did come. It came in the mail. It was a letter from Richard, a letter that brought rays of hope for the island.

Barry was elated. He found Eléna sitting in the garden, and ran up to her, waving the letter and shouting the news. 'You remember, darling, I told you all about my meeting with Canning? Well, he raised the issue of Trinidad in the House! Richard says it was a great landmark in the fight for abolition of the trade, and a step, a small step, towards final abolition of slavery. The House passed Canning's motion on the distribution of land in Trinidad. I quote, 'With the stipulation that no negro imported from Africa can be employed, and no further grants of land will be made in Trinidad until Parliament can decide on the suitable regulations for the importation of labour to the island.'

'Can you believe it, Eléna? Listen, there's more. "Prime Minister Addington has announced his intentions of appointing a commission to run the island, and to acquire information that would lead to a decision on the course of the island's future." Oh Eléna, Picton's days are numbered! Oh my darling!' He swung Eléna up in his arms and spun around. 'It's only a small victory, and we can't tell if it will work, but it's a victory nonetheless!'

'Yes, Barry. It's a great victory, and the best news we've heard in years. It's wonderful, wonderful news! Oh, if only we could see into the future and know, really know, what's in store for this land of Kirie, this beautiful Trinidad. And what the future holds for us too. When we leave, Barry, will we never, never come back?' Her voice grew suddenly sad.

'Of course, we'll come back. I promise you.' He let her down and they walked arm in arm back towards the house, stopping only to look up to the sky as two screaming macaws raced each other overhead. Without warning, Eléna stopped and turned to her husband. She asked the most unlikely question he had ever heard. 'Barry, did you ever eat the cascadura?'

# POSTSCRIPT

The story of Barry and Eléna, and the many characters with whom they interacted, is of course fictitious, although the political characters are modelled on actual historical figures. There is therefore a liberal mixing of factual and fictitious circumstances and events.

Because so much of the history did occur, however, one may legitimately ask: What happened next? So, for the curious or the history enthusiasts, the following historical facts are offered.

- The commission of three appointed by Prime Minister Addington ran the country for less than one year and broke up in chaos, but it did exert a tremendous effect on Picton's governorship.
- In 1803 General Picton returned to England, where opinion (aroused by condemnatory printed propaganda) was already high against him. Through the agencies of one of the above commissioners, he was brought to trial for the torturing of Louisa Calderon. He was convicted on 24 February 1806. On appeal, however, he was retried two years later and was acquitted. He went on to become a hero at the Battle of Waterloo in which he was killed.
- Begorrat held governmental office until 1813 when he was finally dismissed. He remained a planter, recorded as full of loud protest on his financial ruin.
- Of Don Chacon, it is known that through the efforts of a nephew he eventually obtained a pardon. But, already a dying man, he ended his days in exile, in Portugal.
- In 1805, a massive slave underground network was uncovered and subdued, before an alleged planned uprising of vast proportions.
- The position of free coloureds on the island grew steadily worse until a dozen years after our story, when liberal attitudes towards them were initiated by the British government.
- The attempt by the British at Latin American revolution, hinted at in the early chapters – a project that was apparently dear to Picton's heart – was eventually abandoned. The British had to turn their attention to the invasion of Spain and Portugal by Napoleon.
- Napoleon reintroduced slavery in Guadeloupe in 1802, but not without violent resistance from the African slaves there.
- In 1807, just five years after the curtain fell on our story, the British slave trade was discontinued. Slavery was finally abolished on 31 August 1834: thirty-two years after our story, some fourteen years before French abolition, fifty-two years before the Spanish finally

277

freed the slaves in Cuba, and thirty-one years before the American Civil War ended slavery in the United States. True slavery in Trinidad had, therefore, lasted for the relatively short period of fifty years.

The island of Trinidad became the first experimental Crown Colony.

# ACKNOWLEDGEMENTS

Many people helped in large and small ways in bringing this novel to fruition. I especially wish to acknowledge the support and encouragement of Dr Bridget Brereton (Historian), Professor Kenneth Ramchand (Professor of English Literature), Mr Jeremy Taylor (Literary critic) and that of my editor, Ms Vicky Unwin. A world of thanks also to my father, Dr Horace Charles, and my aunt, Mrs Carmen Blugh-Le Maître. Thanks also for the help of my many friends: Virginia Saney, Pelham Warner, Peter Espinet, Ann Ince, Desmond and Cyrilla Brunton, Dolores Thompson, Miguel Brown and Hazel Mann.